THE BOOKS OF THYME

by

Trudi Ann Smith

Ancient Egyptian mythology is also as real as mythology goes! My descriptions, spells and imagery however, are all imaginary or widely known and taken from the following: The numerous documentaries watched on all things Ancient Egyptian, which has fascinated me since childhood. From scriptures and hieroglyphs carved or painted into the tombs and temples around Egypt. From many books I've read on the subject and from my fond memories of my many visits to Egypt. From physically climbing the pyramid steps with my brother (in the days you could!) and clambering around dry, dusty tombs. To the many hours reading and studying the artefacts in the Cairo Museum. Carrying the enormous papyrus colourfully painted, depicting the scene of the weighing of the heart, through Cairo airport, back to Heathrow was no easy task. Nor was precariously mounting it at the top of my stairs in a huge, heavy picture frame where it remains hanging to this day, reminding me of the start of my own literary journey.

My spiritual, pagan and witchy friends have taught me how kind and wonderfully magical their realm is. My own links to spirit have taught me we are not alone in this New World, nor should we ever dismiss the unknown as being impossible. We just haven't discovered everything in life and death yet, therefore our understanding is extremely limited.

It is here I'd like to thank all those people that have helped make this book possible:

My hubby Chris, for giving me the opportunity to write and for supplying munchies during my long hours at the computer. My friend's son Dan, who read the first draft and my mate Kirsty who gave valuable feedback and encouragement. To my dear friends who have taken time to read it in draft form. To my kids (Rehs and Tia) for cleverly avoiding reading any of the manuscript. I am hoping they succumb once I wave an actual published book at them! Thanks Sean, my eldest, for artistically creating my front and back covers. Jennifer, who loved the story so much she put me onto the one person who finally made my dream possible....Karen Stanley (Mabel & Stanley Publishing), who guided me through the scary process of 'manuscript to publishing'. Thanks also to Steve Dunn from Dunwrite Author Services for the technical side of things.

Lastly, thank YOU, for picking this book from the multitude of options available. Now settle back, let your senses grab you and set your imagination free…

Lesson 85

Taken from
The Book of Our Ancestors

*How much of our world do
you know?
Do you believe other worlds
are out there, waiting to be
explored?
When you are ready to
explore, then you are ready to
grow.*

*How vast can existence be?
Our physical world is only a
small part of existence.
This is where we experience
with five known senses.
But what if there is so much
more to reality than we
already know?
So much more that our mind
can discover.*

The familiar is safe.

1

*Think of all the possibilities
you could explore
If you were guided by your
many other senses;
And are brave enough to
venture into the unfamiliar.*

*Far beyond everything we
know and believe
Are worlds our unknown
senses can explore?
Places you would not even
imagine could exist.
It is here we need to venture
and to experience.
Places our imagination can
reach, can feel, can touch.*

*If you truly believe in magic,
then it is there for the taking,
A place in Thyme where
everything is possible.*

*When it is your time, will you
be brave enough to go where
your
Senses fear it is unsafe, just
because it is unfamiliar?*

I'm not sure how it all began; no one really knew where or how. Yet the sequence of events that brought us to where we are now was catastrophic. It hit us swiftly and they hit us hard. We feel like scattered seeds waiting for the sunlight to dawn on us again so we may grow, re-harvest and flourish once more in the gentle breeze. It did not matter if you were strong, or wise. What mattered was bravery, knowledge and the belief that carried you onwards towards hope. You are not alone. We will find you and bring you home.

THE BEGINNING

Reaching out he could feel something with his fingers. He tried to stretch into the shaft a little more but couldn't quite get a grip on the object he so badly wanted. Still on tiptoes, he looked around the tomb for something solid to stand on, but nothing. He had been told it was here. He had initially been hesitant on coming, knowing the risk, yet he came. Finding it would be one thing; getting it home was a completely different story. He'd never been a gambler, but this, this was indeed a special moment. He was so close to discovering the truth, to touching and having the most important historical artefact ever to be found, but he couldn't quite reach it. This need to own it, to possess it, to understand it, captivated his want to continue stretching further.

The small stone that had once covered the shaft had been removed long ago and the man prayed all day that its contents were where he was told it would be. He had ventured down a seemingly dark and narrow, insignificant passage. It went nowhere after reaching this bare room. Rocky sand covered a spot that housed an ornament; a small stolen article that once helped a dead body on its journey home. All around him were chiselled walls and disturbed alcoves, holes,

4

rocks and displaced sand, oh so much sand. He had believed it was here, he now knew it was here, yet still he couldn't quite reach his treasure in this particular shaft.

The ancient chamber the man stood in, had been ransacked before. Seemingly again, in modern times, it had been completely stripped by the Authorities to its now state of disarray. Now nothing tangible remained, barring the rock and the 'oh so much sand' but more importantly, the historical energy that circulated within its walls, oblivious to mankind, still radiated throughout the tomb.

The walls were still carved with hieroglyphs depicting the lives of the ruling pharaohs but time and intervention meant many were now faded and chipped. One vibrant scene remained showing the story behind the artwork. Semi-clothed figures were painted side-on, offering fruit and perfume to their gods and a pharaoh stood proudly in his chariot, riding against his enemies. The captured were shown cowering as slaves in front of the heroic pharaoh as his might thrust upon them. Osiris, god of the underworld, stood majestically wearing the double crown of Egypt in a colourful scene of judgement. His thickly, black eye-lined eyes gazed upon the living man whose thoughts were foolishly not on the splendour of the pictures, the ancient writing nor on the magical meanings behind the scriptures.

The man was alone and intent on getting what he came to claim. He didn't stop and contemplate the extent of knowledge the ancient Egyptians held. How they built such splendour, how they carved such magnificent scenes and how many thousands of years before, men had walked the passageways and chambers he now trod. He wasn't interested in their history; only in what the future would hold for him if successful in his find. Oh the power he would have. The kudos, the wealth – all here for the taking, if only he could reach it!

The tomb was hot and stuffy and void of all natural light. Two dim light bulbs hung from wire; one over the entrance, the other in the far corner of the room. Placed there many years ago for the archaeologists who thought the tombs and passageways still housed ancient treasures. There were, of course, no more gold or gifts for the dead pharaohs. The tomb had been robbed of all its antiquities but not of its secret. That was until now. The last piece of the pie, the very last puzzle to death and beyond, rested just a few centimetres away from one man's reach.

Sweat began to trickle down the man's brow. He quickly wiped it away with the back of his hand.

He was well dressed, maybe a little over dressed for the climate, but you could tell the man had class without even looking at the labels sewn into the lining of his clothes. He looked well-read and clean shaven. His fingernails were clipped and his jacket fitted to perfection. The colour of his clothes though, had been dusted yellow by the sand in the desert and from his journey above to below; down into the chamber he now inhabited.

He had not informed anyone of his mission. Initially, he had fought the decision to come, knowing the consequences, but when it spoke again, he came. Like a calling, this man couldn't give up now and he couldn't turn back. Time was limited and he grew agitated. He *knew* it was in the shaft, he had been told, yet he couldn't reach it. There was nothing evident to stand on. His frustration was immense. He was so close, yet still a few millimetres too far.

His curly black hair was damp. The air thick and oppressive inside the chamber. Lighting in the chamber was too dim to highlight the droplets of sweat on his hair follicles. He knew they were there with him and this made him sweat more. Having been spontaneous and not dressed appropriately for this task, the heat became unbearable. There was no air conditioning unit, nor window to open allowing cool air to circulate. Air outside was as hot as the air inside and the adrenaline running through his body added to the accumulation of hot sticky sweat now drenching the cavity under his arms.

An idea flashed through his mind.

"Shoes!" he thought.

He whipped off his jacket and folded it against the stone wall. Almost toppling over, he bent down, raised his left leg, then his right and without stopping to untie the laces, ripped both shoes from his feet. He was lucky that he had worn the shoes with man-made uppers on this particular day. Leather shoes or sandals would have been too soft or low for the task and would have given way considerably under his weight, losing him those much needed millimetres. He placed his shoes one on top of the other. With time rapidly running out and panic taking over, fumbling, he climbed onto his jacket and shoes and wobbling slightly, again stretched his arm into the hole.

Outside the tomb, silence filled the air. Neither human nor animal could be heard. The small villages lining the west bank of the Nile were too sporadic and under-populated to cause noise pollution in the desert and the people in the city were too busy attending to their daily routine to worry who could be stealing what, on this very, very hot day. A small breeze began to gather around the entrance, swirling fine particles of sand onto the first stone step down into the encroaching darkness of the tomb. The breeze continued spiralling downwards, towards the corridors and chambers below the desert.

This time his treasure felt slightly closer. He could feel it. He knew it was there. It was close enough now to flick nearer with his fingers. He brushed a little more sand away with his fingertips to expose it a little more. Adrenaline rushed through his body. Without warning, the shoes gave way beneath him and the man slid off. Slightly twisting his ankle, he fought to regain his balance on the uneven floor of the tomb. Without hesitating for a moment, he again placed the shoes one on top of the other, pushed them and his jacket as far as possible to the wall and stepped up. Reaching into the darkness once more, he began flicking the corner of the object again and again until eventually he could grab enough of it to pull it towards him back down the narrow shaft.

It was out. He tumbled awkwardly from excitement and nervousness. His jacket was now covered in rock debris; his shoes slightly squashed. Adjusting his posture, he began urgently rubbing the dusty sand from his find. Held in his hands was a papyrus cloth, loosely tied by a brown fraying piece of ribbon. The sound of his heart beating heavily now echoed around the chamber. He paused for a split second as he viewed the object in awe, then he tugged at the ribbon eager to reveal its contents. The decaying tie ripped easily and the papyrus unfolded. The contents fell to the floor as he lost grip of one end of the papyrus. A gasp escaped from the man's mouth. Lying on the ground at his socked feet, was *the* book. It was magnificent yet jagged at the edges, with the kind of smell that was reminiscent of age. It had been untouched and undiscovered for thousands of years. *He* had found it. He had believed and had found it. His adrenaline now flowed stronger. Hairs sprung up from the back of his neck and on his arms.

'My God,' he thought as he stared at his find, 'it's true!'

The large rocks of the tomb, which on first sight caused wonderment to the onlooker, amazed by their ancient, artistic splendour, creaked. The man flinched. With eyes wide he yanked his head from side to side scanning every direction.

"I'm overreacting!" he thought to himself, "just nerves."

In the dim light his eyes squinted to make out movement of sand, slowly seeping from tiny cracks between the walls and the ceiling. At first he couldn't believe his eyes. All this was reminiscent of a scene from an action movie. He was not an actor, nor was this a movie scene, it was real. A gentle breeze circled around him and a rumbling noise began as two of the walls began slowly sliding towards him. Their aim was to kill but the man certainly had no intention of remaining within the tomb a moment longer. A high pitched shrill echoed around the chamber ricocheting off the moving walls. Unlike in the movies, full of fear, this man was gone. Leaving his shoes behind, he ran for his life. He didn't need them though.

The scream and the wind had followed him out. Overtaking him with such ferocity, the wind had blown his sweat-soaked shirt away. Ripping it with such force he was semi-naked before he had even cleared the slope to the tomb's entrance. Gripping the book, he ran for his life, faster than he had ever run before but that was not enough. The wind came back to finish him.

He took a chance on coming, knowing the risk, but the prize outweighed the risk. Now just a heap on the ground, the man's skin peeled away with the spiralling of the wind and sand. Then his bones crumbled to dust. The remaining pile of man-dust was eventually also blown away and mingled into little sand particles as the wind finally ceased. On finishing its deadly task, it returned to just a gentle breeze in the dessert air.

Silence followed. A weird kind of stillness in the heat of the day could be felt for miles. The sun's rays, too dangerous to be directly looked at by the human eye, beat down, heating the sand. The book, once grasped safely under the man's arm,

11

was now dangerously laying alone and silent outside the city in the desert dunes. Alone, waiting for the next chapter…..

To my daughter Jilly
These blessings I give you

That you may read the magic book
And taste the witches brew

Then when you get much older
And leave the magic wood

Remember all the spells you cast
Must only be for good!

Spell for Age of Transition

Taken from a
Book of Thyme

Chapter 1

Jilly was tired. She had been picking mushrooms all afternoon for her mother and dusk was drawing in. Scooping the long, dark curl that swept across her forehead, she stood up and stretched towards the sky. She yawned and gave a slight groan. The curl fell back across her rosy cheek.

"Come on Gyp!" she cried, "race you home."

Grabbing her twig-entwined wicker basket, Jilly set off, grinning back at Gyp as she quickened her pace.

Jilly was still much younger in heart than her sixteen years but her body gave away her age. It had suddenly taken shape and her clothes began to fit even more snugly than before. She always looked neat and well groomed, even when muddy from tramping in the woods during the rains, but a certain shyness was beginning to emerge. Her facial features were still delicate which gave rise to comments such as *pretty* or *cute*. *Beautiful* would have to wait until she was older. Her mother though, *was* beautiful. Her father, well this was something she could not comment on if asked. She didn't know him!

A few mushrooms fell from her basket as she ran along the edge of the forest trail but neither she, nor the black cat racing her home, stopped to retrieve any.

Jilly loved days like these spent in the forest with Gyp. He often sat peering down at her from a log or a branch if he was feeling particularly brave that day, while she collected nature from the woods. This always made her feel safe. Other times he would stay by her side and occasionally rub himself around her legs until she paused from her task and stroked him. They had grown up together. She had no memory of him not being around, and yet, he seemed to have old eyes and knowledge of life that spanned way beyond his years. Jilly loved him with all her heart. Gyp was *her* black cat. He, in turn, loved her back with all his heart but often his thoughts were elsewhere. On some occasions, no matter what Jilly did, his only response would be a flick of his black tail or a quick sly look that informed her he was busy in his own thoughts and was not interested in being disturbed.

A couple of times on the way home, Gyp stopped and glanced back. He felt uneasy, but had no idea why. Woods were woods and mushrooms were just mushrooms, but he couldn't shake off the feeling that someone, or something was in the woods with them, watching from the trees.

"I'm home Mum!" Jilly called as she slipped in through the cottage door.

Gyp had, as usual, won the race and beaten her home. Already curled up on his favourite mat in the lounge he decided not to respond to her arrival. He always beat Jilly home and had headed straight for his comfort area; somewhere nice, warm and cosy and smelling of his own scent.

"Did you remember the stinging nettles dear?" her mother asked as she came into the kitchen.

"Yep! They're in my pocket."

She placed her little, feminine hand inside her so called 'practical' pinafore pocket and pulled out a cluster of stinging nettles complete with roots. She wore this pinafore on many such occasions due to the extra-large pocket sewn on the front. Nettles and various herbs fitted neatly inside leaving Jilly's arms free for carrying the basket for mushroom or flower-picking. Jilly wasn't really a pinafore kind of girl anymore, but practical she definitely was. Wood days needed practicality.

"Excellent!" said her mother gleefully, "pop them into the cooking pot, and don't forget to stir them in well."

Jilly made her way over to the kitchen sink. Plunging her hands into her pinafore pocket she grabbed the nettles. Flicking them above the sink, she removed any loose earth from the leaves and roots. Instead of washing them, she immediately turned to the stove where a huge, polished, copper cooking pot sat bubbling. Every now and then a large bubble would blow up from the depths of the pot, spurt, and let out an almighty squelching noise. Standing on her *tippiest* of toes, Jilly peered into the pot and dropped the stinging nettles into the bubbling cauldron. The pot hissed back at her loudly sending a little spit of fluid towards her face. Jilly squeaked as she withdrew her face from the line of fire and landed back onto her feet.

Very slowly the boiling liquid began to change into a murky, vibrant green colour that swirled anti-clockwise, mixing in the browns and reds of the ingredients her mother had previous added.

"Don't forget to stir it," Penedora repeated anxiously, "or the nettles will take over!"

Jilly grabbed the large wooden spoon resting on the inside edge of the pot and with two hands began to stir the mixture. Stirring caused the thickening liquid to settle and return to its brown squelching substance which randomly popped and squirted towards the ceiling.

Jilly peeped into the pot again, mesmerised by its evolving patterns.

"You've made enough for the whole hollow, Mother," she laughed, resting the wooden spoon back against the side of the cauldron.

Penedora patted her daughter on the shoulder and stretched over her to reach for the little salt jar sitting on the sideboard.

"Just a small pinch of this," she said adding some salt to the liquid, "and the mixture will be ready."

Penedora rubbed her hands down her kitchen apron to remove any salt residue from her fingers, turned her elegant physique to the stairwell door and left the kitchen.

Jilly peered back into the copper pot and continued to watch the gooey liquid as it changed from brown to red, to orange and then to a light brown, rather scrummy chocolate-looking substance. Jilly like chocolate. They both liked chocolate!

Their cottage was a homely little place, full of interesting ornaments with nooks and crannies filled with charming objects, gifts and collectibles. Penedora was a gatherer of 'things' but her items were not left jumbled up and forgotten about like most hoarders. Penedora stored things and kept things for a reason. She was a good homemaker and a very proud one at that. Jilly followed her mother's footsteps in her creativity with the so-called feminine touches around the home and often arranged the colourful array of flowers in the vase on the coffee table. Flowers also added a fresh fragrance to their homely, quaint lounge.

Outside the garden was well established and the herbs were arranged in rows. Each row had a little stick label where the seedlings had established themselves. Jilly collected wild herbs for her mother from around the woods but Penedora grew selected ones for those special spells and potions, and kept them all in meticulous order, both inside and outside of the home.

Jilly loved the whole business of spells and cooking pots and the whole essence of magic. She had reached the age of Crossover, where like previous generations before, it was time for Jilly to accept she was *growing up*. Slowly disappearing were the days of climbing trees and throwing balls of wool to the cat for entertainment. Gradually her childish fun days were being replaced by ones where reading by the river and watching Gyp as *he* climbed the tree alone were more enjoyable than climbing the trees herself. Jilly enjoyed the challenge of becoming a young lady and learning the magical ways of Thyme but apprehensively she was beginning to notice the boys! They used to be just friends she had grown up around, but now they were *boys*! For Jilly, for now, magic would always be her one true passion and Gyp, her one true love.

Shortly, Penedora returned with two beautiful crystal jars. She removed their cork tops and placed them on the work-surface. She pulled open a kitchen drawer and fiddled around in it for the ladle.

"Got it." She smiled, pulling it out and waving it in the air.

She carefully held one of the jars over the cauldron and, using the ladle, emptied some mixture from the copper pot into it. Carefully trying not to spill any of the mixture on the outside of the jar, she did the same with the other one. Squeezing the cork tops into the openings to re-seal them, she carefully placed the jars onto a silver tray sitting on the kitchen table.

"Let's give blessings." Penedora whispered to Jilly as she carefully carried the tray out of the room. Jilly excitedly followed behind.

Heading upstairs, mother and daughter entered a little back room. It was a pleasant, small and simple room. The mint green décor was soothing but plain. It was dimly lit due to only having one small window at its far end. Unlike the clutter of the kitchen and lounge, this room was almost bare apart from a low, sturdy, oval table in its middle. A neat purple cloth lay across it, and a large, green book, untitled, lay on top. Some purple candles were waxed onto four little glass bowls and placed on the floor in each corner of the room.

Jilly made her way around the table and unlatched the window at the far end. She picked up a box of matches left on the window ledge.

Striking the matches, Jilly bent down in each corner of the room, and lit the four purple candles. As she ignited them, Jilly whispered under her breath, "*Candles glow, strong and bright, give us a spell from love and light.*"

Penedora had placed the crystal jars onto the purple table cloth beside the book and put the tray onto the floor. She knelt down in front of the table, opened the book to the first page and then raised her arms above her head. Offering the palms of her hands up to her angels and ancestors, Penedora spoke to the book:

"Cwym yun am ochorios
With love and light I ask thee, to share thy words
so true.
A spell for love and marriage is what I ask of you."

Penedora lowered her arms and steadied herself with the edge of the table as she stood up. The room lay silent. Jilly and her mother then waited in anticipation for the book to respond.

BANG! The small window at the far end of the room blew open and the wind circled in, bringing with it dust and leaves from outside. It rapidly grew in momentum hurtling around the room and lifting Jilly's dark curly hair and swirling it above her head. She laughed. The candle flames flickered and danced in a magical trance with the wind. The wind directed itself to the book on the table and its pages, now caught with the swirling disturbance, began to flick from right to left. Penedora stood her ground as the wind spiralled around her skirt, whipping her legs in the process. Penedora had long brown curly hair like her daughter's but it was often tied back. The wind had caused great lumps of hair to escape from the hair clasp she was wearing on this occasion. Jilly looked as though she had been pulled through a hedge backwards! Penedora, as usual, looked just naturally windswept!

Almost as quickly as the commotion began, calm suddenly returned as the window banged shut. The book now lay open but still and a calm silence filled the room. They waited eagerly. Words began to slowly emerge from the depths of the open pages, written in the most beautiful, golden writing ever seen.

"Excellent!" Penedora gasped with glee. She fumbled to replace some of her loose hair and straighten her skirt. When the writing had finished appearing, she picked up the crystal jars, held one in each hand and then read aloud from the new scripture in the book.

"These wedding gifts are for you both, from the heart of a loving friend.

*May they protect you from life's troubles, so your
love will never end.
Drink heartily you both, from the jars now blessed
this eve.
So your marriage will be filled with love, until you
no longer breathe."*

What strange words, thought Penedora.

What lovely words, thought Jilly. "Carmel and
Joseph will love these wedding gifts," she said
softly, "kind of like a 'til death us do part wedding
vow' from the New World."

Penedora had a knack of choosing perfect gifts
for people and her spells were always made with
such thoughtfulness.

Jilly admired her mother deeply and hoped that
one day she too would bring happiness to people
with her gift of reading the book. At least she had
graduated from just lighting the candles to asking
the book for a suitable spell, but her mother hadn't
let her cast any actual spells received yet, just in
case they went wrong. Jilly knew one day the
opportunity would come and she would be
allowed to chant the words and complete the
whole ceremony. Her Age of Transition was
nearing.

Carmel and Joseph's wedding day was also
nearing and the residents of Thyme Hollow were
becoming more excited. The happy couple had

been childhood sweethearts and their love had grown with the seasons. Jilly had a soft spot for Joseph. He was like the big brother she never had. He taught her about mushrooms and berries, how to talk to the trees and listen for messages in the wind; as well as the general helping with school homework that older siblings tend to do. Joseph's little fledgling couldn't wait for the wedding celebrations. Excitement filled her heart; thinking about all that singing and dancing and the gift of her mother's love potion!

Penedora returned the crystal jars to the tray as Jilly re-latched the spell room window shut. She blew out the candles while Penedora fetched a dustpan and brush from the landing cupboard. She swept the leaves that had come in on the wind. When finished, she handed Jilly the pan of leaves to take outside and, picking up the tray, both made their way back downstairs.

Behind them, their Book of Thyme flicked its pages and slammed itself tightly shut. Inside, the beautiful scripted words slowly disappeared from its pages.

Time whisked briskly on and after the events of yet another busy day of preparations and chores, Jilly retired to bed with Gyp closely by her side. Penedora shortly followed them into the bedroom and bending down kissed her daughter goodnight.

She tucked the bed sheet around her shoulders a little tighter and gently caressed Gyp's head a couple of times before leaving the room. After Penedora had closed the door behind her, Jilly rolled over on to her side and curled up her knees. Gyp nestled in closer to her stomach, curling round like a sleeping snake; his contented purr vibrating against Jilly.

"Goodnight Gyp," she whispered to him.

Gyp responded with a slightly louder purr but any other acknowledgement than that seemed too much effort after getting himself so comfy. He would normally nuzzle Jilly's hand over and over again as a hint for her to stroke him. Tonight though, he wanted to sleep. He had a right to sleep. He was a cat and all cats had a right to sleep. He also felt he had a right to demand owner-affection whenever he wanted stroking and the right to demand food when it was feeding time! Tonight though, he decided sleep was higher on the agenda.

Jilly's bedroom was neat and pretty and was reflective of her nature. Lemon-coloured walls made the room feel light and airy in the daytime and at night they glowed a soft yellow hue under the light of the moon which shone through her window. She had a small wooden wardrobe and chest of drawers for her clothes, which of course were mainly home-made apart from the odd pair of jeans someone had brought her back from the

New World. Jilly liked jeans. Penedora, didn't like them as much!

She closed her eyes and allowed her mind to wander. Shortly, her breathing slowed in pace and her whole body began to unwind, relaxing itself naturally for the process of sleep.

Downstairs, Penedora settled herself also. Looking around the living room she sighed and closed her eyes for a moment, taking in the air and stillness of her surroundings. Then stretching each arm in turn behind her head she could feel the tension in her neck. Her hands shifted and rubbed each shoulder to soothe them from their hard day of chores. Penedora, sauntering over to the comfy armchair in the corner of the room, slumped down into it and breathed out gently. She was tired, but it was too early to retire to bed. She decided to stay up a little longer. This hour of the day was always hardest for Penedora. This was the time when she wished Jilly and Gyp goodnight and ventured downstairs on her own. She loved to be busy, she loved the company of her daughter and her friends from Thyme Hollow, but she held a sense of loneliness deep inside. It was particularly at this time, the end of each day, Penedora felt completely alone.

Being careful not to knock over the vase of flowers, Penedora bent over and picked up her reading glasses from the coffee table beside the chair. She placed them over her cute pointed nose with one hand and completed her task by scooping up a small reading book from the table with the other. Her deep, brown eyes, hidden beneath thick lashes, blinked behind the glass. She grabbed the tassel which hung out the book and ran her fingers along the page's edges opening it up to reveal the page marker. She was at the stage where she kept reading the same page over and over again, each time forgetting she had already passed a particular paragraph. It showed that she didn't really have time to just sit and read and if the odd occasion arose where she was allowed to do just that, the novelty lasted only a few minutes at a time. The guilty feeling of having to do a much needier task at that precise moment was too great for Penedora. Her mind was always elsewhere, hence the repetition of the paragraphs. Tonight was different though. Tonight she wanted to read her book, get whisked away in the fantasy of it. Tonight she thought all other tasks could wait until the morning. Her mind swiftly caught up in the realm of fantasy, captivated by the thrills and imagination each page offered her as she read. Behind the back of her chair, two crystal jars containing cast love potion sat motionless on a shelf. Their liquid now remained dormant, waiting for the impending wedding celebrations.

Upstairs, Jilly was also caught up in fantasy. Her dream though seemed so real as if she could actually see the bright colours circling around her head. *She could smell the perfume of the flowers and the freshness of the meadow and she could actually hear the voice softly calling her name in the distance.*

"What a wonderfully floaty dream," she thought as her body flew in and out of the puffy white formations in the sky. Very slowly, sinking gently, downwards towards the earth, she landed softly on the grass below. A voice was calling to her in the wind…*

Agitated, Gyp woke up. He moved a paw away from his body and stretched a leg, its claw just gripping the cover that he was sleeping on. Flicking his paw back in again he decided to rearrange his position. He manoeuvred, arching his back and turning full circle, then came back down to rest on the bed again. He licked the same paw, tucked it back into his warm body and snuggled closer to Jilly.

'*Another restless night ahead,*' he thought closing his eyes once more.

Chapter 2

If it wasn't the sun that woke you early in Thyme Hollow, it was the dawn chorus of the wood pigeons and other wildlife that wandered by aimlessly rummaging for breakfast. Crows in the twilight, owls by night, and other beasts by dawn, all chatting loudly beneath and above the cottage windows. Jilly loved mornings. The sweet smell of dew and its freshness warmed her heart. She wasn't scared of the night, but the voices in her head would sometimes catch her unawares, making her feel uneasy. Her mother had once comforted her and explained in depth that one day she would be able to communicate with the voices and that they were only here to help her. At this particular span of time, she didn't seem quite so agitated by the voices blowing in the wind. These she believed to be her ancestors, but the ones that came from within her head disturbed her a little as she felt these invaded her privacy. Her friend, Joseph, had also helped her to listen when the voices came and how to understand them. Like her mother, Joseph also taught her to be patient. "You won't hear them all the time," he explained, "but when you do you have to listen carefully. Sometimes you'll understand what they are saying, sometimes you won't. It takes practise to blend with the voices and hear them clearly."

"Practise makes perfect!" *they* commanded. So, she would practise when they came and patiently learn.

Spending all her spare time enjoying life, feeding on knowledge from the world around her, Jilly took in everything, hoping that one day she would gain the same respect within the 'circle' as her mother had. Obviously, the elders of Thyme Hollow Wood had far superior knowledge to even her mother, but everyone was important in their own right, and everyone was special in their own way. Jilly was excited to discover how far her knowledge would extend and how high in 'circle' she would eventually end up. Her speciality was though, at 16, still a little mystery.

Unlike Jilly, Penedora had slept quite well and was raring to go this particular day. Both had been up, cleaned and dressed for some time and Penedora was now in the process of wiping the rim of the washed herbal teacups. She had already stacked the breakfast bowls back in the cupboard, dusted, made the beds and finalised a few other chores on her busy agenda.

"I thought I'd pop down to the stream before all the commotion starts this afternoon. Perhaps meditate or read my book of poems. Is that ok with you?" asked Jilly.

Penedora pondered over the question for a little while then nodded. She knew when Jilly went wandering into the woods or headed to the stream with a book, she would be gone for hours. Jilly's mind was often swept away with the magic of Thyme Hollow. Safety was never an issue; timing was, though!

"No problem, but don't be out too long today."

"I'll be back in time for the gathering," Jilly said, kissing her mother softly on the cheek. "Sure you don't mind me not preparing the food with you? I know I'd only get in everyone's way."

"No, honestly. Beverley's coming later to help out with things and you're right, you'll only be in my way while I'm cooking. Go on. Relax by the stream."

She reached over and removed the long curl hiding her daughter's face and hung it over her left ear. "You look tired," she said, "and it's going to be a late night for us all."

Jilly slipped out the front door clutching her book and headed along the path and into the trees. She decided to head down to the stream today and sit where the large rocks made miniature rapids. The noise of the frothy water was quite soothing to her and she needed to just chill after such a restless night's sleep. It was a little further to travel, but it was peaceful there. Peace was something Jilly knew she was not going to get tonight with the girls coming over for the Wedding Gathering Party. The girlie chatter was going to be joyous and loud.

Jilly often came to sit by the stream to read her book, meditate or just listen to the wind while the background of the trickling water relaxed her completely. Today she had taken along her book of poems and quotes. These often inspired her. This particular book had been given to her as a birthday present one year from Joseph. He had brought it back from the New World and instead of dedicating it to the Thyme library, he gave it to Jilly. He knew she would personally appreciate the beauty of the poetry and learn from its section on *quotes*.

Again, Gyp was by her side as she trundled along through the trees to the stream. Today, Gyp felt *stroppy*. He would rather have slept in on this particular day as he also had a disturbed night but he decided to tag along for the company of his best friend. He had been fed early and then washed himself clean thoroughly after. He had even managed another quick nap before Jilly picked up her book to go out. Most cats did what they liked each day, be it sleep, hunt, or sleep! Gyp always seemed to be at his happiest tagging along with Jilly. If, on the odd occasion they did go their separate ways, his heart was always with her and hers remained with him until they met up again.

The journey to the stream was really quite pleasant. Most of the wooded area of Thyme was a delicate splash of nature mixed with slightly rough edges. Unfortunately where nature resides, there were also some *not-so-nice* bits. Water collected in hollows along the footpath where the trees were too dense for light to dry any puddles quick enough before the next rain. Some parts of the pathway leading to the stream were therefore very muddy and on very hot summer days, large areas of mud were dried forming gullies and ridges, which often twisted many a misjudging ankle. The rain caused most of the problems in the wood such as wet slippery leaves, slippery moss and the annoying task of cleaning muddy shoes back home. Everyone in Thyme Hollow was aware though of the importance of the laws of nature and so the rain was actually welcomed. It meant the vegetation grew faster and healthier thus feeding the animals and giving the people of Thyme plenty of substance for their cooking and potions. The dark areas of the wood provided the mushrooms and the lighter ones the wild herbs. The animals brought companionship, the vegetation supplied the food for the hungry vegetarians and the wind brought voices from the spirits. Nature brought harmony to the villagers and the New World brought them their thirst for knowledge. It also brought them handy stuff which helped ease hassle of the old ways. Penedora's favourite New World item was her fridge. She didn't understand all the technology that accompanied having one, but its practicality was immense. Jilly's favourite item was *all* of her New World clothes. She wasn't ungrateful for the clothes her mother made her. Quite the contrary, they were practical and made with love, but the modern materials had so much more colour and texture and shape and well, everything really! Jilly liked torches too, especially if she was heading home late in the dark of winter.

The New World was the place they gained their science and teachings of new ways but the people of Thyme Hollow felt saddened knowing that those in the New World had long forgotten their old ones. Ways which could so help them in their current fast, stressful and often diseased lives. This was a reason nearly everyone in Thyme still held their old ways in highest regard, never to be forgotten - ever!

On reaching the stream, Jilly saw the sun rising high into the blueness of the sky and its rays glistening through the trees, swaying in time with their branches and dancing on the ripples of the water. She felt the warm on her face and smiled.

"There is going to be no rain today," she pondered happily. Gyp scanned the area for a suitable place to sleep while Jilly climbed upon a couple of the larger rocks. Steadying herself with one arm and trying not to drop her book into the water with the other, she managed to prop herself on the highest rock. Her feet dangled over its edge. The grass verge was a little wet from splashes and the rocks gave her a stable base to perch on and take in the relaxing surroundings. Gyp remained by the trees, exploring and practising his scratching techniques before settling himself. Neither noticed the two dead fish silently slithering down the stream between the rocks, occasionally snagging their once mobile fins on the sharp edges. A set of smaller rocks blocked their progress for a split second until the movement of the water pushed them along on their way again downstream.

Time trickled slowly by as Jilly's fingers scanned the pages of her book. She often paused to close her eyes and concentrate on learning or memorising the written words contained therein and the meanings behind them.

A long curl made its way past her fringe and fell over her eyes obscuring her vision. Trying not to lose her momentum in reading she quickly hooked it back behind her left ear. This felt strange on her head as the piece of hair had obviously fallen from the right side of her head. She unhooked it again, held it out in front of her face and made the decision that it belonged on the right side. She then hooked the piece of hair over her right ear but this too felt strange. She sighed with the effort and took the opportunity to stop and rub the back of her neck with her hand. It felt tense so she used her fingers to knead into the flesh, massaging the whole area that ached. Her posture on the rocks didn't help her aching neck, nor did the repeating dream she had had last night. The tension, which often gripped her neck when she woke after such dreams, remained with her throughout most of the following day.

A cloud floated by, partly covering the early afternoon sun. Jilly shivered slightly, turned over the next page and continued reading. A fresh wind chilled her, again making her shiver. With all the niggling disturbances, she eventually looked up from her book for a rest.

"*Wey narvea*," the voices whispered to her across the water, "*Wey narvea imbrew*".

Jilly didn't quite catch them the first time around and tried hard to listen more carefully. She remembered Joseph's teachings and how to link into messages from her ancestors in spirit but she felt the energy of these messages were lighter and more distant than she hoped for with all her practice.

"*Wey narvea imbrew*," they repeated to her. Then they were gone. Jilly hadn't really grasped the old language fully and was confused by the message. She decided to ask her mother on returning home what the message meant.

"Wheaooow!" Gyp screeched in a high pitched tone as he fell from a tree. His rapid descent through the branches had scraped one of his front legs leaving some fur behind on a jutting twig. Unlike most cat landings, Gyp had landed awkwardly and looked dishevelled. He fell from far up leaving his pride high above him. Jilly leapt up, throwing down her book on the rock behind her, headed rapidly in his direction.

"Are you ok Gyp?" She looked up to where he had fallen from. "You idiot!" she scoffed. Gyp was already licking his wounds when she finally reached him, his pride hurt more than his leg. Bending down she held out her hand to pick up his front leg to see the damage.

"Let me see."

Gyp flicked his tail at the offending tree and turned away from her. "I don't need your sympathy," he thought to himself as he huffed off in a homeward direction. He'd had enough of climbing today and sleeping and generally waiting for Jilly to finish her book. He was tired, stroppy and bored. That's most likely why he slipped out of the tree, sheer boredom!

"Don't go Gyp," Jilly beckoned him, "let me have a quick look at your leg."

Gyp took no notice of her comfort, his pride was still dented as everyone knows cats don't fall, they jump and land with dignity.

"*My* wounds?" he questioned, "I'm not wounded; mere scratches! I'll clean up my very small scratches later. Maybe much later when they don't hurt so much!"

He sauntered off in a huff.

"OK then," Jilly sighed reluctantly, "If you want to go home, then I suppose I'll come too."

Jilly so wanted to stay a little longer and read, but she knew if Gyp had hurt himself she should follow. He generally looked out for her and so she should him. They were best of friends and treated each other as such.

"Now look what's happened!" she gasped, as she returned to the rocks to fetch her book. "My book's fallen into the water."

It had slipped down and jammed itself between two smaller rocks. Unfortunately for Jilly though, it had fallen low enough for the stream to cascade merrily over it. Now slightly miffed with the disturbance Gyp had caused, Jilly reached between the rocks. Leaning over, her reflection could be seen from beneath the water. She managed to retrieve her now thoroughly soggy book without losing her balance and fall in.

"Great, just great!"

She flicked it in the air trying to regain some element of dryness but realised this was a total waste of time. Her book needed some serious drying out technique! She huffed loudly enough for Gyp to hear her and turned to follow him home. "Why did you climb up so high?" she called after him.

The voices in the wind began whispering again. By now, Jilly was too preoccupied with the salvaging of her Book of Poems & Quotes to listen.

Back home, Penedora was finishing the last little touches to the kitchen table. She placed the salad bowl in the centre of the spread, stepped back and weighed up its position. "Umm," she sighed and promptly moved it! Replacing the salad bowl with the basket of bread, she put the salad bowl into another space and again moved various dishes to fill in the surrounding gaps.

"That's better," she thought and smiled proudly to herself. Most of the morning had been spent cooking and preparing. She'd worked really quite hard but Penedora was never afraid of hard work. She liked it because it kept her mind busy and a busy mind kept her from thinking about him.

Looking much younger than her thirty-six years, Penedora was naturally beautiful and had a figure to match. She was quite a mature and homely woman and she believed things had to be just right. Gatherings at Thyme Hollow were particularly enjoyable to all those who attended, especially when food was on the agenda. Penedora's specialities were her 'brewed' magic concoctions but everyone still enjoyed and complemented her in abundance on her old-fashioned cooking. Visitors often popped into the cottage unannounced and Penedora always offered to feed everyone who visited, hence her homeliness persona. Hospitality was a high priority in Thyme Hollow, especially at Penedora's. Her cupboards and 'New World' fridge were always full of freshly baked cakes, jams and old-fashioned stews. Her larder was also full. It was crammed with jars of specialities, each neatly labelled and each relating to a New World remedy or Thyme Hollow spell.

It was an unspoken rule in Thyme that spells and potions were only used for good or for advancement, which would guarantee a good outcome. Vindictive spells, those causing hindrance or hurt or indeed any spell cast with a bad attitude or intended outcome was definitely not allowed. The general welfare of others and thoughtfulness made Thyme Hollow such a wonderfully magical place to live in. Of course, there were the odd, infrequent, trivial problems between friends or neighbours, but the Council was there for those seeking advice and an acceptable solution to every problem could always be found.

The lifting of the back door latch caused Penedora to look round as her daughter entered the cottage.

"You're back earlier than I thought you'd be."

Jilly curled up her nose. "Gyp fell out of a tree and scratched his leg on some branches on the way down. I think he hurt it quite badly. He didn't want to stay anymore."

"Meaning you had to return too?" her mother finished.

Gyp followed Jilly into the room and ignoring Penedora in the process, made his way to his favourite mat in the lounge. He couldn't be bothered with any fuss from her, his leg was still sore and he definitely needed a rest! Both watched him as he meandered his way past them.

Jilly took the opportunity to show her mother the book. Holding it up, she screwed up her faced in disappointment.

"Stream?" enquired Penedora, as her face followed suit in an '*ouch*' kind of response.

"Yep!"

Her mother took the book from her and, holding it between her thumb and forefinger, held it away at arm's length. She positioned it over the top rung of the clotheshorse tucked in the kitchen corner.

"You know the pages will go crispy when it dries," Penedora informed her.

Jilly nodded but was grateful that she hadn't completely lost it in the stream. Most things accidentally dropped in the stream were usually found at a later date washed up near the shingles. This was an area at the far end of Thyme Hollow where the stream became very shallow over a bed of shingles, a place where everyone splashed about on hot summer days.

Having now noticed the wonderful spread her mother had set at the table, Jilly's face lit up. "Wow! Look at all that delicious food." She scanned the tray of cakes. Eyes bright and focussed on the display of goodies, it didn't take her long to become distracted from the question she was going to ask her mother. Food and the looming gathering was now top of her agenda.

"What time is everyone coming?" she asked excitedly.

"At about four," her mother replied as she placed the last bowl onto the table. Penedora slapped her daughter's hand as it reached for a crisp. Jilly's hand flinched and she smiled.

Penedora opened a draw, and reached in for a long thin box.

"You can help me cling-film these bowls," she said as she popped the cling-film box into Jilly's hands.

"Broach is going to collect Carmel up on the way. Hopefully everyone will be here by then," Penedora continued. "Joseph is going to Uncle Gustus' up on The Ridge. I'm not sure how many they have going to their feast, I think he's kept his one quite small too."

Jilly quickly sneaked a crisp when her mother's back was turned.

"Why can't Gyp come to the wedding?" she crunched. Penedora ignored the small crisp crumb she noticed resting on Jilly's chin.

"Don't be silly darling. You know pets think weddings are just human things and I'm not sure Gyp is in any fit state to go now." She raised an eyebrow in Gyp's direction and Jilly's eyes obeyed. They both smiled as they spied him through the large archway leading to the lounge. He sat at a weird angle on his mat, licking his wounds and flicking his tail in anger.

"Would you like some ointment for your leg?" Jilly called to him. "You fell quite far."

Gyp flicked his tail twice from left to right and starred back through the archway at her.

"I think he's embarrassed," whispered Penedora, "cats don't generally fall out of trees. Get stuck in them, yes, but slither down uncontrollably, no!"

"Oh he didn't slither downwards, he literally fell." Jilly's hand replayed the trajectory of Gyp's fall from grace from a great height. She chuckled as her mind replayed his falling from the tree. She knew it wasn't funny as he had actually hurt himself, but it was one of those events that became funnier the more you thought about it.

"Maybe it's best he doesn't come to the wedding; he'll probably still be miserable. Is Frank going?"

"No," Penedora tittered. "I'm sure Joseph won't be taking Frank to his wedding."

Frank was Joseph's frog. His colouring was indistinguishable and could only be described as a dirty, murky, brownish, green blend. Frank just sat and croaked at them whenever they visited. Joseph kept him on the bay window seat with a shallow bowl of water where he would sleep all day and only move his tongue by suddenly flicking it to catch a passing fly. Frank wasn't really bothered about venturing into the garden or playing in the pond. He was more of an indoors, home-kept frog.

Gyp and Frank hated each other. Mainly because Frank sat on the seat where Gyp wanted to snuggle down when he and Jilly visited. Both animals were stubborn and intimidating to each other. Gyp would always threaten to eat him if he didn't move and Frank, undeterred by the threats, would open an eye and croak back. He knew he would taste extremely unpleasant and to him; Gyp was just another old, stroppy cat with attitude.

"Did *you* have a pre-wedding feast?" Jilly asked her mother inquisitively.

Penedora raised her eyebrows. Memories flashed in her mind and she smiled warmly.

"Yes. We had so much food and drink I was worried about being able to jump the broom the next day!" she laughed.

Penedora removed her apron and hooked it up carefully behind the kitchen door. Earlier she had managed to change into something more attractive while the cakes were cooking. The messy preparations had been finished and the apron was put on so as not to spoil her smart clothes while laying the table. A small amount of makeup finished her outfit but Penedora had decided to keep her hair tied up for the gathering as she would be passing food around to the guests. Jilly had noticed her mother tying her hair back more often lately. She looked less like a mum when her long brown curls were loose.

"Did anyone gift you love potion on your wedding day?" Jilly continued searching for answers but made sure her eyes didn't meet her mother's when she asked the question. She knew her mother would feel pain from these memories. Memories of her father always brought hurt to her mother. Penedora returned to the table pulled out a chair and sat down on it.

"Yes," she answered affectionately. "Your father and I drank the potion. We didn't think we needed it though. We were so in love, but then," she hesitated, "most people think that on their wedding day."

She held out her left hand and curled her fingers around Jilly's waist. Jilly moved in closer to her mother and hugged her.

"It's been ten years since I last saw Steven. He crossed the stones but never returned and to this day I don't know why."

A tear pricked in her mother's eye and Penedora quickly wiped it away before it fell. Ten years on and she could still so easily cry over her lost husband.

Jilly comforted her mother. Over the years Jilly had grasped the gist of the story of where her father had disappeared but did not quite understand what motive there was for it.

As she understood from the pieces she had gathered along the way, her father had come back over the stones from a New World visit and after popping in to see Uncle Gustus first, had completely disappeared on his way back home. The story continued that her father's pen had been found near to the stones, obviously dropped by mistake from his pocket before he crossed back over again. Jilly had always thought something terrible had happened to him but was too young to participate in the confusion. At that time, everyone thought Steven had re-crossed the stones by choice, as subsequent searches proved futile. No one could understand why he had decided to cross over again, especially without his crystal. Everyone took their sacred crystal with them when they crossed into the New World. This was important. No crystal, no return. No one ever crossed the stones without a crossing spell or their Thyme crystal, unless of course they had no intention of returning to Thyme Hollow.

If anyone had just forgotten or accidentally dropped their crystal then they would have realised in the New World what they had done when trying to return. A spell for crossing over would have protected them while waiting on the other side for someone to cross from Thyme and bring them back. Penedora had exhausted every explanation in her head over and over. Jilly had done the same as she grew up but her faith in her father remained. Steven was never found waiting to return on the other side. This led to the conclusion that he had not intended to return when he crossed for the second time that fateful day and had purposely left his crystal at Uncle Gustus', this side of the stones.

The Council had even tried to contact him via their magic books, asking their ancestors for an answer. Nothing ever came to light. Magic was lost when entering the New World without a crystal or a spell book and by not returning to the crossing over point Steven had become a hidden man amongst millions in a world of modern technology.

Over the years Penedora also began believing it was Steven's choice to remain in the New World. Jilly on the other hand had believed, ever since understanding the enormity of what happened, that for some reason, her father had no choice. He couldn't return, but she didn't know why he was unable to.

"You must still love each other, having drunk the potion." Jilly continued her subtle interrogation.

"Well, at least I know he's alive, as my heart still aches for him so very much from this side. If he had died, I know my heart would be longing for our reunion in the World of Spirit. Your heart tells you of our absences Jilly. Always follow the feeling in your heart." She placed her right hand over her heart to emphasise what she was telling her daughter. "If someone is just away, your heart longs for their return. When someone has died, your heart longs for your reunion. It feels different. That's why I know your father is alive."

Penedora tweaked Jilly's waist again and tried to make light of the conversation.

"Whether or not love spells wear off in the New World, I don't know. Your father crossed for a reason and he obviously had strong reasons to do so." Penedora's voice began to harden. "Maybe it's possible to love more than one person, one here, one there, or more than one style of life. He may prefer New World technology to old ways. Who knows?" Penedora shrugged her shoulders.

Jilly was not satisfied with her mother's explanation or her 'giving up' kind of attitude.

"I believe he genuinely forgot his crystal and then something awful happened so he couldn't get back. I think Dad still loves you and is trying even to this day to return." Jilly finished defiantly.

A knock at the front door broke the tension and was welcomed by both. Jilly raced to answer it.

Much later, up at The Ridge, Joseph's evening wasn't going quite to plan. His party of men had gathered outside Uncle Gustus' lodge. The lights were out and no one appeared to be home.

When Joseph arrived, Zac had already ventured round to the side and back of the lodge to peer through the windows but it was too dim inside to see with clarity. He saw no movement inside.

Zac's elder brother, Marcus, was repeatedly knocking at the front door. He felt uneasy. He couldn't understand it. The party was not a surprise as it had been planned weeks in advance. Theoretically, Uncle Gustus should have been home and if he had popped out for some reason, surely a note stuck to an 'unlocked' door would have been a courteous gesture.

"There's definitely no one in," called Zac, as he returned to the group.

Dellery removed his hat and scratched his head. His little bit of remaining grey hair moved between his fingers.

"I can't understand it," he said, "we arranged this evening a long time ago. Uncle Gustus knew we were all coming here for Joseph's feast."

Uncle Gustus was a loveable old fellow. Similar in age to Dellery but much taller and with more rounded, cheery cheeks each side of his wrinkly face. He was a pillar of knowledge to the community and the name 'Uncle' was given to him, not by bloodline, but because he was like an uncle to everyone. He was, on the whole, a very trustworthy person and a warm character who always welcomed people with open arms. For this reason Dellery was anxious to find out where he had got to. For Uncle Gustus not to be there to greet everyone when a party had been arranged was indeed, very out of character.

"Do you think he just forgot, being old and all?" asked Zac.

"Not everyone forgets things when they get old," Dellery replied, giving Zac a knowing face. Zac immediately knew he had overstepped the mark with his comment.

"I bet he's headed to your house then, Joseph, thinking we were holding the feast at yours."

Everyone just shuffled around for a little while not knowing quite what to do next. Joseph, undeterred by the evening's events finally threw up his hands.

"Never mind," he said cheerily, "I know somewhere there'll be plenty of food on the table!"

"You can't be serious?" Marcus scoffed, catching on to Joseph's thoughts. "We can't go there."

"Why not?" Joseph asked. "Carmel will love the idea. I don't know why we didn't think of this earlier anyway." Joseph turned and headed back down the hill.

"But it's just not right," Marcus called after him.

"Come on everyone," Joseph beckoned as he headed away. "All round to Penedora's!"

Dellery and Marcus exchanged glances. Both thought the younger generation was losing sight of tradition. Even though Marcus was still a young man himself, he was very much a traditionalist. Pre-nuptial Gatherings were to be kept separate. Brides and Grooms never met the night before their wedding and certainly didn't celebrate together until *after* the ceremony.

Marcus raised a hand in acknowledgement to Dellery's disbelief in the disastrous events of the evening and reluctantly followed Joseph and his younger brother Zac down the hill. He became uneasy at the bad luck element of the unfolding events of the wedding evening.

Dellery looked back over his shoulder at the dark lodge. "Where had Uncle Gustus got to?" He thought. He beckoned to the others.

"Hold on a minute," he shouted to them, "I'm just going to leave a note in case Uncle Gustus returns home. He can then join us at Penedora's later."

51

Dellery hurried back to the front door of the lodge. He fumbled in his pocket for something to write on and pulled out a piece of screwed up tissue, which had been festering in his jacket for some time. This was all he could find.

"Has anyone got a piece of paper?" he yelled down to his colleagues.

They shook their heads.

"No!" was shouted back.

He unrolled the tissue as best he could, rubbed his hands across it a few times and found enough smooth space to write on a few words. Removing a pen from his shirt pocket he lent against the front door and wrote a short message:

"*All gone to Penny's*."

He poked the tissue carefully through the letterbox and turned to hurry back down the hill to catch up with the others.

Uncle Gustus couldn't see the tissue as it came through his letterbox. In fact, he couldn't see anything anymore. He lay on the floor of his little backroom, silent and without breath. He was now reduced to being a pile of dust. Another pile of dust, black in colour, was scattered beside him: the remains of his dog, Brin.

Brin had been a trusted friend who had offered protection to Uncle Gustus right up to his untimely demise. Beside the piles of dust a black book had fallen to the floor. It had tattered edges and its smell was reminiscent of age. Also, in the little backroom of the lodge, a spell book, untitled, lay open on a prayer table, no words could be seen on its pages. Its magic had also died that night.

The girls had all settled themselves scattered around Penedora's lounge, eating and drinking merrily, telling tales of past escapades and giggling wildly. Beverley had arrived in the afternoon to help Penedora with the housework. Jilly and Penedora had both seemed a little flushed when she had arrived but they both welcomed her into their home eagerly.

Jilly also mucked in with putting up the celebratory decorations. The other party guests arrived in spits and spurts around five o'clock. Penedora put on some music to help the evening flow. It was a good few hours later when a further knock was heard at Penedora's door. Penedora turned off the music. Everyone looked surprised.

"I wonder who that could be," she pondered, and went to open the front door.

Joseph was right. Carmel was delighted to have the boys join their feast. They were young, in love and found it modern to be able to share a Wedding Gathering feast. Broach was a little concerned, firstly that the boys had turned up to share in the girl's Gathering Party and secondly that Uncle Gustus had let them down. She was sure her husband, Dellery, also shared the same traditional views. She glanced at him as he entered the room with a disapproving look. Dellery gestured back to his wife with shrugged shoulders.

On their unexpected arrival, Penedora spent the first ten minutes fussing over not having enough food to eat or enough chairs to sit on!

Everyone gave their reasons why they thought Uncle Gustus had not opened the door, from being asleep to having gone out for chestnuts, to popping to the New World for something special and maybe just missed them. Zac explained that he definitely saw nobody home when he looked through the windows.

"I hope he turns up at the wedding," whispered Broach to Dellery, "he promised to do the fertility spell as their wedding gift."

Dellery responded to his wife's worries by patting her knee with his hand.

"Don't worry love. We'll find out what's happened first thing in the morning. I promise you."

When everyone was settled and the merriment resumed, Penedora put the music back on lightly in the background to help soothe the worried 'Gatherers'.

Jilly had gone up to her room shortly before the men arrived. She wished Carmel much happiness in her marriage and a lovely 'rest of the evening' but she had suddenly come over all funny. Her mother put it down to scoffing cakes and sickly sweet things since the afternoon but Jilly knew it wasn't the food that had made her feel sick. She had been fighting the tension building up inside her head all afternoon and this had now exploded into a full-scale headache. At one point she thought she could hear her father calling her but immediately dismissed this as coincidence from the earlier conversation with her mother. Jilly had survived the noise of the New World vacuum cleaner, the nattering of girlie chat and the music from the lounge but couldn't escape from the voices and heaviness in her head. She mentally blocked everything and everyone out of her mind, had taken a cup of *feverfew* herbal tea to her room and lay there in her own silence to recover.

The music downstairs had been lowered by her mother later that evening but she could still hear the distant thudding of the drum's beat. Instead of being niggled by the noise, she used it to her advantage and focussed on the rhythm of the drumbeat to drown out the noise of the Gathering, calm her mind and block out any other intrusion into her thoughts.

Her initial rest had been disturbed by all the commotion downstairs when the men arrived and after listening inquisitively at her bedroom door for a while, she too thought it very strange that Uncle Gustus had 'gone walkabout'. Popping herself back into bed, she made the decision to get up

early the next morning, *headache willing*, and
venture over to the lodge to ask Uncle Gustus
what had happened.

It wasn't really her inquisitive nature that
involved her, she just knew everyone else would
be concentrating on the wedding preparations and
she, like most teenagers, would only be told to
keep out of the way! Picking mushrooms and
nettles for someone, like Broach, would be an
excellent excuse to leave early. Her arm reached
across to Gyp and stroked him several times. He
responded with a purr and shut his eyes. He
thought it best to go with her to the lodge in the
morning. He was none too impressed with her
little story planned for Penedora next morning. He
would rather her just tell her mother what she was
really up to. Truth was always best in situations
like these.

Jilly leaned over to her bedside table, picked up
her cup and sipped the last remains of the now
cold herbal tea, replaced the cup onto the table
and then settled herself down for the rest of the
night. Gyp rearranged his position and snuggled
into the curvature of Jilly's covered body.
Downstairs the sound of the merriment continued
and it began to fade slowly in her mind as she
drifted off to sleep.

*Bright colours circled around her head, swirling
like cream mixing in a coffee cup. Jilly was*

floating on the wind, being lifted by a hand, which felt like cotton wool. With her whole body totally relaxed, her mind calm, slowly she began sinking towards the field beneath her. Gently, she came to a rest on the cushion of ground below. It was soft beneath her and she realised it was a field, fresh and green with the sweet smell of flowers all around her. Jilly was smiling from ear to ear, her heart at one with the world and her mind away with the fairies. This dream always began so pleasantly. A voice in the background was calling her name…..

"Jilly!" it called softly, "I'm here, I'm here, please reach into the darkness and find me."

Jilly stirred in her sleep. Gyp knew it was the same dream again. He wasn't aware though of its implications, but it bothered him Jilly always woke from these dreams more restless and confused than when she retired the night before.

Gyp was neither scruffy nor immaculately groomed, he was just, Gyp! His yellow eyes glowed in the dark, but in daylight, you could see one eye had a small mark by its pupil. This was not so much a disfigurement, but a mark of originality. Most cats had markings that distinguished them immediately upon sight. Gyp was completely black with an average shaped face and of an average size. Only the small black mark on his left yellow, cat-shaped eye made him different to most other completely black cats. To an owner though, like Jilly, markings were irrelevant. She knew Gyp from afar and could pick him out from a hundred black cats. They were mentally connected, yet stronger than that, they loved each other. Gyp knew, soon his love for her would be tested, but for now, he moved and curled up closer to her and went back to sleep.

Chapter 3

Didn't want to wake you
Gyp and I have gone out to gather mushrooms
and nettles for Broach

Jilly's note was short, to the point and left on the kitchen table for Penedora when she woke. Purposely, she failed to mention that she was actually going up to The Ridge to find out what had happened to Uncle Gustus. Jilly loved a good mystery, yet deep down she knew this would be deemed as interference by the elders.

It took quite a while to reach Uncle Gustus' lodge and having had no breakfast and another sleepless night, Jilly felt a little weak walking up the steep hill. The path was quite muddy and slippery in a couple of places and her tiredness caused her to misjudge a few of her steps en route.

Suddenly she remembered the mushrooms, the nettle…and her basket.

"Damn!" she thought, "I forgot my basket! Would mother notice the mushroom-picking basket at home? Now, if Uncle Gustus has been hurt in anyway and I can help him, everyone would be pleased with my meddling. But then again, if Uncle Gustus is fine I could just say I'd forgotten the basket!"

Gyp looked up at her. Jilly could tell by his face that he didn't approve of her 'get out of gaol' analysing thoughts.

"OK," she replied reluctantly to him, "I'll tell Mum that as I'd forgotten the mushroom basket. I then decided to just pick a few stinging nettles and as I was already out in the woods, I thought it a nice idea to pay a visit to Uncle Gustus."

At least she could scrunch nettles up into her pockets just like she'd done a couple of days earlier for the love potion. Gyp stared at her then flicked his tail sharply. He supposed this was the best explanation Penedora was going to get.

"What?" her eyes rolled back at him.

Jilly strayed from the path and bent in front of a large cluster of nettles. Reaching out with both hands grasped two large clumps. She screamed! The sudden rush of pain felt between the palms of her hands and up her fingers, came as a complete shock to her. Gyp immediately sprang into action, his senses alert as he scanned the area. He saw nothing. Jilly let go of the nettles and her fingers began painfully pulsating. Small white bumps appeared before her eyes as she unclenched her fists to see what happened.

"I've been stung!" Jilly cried. Tears swelled in her eyes as she tried to keep control. Confusion then swept through her. "But how?"

With throbbing hands, she struggled to her feet. Her eyes scanned the sunlight in the direction of the lodge. Her objective was to reach it as quickly as possible in the hope Uncle Gustus had ointment or some spell to stop the searing sensation of pain. This sharp hurting was alien to her. Gyp felt useless.

Cupping her palms close to her chest she walked briskly towards the lodge. A couple of times her feet slipped in the mud beneath her but she managed to hold on to her footing until she reached firmer, stony ground. Tears dripped from her face but she didn't wipe them away as her hands were too sore to unclench.

The pain was all she could focus on as it prevented her intuition to flow. Gyp on the other hand began to realise something was horribly wrong having now reached the lodge. He immediately noticed there was no dog barking at him from the porch. Brin was absent and the air around them felt still, cold and un-welcoming.

Winching in pain, Jilly knocked loudly with her knuckles then called out repeatedly to gain some attention.
"Hello!" she called as she leant over and peered through the front window. "Uncle Gustus! Are you OK? Is anyone in?"
Silence.

Agitated, she knocked loudly at the door again. "Uncle Gustus are you there?"

A hand touched her shoulder. Her body twisted round at an alarming speed and a loud gasp escaped her.

"Good God Zac!" she yelped. "You scared me half to death."

"I'm sooo sorry Jilly. I was round the back and heard you calling. What are you doing here?"

"Same as you, by the look of it; I came to see if Uncle Gustus had returned."

Jilly smiled in relief that it was him who stood before her and no one more senior. Zac wouldn't snitch on her, but even if he did, they were now investigating together and team work was most definitely encouraged in Thyme! The excruciating pain in her hands subsided just a tad as Zac's presence distracted her focus on them.

Jilly's acknowledging smiled warmed him and he stood for a split second just admiring the view. Zac was actually quite shy. Like his older brother, Marcus, he was a kind and gentle person, but where Marcus was more manly and rugged in his features, Zac still held the boyish charms of full lips and a smaller defined nose. His skin was smooth and facial hair was, as yet, still nowhere to be seen. Marcus took after his father and Zac looked more like his mother, but there was still enough distinguishing features between them that linked them as siblings.

"There's no sign of Uncle Gustus. I managed to force open the back door."

Jilly's pursed her lips and sucked in a little air. She didn't expect that to go down well when Uncle Gustus returned home.

"There's no sign of him having been in all night or having gone out. The front door is actually still locked from the inside."

"That's rather strange," she replied.

"Another strange thing is Brin is missing too."

Gyp purred a little over Zac's astuteness.

Deep down Zac was glad Jilly had turned up. He had noticed weird things beginning to happen in Thyme Hollow and the disappearance of Uncle Gustus emphasised his fears. If something horrible had happened to Uncle Gustus, he felt The Ridge was definitely not the place to be alone. At night, The Ridge was an extremely dark place. Not that anyone in Thyme Hollow feared being alone or going out in the dark. It was just sometimes the mind would spark scary thoughts as the midnight breezes filtered through the trees, whispering in your ears and touching your body eerily as you moved between them.

Jilly thought she could utilise the opportunity of an open back door and for someone to allow her in without the owner's permission. She knew Uncle Gustus wouldn't mind them just going in, but it was always polite to ask before entering. Breaking his back door would have to be a Zac explanation/problem.

"Can I go in? I really need to wash my hands."

Extending her arms she opened her clenched fists and showed Zac the white rashes around her hands.

"They really hurt."

"Oh they look sore." He wanted to touch them but thought better of it. "How did you do that? What happened?"

"Stinging nettles."

"Stinging Nettles? Thyme nettles?"

"They actually stung me!"

Zac looked perplexed.

"But nettles in Thyme don't sting."

"Well the ones I picked today did!"

His strong arms and slowly broadening shoulders, steered her towards the back door. Gyp followed them.

Once inside the lodge, they made their way to the kitchen where Zac turned on the cold tap. Jilly held out her hands over the sink. The coolness of the water soothed her palms a little, but the pain had now reached deep under her skin.

"I just don't understand it," Jilly explained as she waved her hands beneath the flow of water. "I've never been stung by nettles before. I know they're called stinging nettles from folklore and theoretically they should sting but we've never had stingy ones in Thyme before. Why now?"

Zac couldn't give her an answer.

"Where were they?" he asked.

"Just up the path, edge of the woods." She pointed and splashed a little water from the tap in his direction.

Zac laughed as his reflexes weren't quick enough to dodge the droplets.

"Oops! Sorry!" She crinkled up her little nose at him.

"The nettles they have in the New World sting," he explained.

"Do they? Do you think we've got a rogue batch growing over here? Maybe Uncle Gustus brought some back across the stones from the New World and planted them?"

"Possibly! But we have our own so why would he plant New World ones? And Uncle Gustus planting stuff? Unlikely?"

Jilly held her hands under the cold water until she could feel nothing. "Maybe it was for a scientific experiment or something."

Zac lent over her to retrieve a small, slightly dirty, once-cream, towel that was hanging from a hook beside the sink and handed it to Jilly. He could feel the warmth of her breath as he lent across her to turn off the tap. A strange sensation ripped through him causing his cheeks to slightly redden. Jilly felt nothing, as she was focussing on her numb hands. She took the towel and thanked him. Her palms felt a lot better cold but the throbbing sensation began to rise again slightly when warm blood flowed back into them.

"I can't believe they still hurt," she told him while inspecting the poisonous bumps. Zac held her hands in his to inspect the damage.

"I bent down and grabbed two large handfuls before I realised what had happened. Serves me right I suppose. If I hadn't have been so eager I'd have only grabbed one bunch and maybe if I'd brought a basket and not forgotten it, I would only have needed to pick mushrooms." Jilly was waffling as Zac stood gazing at her.

She had found herself doing this waffling stuff around Zac of late. Whether it was to impress him or a kind of embarrassment thing, Jilly was unsure. She just knew she was becoming more and more fingers and thumbs around the boys, especially the ones she quite liked. Jilly liked Zac. They had always got on well. Jilly viewed Marcus as the older, rougher brother but Zac was more shy and cute. She looked up at him. At this very moment, when their eyes met, for just a few seconds longer than usual, she decided she definitely liked cute.

Zac broke their gaze and dropped her hands. "I've got an idea. I'll be back in a minute."

He headed out the kitchen and into the hallway towards the front door.

Jilly saw him cut back passed the kitchen window outside making his way to the woodland edge. She watched as he scouted around the wild plants. There were none immediately around the lodge. In fact there were not many plants inside the lodge boundary at all. The position of the lodge meant you could approach coming uphill from the woods or from the back by a large gravelled area leading from the fields. Either way, it felt secluded and peaceful. Uncle Gustus was not really a keen gardener anyway. He kept the place *neat-ish* and well-swept in autumn but fussy flower beds were not his style. Instead, he chose the simple method of stones, pea-shingle and the natural-looking surroundings with plenty of earth for the dog to play on! He kept his lodge garden free of nettles, mushrooms and most herbs as he felt these should remain wild and not invade his little patch of Ridge rock.

Zac's idea sprang to his mind from visits to the New World and his love of reading. There they had some kind of plant called *dock weed*. The leaves were said to help soothe stinging nettle stings. He couldn't remember what the plants looked like. He did however, remember that they grew next to or very near stinging nettles, so he picked as many different kinds of leaves as he could find, taking great care not to sting himself on any nearby nettles. Any leaves he did recognise, he left. Zac felt very tempted to see if the nettles would sting him too but he chickened out. Jilly's hand's looked quite painful and he didn't want to experience the sensation of a nettle sting.

Jilly peered out the window anxiously trying to see where Zac had gone, and was relieved when he returned. For some strange reason, she felt slightly uneasy being left alone inside the lodge. On entering the kitchen he made his way over to Jilly who was replacing the cream towel back onto its little hook.

"Try these," he said placing a pile of leaves before her on the kitchen table.

Try one? Confused, Jilly leaned over, took some of the leaves displayed before her and popped them into her mouth.

"No!" Zac laughed, "don't eat them!"

She immediately spat out some rather distasteful leaves and laughed too.

"You're supposed to scrunch them up to get the juice out their stems, then rub the juice on your skin over the stings, like this."

She watched him as he picked up a leaf and rubbed it slowly in his palm until a little bit of juice came out of it. He took her right hand and dabbed the juice onto a sore bit. She liked him holding her hand and it didn't matter if the leaf juice worked or not!

"You must think I'm stupid," she said, pushing out the last bit of damp leaf from her mouth.

Blushing, she looked away from him, as he let go of her hand.

Zac smiled. He noticed her blush and instantly knew she too felt the same chemistry he felt whenever he was around her.

"Not at all. In fact I'm the one who's stupid. I can't remember what a dock leaf is supposed to look like. That's why you've got to try all these different varieties until one helps!"

His hands swept proudly over the display of leaves he placed before her.

Zac had gained much knowledge of many subjects through reading and venturing over to the New World with his brother. He was older than Jilly by a little under three years but they had grown up around each other and he had seen her blossom into a delightful young lady. His mind wandered to the night before when he had been disappointed in her not attending the Gathering and how sad he was to hear of her headache. His mind tried to capture other moments before where Jilly had impacted his consciousness. He remembered back to when she was thirteen and had arrived with her mother one day to attend a summer picnic. The pretty yellow dress was still vivid in his mind to this day. Chemistry with this girl had begun for him many years before this moment but her blush had just confirmed she liked him back.

"Dock leaf? Erm… well I know this one definitely isn't a dock leaf," Jilly said picking out a small yellowish leaf from the pile that she immediately recognised. Placing it to one side she continued routing around the pile.

"I'll try this one," she said, waving it at him.

"You should read more books from the New World; they're full of such interesting stuff."

"I do read books from the New World actually," she stated. "But I'm more interested in the old ways. I love spells and magic and poems and stuff like that."

"But you still have to be practical, Jilly. Where would we be if Uncle Gustus hadn't read science books and given us indoor running water and taps? Probably down by the stream trying to soothe your stinging hands."

"But with old ways, I'd probably drink some of my mother's potion and wouldn't have to go down to the stream in the first place."

"Point won!"

They both chuckled.

"I think you are right though, Jilly, someone must have brought nettles back from the New World and now they are growing here."

Jilly looked up at him, her smile disappearing. "They obviously look exactly the same. Maybe our ones have somehow just lost their magic."

The mood in the room changed.

"Do you think something bad has happened to Uncle Gustus?" she asked hesitantly.

"I've looked all over the lodge and around The Ridge in case he is hurt or had left a message but there's no sign of him. It's as if he's disappeared. Poof! Just vanished. Which worries me immensely as this is so unlike Uncle Gustus. He never crosses the stones without letting someone know."

Jilly's thoughts veered off to her conversation with Penedora about the strange disappearance of her father many years ago.

Zac interrupted her thoughts. "I did find this though."

He went over to the sideboard and picked up a book. He turned back and opened it in front of Jilly, flicked through the pages, then shut it again as he handed it to her.

Gyp leapt up onto the table and with arched back, hissed at Zac.

"Get down!" Jilly shouted, as she stood up abruptly and pushed him out of the way and off the table. Leaves scattered everywhere in the commotion and the book landed with a thud on the kitchen floor. Jilly had firm rules about animals on kitchen tables and she extended these rules even to Gyp.

"Sorry about that Zac. You probably just scared him when you flicked the book shut," she said, bending and picking up the book.

Gyp gave Jilly a stern look as he made his way under a kitchen chair. He licked his fur just where she had caught him with the back of her hand. He wasn't happy. He wasn't happy about this situation at all.

"It's OK. Sorry if I scared you Gyp," said Zac as he peered under the chair at the chastised cat. Undeterred by Gyp's cold response, Zac then continued the conversation of the book with Jilly.

"Take a look. It's not Uncle Gustus' spell book. That's still on his back room table, but it is very similar, as it has plain pages. It's obviously a spell book of some sort as Uncle Gustus had it in his spell room, but I wouldn't know how to begin to use it."

Jilly explored the book. There was no writing on it at all. Every page was empty, and so was the cover.

"See, blank pages, just like ours."

She could feel the age of it and she acknowledged its smell by curling up her nose as she drew it close to her face to examine the beautiful stitching of the front cover.

She agreed with him.

"I think you're right. It does look like a spell book. Old though. Much older than any I have seen in Thyme Hollow. Look how worn the edges are. I wonder where it came from and how Uncle Gustus got it."

Zac shrugged his shoulders.

The back door creaked a little as the wind began to pick up outside.

"That sounded creepy." Zac muttered. "I think I better go sort it."

He felt guilty for breaking the hinges and damaging it to force entry. He would apologise to Uncle Gustus later when he returned home and, of course, he would fix it properly as soon as he could. The wind howled a little more outside as Zac bent the latch back into place to secure the door against the frame as best he could.

"This will have to do," he said.

Gyp stood his ground crouched beneath the chair, waiting for something to happen. Nothing did.

"Where did you say you found this book?" Jilly asked as Zac returned.

"In the spell room. It wasn't actually on the table next to Uncle Gustus' own spell book. It's weird, but I found it on the floor next to two large piles of dust by the door. I know Uncle Gustus is not the cleanest of people, but I've never seen him leave little piles of dirt around before. Everything seems a little spooky too me. It felt as if Uncle Gustus had been in the middle of a spell and had just *left*! I wonder why he did and what's going on?"

Neither could think of a suitable answer.

"Do you want to come up and have a look for yourself?"

Jilly declined. The weather had suddenly taken a turn for the worse, the trees were swaying, her hands still hurt, Gyp was acting funny, the back door was still rattling and she now just wanted to go home.

They both decided to head back to Penedora's together so Jilly could get proper medicine to cure her nettle stings. Gyp thought this was a very wise move.

There was a gathering at Penedora's waiting to meet the intrepid explorers. Jilly was a little surprised to see everyone as she stepped in through the door and scanned all the faces. But Penedora was not so surprised to see Jilly return with Zac. Finally, their eyes made contact and Penedora beckoned Jilly with them. Their movements motioned her to take a seat in the corner of the room and remain silent. Jilly obeyed. Penedora knew Jilly had obviously got herself involved with the strange disappearance of Uncle Gustus but now was not the right time to question her, now was the time for adult intervention.

When Zac had followed Jilly into the cottage, Penedora immediately picked up on the chemistry merging between the two youngsters.

Dellery welcomed Zac and passed him a kitchen chair to sit on. "Well Zac, was he there?"

"No."

Dellery shared the worry on everyone's faces. "Did you find *any* trace of Uncle Gustus?"

Jilly realised that Zac had obviously been asked to intervene by the elders. She hoped this would get her out of any trouble with her mother.

"No, Sir," he replied. "I found a couple of odd things though. Brin has disappeared too. There's no sign of him anywhere but I noticed his lead was still hanging up by the back door."

Jilly felt useless. She had bothered to go all that way up to the ridge but hadn't bothered to find any clues as to where Uncle Gustus could be. She had been preoccupied with her hands and with Zac of course. She hadn't even noticed Brin wasn't barking at Gyp when they arrived.

Broach chirped up. "That must mean that Brin has run off somewhere and Uncle Gustus must have gone in search of him. Maybe they're hurt somewhere in the woods and are just waiting for a search party."

"I don't think so Broach." Dellery took the smile off his wife's weathered face with his troubled look and negative words.

"Firstly has anyone here felt that Uncle Gustus might be in danger?" His eyes scanned the room for a response but none came. "As I thought. Secondly, Brin is his best friend and that dog never leaves his side. That rules out Brin running off. Thirdly, did Uncle Gustus mention to anyone about crossing the stones to the New World?"

Everyone present shook their heads. "Did you find his crystal?"

Zac shook his head. Dellery beckoned Zac to continue.

"There were piles of dirt on his spell room floor and then there's Jilly; she stung herself on some nettles."

Everyone gasped and turned to face her. Jilly starred back uneasily. At least she thought she wouldn't have to give an excuse about being there to pick mushrooms and nettles; these nasty bumps were proof enough. Her mother got up and knelt beside her.

"Let me see."

Jilly held out her hands so everyone could see the now reddening rash on her palms.

"The throbbing has stopped now," she said sadly, "but my hands still feel quite sore."

"We tried *dock leafing* them," Zac butted in, "but we don't appear to have any dock leaves in Thyme, obviously never needed them!"

"Dock leafing?" questioned Broach. "Whatever is that?"

"A New World medicine." Zac replied.

Penedora got up and left. "I'm sure I have something in the larder to help this."

The atmosphere within the room intensified as awareness of something very wrong grew in everyone's minds. They waited until Penedora returned with a bottle of mixture and some cotton wool. She poured a little ointment onto the cotton wool and gently dabbed the mixture onto Jilly's palms. Replacing the bottle top she motioned Dellery to ignore her and continue with the meeting. She left the room and returned her ointment.

Dellery's gaze turned back to Zac. "There's more isn't there? Go on, son."

Zac fidgeted in his seat.

"I found this." He reached under his jacket and pulled out the old book he'd found at the lodge. It was too big to fit into his pocket, so he'd nestled it under his arm. He handed it to Dellery. Nervously, Zac placed his right hand into his trouser pocket and fumbled to find his crystal. He rolled it around his fingers feeling the energy from it. The book had put him on edge for some unknown reason.

"It was in Uncle Gustus' spell room. It looked as if Uncle Gustus had left in a hurry and dropped it on the way out."

Dellery passed the book around for everyone to examine. The gathering was puzzled. Nothing made sense to them yet. If something was horribly wrong, why hadn't anyone heard any messages in the wind?

Penedora returned to the kitchen and offered to make drinks for everyone.

Having noted the book's age and flicked through the empty pages, Marcus handed the book back to Dellery. He agreed that it was definitely some sort of spell book.

Zac was thanked for his help and many ideas of what may have happened circulated for some time after. All agreed that a few of the men would search further into the woods later that day in case Uncle Gustus was lying somewhere hurt. Marcus agreed to step into the New World with his friend Julin to see if Uncle Gustus was somehow stuck on the other side and everyone decided it was best not to breathe a word of this to Joseph or Carmel, at least not until after their Wedding.

Strange events from the morning had swiftly passed and the rest of the day was an active buzz for all in Thyme Hollow. Some prepared to go search for Uncle Gustus and Brin while others concentrated on the upcoming wedding ceremony.

Later that evening Marcus prepared himself for crossing over into the New World. His little brother, Zac, had retired early for the evening after his rather eventful day. They had agreed that it would be best if Julin accompanied Marcus across the stones. Julin and Marcus were great friends and had a lot in common. They had ventured across to the New World many times before and it was Julin who had come up with the idea of a Thyme library. The Council welcomed the suggestion that everyone pooled their knowledge and within a year of Julin's suggestion the little library hut was in place. It housed all the New World books brought back across the stones.

Marcus removed his crystal from his trouser pocket and placed it beside his spell book. He was very mature for his twenty-nine years and had taken his 'Age of Transition' ceremony very seriously indeed. He was twenty-two when this happened and his first spell had been a task to bear fruit from a dead tree. Marcus made a point of picking fruit from that very tree every year after passing into adulthood and accepting the ways of the old.

Girls in Thyme Hollow though seemed to reach the Age of Transition earlier. They just seemed more attune to the old ways and able to connect with their ancestors easier. This was probably the reason why there had never been a High *Priest* in Thyme. Marcus was the only hope of this ever coming about. He had gained superior knowledge from the New World, had a great memory for storing facts and was very spiritually connected with the ancestors. His intuition flowed and for these reasons he put off marriage! There had been possible suitors but Marcus had his sights on priesthood, not marriage. He felt in his heart that his calling was to serve his ancestors and the people of Thyme Hollow, not a wife and children!

The Council knew that Marcus would one day join the Inner Circle and lead them. Everyone knew and expected Marcus to be a much trusted and worthy priest. His pathway in life was already being laid by their High Priestess, Nefron. She often prayed for him in his studies and for guidance in his teachings when his time came to take up the order.

Kneeling down beside the little, low table in the back room of his father Edin's cottage Marcus began to whisper gently, *"Crystal shine strong and bright let my wish come true tonight."* Lifting his hands into the air, he spoke aloud:

"Cwym yun am ochorios
With love and light I ask thee, to share thy words so true.
A spell for crossing over is what I ask of you."

The room lay silent for a short while. Slowly a wind began to swell up around Marcus blowing the collar of his shirt against his neck. His spell book began to respond to his call.

As many times previously, the book stopped flicking at an open, empty page and words slowly appeared. Marcus didn't really need to look at them anymore as he had read from his book so often, but tradition was tradition and nobody crossed over to the New World unprotected. He read aloud:

"I carry this crystal across the stone
To keep me safe and return me home
I take only myself and the good within me
And return with the knowledge of things
that I see."

Marcus picked up his crystal from the table, popped it back into his trouser pocket and left the room. Giving a quick farewell to his father, he grabbed his over-coat by the back door and slipped outside. He was running a little late in meeting Julin by the stones so he picked up his pace through the woods, as he headed towards the stream.

At the same time Marcus and Julin crossed the stones into the New World, a crowd had congregated outside Uncle Gustus' lodge. They were also running late. The sun was falling and the wood now appeared very dark in places. The gathering lit hand-held beacons, some turned on their New-World-style torches, others held lanterns. Technology was very mixed in Thyme, some residents strictly retained the old ways and others opted to copy science brought back from the New World. Both ways were accepted as long as the land was not poisoned in anyway or links with tradition broken. The afternoon scout team had returned empty with no clues and reluctantly went back to their homes.

Spreading in different directions, the new group set off through the woods in search of Uncle Gustus.

Meanwhile, Jilly stirred in her sleep. The bright colours circulating in her head returned. Then, as before, she was floating high and without effort. Feeling complete freedom from the world and its restrictions, her thoughts blended with the peace and tranquillity of the moment. Softly, she again came to rest in a field and the distant voice began to call her name. Curiosity made her follow the soft tones calling to her. Calmly, she headed towards the beckoning. Her feet felt like they were made of sponge walking on the thickest and softest, shag pile carpet. Gradually the surface beneath her feet began to feel harder until eventually the sponginess of the meadow grass had gone entirely and she was left walking on a solid pathway. She acknowledged the need to follow it.

Her dream seemed to skip rapidly and without question on to the next stage where there was no longer a path but sand beneath her. Her feet felt warm against the fine grain and she could feel it rising between her toes. She became aware that she was now not wearing shoes. The sand felt important.

"Jilly! Jilly, I'm here. Reach into the darkness and take my hand."

She could hear the voice a little clearer now. "Save me Jilly, help me. I'm here in the darkness."

The voice grew stronger as she headed towards it. It sounded distressed and in need of her help. This intrigued her.

Jilly's way forward was suddenly blocked by a huge rock. The rock wasn't really a rock, or either a wall, in her dream it was just something substantial blocking her path; something wide, solid and imposing. It separated her from the voice. She stood motionless for a while, hesitant on which way to go. Around? Over? She wasn't quite sure. She just felt the need to find a way to the voice. Then she noticed to her left, a hole materialising at the base of the rock. It didn't grow large enough for her to see inside. It stopped opening when it was large enough for a cat or small dog to venture inside and investigate the blackness. She positioned herself in front of the hole and kneeling down, peered into the darkness. The voice came again, asking her to reach in and help.

She had arrived at this point of the dream on several occasions, but now she knew she was able to go on further. On this occasion, the dream was allowing her to investigate the voice more. To venture into the unknown. This time, she reached in. Usually, she was content to just float around with the colours or smell the sweet flowers. Often *she would deviate from the pathway to pick the weird flowers growing in her mind. On one occasion she had ignored the voice and climbed the rock to nothingness. This time though, her subconscious was curious. Who called her?*

As her hand lowered itself into the gap of darkness she could feel a warm glow rising up her arm. She felt good and when the hand from within the darkness stretched out and touched her fingers, she felt enveloped in love.

"Jilly it's me. I can feel you. You have come to save me."

"Father?"

Then it grabbed her. The stranger's hand, which had made her feel warm and safe, suddenly grabbed her tightly and its fingers grew rapidly upwards towards her elbow. Crushing her wrist and entwining themselves around her arm, the fingers took a firm hold. Jilly screamed and screamed trying desperately to pull herself free. The pain in her arm was excruciating, on fire and she knew she had to escape its grip. The voice from the darkness laughed, a sickening, taunting laugh and the evil arm, with great force, sucked her through. Jilly could feel her body crushing and contorting, her muscles, squeezing the bones of her delicate skeleton, cracking. She could feel her blood squirting out from her torn skin as he/it dragged her down into the small black gap and

*the darkness beyond. Jilly let out a final blood
curdling scream in her dream.*

Gyp was jolted off her lap as Jilly lashed out
from her sleep. She sat bolt upright and opened
her eyes. Sweat poured down the sides of her
face. It took her a while to realise that she was
safe in bed and that this had only been a bad
dream. Shaken, she sighed and lay back against
the pillow again. Gyp composed himself and
jumped back onto her lap.

"I'm sorry Gyp," her hand stretched out to
stroke him. "I had a bad dream again didn't I?"

He rubbed himself against her hand a couple of
times and then snuggled himself down again. He
knew the dreams were coming more frequently
but this was the first time she had gone further
than hearing the cry for help. He didn't purr. He
felt too uneasy and afraid of what would happen
to her unconscious mind if next time she failed to
wake up before succumbing to the darkness in
her dreams.

Chapter 4

The atmosphere in Thyme Hollow was very mixed. Both search parties had returned the previous day, still none-the-wiser about the disappearance of Uncle Gustus. Mutterings around the wood about the odd occurrences escalating stirred fear in many. Two piles of undisturbed dust remained in the little back room at the Lodge. Everyone was eager not to spoil the wedding celebrations but the smiles hid many a worried mind.

Joseph and Carmel both had butterflies flittering around their stomachs with the excitement of the rapidly approaching afternoon. Even though their pre-wedding Gathering had last minute changes, their wedding preparations had actually gone quite smoothly. Everything was in place and waiting for the hour of their betrothal. Those who were involved in the organisation of the wedding festival were briefed, poised and ready for the afternoon. All Joseph and Carmel needed to do on this particular sunny day was to get up, washed, dressed and turn up at the clearing in the woods. They were both a little nervous, like most people are on their special day but this was a happy, thrill of a nervous feeling they shared.

Weddings were not just a close family event in Thyme Hollow, everyone chipped in. Sharing was a major part of the community and it was this community spirit that gave Thyme Hollow its soul.

Of course, the community had its ups and downs. Occasionally people would clash over decisions made and the Council and the elders of Thyme were called to smooth out any wrinkles that occurred. Their teachings were not strictly of a religious nature, but of a spiritual one. *'Do unto others as you would have them do unto you'* style of ethics, and the cliché of *'practise what you preach'* was highlighted heavily in the school. It certainly worked. Neighbours were truly neighbours and friends were friends for life. Their love for each other kept the land wholesome and abundant. The occasional hiccups did not last long as forgiveness and understanding of each other's actions usually smoothed any ruffled situation. Spells of harm were not tolerated in Thyme. If a person flouted the 'non-spoken' or stronger 'forbidden' rules then the High Priestess was called upon to decide punishment. Her justice was incredibly hard. Only a handful of times had a personal crystal been confiscated and the perpetrator banished to the New World, never to return. The elders did a grand job in Thyme, teaching the younger ones as they grew. Respect and togetherness held Thyme in hours of need, in which there were few. Magic kept Thyme Hollow alive – until now!

At the clearing, Penedora was busy adding the final touches to the food stall. She was fussing for the sake of fussing. The usual questions of food preparation were buzzing around her head, such as, do I have enough sausage rolls to go round? Are there enough types of cheese? Will the gateaux melt in the sun? She couldn't understand why she doubted herself so much. There was always enough food. The allotments were plentiful and nature provided the rest. The people of Thyme kept their nutrition as natural as possible, but on many occasions visitors to the New World brought back exquisite delights which the younger ones craved. Cream on Penedora's gateaux never melted and congratulatory comments were always expressed to her at every event where she catered and yet she still fussed.

"So delicious Pen!"
"What a delightful spread Penny."
"Aren't your tomatoes full of taste this year?"
etc.

Penedora was a strong woman and good at most tasks she tackled. Having lost Steven so many years ago, she grew independent and capable. She had been both mother and father to Jilly and had done a grand job in raising their daughter.

She chuckled to herself. "I wonder, if I added pepper to the cakes would anyone comment on how foul they tasted, or would everyone still pass pleasant comments to me?"

"What's so funny Mum?" Jilly asked as she handed her mother the last stack of paper plates.

"Oh nothing, just a silly thought," she smirked.

"I almost forgot to tell you," Jilly said, "Broach commented earlier on the lovely spread you'd done. I told her I'd pass her comment on to you."

Penedora shook her head as her smile widened. "Well, there you go!"

Jilly's confused expression followed her mother as Penedora left the food stall merrily chuckling away to herself. Jilly cleared up the boxes and bags she and her mother had brought the food in, then scuttled off back to the cottage to dispose of the rubbish and make herself look presentable for the wedding.

Beverley had also attended the ceremonial site early and was now adding the last of the wild flowers to the 'ring of love' when Penedora wandered over to admire her work. Beverley neatly tied the last two bunches of heather together and stretched out both arms above her head as she stood up.

She was nearing thirty-one but looked much younger than her years. Still slim after having Jacob and feeling fit as a fiddle, she had decided now was the time to think about having another baby. Weddings always brought on thoughts of private matters of the heart and she had stayed awake all night contemplating asking her husband what he thought on the subject of more babies! Jacob was a lovely little boy but Beverley often pondered over the fact that she had been an only child and always felt desperate for a sibling to share her childhood years. She wasn't too bothered if the next baby would be a boy or a girl, either would be great for little Jacob. She felt great joy in the pit of her stomach at the thought of her Terry being delighted with her idea. Of course he was going to be delighted with her wanting another baby. What husband wouldn't be?

Penedora interrupted Beverley's maternal thoughts as she passed by.

"Oh it's beautiful Bev. I love the way you've entwined the ivy around the inner edge," Penedora complimented. "It sets the whole ring off nicely."

She wandered off grinning to herself, but hoping her pleasantry hadn't come across too flippant. Beverley smiled back at Penedora in appreciation. Broach used to be Thyme Hollow's firm favourite to do the 'ring of love' at weddings but as her back was now creaking a little with age, bending and arranging the flowers was now a difficult task. Beverley always took on Broach's ideas for the flower arrangements and even though the touch of ivy was not hers, Bev was not going to let on just yet, she enjoyed the praise! Anyway, she felt kind of good about herself at that moment. She had kind of an inner glow about her that day.

The flowers were woven together to form a ring large enough for the bride and groom to stand inside and for the guests to assemble around the outer edge. Twigs, leaves and climbers formed the main structure of the floral circle and dotted around in an attractive setting were the flowers that bloomed with the colours of that particular season. All flowers were brought to the Council Hall to be placed before the ancestors prior to weaving. Here they were blessed by the High Priestess. A leaf from each variety of flora used was taken and placed on the altar and thanks given to nature for allowing their use in the marriage ceremony.

Penedora made her way to the drinks stall where she had spotted Zac earlier helping his brother unload their boxes. They hadn't long arrived when Marcus saw her coming over and waved. She nodded in response as he went to fetch more boxes from his cart.

"Hello Zac," she said politely.

Zac turned round and a smile immediately appeared on his face. "Hi, Ma'am."

He knew, that she knew that there was an attraction between him and her daughter and his intuition had told him that *she* knew, that he knew, that she knew! That's why he smiled. He actually felt quite nervous in front of Penedora for the first time ever. It was more of an *approval thing*.

"I hope Jilly didn't get into too much trouble the other day; getting herself involved with Uncle Gustus going missing and all?" uttered Zac, pausing for a moment from his task. He wiped his hands down his jeans to remove the dirt that wasn't there!

"She's a very wilful girl," said Penedora, "she likes to play detective. It does worry me sometimes though that she charges into situations before thinking things through. Anything could have happened to Uncle Gustus that maybe Jilly could have stumbled into herself."

Zac bent down and picked up another box of drinks. He heaved them onto the table and began removing the bottles from the box, placing them two at a time on the table in front of him.

"I really came over to say thanks for helping Jilly when she stung herself."

Zac cried for joy inside. He had gained the approval of *the mother*!

"That's Ok. I do think it wise though that Jilly doesn't go off anywhere on her own at the moment."

"You mean you want to escort her everywhere?"

"No!" Zac chuckled embarrassingly, "I meant because of all the weird things going on. Like you just said, she could get into all sorts of dangerous situations on her own."

He leant over closer to Penedora and whispered, "I don't think Thyme Hollow is safe at the moment."

Penedora nodded in agreement.

"What with all the strange nettles, Uncle Gustus going missing, and the fish." Zac continued.

"Fish?"

"Haven't you noticed the fish are dying?"

Penedora was taken aback. She hadn't actually been down to the stream recently and the issue of fish hadn't been raised at the last Council meeting.

Zac explained about the dead fish he'd seen, collecting on the shingle banks where the stream became very shallow. He thought everyone had seen them. He was wrong. Penedora told him she would let the Council know straight after the wedding festivities. She thanked him for the information, bid him farewell, and feeling incredibly unsettled, Penedora made her way back home to get dressed for the wedding too.

The feast was ready for uncovering and digesting. The centre flower circle was complete and the bustle of the morning soon died down as helpers hurried back home to prepare themselves for the festivities ahead.

Joseph eyed himself in the mirror and admired the view. His father also stood looking at him proudly. His white suit looked so stylish.

"Like something out of a black and white musical film," Issac stated, smoothing his son's white jacket at the back. Joseph took a long last look at himself in the full length mirror and turned to face his father.

"Well at least I won't have to waltz around a ballroom," laughed Joseph. "I really don't think I should bend in these trousers."

Admittedly, they were a little tight. The material around the tiny trouser button was stretched to capacity. Joseph had been eating and drinking quite heavily in the run up to the wedding and had gained a little more than the expected few extra pounds around his waist in the process. When Broach had measured him at the first fitting session she hadn't bargained on him putting on *so much* weight.

His father jokingly patted his son's stomach, "You'll just have to breathe in all day."

"We'd better get going now," said Joseph, looking at his watch.

Issac agreed, "Now's a good a time as any."

He was full of pride as he paused for a moment and then took hold of his son. Joseph hugged him back. To finish they tapped each other's backs and then parted.

Before leaving, Joseph stooped over the window ledge, picked up Frank and popped him into his top pocket. His father saw this movement just in time.

"What are you playing at? You can't take a frog to your wedding."

"I thought it would be a laugh."

Studying his father's disapproving look, Joseph reluctantly returned Frank to the windowsill then brushed his top pocket flat again with his fingers.

"Your mother and I have waited a long time for this glorious day." Issac stated proudly. "Your ancestors wanted this wedding and we are so pleased you and Carmel have grown up together in love. Now I don't want you to go spoiling it with your silly ways."

Joseph gave a cheeky grin in response. His thoughts flashed back to the times when Carmel wore pig-tails and he wore braces; when they played by the river together with other children from the Hollow and that special occasion when he had picked her up for their first school dance. All the children from Thyme Hollow grew close as they matured. It was not only their upbringing and respect for their elders which gave them their inner peace, the teachings and knowledge given to them by their ancestors created their harmonious and 'love of life' attitudes.

Everyone firmly believed in the 'what comes around goes around' saying and thus they would always strive to 'please and to do'. Of course, the children did have their spats and tantrums but these were often short lived. Friends were friends for life, even if they all had funny, irritating ways!

Joseph remembered the day he and Carmel pledged their love together by the stones and had made Jilly swear not to tell anyone before the official *Marking of the Hands*. She had sneaked up on them from behind and, realising a pledge was taking place, hurled herself at them, arms out-stretched and grinning from ear to ear. Both were quite shocked at being caught at the time but thought it fun to have someone else share their secret pledge. He and Carmel were proud of Jilly, being so young at that time and so excited for them, yet so good at keeping their betrothal a secret until they both reached the Age of Becoming when they were allowed to be joined by marking of their hands.

Issac snapped Joseph out of his memories.
"Come on son, you don't want to be late for your own wedding now do you?"
The bedroom door was swung open in front of him as his father hurried out of the room. Joseph, taking the opportunity, quickly turned round, reached out and grabbed Frank from the window ledge. He whipped him back into his top pocket.
"No croaking," he whispered, "or you'll give the game away."
Joseph's broad grin followed his father's footsteps out of the room.

Isabella was waiting at the foot of the stairs for her husband and son. There were many momentous occasions in life such as birth, Age of Becoming, Marking of the Hands, first spell at the Transition Ceremony, first trip to the New World etc. This day was one such occasion for Joseph's parents. He was their only son. Isabella was quite a mature woman when they finally conceived Joseph and after his arrival their chance of having any more children had gone by. They had worried that their child spell was missing an important ingredient or they were being punished for something unknown. But they just needed to be patient and learned that time often took its own time in Thyme!

Joseph hugged his mother when he greeted her at the bottom of the stairs and she responded by kissing him gently on the cheek. Isabella tried very hard not to allow the pride-filled tears in her eyes to drop. She sniffed them back in again with a smile, a short cough and a quick wipe of a finger! Her husband, her only son and she departed for the wedding together.

Carmel, in total contrast to her betrothed, had *lost* weight in the run up to the wedding and was one of four siblings. All were older and already married. Her eldest sister had caused a great sensation within Thyme three years earlier when she had fallen in love with a gentleman from the

New World. The heartache of separation was felt by all when her final decision was to marry him and live across the stones. Blessings were sent with her but of course, her past was left behind the day she crossed over for good. Her husband was of the new ways and could therefore never know who she really was or where she had come from. Sara loved the New World and her marriage was quite content but she often longed to tell her husband all about her old life, her upbringing and of her parents and siblings back in Thyme Hollow. She was allowed though to practise New World witchcraft and magic in private and connect with her family and friends through her dreams and meditation. This is all she could do, so did it often. It was obviously not the same as back in Thyme where spells and potions were a way of life. In the New World people had lost the old ways and only a few dabbled in trying to bring magic back into their busy or mundane lives. They had no understanding that it needed everyone to vibrate on the same wavelength to enable the possibilities that Thyme gave to all.

Sara was allowed to teach any children they had, the 'old ways' through her spells, meditation, crystals etc. to keep traditions alive, but the right to return to Thyme for ever could only be done alone. Only physical items, such as cutlery, torches, books and of course, knowledge she'd gained while in the New World could be taken back across the stones. This rule though meant if she ever wanted to return it would mean leaving her husband and any of their children behind. New World People were not allowed to cross. Inhabitants of Thyme Hollow knew they would bring sorrow and change with them, something everyone agreed should never happen.

Unlike many from Thyme who often crossed back and forth, Sara had made a connection in the New World which complicated her passages to and from. She was not cast out from Thyme. On the contrary, she went with much love and blessings. Combining the two worlds was not an option and this gave rise to her having to choose. The risk of her future husband knowing their existence was too great and this responsibility she accepted with a heavy heart, but gracefully.

Today Carmel missed Sara deeply. On this special day, she felt a strong urge to see her eldest sister, one more time.

Jilly had made it home before her mother and was trying on her dress, swinging her hips as far out as she could to enable her to see the back of it. It was beige in colour with subtle brown trimming. Fitted at the waist and cut to a very feminine outline the dress enhanced Jilly's maturing figure. Length-wise, it stopped just at the knees allowing her to show off her shapely legs. This is something Jilly seldom did. She was still mainly a longish pinny *or* jeans girl, practical and yet pretty. This particular outfit was from the New World and it made her feel vibrant.

"Does it look okay from the back?" she enquired of her mother.

"Fine dear, you look lovely."

Penedora's mind was busy with other things, such as food stalls, approaching the subject of Jilly's feelings towards Zac and dead fish, but she did sneak in a quick glance at her daughter displaying herself in front of the mirror. She was becoming a young lady. "Wrong!" Penedora corrected her thoughts. "She has already become a young lady." Next step womanhood and then motherhood, which was going to go way too quickly for Penedora's liking. Then her mind flashed to Zac.

"Are you sure my bottom doesn't look too big in this dress?" Jilly disrupted her mother's thinking, rubbed her hands over her bottom and straightened up the edges of her dress.

Her mother gently smacked it with the back of her hand and giggled.

"Of course not! It's amazing how you've recently become so interested in what you look like," her mother said sarcastically.

Jilly smiled broadly.

"Well, you know how it is? Everyone makes a special effort for weddings and blessings and such like."

Jilly stole one more glance in the mirror to reassure herself that she was looking good. She picked low-heeled shoes, not because she was tall but the clearing often proved an impractical venue for high heels. She added two pearl earrings and a dainty necklace to her attire. Her hair hung loosely around her shoulders and her make-up was subtle and soft. Jilly felt fresh and alive.

When the last of the wedding guests arrived, Carmel was already within the ring of love. She was seated in its centre on the grass, surrounded by her stunning wedding gown and by the beautiful flowers of the ring. She looked like a fairy in the middle of a flower, waiting for Spring to open its petals and free her. Her dress was an ivory-cross-gold colour with tiny pearl beading edging its glory. When the sun poked through the large intermittent clouds above, the pearls within her head-dress glistened softly, adding special highlights to the whole outfit. Carmel looked and felt a million dollars. Her mother looked on admiringly. The beauty her daughter radiated this day made her not only feel extremely proud but saddened by the loss of her little girl, her baby. She was now fully grown and was the last to leave the nest. "Joseph is a very lucky man," she thought.

The guests started gathering around the edge of the flowers and their excitement grew. Soon everyone was holding hands and the chanting began. The soft melody of voices all singing beautifully and joyously began echoing around the clearing. Slowly, the crowd began to sway in time with the rhythm of their tune.

On arrival, Isabella and Issac joined the singing crowd next to Carmel's parents. They all linked hands and closed the circle of people again. Voices lifted high and the movement of the swaying blended with the surrounding trees, almost bringing the whole area into a state of meditation and musical trance. Peace and harmony radiated around the ring of love sending out joy to the couple soon to be betrothed.

When the song had finished Carmel and Joseph's parents dropped their hands causing a gap to emerge once more. They stepped back slightly allowing Joseph to pass through the gap and enter the ring by stepping over the flowers. At the same time, Carmel stood up and held out her arms to greet her husband-to-be. Joseph took her hands in his as he stepped in towards her.

The bride and groom then turned around together to face the High Priestess, a woman who stood out from the rest of the crowd in all her splendour. She was a tall, elegant woman who, at a glance, could be seen immediately as someone of great importance. The red robe, which hung loosely over her shoulders, was fastened around her neck by a huge pentagon-shaped broach. She was stunning to any onlooker but, of course, it was the bride who took centre stage at these events as she bloomed and radiated happiness.

The High Priestess spoke loudly so the crowd could hear.

"Whose hands have been marked for betrothal?"

"Ours have," was their reply, as the happy couple held up their palms to show the High Priestess their Markings.

"Do you enter this marriage willingly?" the High Priestess continued.

"We do," they replied.

"Do you understand the responsibilities of marriage as is written in The Book?"

"We understand."

"Do you wish to be joined in matrimony to each other according to the law of The Book?"

"We do."

The High Priestess turned to a young child standing to her right. Little Jacob had been chosen to hold the basket of petals and ribbons. He was dressed in a smart velvet brown suit with a cream, frilly shirt. His little brown bow tie was slightly choking him as his mother, Beverley, had tied it too tight while dressing him in haste. He kept poking a finger between the bow tie and his shirt collar to try and loosen it but couldn't quite get his finger far enough in between the two to separate them. He kept pulling faces and fidgeting and hoped the ceremony wouldn't go on too long.

The High Priestess took a small handful of petals from the basket. She brought her hand back round to the front of her again and carefully sprinkled some petals over Joseph and Carmel's hands. She repeated this three times while chanting a prayer in the old language. She then reached into Jacob's basket and removed two white ribbons. She tied the ribbons loosely around their hands, sealing their love together. The High Priestess then invited the bride and groom to say their vows to each other.

Joseph spoke first while lovingly looking into Carmel's glistening eyes. Carmel then said her vows back, both promising to love each other for ever.

Upon finishing, Jacob stepped back and retreated into the crowd. He ran around the back of the circle and joined his mother. Beverley patted him on the head and allowed him to stand next to her.

The High Priestess continued the ceremony by addressing the bride and groom once more.

"Do you thank your ancestors and the witnesses here present for the blessings they bestow upon you?"

"We thank them."

Joseph and Carmel reached their hands towards the High Priestess and she gently removed the ribbons. She tied one around the bride's left wrist and the other around the groom's.

"Please join with me now in the thanks we give to your parents for the love they have bestowed upon you in your upbringing and for the joy they now share in this, your special day. May you grow wise together and teach your children the values you yourselves have received."

Joseph and Carmel turned round and embraced their parents, returning their parents' kisses as they wished them good luck and great joy in their life. The bride and groom in return thanked their parents for their happy, joyous childhood.

When this had finished, the High Priestess continued with the proceedings, "Do you now wish to cross the broom?"

Joseph and Carmel looked at each other, their smiles wide and their eyes glistening with happiness as they both replied again, "We do."

The High Priestess raised her arms towards the crowd, saying happily, "Yea martydinium, heni alim el ya omnay. These two children of God and Spirit who stand before me entered the ring separately. They now choose to leave as one. May our ancestors give their blessings to this couple who are now wed in the sight of all witnesses here present and in sight of those in the realms beyond."

The High Priestess stepped to one side revealing a broom lying just outside of the ring of flowers. Joseph and Carmel took hold of each other's hands and, with emphasised effort, together, jumped over it.

A loud cheer went up from the crowd and as the happy couple kissed. Hugs and blessings were showered upon them from all around as they began their new life as husband and wife.

The marriage ceremony was complete and the after celebrations began. Soon the music was playing merrily, hands clapped and the partying commenced. The hustle and bustle of the final weeks of preparations had now come to fruition and everyone began dancing, drinking and enjoying the wedding feast. Gifts were bestowed upon the couple as they were carried away into the merriment of the occasion.

Jilly finally jigged away from the partying section and made her way over to the stand where Zac and Julin were serving drinks.

"Hi!" she called to them both.

Julin acknowledged her with a nod and Zac, pausing from his task, ventured to the side of the table to talk to her.

"How's it going?" he asked her as he manoeuvred himself closer.

"Fine thanks. Where's Marcus?"

Zac pointed to a group of people who were dancing haphazardly to the music. His brother could be seen waving his arms sporadically as other dancers were desperately trying to avoid being swiped.

Jilly caught sight of him and cringed, "He never could dance."

They both laughed as they watched the celebrations around them. Zac served a few drinks in between the small talk and loud chatter.

"I wanted to thank you for helping me," Jilly piped up, "when I got stung, you know, at the lodge."

Zac shrugged his shoulders, "No problem. How are your hands now?"

Jilly held out her palms to show him that she was ok and that the pain hadn't remained for too long after her mother had dealt with them.

"I'm fine now - rash gone – see?"

Zac took hold of her fingers with his as she held up her hands towards him. Then he rapidly retreated. That same flash of chemistry that emerged up at the lodge happened again and his stomach churned as their fingers had touched.

"They look much better," he choked.

"I'd better get on," he said, returning to safety behind the table. "I'm glad they're better now."

Jilly smiled. She suddenly felt good and in control. She became aware of what was going on between them and she knew he had just felt it too. A little butterfly flittered in her stomach. Wickedly, she made sure their eyes made contact again when she bid farewell to him and she held her gaze for a split second longer than normal.

"See you around then, Zac."

Penedora stood frozen to the spot and watched as her daughter left Zac's drinks table and circulated within the gathering. Her daughter had just reached the Age of Becoming.

About an hour later, Jilly finally ended up at her mother's stall where Penedora was busy again serving cake and rolls and explaining what filling was in which sandwich. They exchanged nods and smiles. People were getting hot and tired from jigging about and the drinks and food areas were quite busy now. Jilly looked on, as those still dancing and clapping to the music, swept the happy couple along with the momentum of the festivities. She pondered delightfully, knowing that one day, she too would be a bride.

It wasn't long after Jilly's arrival at the stall that Penedora began paying little notice to her daughter's presence. Her undivided attention was being given to the guests requesting service and small talk. The rolls and cakes swiftly began to dwindle in number. Jilly often glanced over to where Zac was helping Julin serve drinks and it was then, for some strange reason, that Jilly remembered her question. At first her mind couldn't quite catch the phrase that had been spoken to her in the wind, down by the stream.

"Wey nervy something," she thought.

She tried hard to get the words into her brain again. This was 'tip of the tongue syndrome'.

"Wey narvea inbry?"

She nearly had it but the partying in the background kept disrupting her thoughts.

"Wey narvea imbrew. That's it!" She cried excitedly, "wey narvea imbrew."

She moved closer to her mother who was by now madly dealing with a whole host of food requests, listening to the music and trying to see the happy couple amongst the crowd receiving and showing their presents.

"Not now, Jilly!" she interrupted as her daughter tried to grab her attention.

"But it's something I forgot to ask you," Jilly persisted, "it may be important. I heard a message in the wind and I thought you might know what it meant."

Her mother didn't have time to stop and face her as she continued serving. "This slice; no it's not fattening; some of that, no problem."

Penedora wiped her fingers on a napkin nearby

then passed over yet another plate. At the same time she could see in the distance the happy couple picking up her gifted jars of love potion. She tried to look round people in front of her stall to see their happy faces and watch them as they drank.

"I'm a bit busy at the moment Jilly." Her mother's voice was a little raised. Not only because her daughter was interrupting her but also the music and laughter was becoming louder and trying to concentrate on everything at once was slightly agitating.

"What does 'wey narvea imbrew' mean?" Jilly shouted.

Her mother's gaze was suddenly fixed upon Jilly's face. She stood bolt upright and the knife in her hand froze against the side of the half-sliced piece of cake.

"I beg your pardon, Jilly. What did you say?"

Jilly was taken aback. Her mother was not usually so snappy with her. A feeling of dread filled her stomach and she was now wishing she had not brought the subject up at this inopportune moment.

Hesitantly, Jilly explained herself. "I heard voices at the stream. You know the day after we did the spell together. I'd totally forgotten to ask you what they meant but I've just remembered, you see."

A wedding guest interrupted them and requested a roll, but Penedora put her hand out to halt their request.

Penedora waved her other hand with the knife in a circular motion, beckoning Jilly to speed up her conversation.

Jilly took no notice of her mother's request to speed up. Her voice grew quieter and slower as she reached the end of her sentence. "The voices were saying - wey narvea imbrew."

Jilly now noticed her mother had gone a very light shade of white and it was then that she watched the following events as if they were all played in slow motion.

Her mother screamed at the top of her voice, the knife left her hand and fell to the grass as she manoeuvred around the table and darted towards the people surrounding the bride and groom. Those at the food stall turned towards the commotion going on around them. They stood dazed as they watched Penedora, shouting at the top of her voice, waving her arms frantically in front of her, as she ran away from them towards the happy couple.

"Don't drink the potion!" Penedora screeched at the top of her voice, trying desperately hard to get Joseph or Carmel's attention. "Don't drink……."

Silence fell everywhere. Still in slow motion, Jilly could see the crowd dispersing as her mother drew nearer to them. Shock filled everyone's face as they turned away from the scene that confronted them and gazed at the mad, screaming Penedora running towards them. Hesitantly, a gap emerged in the once-partying group at the centre of the clearing and Jilly could just make out that two figures were lying on the ground not moving. She could see Joseph and Carmel.

Penedora stopped in her tracks. She was too late. One crystal jar had smashed on impact with the ground the other splattered half its contents on the once glistening wedding dress. Joseph and Carmel were lying dead in front of her and the shocked onlookers. A scream was heard, then another. Then the crying and panic began. Penedora put her hands to her head in disbelief. She had poisoned them with her love potion. Realisation of the tragedy took over the celebrations.

"The potion was poisoned," Penedora muttered. "I didn't know. I'm so sorry. I didn't realise. I....I....Noooo!" was the last cry heard from her lips as she fell to her knees clutching her head in her hands. Penedora's sobs blended with the utter confusion that followed.

Jilly stood rooted to the spot by the food stall. Her mouth wide open with disbelief, her stomach knotted, her mind was stung with pain and seemed unable to function normally. Time in Thyme stood still.

Joseph and Carmel didn't move. The poisoned potion had killed them instantly. They both fell to the ground moments after sipping from the jars. Their bodies were now lying together on the ground, motionless. Their eyes starred up towards the sky. Another scream was heard amongst the guests as Frank popped out of Joseph's top pocket. He croaked at the onlookers and feeling totally bewildered by what was going on, hopped away.

Chapter 5

Gyp sat on the grass at the edge of the wood, looking across the stones and focussing on the same time and space as Jilly. Both just sat. Both just sat there numb. Behind them, the shadows on the pathway danced as the sun shone through the trees that were swaying in time with the wind. A small red squirrel leapt from a nearby branch. Gyp looked up as he heard the squirrel move, but didn't take long to return his gaze to the stones. He had no real interest in the squirrel. Today his mind was elsewhere. Jilly kept her head turned and watched the little creature as it hopped along busily with its daily chores. Suddenly the happy little squirrel became aware of being watched and stopped in its tracks. Up on its hind legs its radar of sight and smell swept the area until it had registered the only threats within its immediate vicinity; the black cat and one human. Catching the attention of the two mourners made it edgy and it seemed unusually afraid of happening upon strangers. It stood for what seemed like an eternity fixed looking in their direction. The black cat wasn't interested. It then relaxed. The decision was made that both creatures seemed unthreatening at this particular time, so the squirrel, now undeterred by their presence, bounced off happily and continued with its business.

   The appearance of the squirrel had only halted the process of crying momentarily. As soon as it had hopped out of sight the tears came back. One tiny drop, then another until the girl beside the black cat was in full flood. Jilly sobbed. She sobbed like she had never cried before. Her heart broken, her mind in total confusion and her soul was in bewilderment at the loss of her two friends. The blame was harvesting and the guilty feeling sitting inside of her was immeasurable. Gyp momentarily removed his gaze from the water frothing between the rocks and looked up at her. Jilly's hands now covered her face; her head bent forward allowing the tears to drop freely and the noise of uncontrollable weeping swept through the forest. Gyp felt this was not the time to nuzzle up to her. Whatever anyone said or did at this present time would not take away the fact that she blamed herself. Grief is a hard emotion to control at the best of times but when you blame yourself in anyway, the grief is intensified. These were unusual emotions to Jilly, ones she could never have imagined experiencing. If only she had properly *listened* to the message. If only she had *remembered* the message. If only. The more the image of Carmel and Joseph lying on the ground flashed through her thoughts, the more Jilly sobbed.

Death in Thyme Hollow was often treated with mixed celebrations; one part was joyous for the passage of the dead to the Land of Spirit and Ancestry and the other part given to the sadness of the goodbyes from those left behind on Earth. It was rare indeed for someone in Thyme Hollow to pass over to the Land of Spirit before their time so unnaturally, as in the case of Joseph and Carmel. Ancestors were generally prepared and ready to greet those crossing over to the other side but if the death came suddenly and unexpectedly, confusion followed and the dead soul would be left to find its own way home alone to the land beyond. This period of searching for where it should rightfully be was often lonely and heart wrenching for the soul as it came to terms with its untimely demise. Those friends and relatives left behind were then forced to cope with being denied their farewells and loving goodbyes. Heartache felt, both *here* and *there*, until the spiritual soul had reached its destination beyond and the 'remainders' come to terms with their loss. This was cruel. If death was feared by anyone in Thyme Hollow, this was the only reason. The people of Thyme Hollow were now stuck in the grief of the unknown wait, while Carmel and Joseph found their own way home to their ancestors.

Beneath Jilly's tears the general day to day noises of the wood continued. Lapping water over rocks, birds singing, animals rustling through the leaves and the friendly wind of Thyme made the branches sway rhythmically in the trees. Jilly had momentarily hated her ancestors. She had hated spells and potions and her mother! She had *blamed* everyone else for a split second. She had also *hated* everyone else for a split second. She then returned to the comforting *self-pity* where her reality hit home. Here she just blamed herself for the tragic loss of her dear friends and here she also acknowledged the acceptance of her beliefs where she knew that death was not final but merely just a parting. She knew in her heart that Joseph and Carmel would eventually turn up in the Land of Spirit but today she mourned for their funeral. She mourned for their right to pass over with dignity and timing, with love and with friends to greet them warmly on the other side. Today she mourned for the *goodbyes* that they didn't get the chance to say.

Jilly had cried all she could and her eyes were now sore and her nose dripped. She wiped the tissue across her nostrils and sniffed back the residue. Her throat too was sore from the 'lump feeling' that had been overwhelming her all day. She felt a state and she looked a state. She took time to think of her mother and wondered how she was getting on at the Council gathering. All hierarchy members had been summoned to an emergency meeting in light of the wedding tragedy and the failed search for Uncle Gustus. Jilly's thoughts made her feel uneasy. Something big was going down in Thyme and she felt vulnerable and suddenly very small and insignificant. She needed her mother at this precise time but unfortunately both had been unable to communicate with each other since the fateful event. Penedora blamed herself for making the potion; Jilly blamed herself for not warning anyone in time that it had been poisoned.

Gyp blamed himself too. Not for the deaths of Joseph and Carmel but for being unable to protect his friends from the impending doom. He knew it was coming and it would be coming swiftly. He knew '*They*' were here in Thyme Hollow and he knew what '*They*' wanted.

In a little back room of her house, the High Priestess closed her book. She knelt down in front of her prayer table and bowed her head, her hands meeting her face to cup it gently.

"Please give us the strength to fight this," she whispered into her palms, "please help your children for as long as you can. Guide us to the knowledge we need to see this thing through."

She sat in this position for what felt a life time. Words escaped her now. She just couldn't think of anything else to say or ask. Facing the Council

was going to be hard but she was prepared.
Nefron had done all she could do but now needed
to dig deep for her leadership skills. She had to be
courageous and determined and show strength,
even though what she had just been told was
something no one could be confident about. The
people of Thyme would soon be left on their own.
Yet it was now that they needed their spells, their
link to the other world and their confidence. She
knew that now they all needed a miracle!

The Council had congregated at the communal
hall. It wasn't a grand hall like some in the New
World, but it was grand to the people of Thyme
Hollow. Grand in the notion that the land's wise
and educated ones gathered here to make
important decisions; to make sure the equilibrium
of Thyme was kept. It was a place where
hierarchy reigned and through hard work and
love, anyone from Thyme could gain knowledge
and work their way up towards joining the inner
circle and become one of Thyme's esteemed
Council members.

Everyone present sat in silence while they
awaited the appearance of the High Priestess.
Significant movement eventually came from the
back of the hall as Dellery heaved open the main
door, allowing the High Priestess to enter. All eyes
followed her as she glided gracefully past the
chairs to the front of the main hall. Her long

flowing purple gown dragged behind her on the wooden floor collecting a little dirt just below the seam as she moved. The gown swished to her side revealing the brilliant redness of the lining as on reaching the front she abruptly turned and faced the gathering. Her short, bobbed, auburn hair flicked around her face completing her movement. All eyes of the Council eagerly awaited her prayer. Not a mutter could be heard amongst the gathering but the noise within each mind present was unbearable. The High Priestess raised her arms and tilted her head backwards. Shutting her eyes, she drew breath, drew strength and began.

"Chi Dayoo am Natra. I am Nefron. Chi ley naum investialias. I am of the Old Order. I am pure of heart, strong of mind and my soul is attuned. I call upon the ancestors of our forefathers and mothers to join us now; to advise us; to guide us and to assist in our time of need."

Her energy radiated around the room; her presence calmed the minds of those at the Council gathering.

Adjusting her position and her cloak, she took a quick glance backwards and sat down on the enormous, ornately carved chair behind. It was intricately hand-carved with magical symbols and flowers; each design entwined and pertinent in meaning to her wisdom and power. Placing her arms on the solid arm rests either side of the wooden chair, Nefron re-affixed her gaze towards her audience. Dellery slipped silently down the middle of the group and into his chair at the front of the hall. He made no interruption as Nefron took a moment to scan the faces of the people before her. She then turned to and addressed Penedora who sat patiently in front.

"We hold you not to blame my child. Your potion was made pure of heart and for good and for this you can not be held responsible. Something is happening here in Thyme Hollow which is not of our choosing and not of your doing."

Penedora heard the words Nefron had spoken to her but had not accepted them. She knew Joseph and Carmel's parents blamed her. However understanding or nice they were, however much knowing they had that Thyme was gripped in something that no one as yet understood, she knew they could only attribute blame to the very one known thing, *her. Penedora made the potion. Penedora had poisoned the bride and groom.*

The High Priestess then directed herself to the Council.

"I ask all of you present to refrain from small talk and accusations. Penedora is not to be held accountable for the untimely passing of Carmel and Joseph. What I am about to tell you, affects you all."

Her eyes scanned the room making sure everyone had her attention.

"I have consulted with those beyond through The Book of our Ancestors and I am afraid by what they have told me."

Every eye was fixed towards the front. Every ear was attentive. They knew that the situation was serious by the strange events that had happened over the last couple of days but for Nefron to feel fear and admit to it, was indeed extremely worrying to the people of Thyme.

She continued. "Our stream and vegetation have been poisoned. It has been witnessed that our fish are dying and nature has turned against us. Our links to our ancestors are becoming weaker by the day and soon we will be on our own."

Gasps were heard all around the hall.

"I have been told that we must collect knowledge from each other and from the New World immediately and we must use this knowledge to protect ourselves and make good the situation. In the meantime, we cannot use water from the stream, no mushrooms or nettles from the wood for our spells. I ask also for you to refrain using any wild herbs or any plant from your gardens as we must be vigilant. The poison could already have spread."

Dellery reached into his pocket and clasped his crystal tightly in his hand.

"We must also be vigilant in what we now ask of our Books as our links are fading fast. I have been told that the Gods of Misr have awoken. That we have angered them and our ancestors fear for us because of our actions."

She faltered a little, swallowed and then finished, "The Gods of Misr are stronger than our ancestors."

More gasps. No one was stronger than their ancestors. This could not be!

Agitation grew stronger around the hall as people shuffled in their seats.

"They have the power to sever our links with the world beyond and are doing so in order to punish us until they get what they want."

Cries and panic filled the air. Heads turned from side to side looking around the room for someone to blame. The noise made within everyone's minds as they searched for answers and accountability echoed around the hall in great waves of energy. Who did what? Who was to blame? Why were they all being punished?

"Silence!" Nefron commanded. "The blame lies not with yourselves but with an unfortunate situation that we have gathered unintentionally."

The Council looked confused. Dellery stood up. He turned to face everyone and waved his arms motioning everyone to settle down again. He had earned his title of Council Elder and as this position stated, he spoke for them all.

"Nefron, we do not understand. What have we done to offend these people? Why are we being punished and for what? Can you explain further?"

Nefron shrugged.

"I do not completely understand either," she said. "Apparently we have angered these Gods by stealing from them and using their spells! Our ancestors have informed me that they are unable to undo what is being done and they do not have the power to defend us. Our links are being slowly severed and they can only advise us in what actions to take because the powers of Misr are too strong for them. Our knowledge is not as ancient. We are all unfortunately out of our depth."

Everyone grew more agitated than before and Nefron raised her arm to hush the Council again.

Dellery who was still standing at this point, raised another question to Nefron.

"Who or what is Misr?"

The Council silenced again, and everyone listened for her answer with bated breath.

"Egypt," she replied. "We have disturbed and angered the gods of ancient Egypt and their might is now upon us."

"What have we stolen?" a hesitant voice piped up from the middle of the hall.

"Their ancient spell book. The Book of the Dead."

Penedora gasped. It was a loud enough noise to attract the attention of the High Priestess.

Marcus and Zac's father, a tall, stately-looking gentleman stood up and politely addressed the High Priestess. Her attention was drawn away from Penedora's sudden reaction.

"Yes, Edin?"

"Have our ancestors informed you of who supposedly stole this book?"

"I think we may have found an answer," replied Nefron, fixing her deep green eyes back upon Penedora.

Penedora gulped. "I didn't steal it," she said nervously raising herself from her chair, scanned the room behind her at all the staring faces.

"Do you know who did?" Nefron asked.

"Not quite."

"'Not quite' is not an answer. Do you or do you not know who took the Egyptian Book of the Dead?"

"No."

"Then enlighten us with what you *do* know."

"I don't know much, really. I'm not sure about the stealing bit but I think I might know about the book you are talking about."

At that same moment, Dellery eagerly made his way next to Penedora to give her support.

"I think I can shed some light on this book too," he said. "I think what Penedora is going to say is that it all somehow links to Uncle Gustus and the night of the Gathering."

Dellery and Marcus, who were also present at Penedora's on the day Zac and Jilly had brought them the strange book from the lodge, repeated their accounts of the events surrounding the strange disappearance of Uncle Gustus. It was unanimously agreed that this must definitely be the book in question and that Uncle Gustus had obviously been the one who had dabbled with the spells. This must be why the Egyptian Gods had now awoken and caused havoc but who had originally stolen the book from Egypt was another matter for discussion. It could not be proved that Uncle Gustus had taken it even though it was found at his lodge. How had it got there? Was it indeed the book in question? Everyone gave their opinion on the matter, but no actual fact was evident.

Penedora now remained silent. Too scared to speak, she was afraid of what reaction her words would bring. Memories flooded back to her and she remembered Steven had given a book to Uncle Gustus the day he disappeared. She knew Steven had crossed the stones to Egypt and returned with a book that day, but stealing – no! She couldn't believe Steven or Uncle Gustus would steal anything. *Could they have? Absolutely not!* Her mind refused to give any more credence to that thought.

"Where is the book now?" asked Nefron.

"I have it," said Dellery, "it's at my place."

Fear suddenly swept across his face as he pictured Broach, alone at the cottage. Nefron stopped him.

"Don't panic," she cried. "as long as we have our sacred crystals we are safe from harm; for the time being anyway. This I have been assured of, but I don't know how long till Misr takes away all our power."

She looked to the floor of the grand hall, unable to give any more assurance of safety that she had been told. She knew time was running out and they were losing a grip on the magic of Thyme.

Broach wore her crystal around her neck on a chain that Dellery had given to her as an anniversary present. Dellery decided not to take any chances. Thoughts of his wife forgetting to put on her necklace that morning, or removing it to do daily chores, scared him. His loyalties suddenly changed and he wished more than anything to be at his wife's side and not at the Council Hall discussing a potentially dangerous matter. The High Priestess looked up and acknowledged his need to leave. He excused himself politely, but sharply and hurriedly left the meeting. Images of his wife being 'got' by ancient Egyptian Gods made his little legs travel faster than they had done in a very, long time.

He kept repeating himself all the way home. "Please let her be OK. Please, please, please."

Shortly after Dellery's brisk exit from the hall, Marcus made a wise decision. He was excused also. The Council agreed with him that he should follow Dellery home as a 'safety in numbers' back up. He knew he was the right man for the job. He *hoped* he was the right man for the job. Marcus often came across as a leader and helper in times of trouble throughout the community of Thyme and its people were beginning to trust him, intuitively, confidently and admiringly. Marcus was rapidly gaining respect, from the Council who looked upon him as a very mature, young man. His rise to priesthood was taking shape and at times like this he was always first to step up and take charge. There were also very few now seated within the hall that actually wanted to venture outside into the unknown reign of Egyptian terror.

Penedora was worried; so were all the Inner Circle members. Their High Priestess was afraid and now both hierarchies had left the safety of the Hall: Marcus, their priest in the making, and their oldest *Elder*, Dellery.

Marcus was requested to bring the Egyptian book back to the hall immediately. It was felt that placing the stolen book on a holy altar would offer them all at least some protection until they learned how to and as importantly, where to, return it.

Everyone desperately wanted a decision made as to how to proceed in undoing the dreadful wrong, without anyone else being harmed. Nefron had offered all the advice and information to everyone that she herself had been issued with by the ancestors earlier that day. She didn't know what else to give them.

"Right," she said abruptly after the commotion of Dellery and Marcus leaving the sacred building, "let's think our dilemma through."

She settled the remaining Council members down again; each were worried for the safety of their two missing colleagues, for their family and friends at home and for themselves. Nefron feared most for the future Thyme Hollow.

"Now, we have been told we have to gain knowledge to deal with this situation, and this is what we should do next. Gaining knowledge is what we do best to exist and continue, so let's start with what we are really good at and use this as our weapon. Remember, keeping one mental step ahead of your enemy can win a battle. Let's now gather up our army," she said confidently.

Nefron shuffled back into her chair, took a deep breath filling her lungs with confidence, and began again.

"We know the basics. For example, we know we have a book that doesn't belong to us; we know the people who own it have come for it, and that they are extremely angry with us. We know we have to return it before our links with our Spirits are severed or before we are all killed."

Everyone nodded.

"What we don't know is how to return it or to whom, so let's start at the beginning. If we gather all the information we can on how the book came to be here and from exactly where, we can then build on this to make a possible plan of action. Are we all agreed?"

All agreed.

"Then we shall start with you, Penedora. You must tell us every little detail you know about the book, of Steven's visit to Egypt, and of anything else you think may help us."

Ouch! Penedora's eyes widened as her face flinched. Nefron had remembered Steven's last cross over was to Egypt. Much to her regret, Penedora's hand was forced to tell all and she now took centre stage.

On reaching his cottage Dellery could see no movement through the little windows. His heart raced and adrenaline shot through his body. He hurried through the front door and called his wife's name loudly.

"Broach!"

No reply came. Their little lounge was empty. He called again and again as he ran upstairs searching every empty room. The beds had been made. The bathroom towels were hanging neatly from the towel rails, but there was no sign of Broach. He hurried downstairs again, missing many steps in his haste and then into their back kitchen.

Bang!

"You stupid man!" cried Broach, as they both collided in the doorway.

Pegs scattered themselves across the kitchen floor as they flew out of her hands on impact.

"What's the hurry? Look what you've done!" she screeched.

Dellery rubbed his shoulder which he'd knocked against the framework of the door as he and his wife banged into each other. The impending bruise on his shoulder was irrelevant. His wife was safe. He eyed the crystal hanging around her neck and he smiled.

Dellery then hugged his wife tightly. Broach, still confused by her husband's eager clumsiness, pulled herself from his grasp. She picked up the laundry basket and tipped the dry clothes on top of a growing pile of ironing on the kitchen chair and then replaced the basket under the sink.

"Now are you going to tell me what all the hurry is while you help me pick up these pegs?"

At that point Marcus entered through the front door which had been left wide open by Dellery as he raced through it at great speed.

"Is everyone OK?" he shouted.

"We're fine," Dellery called back, surprised by Marcus' entrance, "we're in the kitchen."

Marcus made his way to the kitchen where he saw Dellery and Broach on all fours gathering up clothes pegs from the floor.

"Now are you two going to tell me what all the emergency is?" she said popping the pegs back in their bag.

"What do you mean we've got the book?" Broach cried out in horror as the story unfolded.

Dellery calmed her down. "Don't worry. I brought it back with us from Penny's. Our ancestors told Nefron that as long as we don't use it and we have our crystals to hand nothing can harm us. Well, for now, anyway."

Broach was not convinced. Her hand clasped her necklace tightly as she reassured herself she was wearing her crystal.

"Get it out of here!" she demanded, waving her arms. "Just give it back to these people."

"We can't," said Marcus.

"Why not?"

"Because we don't quite know who they are, where, or how to give it back," said Dellery.

"But you just said they are Egyptian Gods. Send someone across the stones to Egypt and leave it there." She hung up her little peg bag she'd been clutching throughout their explanation and moved into the sitting room.

Marcus butted in their discussion as he followed them through.

"We can't take that chance until we know what we're dealing with. Whoever goes across the stones with the book may not come back safely and who's to say if we just dump it on the other side, someone in Egypt may innocently pick it up and then the Gods will go after them."

"That's their problem!" she spat.

"Broach!"

Dellery was quite surprised at his wife's flippant attitude.

"We can't just palm off our problems dear. Firstly, we have to return it to the right people and ask forgiveness. They may decide to still kill us all off, even after returning it. Who knows? We're dealing with a very powerful force, Broach, and an evil one at that. We must be guided by Nefron and our ancestors on this one, for everyone's safety."

"I'll take the book back right now." said Marcus calmly, "*You'll* feel much safer if I do."

Broach liked this suggestion very much.

Dellery reached up and removed the strange old, Egyptian Book of the Dead from the sideboard and handed it to Marcus.

"You kept it on my sideboard!" she shouted.

"It's okay dear. Marcus has it now."

"It's still in my house!" Her voice suddenly lowered. "Say they hear us and know we have it."

Broach went over to the window and gingerly pulled her curtains, peering out the window as she did.

Marcus tapped the book with his hand. "I'll take it back right now. I promise you'll be safe, but please remember, no spells. Do nothing magical or eat anything you've picked recently, just in case."

Dellery followed Marcus to the front door, "Be careful son."

Dellery shivered. He had felt the power of the book at Penedora's and knowing now how dangerous it was, wanted rid of it from his house more than anything. The strange book was no longer the old interesting article found up at The Ridge. It had become something evil. It felt older now, it looked older now and it radiated power from within its pages. Marcus turned his nose up at its smell.

"Are you not coming back to the hall Dellery?" he whispered.

"No. I'd rather stay with my wife, she's a little shaken."

Marcus could see Broach was none too impressed with the danger her husband had placed them in. He nodded a quick farewell to them both. Apprehensively, he set off back to the Council Hall, clutching danger tightly in his right hand.

Marcus started briskly. He was frightened; he admitted this to himself but the chilly wind that began to swell up around his feet scared him even more. His eyes scanned everything around him as he made his way along the paths. Halfway back, Marcus broke out into a run but made sure there was no way he was going to lose his footing and fall. Adrenaline shot through his veins as he could feel the energy of something different surrounding him. The book was tight in his grasp and his crystal was safely in his trouser pocket. He prayed as he and the increasing wind following him, hurried back to the Council.

The atmosphere in the hall had become very tense. Marcus entered just as the accusations started flying in Penedora's direction. He felt safe again; she, less so. Penedora had been verbally defending herself very well up until that moment. All the information she had given freely to the Council was now being thrown back in her face. Everyone was standing and the flying accusations were increasing the already raised volume within the hall. Penedora finally lost her temper when someone put the blame solely on Steven.

"You can't prove that." she shouted in defence. "How do you know that is the actual book the Egyptians want back and maybe the one Uncle Gustus had was a different one, from another trip?"

"*He* brought it over the stones," came a sharp reply from the mob.

"That doesn't prove he stole it." Penny cried in desperation. "Maybe he found it. Have you thought about that? Maybe someone gave it to him legitimately."

"Then that person could be dead too."

Everyone went silent. Penedora turned white. *Dead? Maybe Steven was dead after all.*

The shocking revelation that if Steven had had something to do with the strange book then he could possibly be dead suddenly became very real indeed to Penedora. She looked pitifully at Nefron for help, for someone to be on her side but none came.

"What have I missed?" Marcus asked inquisitively as he made his way to the front of the hall. He gave Penedora an acknowledgement with his eyes as he approached. This reassured her that at least one friend remained in her corner of the circle! The Council reacted to his entrance by moving away from his path. Some returned to their seats, other gasped or just starred at the book as he passed. He held it tightly in his hand. Everyone was understandably afraid of it.

"Is this the Book of the Dead?" asked the High Priestess as she got up from her chair to greet him.

"Yes, we think so." Marcus held it up to her and she took it from him. She could feel the power of its magic and the book could feel the power of hers. The sudden rustling of the trees outside the hall caught everyone's attention as the wind, which had followed Marcus back to the hall, rushed around the roof at great speed.

Bang!

Someone let out a scream.

A window at the far end of the hall flung itself wide open and everyone turned their heads in its direction. Beverley let out an almighty scream as the bang from the window frame hitting the hall wall to her right made her jump. She was nearest to the window's great thud, and she got the full force of the wind as it rushed by her. It swirled high and fast. Anyone with lose items lost them as the wind whipped around the group. Nefron quickly turned and headed for the altar. She slammed the book down. It now lay upon a beautiful silk cloth in between the candles and crystals which adorned its majesty. It was truly a holy place where many a prayer had been said and Nefron knew the power of the altar could prevent the evil surrounding the book from penetrating the hall walls; at least for the time being. Links with their ancestors and land of spirit was growing steadily weaker and her magic would soon no longer give protection. She knew that even her altar would provide no safety to them as long as the book was kept in Thyme.

Slowly, the wind died down and calm returned. People scrambled to retrieve their belongings. Luckily no one had stood on the round spectacles on the floor. Beverley placed her hand over her heart and sighed in great relief. She smoothed her dress down again and combed her wind-blown hair with her fingers. Terry comforted his wife.

"It'll be okay Bev," he whispered. He reached up to the window and, carefully shutting it, replaced the catch and secured it further in the lock position. He returned his right arm around Beverley's shoulders and squeezed her safely. He then gently patted her stomach with his other hand and looked lovingly into her eyes. "It *will* be OK." Both could only think of their son Jacob back at the crèche. They silently prayed for his safety and that of their unborn child.

Marcus inwardly prayed too, thanking spirit for his safe return to the hall. He placed his hand into his trouser pocket and rotated his crystal around and around between his fingers wishing never to let go of it.

The hall was filled with confusion and fear.

"What the hell was that?"

"I've never seen wind like it. Where did it come from?"

"We're all gonna die!"

"I think it would be best if we all calm down and sort this problem out in a civilised manner," said Nefron, holding out her hands to the Council and motioning everyone to settle in their chairs.

"Now where were we? Oh yes, Steven. However Steven obtained the book is now irrelevant. What matters is that he brought it across the stones and we have to return it before it destroys us all."

Marcus scanned Penedora's face for questions. He had certainly missed a lot when he went to fetch the book. He was a bit confused by all this.

He moved to where Julin was sitting and sat down beside his friend.

"What has Steven got to do with this? I thought he disappeared *years* ago," he whispered. "That's true," Julin whispered back, "we were just discussing that bit when you came in. We think Steven may have brought the book back and gave it to Uncle Gustus. Unfortunately neither are here to ask about it."

"But that was years ago. Are you saying we've had the book in Thyme for at least ten years?"

"Looks like it."

"Then why is everything going wrong now?"

Julin shrugged his shoulders.

Penedora remained standing as everyone silenced themselves in their seats. She then continued her story. Tears pricked in her eyes as she again tried to explain her reaction to the mention of Egypt. Egypt had been the last place Steven had crossed over to, she admitted this to them all but reiterated that she, like them, did not know how Steven had come to be in possession of the book. Nor, if this was the same book he brought across. Penedora began to jog everyone's memory as she recalled the events surrounding Steven's strange disappearance that fateful day. Could what was happening now be instrumental in the event that took her husband from her, after he visited Uncle Gustus late one night, almost ten years earlier?

Chapter 6

"Where'd you get the book from?" Uncle Gustus enquired as he turned it over in his hands examining it more closely.

"Egypt," Steven replied, "don't laugh! But a man shoved it into my hands as he was running past me in the market place. I know I can look scruffy at times but surely I don't pass as a beggar!"

Uncle Gustus laughed. "So, you are telling me, a man just gave it to you."

"Not gave, thrust it at me, but yes! Funny eh? I called after him, thinking he'd mistaken me for someone else but he just kept running."

"Maybe you should go back and try again. Scruff your hair a little untidier and you might get more things! I must agree with you though, you've definitely got yourself a catch here Steven. Literally I mean!"

"Oh har! Har!"

Uncle Gustus removed his glasses and balanced them on top of his head causing a little grey piece of hair to stick up at a funny angle as he did so. This enabled him to take a much closer look at the book. Unlike many older people who have to hold items at arm's length to see properly, Uncle Gustus needed to almost touch his nose to bring clarity.

"It bears an uncanny resemblance to our spell books but the smell and roughness of the paper appear to make it so much older."

"How old do you think it is then, fifty, hundred years, couple of centuries?" Steven asked him.

"Good God, no!" exclaimed Uncle Gustus, "I think we're talking thousands of years!"

Uncle Gustus was very well read. He had been gaining knowledge from the New World for many, many years and the people of Thyme respected his opinions and advice. He was the obvious choice for Steven to show the book to. Not only was he most likely to know something about it with his years of built-up knowledge, but he was the most likely person to have already come across a book like this. It appeared not on this occasion as Uncle Gustus was stumped and could only surmise on its origins and use. It was Uncle Gustus who first put the science of running water into place from technology he had read about in New World science books. Parts were salvaged from dumps and given by kind inhabitants of the New World. Now almost all of Thyme Hollow's inhabitants had taps and sinks. He had also gone on to incorporate his teachings into new fandangled things such as toilets and washing machines. Not every one though had accepted his borrowed ideas and inventions. Laying of pipework was considered intrusive to nature. Some still used the old, hard graft ways, *of washing their clothes in the stream or using water from the wells. Everyone had choice in Thyme Hollow, and everyone's choice was respected. Uncle Gustus found the younger generation to be more willing to accept science from the New World and more eager to cross the stones and learn for themselves. Keeping their knowledge, their sixth sense and magic was very sacred, but just making life a little easier with modern technology was becoming more acceptable. The balance from both worlds, was so far, still intact.*

The two men retired to the lounge and spent most of the afternoon discussing their knowledge of Egypt, its ancient teachings, of the trips they had there and of the strange book Steven had acquired. Neither could come up with an answer as to why the Egyptian man wanted to throw it away at the market place but both agreed it had an energy and a certain smell of age about it but, like their spell books, both agreed it should be treated with upmost respect.

"Fancy a beer?" Uncle Gustus politely enquired, as he went to fetch one from the kitchen.
"I should really be making my way home," muttered Steven. He um'd and arrh'd for a split second, pause, then made his decision.
"Oh go on then."

Steven settled himself more snugly into one of Uncle Gustus' armchairs. His blonde hair was comfortably trapped between his head and the back of the chair. He closed his blue eyes for a second and his clean shaven chin turned up to meet his laughter lines around his eyes as he thought of Penny. He loved her very much and just thinking about her made him smile, every time he did.

His strong arms lifted him back into an upright position as Uncle Gustus returned to the lounge holding two bottles of beer in one hand and a bottle top opener in the other. In one sharp movement he wiped the top off one bottle and handed the beer to Steven. He then repeated the exercise with his own bottle and placed the opener, plus the two bottle tops onto the small table in front of them.

"Cheers to the New World," he said to Steven as he offered his bottle.

Steven raised his and they clinked them; both men taking a quick swig from their respective bottles.

Steven told Uncle Gustus how weird he had felt while crossing back over the stones that afternoon and that he was sure someone had followed him over. He had looked but couldn't see anyone.

"I got really spooked for minute," he explained, "I had strange thoughts that the book was evil or

something and felt all cold and shivery for a moment." He laughed. "Then I realised it was the cold wind blowing as I crossed over that had made me chilly and nothing more sinister after all."

"Sometimes your intuition can take over and your mind makes things up to scare you." Uncle Gustus commented. "I remember the time I was walking back through the woods really late one winter and I could have sworn I saw a man on a horse up ahead of me. It was actually a tree that I'd passed many times before but this time it just caught my eye and my mind decided to spook me. It was my own fault for watching scary horror films in the New World."

"Did you ever see that one about a group of youngsters camping in the woods? Can't remember the name of it, but eventually they all got bumped off, one by one by a mad man?"

Uncle Gustus screwed up his nose. "Was that the one where they set light to him at the end and he still came back for more?"

"Yes. Gross wasn't it?"

"Did you see the one about the headless horseman who terrorised erm, let me think now, it was similar to Thyme….. Hollow something, that's the one I saw horses in the woods after watching. Plays with your mind, these scary films," said Uncle Gustus, tapping his finger on his brow.

"Sleepy Hollow?"

"That's it," agreed Uncle Gustus raising his beer again in confirmation, "The Legend of Sleepy Hollow. Bit different to Thyme Hollow as we're not very sleepy here."

"Nor do we allow men without heads on horses to go charging around late at night."

"Could you imagine that," he giggled, "headless horses running amok!"

Steven laughed at him, "I'm sure Nefron would have something to say if our horses had no heads."

Both chuckled loudly. They understood now why the people in the New World found these films so entertaining; you just needed to add beer and some mates when you watched them.

The clock ticked on and eventually eleven bottles of ale had been scattered around the coffee table, two had found their way onto the floor. On finishing his third or maybe it was his fifth drink, he couldn't recall, Steven thought it best he made polite excuses and head home. It was now very late and he knew that Penny would not have waited up for him. He decided he would have to sneak in so as not to disturb her and tell her about his latest trip and the running man in the morning. When he had sobered up of course!

Uncle Gustus had placed the Egyptian book on his dresser in the main room of his lodge earlier *that evening and both had forgotten about it by the time it had come for Steven to leave.*

"Are you sure you don't want to crash here for the night? Are you even capable of getting home?"

"Ha ha, you've drunk way more than I have. Thanks for the offer though Gus, but I should get back."

It was only when Uncle Gustus had waved Steven farewell, shut the front door and attempted to pick up two empty beer bottles from the floor, that he realised Steven had forgotten to take the Egyptian book with him. Not only that, he had also left his crystal on the coffee table. He couldn't be bothered to chase after him or finish clearing up that night. It had taken him long enough to stagger to the front door and back again due to the copious amounts of alcohol he'd consumed that evening, so he decided to drop Steven's things round in the morning. Neither men thought about the dark and how Steven was going to manage his way home through the woods. Intelligent planning had been soaked away with the drink. Uncle Gustus staggered up to bed.

Steven felt uneasy as he ventured back down through the wood from The Ridge. It really was quite dark in places by the time he left and his coordination was much less than one hundred percent due to his alcohol consumption. The full moon showed his path home but that came in spits and spots where the trees were thinner. He tripped a couple of times as he tried to avoid jutting roots and mud patches on the pathway. He shivered a little in the coolness of the night and felt the wind beginning to stir.

His heartbeat began to increase, as he became more nervous of his homeward journey. He kept telling his mind to calm down. All the talk of people being hacked to death hadn't helped this situation. A couple of times he looked backwards to where he had just passed. The feeling that he was being followed intensified. The wind began to blow stronger as he stumbled his way home. Once more he put the uneasiness down to drink, darkness and a drunken, vivid imagination.

Twigs cracked beneath his feet as he fumbled his way out of the wood and into the clearing by the stones. The moonlight was bright here and reflected off the stream. Steven could see it clearly ahead and recognised the soft rippling noise of the water over the rocks. He quickened his pace. He turned his head to look backwards again, relieved that he had cleared the woods leading from The Ridge and was now half way home. Just another jagged path to his cottage remained. The wind had died down and the trees behind him were now still. He took a deep sigh of relief as he turned to face forwards again and *continue on his way. There was a sudden rush of adrenaline within his body and a slight scream leapt out of Steven's mouth as he collided with the very tall figure who blocked him. The sudden collision caused Steven to fall backwards to the ground; his pen was knocked out of his top pocket on impact. Steven immediately froze as he saw what stood before him. Fear gripped him as he scrambled deep within his pockets for his crystal but it was missing.*

Standing, towering over him, was the Egyptian God, Horus. From where he fell, Steven could see the body of a man, dressed scantily with a short white skirt wrapped around his deep, olive skinned waist. There were no shoes on his feet. His arms were also bare apart from fat golden bracelets adorning both wrists and another on his upper right arm. A matching necklace of equal magnitude hung around his neck glorifying its richness and splendour. The night was dark but the gold bounced off the moonlight. The figure was carrying a long golden sceptre in one hand and a large ankh, an Egyptian symbol of life, in the other.

Then Steven gasped. His breath sucked in the cold night air so quickly it didn't have time to warm before reaching his lungs. As Steven had looked up he saw that the head of the figure was not that of a man but a falcon. Standing before him was someone or something half-man, half-

bird. He had never before seen such a person, such an animal. His eyes couldn't decipher what he was actually looking at. Then it dawned on him. He had seen this figure before. Yes, he had, maybe in a book. Or maybe it was drawn on a wall somewhere. He tried to think. He scrambled for the answer in his head. All this happened within an instant. One minute he was walking, then he had bumped into something, then he was on the floor. Confusion. All in a split second his mind had thought of a thousand things. 'Yes', he thought again. I've seen this man before in Egypt. He was just like an ancient carving he had seen of one of their gods. His eyes grew wide as realisation hit him.

"Oh my God!" cried Steven, covering his head with his right arm in protection as the bird-man suddenly swooped down and engulfed him.

~~ ~~ ~~ ~~ ~~

Penedora tried to recall the events as clearly as she could. She remembered Steven crossing the stones to gain knowledge on Egypt and its history. She also remembered Uncle Gustus turning up at her house the next day with Steven's crystal and a book, which he had brought back from the New World. Uncle Gustus had explained to her that Steven had left the items at his lodge. Penedora informed the Council that she still had Steven's crystal at home but had allowed Uncle Gustus to keep the book, as he was keen to study it some more.

"I didn't mention anything about the book when Zac found it at Uncle Gustus' recently because I'd totally forgotten about it and I hadn't really taken any notice of it when Uncle Gustus originally showed up that evening. It was just a book and bared no relevance to my husband's disappearance. It was so long ago and I was more concerned about Steven at the time." She hesitated a little. "I'm sorry. I wasn't aware it was the same book, that it was magical or that it would be the cause of these horrid things happening to us all now."

Penedora tried to regain composure as a small tear gently trickled down her cheek.

Nefron motioned for her to continue.

"I'm sure everyone remembers searching for Steven and coming up with all those theories of him crossing back over the stones. I've believed all these years that he had chosen to leave Thyme and he was still alive somewhere happy, but now, if he's linked in any way to what's going on I can't bear to think. Her eyes swelled up more and Beverley, who had left her husband's side, quietly edged her way over to Penedora and handed her a small, delicate white hanky with the letter B ornately sewn on it. Penny wiped her tears with it as they fell onto her cheek. She then crumpled the hanky into her palm.

"I'm OK."

Penedora sniffed as she thanked her friend Bev for her assistance.

Marcus interrupted and enquired as to why there had been no trouble for the last ten years, especially as Uncle Gustus had still got the book.

The whole business was confusing and there were so many pieces of the puzzle still to connect. Putting two and two together, without any proof, the conclusion was eventually made that Uncle Gustus must have used the Egyptian book for his wedding spell and not his own spell Book of Thyme. No one could come up with why Uncle Gustus would suddenly mistake his book from the Book of the Dead, or why he would use it for any spells. Intentional or not, whatever his reasoning for dabbling was, they were all in agreement, his actions stirred up the now escalating wrath of the Egyptian Gods. The Gods of Misr.

"Dabbling with other people's spells is something you just don't do." Julin pointed out. "They obviously got used to the idea that their book was quite safe here until, stupidly, one of us had to have a go!"

Nefron swooped in to defend Uncle Gustus. "Stupid is something he is not. I'm sure Uncle Gustus has his reasons to try and cast from that book." Her hand stretched as she pointed towards the old, black, smelly book with jagged edges, on her alter table.

Penedora agreed, "Surely the past is irrelevant now. Surely what *is* important is returning their book and somehow letting them know we are happy to give it back."

Nefron nodded, "I think you are correct Penedora. Our ancestors have advised us to seek knowledge to help us and I think this is what they mean. Going over old ground has given us an understanding of our current predicament. But now, now we need to know everything about who these gods are, or where they are and how to communicate with them."

A large gust of wind flung itself against the back door. The group inside jumped. They could hear the wind once more blowing against the hall walls.

"They must be listening to us," cried Julin, "surely they know we are trying to sort all this out."

The wind then spiralled its way up to the roof and circled around it removing some roof tiles in the process. The group inside listened horrified to the clashing of tiles hitting the ground, their ears waiting nervously for another window or door to bang open, but after a short while the wind eased, leaving the Council Hall surrounded by another period of silence.

"I think these are just warnings," said Julin, as he peered through one of the windows. "If they really wanted to they could destroy us in one quick gust. I mean, we're only mere mortals with knowledge of the old ways and they're... well, they're Gods!"

"I think Julin is right," agreed Penedora. "They're just warning us. They must have thought their book was in a safe place here in Thyme but are obviously just not happy with any of us using it."

"Unless," said Nefron trying hard to remember all what the ancestors had told her. "Unless, they were unable to do anything about it, until now." She thought harder. "Just think," she mused, "crystals offer protection. Was the book placed beside Uncle Gustus' crystal collection? If it was, then there was nothing they could do to retrieve it."

"Until," Marcus piped up enthusiastically, "Uncle Gustus removed the book from its ten year resting place to try a spell."

"The possibility is there," continued Nefron. "Unfortunately, dabbling with the book maybe opened their channels to our world. It could have given them a window of opportunity and hence they are now here. Remember time has no meaning in our spirit realm, maybe the same is said of them. Ten years to us may seem like a passing of a day to them."

"That would explain why they are still so angry," gasped Marcus, "So in theory, we took their book yesterday and today they have come to collect it!"

A story of some sort was beginning to unfold as more ideas were thrashed around the hall but the sound of the wind that circled outside still echoed around the hearts of those inside.

"How long do you think we have until our link to our ancestors run out?" Beverley asked nervously.

"Considering they have already poisoned our land and shown us what they are capable of, I don't think we have very long," said Nefron. "I think it is time we protect ourselves further."

The gathering watched as their High Priestess took action. She approached the high altar where the Book of the Dead lay watching her every move. She then clasped both her hands around a small crystal pot, which sat on a shelf just left of the altar. Doing a quick count with her eyes she made sure there were enough tiny crystals for all and carefully picked out any that were larger than a hazelnut. Nefron closed her eyes, raised her arms, palms showing to the Land of Spirit and said out loud.

"Am yeah si kalian queck. O yeah cwym anton. Hear thy words and blessed be."

She circled the pot around the flame of a candle three times then lowered it to her chest. She peered in, closed her eyes and prayed inwardly, hoping that the plan would work. Explaining her idea, the gathering passed the bowl between them around the hall and in turn everyone present took one of the tiny crystals.

When the bowl was finally passed back to Nefron she returned it to the altar and, raising her arms again in thanks, said another prayer to the ancestors and spirit in their old language. Nefron then popped a tiny crystal from the pot into her mouth and swallowed it. Everyone followed suit. Penedora found it really hard to swallow the one she had picked and it took many attempts and a lot of saliva to succeed. Beverley was unsuccessful with hers. She had never been able to swallow anything on demand and always had to rely on liquid potions rather than pills to cure any ailments. She shoved the tiny crystal into the lining of her cheek and it sat there like food stored by a hamster.

"This will ensure that no one goes out of this hall without added spiritual protection," said Nefron, "and no one loses their protection if caught off guard by the wind."

Hours had now passed since the Council had congregated in the hall. The next vital twenty minutes were spent drawing up an action plan. They had been told by their ancestors to seek knowledge and this was agreed to be their priority. Marcus and Julin volunteered to cross the stones together to visit the museum in Cairo to find out as much as they could about Egypt, its history, and most importantly about their ancient Egyptian Gods.

Penedora and Nefron wanted to try and make contact with their aggressors and find out how to return their book but everyone unanimously agreed this should not be attempted until the men returned from the New World. No one underestimated the power of these Gods and the thought of more deaths or disappearances scared them all.

"Let's just find out what we are dealing with first, and go from there," demanded Edin, "the quicker my son Marcus and Julin gain the knowledge we need to clear up this mess the better. I also think I speak for us all but I will not allow even the slightest chance of anything bad happening to Nefron due to our own ignorance. You cannot call upon these Gods, Nefron. You do not know what they are capable of once you allow them into your soul. We could lose you like we did Carmel and Joseph. That would not be good. Not good for any of us in Thyme."

Nefron was honoured that Edin felt so strongly for her welfare. He was right. She may hold the highest of order throughout Thyme Hollow and hold divine connections with the ancestors but she too was unsure of the power that the evil entities were capable of, especially if she connected with them spiritually. They had only ever known peace and circumstances like these were new to them all. War only happened to those in the New World. Accidents, yes, but untimely death from murder and disease only ever happened to other lands, somewhere else, indeed everywhere else, but never in Thyme Hollow.

The collective brave decision was finally made to leave the hall and return to their respective homes and to remain there until Marcus and Julin had made the crossover and returned. Marcus opened the hall doors and peered outside. The congregation stood back and watched as he did. The wind had died down to a gentle breeze. Marcus' thoughts came to a conclusion that maybe Julin was right and these Gods were listening to everything they were saying. Maybe if they understood their intentions they would not harm anyone further. He was as unsure as the rest of them, but nervously, he and the gathering left the safety of the Council Hall. Each prayed for a safe journey home. Each gasped and shivered as the chill of the wind circled their legs on the way out.

Penedora hesitated before she ventured out last. She felt that no one really cared if anything happened to her on the way home. Her heart knew they all blamed her, or at least her Steven. She *had* to return that book. How, she did not know, but she knew it was her responsibility to end this business and take whatever punishment was due to her for Steven's initial involvement. Not only did she wish to prove her worth in the community again, she wanted to gain back pride for her family and undo any wrongs. Penedora prayed that these Gods of Misr understood what

she was feeling and stepped defiantly out into the
wind.

Chapter 7

The crowd shuffled forward. Loud *Ooos* and *Aarrhs* echoed around the upper corridors as people hustled and bustled to see the great marvels before their eyes. The whole area gleamed with gold; gold statues, gold chariots, gold adornments and gold coffins. Jewels encrusted with gold leaf, gold-plated or just plain gold, it didn't matter. The sheer expense of it all, the sheer splendour of it all and the sheer history engraved on every piece of artefact said it all. These objects belonged to a once-incredibly-powerful nation. Everyone was excited that they were party to the wonderment of the history of these ancient people.

Marcus caught Julin's attention and motioned with his eyes where he wished him to follow. They had reached the part of the museum that they were heading for and no longer needed the crowd as cover. As the tourists moved swiftly onwards down the corridor to the next display cabinet, ushered vigorously by their guide waving his pamphlet at head height, Marcus and Julin slipped unnoticed through an archway and into another but smaller display hall. Here the shelves were lined with many tools. In fact, the corridor was long enough to display hundreds of these artefacts, each one labelled and carefully mounted to depict the everyday lives of the ancient Egyptians. This part of the museum was darker and quieter than the larger corridors of the upper floor. The tourists seemed less interested in clay pots and kitchen utensils. Tools were made of metal or wood. The tourists missed the cleverness of the ancients' ability to make these tools and the consequences of the items made from their plain and simplistic designs. They came from miles to view the gold pieces and the ornate sarcophagus in which the rich pharaohs once lay. The museum also had an area especially designated to house the bodies of these pharaohs. Even though the bodies were thousands of years old, the mummification process had preserved them well enough to be shown as if lying in state, hands crossed and wrapped to the toes in muslin. The tourists found this section fascinating. *This person was the well-known pharaoh 'someone' who ruled Egypt in 'that particular' dynasty and the other one over there was alive at the time 'that particular' pyramid/tomb was built etc.* Ending up as an exhibit in a museum was certainly not the intention of these great pharaohs. It had taken decades to build their tombs and engrave the walls with hieroglyphics. They had carefully prepared themselves for death and organised their resting place down to the finest details, inscriptions here, food to be placed there, gold ornament to be placed there etc. Mourners of the dead pharaohs had then carefully prepared them for their journey into the next world and, after mummifying the body, would go to great lengths to bury their pharaoh in their secretly located tomb. Yet still, with the best preparations money could buy, only a few escaped the undignified act of being raided, violated and eventually displayed in a museum for these noisy, voyeuristic tourists, all hustling and bustling to get a closer look at their decayed body.

Marcus and Julin had not come to the Cairo museum to look at the exhibits. They had come for knowledge. They were hoping to find the answers surrounding the book, which had brought trouble to Thyme Hollow.

A young couple whisked their way through the tool section hurriedly, half scanning the walls and taking in little of their surroundings as they passed by. A map in hand was directing them to the gold! Marcus acknowledged them with a quick polite nod as they caught his eye. Then they were gone. The two men made their way to the end of the section and veered to the right. In front of them was a large stone staircase leading to the lower floors and to the back of the Egyptian museum.

A spacious landing separated the first floor, on which they stood, and the ground floor which held the largest statues and heavy empty coffins.

"That's where we're heading." Marcus pointed to a door in the middle of the gallery landing. A sign hung just above the doorknob. It said 'private' in three languages. They hung around the steps for a short time while avoiding the gaze of the guard on the other side of the gallery landing. It wasn't long before another group of tourists came hurriedly towards them up the steps heading for the upper level. Marcus and Julin seized the moment, headed for the private door and slipped through it as the crowd passed by. The museum guard didn't see them enter the room and assumed they had headed back up the stairs with the noisy tourists.

With the hustle and bustle of the busy museum behind them, once safely inside the room, Julin fumbled in his backpack for his torch. They had to make sure they didn't attract any attention from museum staff; no noise, no lights. Julin turned it on. Marcus did the same with his and both men stood with their backs to the door surveying the room with their lights.

"Wow!" Julin gasped, "how on Earth did you find this place?"

"By luck. The museum map doesn't list every room, especially those not open to the public, but fortunately for us, this room is."

He pulled the small museum map out of his jacket pocket, flicked it open with his left hand and then shone the torch over the section they were standing in.

"It says 'old library' for this room which is exactly what I was hoping for but just along the corridor here." He fumbled with the museum map a little as he shone the torch further up the plan. "It says *book shop*. If we don't find what we're looking for in *here*, I suggest we head *there* next."

Julin shone his torch on the map also and nodded in agreement.

The room was neither small nor large but it was incredibly cluttered and disorganised. Some of its books were neatly arranged and clearly labelled while others were scattered around in no particular sequence. It was in a kind of chaotic mess with a filing system that only the museum librarians would understand. There was no window in the room so no natural light entered.

"I can't see any computers in here," whispered Julin as his torch flickered across the desk areas. "I suppose that means we'll have to flip through mountains of books and paper."

Julin had always gained his knowledge the easy way. Type in a word on a computer, up comes a list and search further for your information from there. He was very aware of the technology of the New World and loved it. Marcus on the other hand preferred the old ways and held them in high esteem even if some were a challenge. He loved books, especially ancient and grubby ones like the ones he could see stacked before them. This was ironic, as Julin had been the one to set up the Thyme Library.

Marcus looked at his friend with one eyebrow raised. "I'm not sure if a computer would help us any more than books would anyway. I suppose if we were able to type in *'Book of the Dead'* it may come up with a list of say, a) articles about the book, b) how to dispose of, and c) names and addresses of owners!"

"Okay, okay!" Julin remarked. He acknowledged his friend's sarcasm and shrugged his shoulders. "We don't quite know what we're looking for do we?"

Marcus sighed, "Not really, but there has to be a link to the whole scenario somewhere here in this library so we'll just have to look until something triggers a connection. Just don't find another Book of the Dead."

"Do you think there would be more than one?"

"I'm not sure. We each have our own Book of Thyme. Who knows? Just be careful, that's all I'm saying."

They set to work. Both took to a separate shelf and began slowly scanning the titles and the pages within the books hoping to come up with something that could help them with their dilemma back in Thyme.

They picked out books they believed would hold relevant information and read the pages by torchlight. They were careful not to shine their lights towards the thin gap at the bottom of the door. Today they couldn't take the risk of being caught. Neither had brought any New World money or identification with them and involvement with authority of any kind could prove detrimental to the secret existence of Thyme Hollow.

A long time passed and the boys completely submerged their thoughts into their search for knowledge.

"I think I've found something," Marcus finally whispered, a little louder than he wanted to.

Julin swivelled around in the chair he had commandeered and leaned over to his colleague.

"Take a look." Marcus sat upright and moved the book he was reading to enable Julin to see it better. "It says here that to enable a soul to pass safely through the kingdom of the underworld, meaning the life after death, scriptures from the Book of the Dead were engraved around a pharaoh's tomb."

"Bingo!" cried Julin.

"Not quite. That's all it says. There's just a picture of a pharaoh and some hieroglyphics on the next page and then it goes onto the art of mummification."

Marcus flicked the relevant pages over in the book to show Julin the little piece of information he had found.

"It doesn't list any of the engraved scriptures here or where the Book of the Dead comes from or anything more useful to us."

"Don't be so quick to dismiss the information," Julin scorned his friend. "Look! I found this."

He in turn showed Marcus what he had found. "We've got a picture here of a pharaoh, O-, Osi-, Osiris I think it says underneath? Yes, Osiris, God of Vegetation and of the Underworld. I can't quite make out what the word is. The book is so worn. Anyway, you start with him. There's bound to be books on pharaohs somewhere in here and I'll search for scriptures to do with the underworld and maybe find some pictures of tombs and their engravings."

Julin became excited. He enjoyed exploring and delving into knowledge. He never told people that he actually quite liked flicking through books and reading them but in preference, his higher passion was still computing. As well as having the initial idea, it was Julin who set up the library in Thyme. He wanted everyone to experience his enthusiasm for the modern knowledge the New World had to offer, but the elders resisted his attempts to add a computer to their library. He brought back books on computing and programming etc. but was not allowed to actually bring back a computer. They agreed such computer books would provide great reference for anyone wishing to learn the art and use the technology in the New World but Thyme was not yet ready for such science. Their reasoning was sound. There was to be absolutely nothing brought into Thyme Hollow that could show their existence. One small chance of any computer from the New World linking into theirs could jeopardise everything. Julin respected this decision and so crossed the stones often to fuel his thirst for tapping into 'programs' and surfing the *New-World Wide Web* there. He did though miss having a computer to hand at home. Just tap in a word and up the information comes. Scroll through your screen and bingo! "So easy," he thought, "maybe one day…"

They set to work again. Marcus shone his torch around the shelves looking for anything on pharaohs, and Julin did the same on tombs and inscriptions.

Hours passed. Marcus and Julin had become so engrossed in their research neither had noticed the noise levels diminish outside the room. Much time had also passed since their crossing from Thyme Hollow to the corridors of the museum and now the museum had closed its doors to the general public. Julin paused from his task and rubbed the back of his neck. He eased the stiffness in his shoulders where he had been hunched over the table as he scanned book after book, page after page. Through the thin crack at the bottom of the door a shadow could be seen as it moved slowly passed their room and up the stairs towards the upper floors of the museum.

"How are you doing?" Julin enquired.

"I've found heaps this end, what about you?"

Julin swivelled his chair round again. "I've come to the conclusion that we're dealing with something even more sinister than we first thought."

"You mean there is something more sinister about the book or about the people who are angry we have it?"

Julin paused. "Both. For instance our ancestors told Nefron they believed we had the Book of the Dead belonging to the people of Misr. Now if someone had one of our spell books and we wanted it back, we certainly wouldn't go poisoning their vegetation and killing people to retrieve it."

Marcus agreed strongly.

"Therefore, these old Egyptians have shown they are obviously not from the realms of spiritual light. Everything mentioned in here of The Book of The Dead show illustrations of a book with words and pictures. But, if you notice the Book of the Dead we have back in Thyme is very similar to ours in the fact it has no visible writing, just blank pages."

"Meaning?"

"Meaning it must be an original and is obviously used in the same way we use our books, with prayers or chants or something similar, to connect it to a higher source. Thus, the higher entity responds to the request of the reader to enable them to read from its pages."

"What makes you think there is something more sinister to the Egyptian book than the ones we use? I thought the whole reason for our troubles is that they are just angry we stole it."

Julin thought carefully. "Maybe, but think who the book belongs to. If I'm right it certainly isn't a book that casts love spells and brings happiness. We are dealing with a sacred book that belongs to a group of dead people that possibly run the underworld and," he continued hesitantly, "these dead people don't appear to be very nice, especially if they are the same dead people shown in here."

Julin held up a large picture book he'd found and pointed to a picture within it he was currently studying. His index finger scanned over the fire-breathing serpents and the demons that related to the underworld. He then turned to another page and pointed to a picture depicting twenty slaves and four dead men with mummies guarding a gate.

"I think you're right." Marcus agreed as he screwed his face up. "They're certainly not shown as loving angels and spirits of light. Death to these people seem so dark and dangerous."

"Also," Julin continued, "I trust my intuition here, but I think there is something more sinister going on, something more than us just having a sacred spell book that a load of nasty spirits want back."

Marcus was impressed with the information his friend had collated but was now beginning to feel very uneasy, especially if it matched with the information he had uncovered.

Julin swivelled back to his table and rummaged around the books he had laid out in front of him. He picked one up and turned back again to show Marcus.

"It states in here that the scriptures, which were carved on the tomb walls, were also written on old paper called papyrus. The Egyptians buried these along with the dead so they could read them to pass through each gate safely in the underworld."

"Gate?"

"Gates, being the passages they went through as they sailed on a boat through the underworld at each hour of the night. Twelve hours, twelve gates!"

"On a boat?" queried Marcus.

"Look! Read this."

Julin passed Marcus the book in his possession, carefully holding open the relevant page he wished him to read. Marcus studied the passage carefully.

"So the dead souls sail on a boat, which is guided by the Egyptian Sun God Ra."

"Correct. Carry on."

Marcus did.

"At each hour of the night they have to pass through a gate which is guarded by something horrid, into the next hour."

"Serpents and such like, until midnight," explained Julin, "this is the sixth hour and this is where that God Osiris fits in."

Marcus raised his eyebrows as he half read the passage and half listened to the explanation being given to him at the same time.

"It says that Osiris sits in judgement at the sixth hour in the Hall of Truths. This is where he weighs the heart of the dead soul. If it is lighter than a feather the soul is proclaimed good and may continue on through the night to the underworld. But if his heart weighs heavier than the feather, he is doomed in damnation forever."

"So, let me get this straight," said Marcus, getting his head round the information. "The Book of the Dead…"

"Which we have in Thyme," Julin interrupted

"Which we have in Thyme, connects to the Egyptian underworld."

"Where you go when you die here…" said Julin pointing at the floor.

"…and the boat passes through twelve gates towards…..?"

"Don't know!" Julin shook his head.

"But at midnight…"

"The sixth gate."

"…you get to Osiris and the Hall of Truths… where they weigh the dead soul's heart."

"Correct."

The puzzle was slowly fitting together as the two men shared the information they had searched for all afternoon. They had discovered a possible *who* (Osiris) and *where* (the Underworld) but neither had yet pieced together the *how*. Both were now hungry and both were tired from being hunched over the many books they had waded through. Both were still relying on their torches for their light but neither had noticed that the museum was now empty of visitors. The day guards had all gone home and the night security officer was now on duty. The tourists had returned to their hotels. Only polished antiquities and the dead remained behind the very heavy, tightly locked, Egyptian Museum doors.

Back at Thyme Hollow, Nefron was nervous. Marcus and Julin had been gone a long time and she was worried for their safety. Dellery comforted her. He and a few others had congregated back at the Council Hall to await the boy's return from the New World.

"They'll be fine," he commented, "both have their crystals with them and have protection from our ancestors while over the stones."

Nefron faced him. She closed her eyes and shook her head slowly.

"I lost contact with our ancestors an hour ago."

Dellery put his head in his hands and sighed deeply.

"I lost my link during my meditation and I could feel a band of evil blocking my path to the light."

Dellery looked upwards towards the altar at the book and sighed again. "Then we are all now on our own!"

"…and so are Marcus and Julin," she finished.

Back at the Egyptian museum Marcus was showing Julin more of what he had found out about the God Osiris.

"To cut a long story short," Marcus explained, "this Pharaoh or God, whatever you want to call him now, Osiris, had a brother called Seth who was jealous of him. The legend states that at a party, Seth tricks Osiris into lying down in a large chest. Seth then immediately seals down the lid of the chest with the help of his conspirators. They throw this cast into the Nile to be rid of Osiris. Seth then becomes ruler of Egypt. Meanwhile, Osiris' wife Isis, searches for her drowned husband, finds him and, using magic, brings him back to life. They then have a son and call him Horus. He plays a big part in the story later. Anyway, the wicked brother, Seth, gets angry that Osiris is back and murders him again but this time, cuts him into fourteen pieces and scatters him around Egypt."

"Wow, who'd want a brother like that?"

"Well, Isis again goes in search of her husband and eventually finds all the bits of his body barring one, which had been eaten by a fish. Unfortunately this was the bit that helped her conceive Horus, if you get my meaning!"

"You mean...?"

"Yes, I do."

Julin winced at the thought of a fish eating his manhood.

"Anyway, Isis brings him back to life again with the help of another magic ritual."

"Hence the Spell Book," Julin exclaimed as he began to catch on to the significance of the Egyptian myth, Marcus was explaining to him. Spell books, the dead, reincarnation. It was all fitting together nicely.

"That's right. But *this time*, she brings him back to life in the Underworld to safely rule as pharaoh there. Isis brings up their son, Horus, in secret until he is old enough to avenge his father's second death. Eventually Horus and his Uncle Seth do battle but no one wins."

"So if no one won, what happened next?" asked Julin.

"Well they go before a judge called..." Marcus flicked back through the pages of the book he was reading from. He found it quite awkward balancing the book on his knees and trying to turn the pages with one hand while holding a torch in the other. "Here he is. The God Thoth."

Marcus continued the story. "So in court, this Judge, Thoth, gives the verdict of guilty to Seth and banishes him to live forever in the Underworld under the rule of Osiris. He then declares Horus as King of the Upperworld. So now father and son rule both kingdoms. Osiris rules the dead and Horus the living."

"It's all beginning to fit," whispered Julin. "Vegetation, the fish, love, magic, all these things have recently been affected in Thyme. And, all these things link back to the legend of Osiris."

"Correct. But this is the really interesting bit," said Marcus as he drew his torch in nearer to the pages he was about to read to Julin. Hairs on the back of his neck began to rise slowly sending a small shiver down his spine. He hunched over the book and began to read.

"Homage to thee, O my divine father Osiris, thou hast thy being with thy members. Thou didst not decay, thou didst not turn into worms, thou didst not rot away. I shall not decay, I shall not rot, I shall not decompose, I shall have my being, I shall live, I shall wake again."

"Goodness!" cried Julin, "Sounds like some kind of spell?"

"Kind of," replied Marcus, "apparently the old Egyptians invented magical words and ceremonies with the sole object of giving the human body the power necessary to raise itself from the dead. That's how Isis brought Osiris back."

Julin clicked to the link between the legend and the events in Thyme.

"You mean that the book we have is not The Book *OF* the Dead, but The Book *FOR* the Dead. An actual spell book to bring someone BACK to life?"

Marcus nodded. "Someone discovered something that had been lost for thousands of years and possibly lost or buried for a very good reason. Then somehow Steven gets hold of it and, unaware of its power, unknowingly brings it across the stones to Thyme."

"So these Egyptians are not after us because we *stole* it, they're after us because we have it and they *want* it. Do you think they want to bring someone back from the dead?"

Marcus nodded again.

Fear appeared on Julin's face as realisation of their situation crossed his mind. "Seth?" He shuddered at the thought.

Marcus agreed, "It's a strong possibility."

"Everyone in Thyme is looking for a way to get the book back to these people, that's why we were sent here. My God, we have to get back to Thyme to warn them. That book has to be destroyed, *not* returned. Can you imagine what could happen if anyone banished to hell or the Underworld, whatever you call it, got hold of it to bring evil back to life?"

Marcus calmed his friend. "Let's just hope the book is still safely sitting on our high altar surrounded by crystals of pure light."

A sudden noise outside the room made them both jump. Then silence. They froze in the dim light of the room and stared at the door. Fumbling, they turned off their torches and watched the shadows, they could now see under the door gap, moving around outside. Their heartbeats quickened pace as they saw the doorknob slowly turn.

Chapter 8

"Which bottle? The blue or the purple one?"
Jilly shouted loudly to her mother.

"The purple one!" came the reply.

Jilly's fingers had fumbled their way along the
shelves in the larder and she had picked out two
bottles with the correct labels as requested by her
mother: one blue, one purple. Having opened
each bottle and smelled the contents of each, she
could tell their scents were very distinctive. She
popped their cork tops back on tightly and wafted
away the little puffs of smoke that she had allowed
to escape from them. She was unsure as to why
two mixtures with the same contents bearing the
same labels could turn out to be so different in
colour and smell. Penedora thyme meticulous in her
labelling and mixtures and Jilly knew that their
differences must have come from the spells
placed before them on the prayer tables upstairs,
not from an error on her mother's part. Jilly
wondered if one day she would be as competent
as her mother in the old ways. Penedora seldom
needed recipe books and seemed to know the
words from her spell book before the book had
finished displaying the sentences.

"Practice," thought Jilly as she replaced the
blue bottle on the shelf and jumped off the stool
she had used to reach them.

She headed back up the stairs and into the little spell room where her mother was standing over the prayer table. Jilly handed Penedora the small purple bottle. Penedora checked the label. She carefully guided the cork from the bottle's neck and a small hissing noise escaped with a little puff of smoke. Penedora poured a little of the potion from the bottle into an ornate, oval silver dish she had previously placed on the table, next to her spell book. In the dish lay a little pink crystal. Immediately the mixture hissed and bubbled as it made contact with the crystal and, with a small *poof,* gave off a much larger purple cloud of smoke. The smoke slowly began to disperse as it rose towards the ceiling. Jilly and Penedora quickly waved their arms out front wafting the purple smoke back towards their chests before it totally dispersed. They waved the lingering essence of the smoke over their heads and breathed in its fumes.

As the smoke had slowly faded so did the words that had been beautifully inscribed on the spell book. The beautiful writing had listed the ingredients needed for Penedora's request. A page of the book flicked itself over from right to left and then more words began to slowly appear.

They waited patiently until the writing had finished. It read,

*Take Egypt with you he hath the knowledge of
Shat En Sbau
Thy journey will begin at Amentet
Take thy souls up the river of Tuat to the Hall of
Truths
Here you will giveth the book to the righteous
Trust only in thy higher self*

"What does it mean?" Jilly asked her mother.

Penedora curled her lip, "I have absolutely no idea."

They stood together reading the words over and over again, trying to make sense of them.

Penedora had borrowed a book from the Thyme library and had placed it on the window ledge in the little spell room. She went over and picked it up.

"Your father brought this book back from Egypt many moons ago. I've been thinking about it ever since Nefron mentioned the connection to Egypt and the ancient gods. I scanned over it a few times since yesterday." She showed it to Jilly.

"Is it a book about the ancient gods of Egypt?" Jilly asked.

"No. It's called The Book of Ieu." Penedora showed her daughter the front cover. It was an average-sized book, yellow covering with an artistic sketch of a wizard on the front cover. Other than the name of the author and artist, there was nothing more to describe it.

"It's actually a modern version of the Book of Ieu with no real importance at all. It also fails miserably in trying to decipher the ancient texts from the original book." Penedora laughed. "It actually tells the reader in one section to use the eye of a toad and the wing of a bat to cast a spell!"

"Yuk!"

"Sounds horrid I know but *some* of the text is very close to the original Book of Ieu and in one chapter it mentions Pistis Sophia."

"Pistis Sophia. What's that?"

"Ancient Coptic literature. The early Egyptian Christians, much like the ancient Egyptians who worshipped many gods, wrote down their beliefs and doctrines for future generations. Where the ancient Egyptians wrote their texts in hieroglyphics on walls and papyrus, Coptic scriptures were written on scrolls and then passed on down the generations that way."

"I'm lost," admitted Jilly.

"Let me explain. This book is a modern version of the Book of Ieu." Penedora waved the little yellow book at Jilly. "The *original* Book of Ieu contains the ancient wisdom of the Gnostics who were occultists. They had much knowledge and studied the old ways, like we do here in Thyme. Now this book also mentions 'Pistis Sophia' and a few *other* ancient religions. I began thinking and came up with a theory that *all* religions in some way or another overlap each other. This being in a large way or even one tiny detail such as saying prayers to a higher order, believing in life after death or just burning incense."

Penedora raised an eyebrow at her daughter to see if she was keeping up with her theory. Jilly nodded in response.

"Well, it made me think that our beliefs here in Thyme could also possibly cross over to other religions. It then occurred to me that if our links to *our* ancestors were being cut by the evil here in Thyme then maybe we could link up to *another* source that could help to protect us."

"You mean asking help from spirits of another faith, from the unfamiliar?"

"Yes."

"My God that could be so dangerous!" shrieked Jilly.

"Yes…and no! But it was a chance we had to take and it appears to have worked."

Jilly looked across at the prayer book on the table and at the silver tray, which was now empty of potion but contained a tiny mauve crystal.

"You mean we've just delved into something we know nothing about and cast a spell via someone else's ancestors? A magic realm we know nothing about yet?"

Penedora sighed. She tried hopelessly to soothe her daughter's anguish.

"I know it was dangerous Jilly but I *had* to take that chance. Someone had to. I only called upon other spirits of the light to help. There are no demons here, look! We connected successfully and have been given guidance on how to return the Book of the Dead."

Jilly's anger at her mother's apparent stupidity grew. "And you tell *me* not to play with fire!"

"I had to try something!"

"How do you know that this guidance is not a trick? We could have opened ourselves up to anything. What a stupid…"

"Don't talk to me in this way," snapped Penedora. "Do you not think I gave this a lot of thought *before* I delved?"

Jilly was flabbergasted by the foolish actions of her mother. She had been brought up to respect the ancestors and the old knowledge and here was her mother calling on spirits from God knows where. Jilly stormed out of the little back room and hurried down the stairs. She huffed into the kitchen and poured herself a drink of water, crashing and bashing as she went. She rubbed her hands down her clothes and through her hair hoping to remove any residue of smoke from the purple stuff they had just dabbled with. Jilly felt spooked. She drank the water in one quick swig and leant her body over the kitchen sink. She sighed loudly and her mind raced.

Penedora appeared shortly after and placed her arms on her daughter's shoulders. Jilly relaxed her tight shoulders and put the empty glass onto the draining board then turned to face her mother. They hugged.

"Sometimes you have to take risks to succeed," Penedora said softly. "If there's any chance your father is alive, I'll take every risk possible to get him back. However stupid, I will take that chance. Don't hate me Jilly. God, I feel so alone right now."

"I don't hate you, I'm just scared, and you're not alone."

Penedora pulled her daughter in closer to her beating heart. Tears began to fall down Jilly's cheek.

"Are we all going to die?"

"Trust your higher self, Jilly. My intuition is telling me we are *all* going to make it."

Penedora rolled her eyes upwards and closed them slowly. Her intuition was certainly not telling her these things but she hoped her little lie would bring at least some comfort to her daughter. They hugged for a little longer and as they parted, Jilly wiped under her eyes with her fingertips and her nose with the back of her hand.

"Go wash your face and change into something comfortable. I'll make us something to eat now as I'm not sure how long we'll be gone for."

Jilly did as she was told and made her way back upstairs towards the bathroom for a quick freshen up.

Within the comfort of her bedroom, Jilly bounced down onto the bed and leaned over to remove the hairbrush from the top bedside cabinet drawer. She began brushing her hair in singular strokes down from her scalp to the ends. The curls bounced as each hair was brushed and her natural oils were swept down the hair shaft making the hair fuller and softer. Replacing the hairbrush, she made her way to the wardrobe and picked out a pair of jeans and her favourite baggy, burgundy sweater. For her feet she chose a pair of black ballet-style shoes. They had no clunky heels to contend with and as they felt as comfortable as slippers. She knew she could walk long distances in them and she certainly had no idea how far they would be walking. Neither she nor her mother knew what lay ahead of them over the stones but she was sensible enough to go prepared and wear sensible clothing. Grabbing the small haversack from the back of her bedroom door, Jilly left her bedroom and went into the small backroom where her mother's spell book lay on the oval table. She folded the corners of the purple cloth across the top of her mother's green spell book and tied a simple knot on the top. Carefully she put the book inside her haversack.

Gyp watched her from the second step down on the stairs where he had settled himself earlier. His eyes scanned her movements as she went from the bathroom to her bedroom to the little back room and back onto the landing again. He remained perfectly still as Jilly gingerly stepped over him to the step below his. As she made her way down the stairs his eyes closed tightly again as if he was going into some sort of meditation. Gyp knew it was going to be a long night. As his tail dangled onto the step below he slowly flicked just the tip of it. Up and down it went repeatedly in a slow, rhythmic movement.

Penedora had finished making two sandwiches, placed them onto plates and was pouring out a couple of drinks when Jilly entered the kitchen. She sat down at the table and her mother brought over two warm herbal drinks.

"Thanks," Jilly said as her mother sat down next to her to eat.

After finishing their supper, Jilly placed her empty plate on top of her mother's and placed them on the draining board with the empty mugs. She sat back at the table where her mother was fiddling with a piece of paper. Earlier, Penedora had copied the words remembered down from her spell book onto the piece of paper she now displayed at the kitchen table. She slid the paper across the table towards Jilly with her index finger.

"Do you have any idea where Amentet is? At least if we work that one out we'll know where to start."

Jilly read the text carefully and shook her head. "I didn't understand the message at all. I've no idea what Amentet is. To be honest, I don't even understand the first line. '*Take Egypt with you*'. How can you take a country somewhere?"

"Oh I understand that bit," exclaimed Penedora excitedly, "that relates to our Gyp but I'm unsure what 'Shat En Sbau' means. I hope it's not some sort of cat language!"

Jilly was still confused, "Gyp? How does this relate to Gyp?"

"Gyp's original name was Egypt. I named him Egypt when he first arrived but because you shortened his name to Gyp, I started to call him it too and eventually the name just stuck. He followed you everywhere and basically became adopted by you as *your* cat."

"What do you mean arrived? I thought we got Gyp as a kitten from someone in Thyme?"

"No. Gyp turned up at the cottage one evening. He was already an adult cat. I asked around but no one knew whom he belonged to. He was very hungry so I fed him and he's stayed ever since. Don't you remember?"

Jilly shook her head. She didn't remember much around that time. She supposed losing her father at six years old made everything become a blur of memory and pain.

"Why did you name him Egypt?"

"Because he arrived the day after your father disappeared. I called him Egypt, as it was the last place Steven had crossed the stones to. At one point I thought Gyp's arrival was a bit of a strange coincidence but I remembered the Council's guidance. All things are for a reason and everyone thought that the ancestors had shown him the way to our door to give us comfort and love in a difficult time. The way you bonded with him so easily certainly took away some of your tears for you missing your father. Egypt used to curl up on my lap at night when I sat crying in my chair and I'd stroke him until I fell asleep. Every time you went to play in the woods, Egypt followed and I felt you were safe in his company. He knows I'm grateful for his turning up out of the blue at the right time. Isn't that right Gyp?"

Jilly flinched. She looked up and saw that Gyp had been standing in the doorway of the kitchen listening to their conversation. But she couldn't work out how her mother had known he was there. She had her back to him and the entrance to the kitchen from the hallway.

Did she hear him creep down the stairs? She wasn't sure. Jilly relaxed again. She knew she still had a long way to go before her Age of Transition but she was so eager to get there. Her mother was so in tune with the old ways, of casting spells and her intuition was among the best in Thyme. That's why she sat on the Council. Jilly's fear of the situation at hand was subsiding. She was becoming eager to get to the bottom of the mysterious Egyptian book. She was eager to cross the stones on an adventure that would possibly lead her to unknown realms of Spirit and she was more eager now than ever before to find her father. He had to be alive, she knew it. Or at least, she hoped it.

"Well it's a shame you can't talk to us." Jilly waved the piece of paper at Gyp. "Then you could tell us what Shat En Sbau is."

"I think our best course of action is to go to the Hall and wait for the boys to return," said Penedora. "They might be able to shed some light on this." She whipped the piece of paper out of Jilly's hand. "We'll have to go to the Hall anyway to get the Egyptian book. Did you pack my spell book?"

"Yes."

"Good. I'll feel much safer having it with us across the stones. Are you ready to go?"

"Yes."

"Give me just a couple of minutes to get changed and make sure Gyp has eaten, we're taking him with us."

She winked at him as she passed him, and Gyp blinked slowly back at her.

Penedora quickly went upstairs and changed into slacks. She too wore flat, practical shoes. She brushed her brown hair and the few odd bits of grey, then like she often did, tied it back. Her hair was stunning, but since Steven had gone, she didn't feel the need to let her locks flow beautifully over her shoulders. Leaning over to a pot beside her bed, Penedora grabbed a couple of extra crystals for Jilly. "Better safe than sorry," she thought. Her eyes caught sight of Steven's crystal gleaming up at her from the pot. Her fingers hesitated as they went to touch it. Memories of him filled her head. Then she swiftly grabbed it to take along with them. Downstairs Jilly and Gyp were waiting for her.

"Right, let's go?"

Penedora took a quick look behind her to make sure everything had been turned off and that nothing important had been left. She shut the door behind them and the three brave souls headed for the Council Hall.

By early evening, the boys had still not come back from the New World and Nefron and Dellery had been waiting at the Council Hall for many hours. A few other villagers had turned up to await news. Everyone in Thyme Hollow felt edgy while waiting for Julin and Marcus to return from the Cairo Museum with advice on how to stop the evil madness that had descended upon them all.

As dusk was rapidly approaching, a strange, eerie fog began to slowly roll its way across the stones. The small spiralling film of mist gradually thickened as it swirled over the stream, in between the rocks and up the side of the bank. Soon the fog thickened enough to shield the stones and stream from view and only the trickling of the water could be heard beneath the strange, white blanket. Ahead, the woods looked peaceful and silent in the stillness of the approaching night. The mist continued on, curling its way through the trees, bending and entwining itself around every branch, tickling its white fingers along every notch in the bark. It made its way along the pathway that Jilly often took from her cottage to the stream. Inch by inch, the mist continued to thicken and stretch, covering everything in its way. Its spooky white arms reaching out, swirling and clasping every space it covered as it slowly continued through the woods towards the Council Hall.

Broach opened her back door and stepped outside into the evening air. She made her way to the middle of the garden and reached into the washing up bowl that was resting under her right arm. She pulled out some carrot and potato peelings with her left hand and scattered them over the lawn. She never wasted a morsel. Whatever she and Dellery didn't need or finish eating, she would share amongst the wildlife of Thyme. 'Waste not, want not' was her motto and secretly she just loved to see the little nocturnal animals come pecking at the peelings and stalks each evening and the early risers rummaging around each morning for their breakfast.

The vegetables were sitting in their pans of water ready to be cooked. The meat was inside the oven in a tray turned on low and cooking slowly waiting for Dellery to return home. He had been gone most of the late afternoon and she had no idea when to expect him back. They had a little spat before he returned to the hall. She was not happy he decided to go back there. She was not happy at all. And, she told him just that, but he still went. *Why can't people just stay safe at home*, she thought, *all this coming and going to the hall was not healthy or conducive to sorting out this mess they were in?* She just prayed over and over in her mind, that Dellery would indeed return home safely, and in time for them to eat dinner!

After scattering the last morsels, Broach tipped the washing up bowl upside down over the grass to remove any last peelings that remained in the corner of the bowl. She turned and headed back to the kitchen, totally unaware of the mist that had made its way into her garden. As she stepped inside the house, it twirled closely passed her ankle and stretched towards the walls and back door. Broach slammed the door behind her and made her way to the kitchen sink to return the bowl.

"Mummy look at the frog!" called Jacob to his mother from the garden.

Not looking up from her task she smiled to herself and replied loudly, "That's nice dear. Is it a nice green, fat frog?"

Beverley was preparing a juice for Jacob to drink. He had already eaten and Bev had allowed him to play outside in the garden for a little, while she washed up the dishes. It would soon be his bath time and then bedtime with a story; if Daddy felt in the mood to put on his silly voices while reading. Terry was much better at reading stories than she was. Often funny faces would accompany his funny voices and Jacob's giggles made her giggle too.

Terry was upstairs in the bathroom. He loved this part of the day when he could spend time with his family relaxing and sharing intimate moments of fatherhood with his little son. One day he hoped Jacob would work in the fields with him and learn about farming and harvests. He would leave teachings of the old ways to Beverley, as she was better at that sort of thing. Terry sloshed the bubbly, bath water around his hands and then turned off the taps. Jacob's bath was warm and inviting. Terry wiped the froth from his hands on the bath towel and made his way downstairs to fetch Jacob.

"No mummy, look at the frog!" Jacob called to her again.

Beverley turned round to see why Jacob was calling her. He often brought worms and frogs into the house. Beverley would allow him to keep them overnight and then it was a strict rule that all animals were to be released again in the morning.

She too wiped her hands dry on the kitchen tea towel, as she ventured out into the garden to investigate how big this frog was. Bev made her way over to Jacob and bent down to where he was sitting on the grass. "Now let me see this frog you've found darling," she whispered attentively to him.

Jacob looked up and pointed skywards.

"Look mummy, lots of frog."

Beverley's eyes followed his little finger upwards and froze. All around the house perimeter was a thick, soup-like mist. She could not see anything beyond their boundary fence. There had never been anything like this in Thyme before and Beverley's instincts told her that this fog was not natural. Immediately, she became alarmed.

"Go back inside the house honey," she ordered Jacob as she helped him off the grass. She put her hands on Jacob's shoulders and turned him around to guide him back to the house.

Beverley screamed. The mist was now behind them stopping their escape to the back door. On hearing his wife's scream, Terry pelted down the stairs and into the kitchen. From the kitchen doorway he could see nothing but thick fog. He stopped and called out.

"Bev! What's happening? Beverley where are you?"

"Terry!" she shouted at him, "don't come out."

"What the-?"

"Don't come out!" she screamed even louder, "it's evil, don't step into the fog."

"Hurry Beverley," he shouted louder.

"I can't. I don't have my crystal."

"But you swallowed one. You are safe. Run, Bev."

Beverley put her arms around her son and held him tightly. She had spat the crystal out of her mouth when she returned home from the Council Hall. She couldn't swallow it there and she could see it in her mind now, sitting on kitchen window ledge. Her own personal crystal was beside her bed, left there from the afternoon when she had changed after the Council meeting. Forgetting to put it back into her pocket had been a huge mistake.

Beverley could hear Terry calling them from the house but could not see him or the house any longer. Her husband called back to her through the white, dense fog. It had come down on them so fast. She looked upwards towards the sky, to the only tiny clear gap around them. Beverley began to pray. She prayed to the Egyptians to spare her son. The fog swirled and thickened engulfing them both.

Terry rushed back into the kitchen and quickly rummaged around in a kitchen drawer. He fumbled with all the gadgets and tools until his hand gripped hold of the torch. It wouldn't light. He waved it in the air a couple of times and then bashed it down hard onto the palm of his hand. It lit up. Without a second more to lose, Terry rushed out into the garden.

"Beverley!"

The early dusk of evening had arrived in Thyme making visibility within the mist impossible.

"Beverley! Jacob!" He kept calling out their names.

The torch gave Terry almost no help at all. The light reflected back from the mist and all Terry could see was the swirling mass surrounding him. He waved a hand frantically in front of him to sweep away the mist but to no avail. It was thick, moving and unnatural.

"Ouch!" cried Terry as he tripped over Jacob's tricycle, scraping his shin on the framework. Terry went down, clutching his leg in pain.

"Daddy!" the little voice screamed out, "Daddy!"

"Jacob?"

Terry scrambled across the lawn to where he had heard his son calling. He frantically felt for him beneath the white blanket of fog. Suddenly his hand grazed over a leg in the fog and he grabbed it. Jacob was alive. He held on tightly as he felt the power of the fog. Terry stood up swooping Jacob up into his arms.

"Bev! Bev!"

Terry's head swayed from side to side as he searched for Beverley but he couldn't see her anywhere. He couldn't see anything. He held tightly to his son as he raced back towards the house, narrowly missing the abandoned tricycle. Terry plonked the little lad safely inside and slammed the door behind them. He knelt down and made eye contact with the frightened child. Resting his hands on the boy's shoulders, he looked deeply into his son's petrified eyes; afraid to ask, but he did.

"Where's Mummy, Jacob?"

Jacob shook his head.

"Where's mummy?"

"Mummy's gone. The bad man took her."

"What do you think is causing it?" Jilly asked her mother as they stood on the path looking back towards the woods. In the distance they could see an eerie mist covering the edge of the woods like smoke in a kitchen after a pan fire. It was hovering around the trees yet at the same time was moving in every direction possible.

"I'm not sure. I've never seen fog that dense in Thyme before."

"It looks kind of spooky."

"Very sinister! It's moving quite fast yet there's no wind to carry it along. Something's not right," said Penedora, "I don't feel good about this at all."

"Where do you think it's going?"

Penedora put her arm on her daughter's shoulders as they both scanned the view before them. "I think it is going everywhere," she said nervously, "if this fog is harbouring the same evil spirits that the wind carried, then I think we better hurry to the Hall."

Jilly clicked her fingers for Gyp to follow as they headed up the hill to the Council Hall. They all quickened their pace.

"Something's happening!" cried Nefron. "I can hear screaming in my head."

Dellery comforted her. "What is it?"

"I don't know but I can feel fear and crying."

"You don't think it's my brother and Julin in trouble do you?" Zac enquired anxiously.

"No, it's nearer. I can hear screaming in Thyme."

The outer door to the Hall burst opened. Everyone present swung round to see who had entered.

Gyp sneaked into the Hall just as Penedora and Jilly slammed the door shut.

"There's a fog coming," Penedora told them as she swept passed the people in the entrance lobby. "We must hurry."

She made her way into the main room and over to the altar. Those gathered followed her movements. Zac caught hold of Jilly's arm as she passed by him. She stopped and looked at him.

"Are you ok?" he enquired softly.

"Yes, I'm fine."

"Your mother said there was a fog coming. What did she mean?"

Jilly waited as the remaining few made their way into the large hall leaving her and Zac alone. She tried to explain what they had seen on their journey.

"There's a kind of mist coming this way from the woods. First the wind; now the fog. It looks very sinister Zac. Come and look." She took his hand and guided him back to the door.

Zac peered back over his shoulder towards the commotion going on at the altar as Jilly guided him to where they had entered. She carefully opened the door and peered out. There was no fog yet. They both stepped out into the dim light of the evening. Zac could see the mist in the distance.

"You say it's coming this way."

"Definitely. It seemed to be flowing in all directions from the wood, we watched it spread out and then it seemed to come in our direction and follow us. Like it had a soul and knew we were there, and coming here! I don't know but we figured whatever it is, it knows this is where their book is."

"You think it's coming for the book?"

"Yes."

"What is your mother planning to do? She seemed in an awful hurry."

"Give them back their book before they kill us all."

"How?"

"I don't know, nobody knows yet."

"So we don't know how, and we don't know who to give it back to and we have an evil fog coming our way. Great!" Zac grabbed his hair with both hands and spun around randomly searching for answers. He had never raised his voice to Jilly before but the situation caused much anxiety in everyone in Thyme Hollow and these youngsters were no exception.

"Can't we just leave the book outside?" Zac shouted.

"Don't you think the elders would have already thought about that Zac?" she shouted back. "We can't just dump it outside. You've heard what everyone's been saying about Uncle Gustus dabbling with it. They've come to kill us all as punishment. We have no choice, Zac, someone has to return it to the New World."

"But no one knows where in the New World we have to take it."

"My mum has an idea, but she needs more information from Marcus and Julian before she crosses."

"She's crossing the Stones?" Zac asked in disbelief.

"We both are."

Zac looked horrified at the thought of letting Jilly go across to the New World with her mother under such terrifying circumstances.

"This has all become such a mess. Why us?"

Zac clenched his fists by his side to calm himself down. "Remember," he continued, "Nefron told us all to wait for Marcus and Julin to return before we did anything dangerous."

As far as he was concerned nobody contradicted the views or wishes of the High Priestess. The honour of attaining that level of leadership in Thyme was acknowledged by all with utmost respect and obedience.

"You mean they haven't returned yet?"

"No."

"You don't understand, Zac. We have to do something now. Pronto! Mother won't be pleased to hear that they haven't returned. She was hoping to exchange some information here before we proceed across the stones."

Both seemed lost as to what action to take next. Everything had depended on the return of

Marcus and Julin from Cairo. It was now getting late. Night was drawing in. Jilly's next remark cut through Zac like a knife.

"Something has obviously happened to them. How do you know your brother is going to return anyway? Uncle Gustus didn't. My father didn't."

"Of course they'll return. Just give them a little more time," Zac argued back curtly.

"We don't *have* any more time."

Jilly was so frustrated with his lack of action. She was becoming bothered by everyone's lack of action and the way that everyone in Thyme did things the correct way, the proper way, the slow *'let's all make an agreed decision first'* way. No one seemed to just get things done. Everything took time and *time* was certainly something Thyme did not have at this precise moment. She understood now why her mother took such a risk. Penedora was right, someone had to.

"Can't you see the mist for yourself? I told you, it's coming this way. Nefron said we are losing contact with our ancestors. We can't just leave *that* book sitting here while these Egyptians punish us or kills us all for taking it. We have to get it out of here. We have to do something now."

"Like what?" he snapped. "What can you and your mother do that Nefron and my brother can't?"

Zac grabbed her arm and Jilly responded by turning her gaze sharply towards him. Her big brown eyes penetrated his soul.

Then she told him, "We connected with the world of spirit and they told us what to do."

"But you just said no one knew what to do and now you are saying you do."

"Yes and no!"

Zac let go of her, swung round in despair and flung his arms out in disbelief. His hands came to rest on his head again and he turned to face her.

"Well its either you do know what to do, or you don't."

"Well, not exactly. We didn't understand what they were trying to tell us. It was all kind of in code. Anyway, if Marcus and Julin haven't returned yet from Egypt, we'll just have to go and meet them there instead, we need to find out what information they have so we can plan our next move."

"Are you mad? You'll be killed before you even cross the stones. There's a killer fog coming!" Zac waved his arms in the direction of the fog. "You said so yourself!"

"No we won't," she said shouted back at him, "we are protected. We cast a protective spell."

"You did, did you? Contacted to our ancestors in spirit did you? How did you manage that then? If you had been here earlier you'd have known that Nefron has lost contact with our ancestors, so what makes you think your mother could get through when our High Priestess couldn't?"

"We channelled to another spirit level."

Jilly looked away from Zac's disapproving face. This was blasphemy. Other religions were regarded with great respect and secrets of the old ways were not given to anyone outside of Thyme Hollow. Studying other cultures was accepted, but to cross the line of connection between spirits of Thyme and others beyond in different spiritual worlds was absolutely forbidden. It was believed that connecting elsewhere could open up the doors to anything unknown, especially spirits from darkness such as demons, wicked souls and fallen angels. Penedora knew her actions would shock the Council and was wrong, oh so wrong, but it seemed the only option they had left.

After Jilly's initial shock at what her mother was planning earlier had ceased, she too agreed it was their only solution. She now hoped Zac would recognise that fact also. He didn't. He couldn't believe his ears. Yet as he looked at the rising mist in the distance, he knew in his heart that Penedora and Jilly had acted out of fear and love for them all. His anger succumbed to another emotion.

Zac held out his hands and Jilly took them. He pulled her close to his body and wrapped his arms around her tightly. "It's no good. I can't let you go alone. I'm coming too," he said softly to her.

"You can't. It won't be safe for you."

Zac looked down at the young woman he was holding and he felt a rush of anger because of her actions and, at the same time, a strong sense of protectiveness towards her.

"Now I've found you in my heart Jilly, I don't want to let you go." He lowered his head slowly towards her and kissed her on the lips. Jilly was shocked at the initial contact Zac had made but she was quick to respond to the softness of his lips. She closed her eyes and felt the warmth radiating from his arms, his mouth and his whole body. A comforting shivering sensation circulated around her body and she entwined her arms around his back. Their timing of this special moment was incredibly bad, but Jilly had sealed her Age of Becoming with Zac and that short kiss now made her his.

From outside, Zac and Jilly had missed the gasps and loud opposition to her mother's earlier actions and Penedora's response on finding out the boys had not returned with a solution for them. Nefron had calmed the few gatherers within the hall. She understood why Penedora had called upon other realms of spirit and commended her bravery in front of the others but knew it had been an extremely dangerous thing to attempt.

"Such actions can be most foolish but under these circumstances I believe we need all the help we can get. Let us pray that you connected to spirits of light and that they show you the true way. Of course," Nefron frowned, "if you are wrong and are being called into the realms of darkness, we cannot help you. When you cross the stones Penny, you will be on your own."

"Thank you Nefron."

Penedora hugged the High Priestess and backing away bowed her head in acknowledgement and respect.

"Go with the Council's blessings. Go with love in your heart and not fear. Thy mercy will be upon you and the children of Thyme."

Penedora carefully took the book from the altar and looked around at the faces starring anxiously into her eyes.

"Be careful," whispered Dellery, embracing her.

"I will."

"Gods bless your journey, Penny," came another voice, "save us all and come back safe."

"I will."

Penedora was quite surprised that the Council had taken the news of her spell more openly than she had imagined but then she knew they were all fearful of their fate at this time. The boys had not returned and Nefron was right, any hope was better than no hope. Nefron had lost her links to their Ancestors and Penedora, at this moment in time, was now their *only* hope.

"I'm coming too," called Zac from the back of the hall as he and Jilly entered.

Penedora looked at him and then moved her gaze to Jilly and back again.

"It's too dangerous Zac," she responded.

"It's no good. I've made my decision."

"You must stay here in case we don't find your brother across the stones."

"I've made up my mind," he said authoritatively, "I'm coming with you and Jilly and I'm sure when we find Marcus and Julin they will help you also."

"But you haven't been protected by my potion."

"It's my choice to take that chance."

Penny sighed. Holding the Egyptian book tightly in her arms, she looked straight into his eyes. Zac understood her eye contact. Penedora was not going to carry him through this dangerous mission. When he stepped out into the mist he would be on his own. Her priorities were Jilly, Gyp, returning the book and also to find Steven. Zac starred back in acknowledgement of her thoughts. He understood the risks involved but couldn't bear the thought of letting Jilly go across the stones without him by her side. Penedora sensed she was not going to change his mind. She knew he wanted to protect her daughter but felt being a hero at this time would not help either of them. Zac held his ground. Penedora succumbed to his stubbornness.

"Then let's hurry to Cairo."

Penedora brushed passed them both. She called for Gyp to follow. Once more she stepped out of the Hall and into the unknown.

It was playing out like a chapter from a horror novel. The three intrepid heroes, with a cat in tow, clutching an ancient Egyptian book, stepped out into the night and headed towards the mist. Behind them the people watched anxiously as the trio walked briskly to their fate. This *wasn't* a novel though and all three were actually scared as the mist engulfed them. When they got deeper and deeper into the swirling mass they could no longer see the Council Hall behind them or the gathering, who had watched them depart towards the unknown.

The fog was neither cold nor warm to touch but it was thick, causing visibility to be almost non-existent. The group had travelled to the stones through the woods on many occasions and this was the only reason they had a clue to the direction they were heading. They knew that if their feet kept to the path and each person kept near the one in front, they would all make it to the cross over point. To stray off the path would mean becoming disorientated within the mist and no one knew what or who was lurking within it. They all felt some level of fear and apprehension but the need to succeed drove the group on forward. Determination kept them stepping towards their way out of Thyme. The mist swirled and thinned around them as if to allow their progression towards the stones. Penedora sensed that the fog knew they had their book with the intention of returning it. She just knew it was going to let them through. If it wasn't, they would have all been dead by now.

A scream rang out from the vicinity of the Hall; then another. They stopped suddenly and looked backwards. They could see nothing behind. Jilly held tightly to her mother's arm as they strained their eyes to focus on something behind them.

"What do you think that was? I can't see anything," said Jilly nervously.

A sound of breaking glass echoed through the mist and another scream followed. "Keep moving," shouted Penedora and she ushered them on through the fog. "There's nothing we can do. We must hurry."

Zac was wearing four crystals about his body and he checked them all with his hand as they fumbled on through the density.

They finally reached the clearing by the stream and Penedora came to a sudden halt. "Be careful. We should be near the stones but I can't see them."

"I can hear the water," said Zac, straining to listen.

"Wait! What's that?" Jilly grasped her mother's arm again. "Something's happening."

Up ahead, the mist began to slowly disperse. It was as if someone had brought along a machine, like a vacuum cleaner, that sucked up the rolling fog. First they began to see each other clearly again, then around them the mist began to roll away quite quickly. Behind them, a narrow passage free of fog emerged. As it widened they could see the ground beneath them and where they had just travelled through the woods. The stones were now visible in front and their way out was just up ahead.

"Let's go." said Penedora picking up the pace.

Behind them the trees emerged.

"I don't like this," whispered Jilly.

Gyp hissed at something behind them. Zac gasped. In the distance he could see a man from the direction they had come. He couldn't quite make out the full extent of his costume but the man appeared half-naked with a golden robe around his middle. His hair was jet black and long. He held a spear which he was waving towards them in a threatening manner.

"Run!" screamed Zac, realising the danger. He turned and pushed the girls forward with his arms. Jilly picked up pace, her heart pounded. They all ran as fast as they could towards the stones. As the evil man stormed closer, Zac looked over his shoulder as he ran, but wished he hadn't. He saw the man was much closer and watched in horror as his facial features change from man to beast. The evil grew larger and his anger grew until the half, naked beast-man with a long pointed face and golden cloth around his middle lunged towards the frightened group.

Jilly followed Gyp as he leapt onto the first stone. Penedora jumped next, closely followed by

Zac who was still shouting at the top of his voice to run!

Eerie shrills could be heard in the distance behind them as they all fled in the nick of time from Thyme.

Chapter 9

The door knob stopped turning and the door was rattled from the outside.

"I think it's locked," someone whispered.

"Here let me have a go."

The door knob turned slowly again.

"It's not opening for me either!"

The occupants of the room were frozen to the spot as the door rattled. Someone was trying to get in. They could hear their hearts beating in their chests as the tension grew. There was no escape and nowhere to hide and neither had an airtight explanation as to why two random members of the public were rifling through paperwork in a private museum room.

"Try turning it the other way."

The door knob turned slowly again but in the other direction. This time, with a shove, it was opened. Zac fell through the doorway and into the small library. He had shoved a little too hard!

"My god, you scared me half to death!" Marcus shouted at his brother as Zac scrambled to his feet.

Julin sighed with relief as he held his hand over his chest, "Me too!"

"Sorry!" muttered Zac as he brushed his clothes down with the palms of his hands, which were dusty from the library floor, "Penedora had trouble opening it. The door knob was quite stiff to turn."

"What the hell are you doing here and how did you find us?" Marcus asked.

"We knew you were in the Cairo Museum somewhere, so we split up to look. Penedora heard you whispering behind the door and hey presto, found you!"

"Did anyone else see you come here?"

"No, the museum is shut. It's deserted."

Marcus stepped passed the new guests and peered through the door. He looked around the stillness of the stairwell. Julin was surprised that they had been there so long. "I didn't hear everyone leaving. We must have been here for ages."

"Hey Marcus!" Jilly called. She caught sight of him, peering out from a door on the gallery landing of the stairs. She waved to catch his attention and hurried around the perimeter of the upper landing to join the others. Gyp pounded down the stairs ahead of her.

"Sshh!" he whispered loudly to Jilly as she grew nearer.

"It's alright. The night guard is on the ground floor by the sarcophagus section. He's snoozing like a trooper!" she told him, brushing passed him into the room where everyone was now congregated.

"Is anyone else here?" Marcus asked inquisitively, scanning the stairwell and beyond.

"I don't think anyone else escaped," replied Zac.

Julin raised an eyebrow. "What do you mean, escaped?"

Marcus closed the door behind them and switched on the light. He looked at Jilly. "Are you sure the guard is asleep?"

"Yes, I'm sure."

"What's going on?" he enquired worriedly, looking at Penedora.

Marcus and Julin starred in disbelief as the others shared their story of the events in Thyme.

"So what happened to the book when you fled?" asked Julin.

"I have it here," said Jilly, swivelling her shoulder round to reveal her haversack. "I have both books with me, ours and the Egyptian one."

"You brought it with you?" gasped Marcus.

"We're quite safe." Penedora butted in. "Jilly and I have been covered with the purple essence of Romanihum. It's an old potion that ancient witches used to use."

"Romanihum? I haven't heard that name in years," said Marcus. "I'm sure I've read somewhere that the people of Thyme needed this protection to cross the stones in the middle ages, before crystals."

"How on earth did you get it?" Julin enquired.

"Arrrh, family secret," she replied, putting her index finger to her mouth.

"Isn't it really powerful stuff?"

"I hope so," said Penedora. "If it saved our friends from hanging and burning during the dark ages in the New World, fingers crossed it will protect us from the dark forces working here in Egypt now."

"And you still have the spell recipe in your family?" Marcus sucked in his lips and rolled his eyes in amazement.

Zac interrupted, as he flicked through some of the books that lay open on the table in front of him. "Why have you two taken so long?" He sat down where Marcus had been sitting and held up a book. "*The Myth of Osiris, God of the Underworld*; Osiris, God of the Underworld? Sounds powerful, and intriguing stuff."

"We didn't realise how long we had been but I must say we've gathered enough to know that the old Egyptian book is not what you think it is."

"What do you mean, Julin?" asked Penedora. "What knowledge have you gained?"

"We thought it was the ancient Book of the Dead but it's actually a spell book to bring back the dead."

Penedora gasped and Jilly caught the look of surprise on Zac's face as he turned to his brother. "Are you saying we have an Egyptian book of black magic?"

"No," explained Marcus, "what we are saying is, it's just like any other spell book." He continued, "Any spell book is either good or bad depending on the reader and how that reader uses the knowledge from it. Their book is not about spells like the way we use ours, but it has one agenda and that is to raise the dead."

"So you are saying it could be a good thing *or* a bad thing?" asked Penedora.

"Or just a bad thing?" asked Jilly.

"I most definitely think bad," Marcus replied. "The people after the book are obviously intending to raise someone of a negative nature, otherwise what you have just told us would not be happening in Thyme. Good people do not poison bride and grooms. Personally, I think the book must be destroyed. At least we now have it here so we can burn it."

He looked at Jilly beckoning her to remove the book from her haversack.

"Wait a minute. Let's not be so hasty on this," said Penedora, holding up her hand to stop Jilly removing the book from its safe location. The only link to her finding out what happened to Steven was on Jilly's back and nothing was going to jeopardise her plight. Not this early in the game anyway!

"Not necessarily," said Penedora.

She fumbled in her pockets and pulled out the paper on which she had written their message from her spell room. She handed it to Marcus. "I believe this is our answer to returning the book to the rightful owners."

She explained about the spell to another realm and how her instincts told her that they should follow through with the directions on returning the book.

"I really don't believe it's a trap and having thought long and hard over this, I believe that the evil presence in Thyme is not the same as those we are required to give the book back to. There are two forces here, and I don't really think it is our right to destroy the book."

"But you've personally seen the power of what it can do," Julin butted in.

"In the wrong hands yes, but…"

"Penny's right." Marcus looked at each person in turn, waving the little piece of paper at them. "Your cast message would have warned you and told you to destroy it there and then."

"But it didn't."

"But it didn't," he agreed with her. "We have their book, we have our crystals to protect us; this means we have the power of negotiation. The evil cannot harm us while we have protection and the good can only praise our courage when we return it safely to them."

"And if the others get to us first….the evil ones?" Julin asked Marcus with a raised eyebrow.

"We'll cross that bridge when we come to it."

"You've read the power of the evil we are dealing with here Marcus, how can we possibly fight them?"

"I'm just agreeing with Penny. We must proceed to the conclusion and undo what Steven unfortunately started." He looked at Penedora and their glances reassured her of the respect he still held. She knew he hadn't just said what he did in spite and that he did not hold Steven entirely responsible for their predicament. She agreed with the unspoken message in his gaze; it was her responsibility to end the mess Steven had started.

"If we destroy the book we could finish this awful business right now," continued Julin in his fight for corrective action. "If the good are good, they will understand why, and the bad will not succeed in raising their dead. Surely the good guys will be happy with that."

"Think of the repercussions though," said Marcus, "if Penny's right and the book *does* belong to someone righteous, we have no right to destroy it."

"And if the *not so righteous* get hold of it in the meantime, what then eh?" Julin felt uncomfortable with their decision. He felt he was not getting through to these two supposed higher spiritual souls standing before him.

"We'll just have to make sure it's returned to the right people."

"And how do you suppose we do that Marcus? Say, excuse me, are you the nice guy or the evil one? We could bring doom to heaven-knows-where if we fail. None of us know what's left of Thyme Hollow and think of the people here in the New World too. Especially as we are fighting this negativity here amongst people who have no idea about the power of magic."

"We have to take that chance."

"Marcus is right," said Penedora, "we have to try. Just think what could happen if one of our spell books fell into someone else's hands, I'm sure we would want it returned to us and not burnt?"

Penedora was more fearful of the repercussions of destroying the book than the fear of continuing her journey to find Steven. Blinded by love, she was adamant their decision was correct.

"There he is!" Zac shouted as he flew from his chair and shoved a book into Julin's face. "That's him! The Osiris chap," he said, pointing to a page. "This is the figure that ran after us as we crossed the stones. He was a man and then changed as he tried to grab us. He changed into this thing."

Julin stepped back a little as he tried to view the picture thrust into his field of vision.

"Let me see!" asked Jilly.

They all gathered around the book to see what Zac had found.

Julin shook his head, "This isn't a picture of Osiris. This only confirms what Marcus and I believed earlier. If this God is responsible for all the evil in Thyme what chance do we mere mortals have?"

"Is it...?" asked Marcus hesitantly as he took the book in his hand and studied the figure in the picture.

"Yes, it is," Julin confirmed. "Seth!"

Zac looked from his brother to Julin and back again searching for an explanation. "Who's Seth?"

"The brother of Osiris. This man killed his brother and now roams the dark side of the underworld, causing chaos and grief."

Marcus and Julin then told the others of the story of Osiris and Isis and how Isis had brought her husband back to life after Seth had killed him. It became crystal clear that all their pieces of information clicked together like a jigsaw puzzle. Together they had discovered the 'Who?': Isis had dabbled with 'bringing back dead husband spells' so they figured she must be the true owner of the book and it was to her they would attempt to return it. They unanimously agreed, Seth was definitely NOT the one who should gain control of it.

Swiftly moving on, they then tried to analyse the message from the spell book which Penedora had copied on her little piece of paper.

Julin had a fair idea of the meaning of some of the words and looked through a few of the books within the library to confirm.

"Yes, now, Amentet means the underworld and Osiris, is Khenti Amentet – Chief of the Underworld. Now Tuat," he tried to remember where he'd seen the word, "oh yes," he picked up another book and read from it:

220

"*The tuat is a dark, narrow valley which begins in the West at sunset and ends in the East at sunrise. A river runs through it and at each hour of the night the dead, accompanied by the sun god Ra, pass through the twelve gates by boat. The boat is pulled by four beings of the Tuat.*"

Julin then explained to the others about the twelve hours of the night and the weighing of the heart in front of Osiris at the sixth gate.

Penedora was impressed with the knowledge the boys had discovered and realised now why they had taken so long. She felt positive that the prayer to other spirit realms had indeed been active in its response. Little by little they were getting closer to knowing the rest of their task— the *Where* and *How*.

"That just leaves Gyp and the Shat En Sbau," she said proudly.

They all turned and look at their furry black friend, who had all this time been sitting on one of the shelves licking his paws while shrewdly listening to their conversations. He paused from his cleaning duty and starred back down at them all. "What?" he thought!

"How can a cat tell *us* anything," Zac sneered sarcastically, facing him. He never really liked cats. He always mistrusted them and was more of a dog person. "Is he going to write it down for us in paw language?" he smirked.

Gyp leapt off the shelf and landed claws first, on Zac's chest.

"Ooow!" Zac threw Gyp off him, "you horrid…"

"Serves you right teasing him," laughed Jilly.

She bent down and picked Gyp up and squeezed him tightly. He responded to her love by nuzzling under her chin and purring. He then returned his gaze to Zac who was still rubbing his chest from the claw marks Gyp had left behind. Inwardly Gyp smiled. He was a little jealous of Zac's affections towards Jilly and scored this episode as a little one-upmanship between them. He knew though, in his heart, that Zac was good for Jilly and that he had nothing to be really jealous of, but for now, at least for a little longer, *he* was to be Jilly's number one.

"I have no idea why Gyp has a problem with you though."

She reached up and carefully returned Gyp back on the shelf. He wobbled a little at the handover and then steadied himself on all fours.

"We need to know what Shat En Sbau means," she whispered to him softly.

Gyp looked around the room at all the books displayed. There was not enough width to fit some of the larger books on the narrow shelving and thus they extended further than the edge. To manoeuvre himself around these larger books he jumped from shelf to table and back again looking for their answer. His whiskers vibrated and his tail flipped from cover to dusty cover. Zac couldn't believe his eyes. This cat was actually looking for something. Could he read? Surely not. It was a cat!

It didn't take too long for the answer to come. Gyp paused at a book that Julin had earlier been reading. He turned to Jilly and blinked. Swishing his tail at the book in question he gracefully landed back onto the table and began licking his paws again.

'No I'm not going to write it down for you,' he thought smugly to himself, 'I have a body of a cat; paws not hands, and everyone knows cats can't hold a pencil.' His yellow eyes squinted at Zac and a cat-like smile appeared on his face.

Zac was becoming apprehensive of this animal. "Surely this cat can't read my mind too, can it?" he thought suspiciously.

Jilly responded intuitively to Gyp and reached up to the book in question. "See, I knew he could do it," she smiled.

"I read that one earlier but I don't remember seeing the name of a place Shat En Sbau in it," Julin told them, recognising the book Jilly passed him.

"It's not a place," she told him knowingly, "it's the book or the name of the book. The words said '*Gyp hath the knowledge*'. Remember knowledge comes from books, therefore this book *is* the knowledge."

Penedora was proud of her daughter. Jilly was quite impressed with herself as well!

Gyp had chosen the *Book of the Pylons – Coming Forth by Night*. Julin opened it and read a little. He soon remembered it was all about the twelve gates of the night.

"Another spell book," he said, "look it's full of spells!"

He flicked the pages to show everyone. They gathered round as he scanned the contents.

"Each spell relates to a certain hour of the night. So these must be the spells written on papyrus and carved on walls in the burial chambers. They are meant to help the dead souls pass safely through the Tuat towards the Hall of Truths. Pylons, Gates, Hours, they're all the same thing."

Then it clicked in his brain. "Of course! This is it. We have to go to the underworld and pass through the Tuat to Osiris at the sixth gate to hand over the book." Julin poked the book in triumph. "That's where Isis will be; at the sixth hour with her husband, Osiris."

Jilly stroked her cat on the head.

"Well done Gyp! Now we know the "*Where*.""

"Let's go then," cried Zac as he made his way to the door.

"Hold on," Marcus said forcefully to his brother, "where are you actually going?"

"To the Tuat."

"And where's that exactly?"

"In the underworld," Zac paused thoughtfully for a second. Marcus was right. How *do* you get to the underworld from the Cairo museum?

"So? What now?" asked Julin, "does anyone have any bright ideas?"

Zac let go of the door knob and stood with his back against it. Every time they were close to answers, another problem held them up. They all felt they were so near to solving the whole riddle, yet so far from ending this terrifying situation.

"Actually, I do," said Penedora suddenly, "I suggest we start where the dead Egyptians started."

They looked at her with great anticipation for the answer to come. Penedora smiled at them all, this bit was easy she thought.

"Where all the dead Egyptians are laid to rest for their journey to the underworld?"

Everyone was looking at her eagerly waiting the answer.

"Cairo?" asked Zac.

"In a burial chamber." Penedora smiled back.

"Great excellent idea," agreed Marcus, "but which one?"

Penedora shrugged her shoulders.

"The nearest tombs are at the Valley of the Kings aren't they? We could travel down the Nile tomorrow, start with the first one we come to and go from there."

"I know somewhere much nearer," smiled Jilly.

Julin cottoned on quickly too. "Somewhere just across town we could get to tonight you mean?"

Jilly nodded.

Penedora looked puzzled. "I didn't think there were any tombs within the city of Cairo."

"Not underground ones," she replied, "but huge, tall ones on top; the Pyramids of Giza."

Marcus' face lit up. "Well done Jilly, yes, the Pyramids, they are indeed tombs. Ancient burial chambers. So," he looked at them all in turn, "to one of the Seven Wonders of the Ancient World it is. We folks, are off to the Great Pyramids of Egypt."

Everyone gathered up everything they needed and lined up by the door.

Zac opened it just a little and carefully looked out. All seemed quiet. The guard was either still asleep downstairs or on walkabout at another part of the museum. No movement could be heard near them so they decided to take their chances to leave the little room of safety and venture out of the museum into the cool Egyptian night. Everyone followed Zac out onto the landing. As she left last, Penedora flicked the light switch off and closed the old forgotten library door behind her.

Huddled on the great landing stairwell, Marcus and Julin switched on their torches to light the steps and shadows of the corridors ahead of them.

Gyp brushed passed Zac's legs and hurried downstairs in front of them.

"Let's go," whispered Marcus as he took the lead.

"You don't have any munchies in your bag do you?" Julin whispered into Jilly's ear, "We've been here so long, I'm starving."

"Sorry, I don't. We ate before we left."

The basement and building lights were off. The exit signs glowed in the darkness of the museum above doorways and alcoves. They made their way silently down to the ground floor and towards the main entrance. The museum was grand with high ceilings and wide stairwells. Each corridor was lined with tall, elegant or just awe inspiring statues set on plinths, and figurines each numbered for cross reference or labelled with explanation for the tourists. There were glass cases housing amazing artefacts oozing with historic importance or relevance to their display stand. The vast halls were arched and pillared giving rise to the overall experience of grandeur. This building was truly perfect to house such ancient treasure. A modern, square, glass building of any sort would have spoilt the ambiance and historical importance of the antiquities.

"Everyone, sshh!" Marcus had seen something to his left, his raised hand motioning his colleagues to stop. The hall to their left was vast but he could make out a small flickering light up ahead.

"I think it's a torch." He quickly turned his own one off and Julin fumbled clumsily with his torch's off switch. They stood rooted to the spot for what seemed like a lifetime in the hope they hadn't been spotted. The beam wavered at the end of the hall then flickered off into another direction.

Julin peered towards the vanishing light in the distance. "Security?"

"Think so. He must be on his rounds."

Marcus motioned to his brother to usher everyone along. "We'll have to hurry before he makes his way back down here."

They sped along the corridors and steps quickly and as quietly as they could. On reaching the main entrance, they discovered the main exit door was firmly bolted from the inside and one other door near to the museum shop was chained.

"What now?" whispered Julin.

Marcus looked around. A room to the right was sign posted "Shop" and "Exit".

"Let's try through there," he pointed.

They all followed as he made his way into the shop. His hunch paid off. There was a large glass door to the outside. They could see through to the night and their destiny. Unfortunately this entrance was also securely locked. Marcus looked to find a button or mechanism to open it, but found nothing. Looking around again he noticed another room off the shop. He ventured over and entered. It was a storeroom. He shone his torch around the room. Boxes and books, sealed in transparent wrapping, littered the floor and shelves. In one corner there stood a sink and draining board. On top, draining, were two coffee cups. Beside them, a little jar of coffee and an opened bag of sugar with a plastic spoon standing up inside it. He spied another door in the corner, which assumedly led to the outside. There was no window in this one, but a handle and small key hole.

"There's another way out, but it's also locked. We're not having much luck getting out of this place are we?" he huffed angrily.

"Surely we must be able to open it from the inside," said Penedora.

"No, just a door knob and key hole. There must be a key in here somewhere as it's not in the door!"

Marcus ordered his brother to keep a look out for the guard returning from his patrol. They split up and surveyed the storeroom and the shop for any key that resembled the shape of the keyhole.

"Found it!" gasped Julin excitedly. He had chosen to look by the cash till. He slid his fingers underneath the till and a key had flicked out onto the work surface beside it. He threw it over to Marcus by the store room.

The key fitted. "At last," thought Marcus, "our luck has changed."

No one had thought of the door being alarmed. Their thoughts were engaged in getting out of the museum before a guard returned. Luckily for them though, no alarm sounded when it opened. The security guard had not set it, as the door was locked anyway.

Julin went back to the desk and replaced the key under the cash till and then followed the others slipping out of the museum and closing the storeroom door behind him. He hoped the guard would not realise the storeroom door was now unlocked!

They made their way round to the imposing front of the building, down the grand museum steps and across the vast open space towards the tourist booths and into the darkness of the night.

From the city hustle and bustle and beeping of car horns, to the stillness of the desert air, the heroes of Thyme set off for the Great Pyramids of Giza.

The eerie stillness was unsettling. There was no wind, no sound: no movement anywhere. Thyme, in every sense, was at a complete standstill. The fog, which had come so suddenly and violently, began to disperse. It was now shrinking back towards the stones; recoiling its evil arms and retreating to its lair. Its pale white arms slithered backwards, gently caressing each tree trunk and blade of grass as it shrank. As each little area of space became uncovered, no damage could be seen. The herbs and wild flowers of the woods remained intact but their vibrancy and healing properties were gone. A pathway through the trees slowly became visible again. The grass, the trees, the buildings were all as before the fog invaded, but something was different in Thyme. The view was the same, but the energy was wrong somehow. What had changed in the wake of the mist was the movement of life.

In the morning there would be no birds singing their merry little tuneful songs. No children would be heard splashing in the stream as they played amongst the shallow shingles. There would be no farmers in the fields digging, no sounds of animals, munching their way through the fresh green grass. No praying, meditation or idle gossip would be heard and no smells of cooking wafted from the little cottages dotted around the wood and to the vast reaches of the Hollow. No more fish would be congregating on the shallow shingles of the stream. Silence and emptiness was all that remained as the mist completely dissolved. No one stood and watched as it left their home that night. Thyme Hollow was now motionless.

__Chapter 10__

Julin stepped back from the entrance and leaned over the edge of the huge rock ledge, Marcus and he were standing on. Far below he could see the dark figures of his friends. He waved his torch to signal it was okay for them to climb the pyramid to the level above and join them. He then turned back round to his friend who was waiting by the opened entrance to a world which stretched back thousands of years. The entrance was well defined from below at the pyramid base and was supposedly the first to be found when the pyramid was explored in modern times. Julin hoped this would be their route to the centre of the pyramid and finally to the underworld of Amentet. He helped Marcus remove some lose stones and pieces of wood laid across the entrance. He handed his torch to Marcus and watched as his friend disappeared into the darkness of the pyramid.

The huge layers of rocks appeared far larger to Gyp than the humans but he seemed to climb them effortlessly. He bounced and scrambled from one layer to another in an upward movement until he reached the required level. Zac helped Jilly and her mother climb as each portion required skill and careful balancing. Four legs were obviously easier than having just two. Either that, or humans were just not built to climb huge boulders. The rocks were not loose or corroded; in fact, for their age, the pyramid stones had survived remarkably well. They were just so large. Some rocks had to be climbed instead of being stepped on like stairs or the explorers had to squeeze their bodies between crevasses for helpful footholds. There was now also no light from the faded evening dusk. The darkness of the night had swept in while they were in the museum and tonight in Cairo there was no moonlight to light their ascent. Only Marcus and Julin had thought to bring torches across the stones of Thyme. Marcus had given his to his brother at the start of their climb, but Zac had decided to turn it off in case an inhabitant in the distance from the town below spotted them during their difficult climb.

"I always seem to be dusting myself down," laughed Zac as he joined the others on the entrance ledge. "I'm covered in sandstone."

"You look fine to me," Jilly nudged him with her hand.

"You can't possibly see what I look like, it's dark," he playfully nudged her back.

"Wouldn't be if you had your torch on!"

"Sorry, are you okay, Penedora?" Zac asked.

"That was much harder than I thought," she puffed.

Bending over, she needed time to catch her breath and take stock of how high they were. In the distance, she could see dancing night lights from the hustle and bustle of the city below. Taking a large breath in, she refilled her lungs once more.

"I'm good," she said.

They all assembled around the vast pyramid's small opening. Marcus reappeared from the darkness.

"There's a corridor into the pyramid, but it is blocked at the end by a wall," he told them as he stepped outside.

Eager anticipation of venturing into the pyramid was brought to a swift halt and Julin shook his head in disbelief.

Zac turned his torch on and shone it into his brother's eyes. "Maybe there's a secret passage inside. You know, a mysterious stone sticking out, something you press and the wall miraculously opens!"

"This isn't the movies, Zac."

"And where do you suppose movie makers get their ideas from?" Zac raised an acknowledging eyebrow to his brother who was in no mood for his brother's banter.

Marcus looked at Julin's disappointed face and then at Zac's excited one. He rolled his eyes and sighed at them both as he reluctantly ventured back into the pyramid to look for a strange stone, or something similar to what pyramids have in the movies! Zac and Julin followed him in. The girls and Gyp decided to remain at the entrance while the boys tried to help Marcus find a secret passage. Jilly ventured carefully from the opening and sat down swinging her legs over the edge of one of the large rocks.

"Careful Jilly!" Penedora called out. "Don't fall."

"It's actually not far to fall, only to the next stone down." Jilly pointed just below her feet.

"It's just that's it's so dark up here and I don't want us separated."

Jilly turned her head and could just make out the figure of her mother standing by the entrance. "This tomb is awesome don't you think? We're not even a quarter of the way up and we're such a long way from the ground. It's enormous!"

Penedora shuffled across the entrance stones and knelt beside Jilly. She looked down to where they had climbed from and agreed that the structure was indeed immense.

"Stay silent for a moment and just feel the energy radiating from this place," she told her daughter.

Jilly did so. The air was still and the noise from Cairo seemed muffled and distant. Jilly also fixated on the city lights twinkling in the darkness below. There were thousands of lives below them, all milling around and attending to their personal needs. The two ladies perched on the pyramid were too small and insignificant in the darkness for anyone below to know they were even there peering down at them. Penedora and Jilly both breathed in the fresh evening air again and they both felt a wave of energy as it slowly seeped deep into their lungs.

"The stones may be thousands of years old and surrounded by modern living but the old pharaohs still remain here," whispered Penedora. She could feel them but was unable to hear them. Their energy flowed with a different vibration to their ancestors and spirit in Thyme Hollow.

Jilly nodded.

"I can feel their presence too."

They sat imagining what it must have been like all those years ago with the noise and activity of slaves, workers and town folk, building and working on something so beautiful and so powerful. Such a magnificent structure built for the memory of one man, one pharaoh. That one person they once looked upon as a God.

"It's no good," called Zac, "we can't get in this way."

The girls swung round sighting Zac emerging from the entrance first. Penedora helped Jilly to her feet.

Julin was surprised the passage was blocked. "This is the old way into the tomb, discovered many, many years before the tourist entrance was made. I can't understand why they didn't carry on excavating further up this passage. It was obviously once connected to various chambers. Remember, the Egyptians would have put in many false entrances to deter grave robbers. This could be one of them," he explained.

"Possibly, or maybe they just sealed this entrance to stop the tourists ruining their national heritage and built a fresh one just for them," said Marcus, as he began sealing off the entrance again. Julin helped him replace the debris that they had uncovered from the opening.

"Do we have to climb back down again, Marcus?" Jilly enquired.

"I'm afraid so."

"Really?"

Jilly's tut echoed into the night.

Marcus put back the last piece of wood covering the entrance and replaced the "No Entry" sign. "We might as well try the tourist entrance before searching the whole of this pyramid for the *real* original one….. and that could take all night!"

They felt the task ahead of them was more daunting than first envisaged. If they couldn't find the entrance into the depths of the pyramid then they would have to wait until morning and try entering a tomb in the Valley of the Kings. Marcus began to suspect their journey was being purposely thwarted every which way they turned.

The scramble back down the stones was a little trickier than the climb up, but they eventually reached the lower tourist entrance.

"Can we open it?" asked Julin.

"It's not locked." Marcus was surprised that the door lock was hanging open with the key in its hole, and the latch clicked freely upwards and as he pushed, the door opened with ease. He shone his torch inside.

"Why did we not try this door first before climbing all the way up there?" Jilly asked.

"Because we need to venture deep into the pyramid to the original burial chamber, not just to the tourist bits." Julin answered.

"And because they didn't think this door would be actually open or unmanned," mocked Zac.

Julin had told them about the tourist police in Egypt and how security of their antiquities was of highest priority to these people. He couldn't understand why the main door to one of the greatest wonders of the world was unguarded and unlocked in the stillness of the night.

"It worries me that we took forever to get out of the museum, yet this entrance is unmanned and open. Do you think it's a trap?" asked Penedora.

"I'm not sure," came his reply. "I feel apprehensive as well. It's been too easy around the pyramids so far. Where are the night guards? Where is everyone? Are we being guided by good or are we being led by evil?"

Marcus shrugged his shoulders, continuing, "all we can hope for is that this is either an oversight by the authorities or someone trying to help us. I don't know which one it is, but we have to go on."

Marcus slapped Julin's shoulder to relax his nerves and he smiled a broad smile to make light of the predicament they had found themselves in.

"Come on," he continued, "I have a little trepidation and a lot of curiosity. We must succeed and we are not giving up on Thyme."

He had spoken the truth. Inwardly, he *was* nervous, but his curiosity to what lay ahead steered him bravely forward. "How many people get chances to play heroes like this in their lifetime?" he thought to himself.

"We'll have to take this slowly," Marcus told the group. "It looks incredibly dark in there so I suggest we have one torch up front with me and one at the back."

Zac, who was holding the other torch, took heed of his brother's words and made his way to the rear of the group. "I can see steps immediately in front as you enter and beyond that I have no idea. I don't know how far down they go or where they lead. So I suggest we take this slowly and that we each hold on to the person in front. The ceiling is also extremely low so mind your heads."

Marcus then bent down and disappeared into the dark stairwell with Julin following extremely closely behind him. Penedora took hold of Julin's belt with her right index finger; Jilly held on to her mother's clothes and Zac held tightly to Jilly's rucksack. He tried to shine his torch ahead of himself to give some light to the ladies but it was an extremely difficult descent down the steps and into the heart of the pyramid. His light shining abilities were really of no use to anyone. He kept lighting up a piece of wall, then the ground, and flicking it between their legs.

"Keep the torch still," Penedora snapped at him.

"Sorry!"

There was a small gap beside the explorers for Gyp to keep pace. Even though his night vision was far greater than that of his companions, this corridor of steep steps was extremely dark for him to focus too. He therefore followed Marcus' light up front and took each step with great care. He hated being in a confined place that was pitch black. Gyp was not afraid of the dark. He was afraid of where he was going. 'After all, the pyramids are tombs and dead people roam tombs!' He kept reminding himself that tourists now visited this pyramid and not the dead pharaohs of ancient Egypt. He tried hard to convince himself that everything was okay, but Gyp hated tombs. He had always hated these places!

A strong musty smell hit their noses as they ventured deeper into the shaft. At some steps the ceiling appeared lower, forcing them to crouch further down. It wasn't a natural position to walk down steps and the darkness of the tunnel slowed their progress. In theory, the pyramid should have been cool in the dark of the night but the inside temperature felt very warm indeed. Mixed with the musty smell, the heat became uncomfortable for the explorers and the men began to sweat first. Marcus wiped his brow with the back of his hand. Luckily, no one suffered from claustrophobia. The stairwell was narrow, natural light non-existent and the heat unbearable. Not the best circumstances to be in while evil was out to get you!

"Ouch!"

"What happened? Are you alright?" Julin held his hands up against Marcus' back as his friend had stopped dead in front of him. The others bashed into each other also like a domino effect. Marcus stood firm and held the rail to his right tightly to stop them all toppling forward down the steep stairway. Holding the torch in his left hand he let go of the rail and raised his arm rubbing his forehead with his wrist.

"I've just bashed into something," he winced. When the initial pain of being donked on the head subsided, he shone his torch above him to see what he had collided with.

"Excellent!" cried Julin. "It's okay, everyone," he called backwards, "Marcus has found a light bulb!"

One little light bulb housed in a rusty metal casing hung precariously above Marcus' head.

"Where's the switch?" Zac shouted back.

Marcus shone his torch from the light bulb and along the wiring, which ran across the ceiling and down the wall. It then veered off down the shaft in the direction they were heading.

"Probably at the *bottom* of the stairs," Marcus called back sarcastically.

He continued his descent and the others, keeping close, gingerly followed on. Halfway down the stairwell, Marcus caught sight of the light switch.

"Found it."

He flicked the switch. Nothing happened. "Typical!"

He shone his torch around to see if the switch was actually connected to the wire and it was. There was a faint flicker in the distance and slowly the corridor ahead began to light up. Little bars of light dotted along the corridor coughed and spluttered and one by one lit up. Last to shine was Marcus' light bulb behind them.

"So this is a pyramid," commented Zac. He turned off his torch and let his eyes gaze up and down the stairs. He had expected something spectacular having seen pictures of hieroglyphics and brightly coloured walls from books on Valley of the Kings, but all he saw here was a mouldy stone incline of steps that smelt horrid.

"Let's keep moving," Marcus ordered.

It felt good to stand up straight at the bottom. The passage ahead of them was still quite low and narrow but at least they didn't have to navigate the sharp gradient in the dark anymore.

A huge stone seemed to be suspended from nothing in front of them and they all had to duck down to get under it. It seemed strange to have a very long corridor with a huge lump of stone separating the ceiling from the floor. Zac turned back round and touched the large stone he had just passed under. It felt cold and clammy yet the heat inside the shaft was stifling. Then he noticed a large gap just above the rock, which seemed to look like another entrance. He turned his torch back on and shone it up at the ceiling.

"Hey look!" he called to the others, "there's a ladder."

The group halted to investigate.

Marcus squeezed passed the girls. He shone his torch above the huge rock as well and indeed he could see there was another shaft going back towards the stairs but above the level they had just come down.

"I wonder how many layers of corridors this place has."

"Many, young brother, many, and probably many of which still remain undiscovered."

"Shall we keep going?" called Julin.

Marcus looked up at the ladder and back towards Julin. He made the decision to continue in the direction they were heading. Marcus squeezed his way to the front of the queue again and continued down the corridor. Eventually the passage ended at an entrance to a huge expanse with an enormously high ceiling.

"Wow! This place is huge," Zac whistled, "but wow so boring too!" He was impressed with the size of the room but unimpressed by the lack of artistic impression within it. He wondered where all the famous hieroglyphs had gone.

The walls were indeed bland, old and cracked and the floor uneven, worn further from years of tourists trekking in and out. The air inside was stale and chewable. At the far end was a large slab of stone tilted on its side leaning against the wall and in front of it was a large rectangular hole. Neither structure was painted or carved ornately in any way. The hole had been dug by hand and was the same size and shape as the large slab, which was obviously the lid for whatever was once housed inside.

Julin ventured over and peered into the hole. "I assume this was where the sarcophagus once sat."

In turn they all peered into the dugout and envisaged a coffin in all its golden glory resting in the now empty hole. This didn't ring true for Marcus.

"It's not right," he said, gazing round the room. "Imagine you're a pharaoh and you spend all your worldly money on a great tomb as your final resting place. Surely after building such an enormous pyramid you wouldn't end up in a plain room at the end of a corridor, in a hole."

"But surely it wouldn't have looked like this a couple of thousand years ago." Zac commented.

"Maybe, maybe not, but this is not right. Where are the hieroglyphics to show the way through the Tuat? There's no weather to corrode the drawings down here. Even if time does fade things, there would be *something* left. Even the oldest tombs have paintings and markings. No, this room is not a burial chamber for a dead king. This is an antechamber or somewhere just dug out for the tourists to view."

Julin agreed with him. "Or maybe even the resting place of say a close servant or hierarchy member of the palace."

Penedora placed her hand on the wall she was facing and pushed at the rocks. She continued along one wall, feeling and pushing randomly. "It's definitely a dead end. Why don't we try back up the corridor on the level above where the ladder went?"

There was nothing to lose. After pushing a few more times on the walls hoping for something dramatic to happen, they gave up and headed back the way they came.

They stopped once more at the stone with the ladder and the brothers shone their torches upwards.

"How do we get up there?" said Julin.

"Let me try," said Zac as he handed Penedora the torch. He put one hand on the handrail to the left of him as he faced the huge suspended rock and, using his feet as leverage against the wall, he tried to scale up the rock towards the ladder. He slipped back down again. Trying a second time he again failed and slipped back down. The rock was too smooth for his feet to gain any grip and just too tall to lever himself over the top with his elbows. Zac couldn't reach.

"Hey let me help." Julin offered himself as a higher starting point and he bent down in front of the rock. Zac again held onto the handrail and carefully placed his feet, one on Julin's back and one on the wall next to him. Julin raised himself slightly and grunted as he propelled Zac in an upward motion. Zac grabbed the top of the rock with his arms and heaved himself onto the next level.

"Well done," called Jilly excitedly.

Zac turned round and leaned over the edge as Penedora threw the torch up to him. He caught it well.

"Tell us what you can see."

Zac stood up and shone the light up the ladder. He could see another long, low corridor but nothing beyond that. It was too dark and angled. As he rested his hand against the ladder it moved. He placed his hand around a rung and shook it. The ladder wasn't fixed at all.

"Excellent," he thought. "Mind out the way, I'm sending the ladder down."

Carefully lowering the ladder down the edge of the stone and holding the top of it tightly, Zac managed to manoeuvre it towards them without dropping it. He wiggled it a little to make sure it was safe to climb.

"Who's first?"

Julin was, followed by Penedora. Jilly placed Gyp around her shoulders as she gingerly climbed. Marcus followed last and it was he and Zac who hoisted up the ladder behind them and placed it back in the same position they found it.

"We can't let anyone notice we are here," he told Zac.

There was no light switch or wiring in the corridor above them, so they repositioned themselves once more with Marcus at the front holding one torch and Zac at the rear with the other.

About fifty paces forwards the corridor turned sharply left and they began descending again. It then veered left once more revealing another chamber. Again, it was huge with a high ceiling and not a hieroglyph in sight. Some workmen had left a few tools in the corner of the room and a few cigarette ends had been stamped into the ground where they had obviously stopped for a work break.

"You'd need more than a hammer and chisel to find hidden corridors in this place," said Zac as he kicked a few tools over with his foot.

There were a couple of wooden crates used for seating and a newspaper had been left beside an overturned flask. Zac picked up the newspaper and flicked it over to reveal the front cover. He shone his torch up and down it.

"It looks very old," he muttered, "it's all yellow and faded. Obviously no one comes up here anymore, that's probably why there are no light bulbs. Do you think they stopped working here when they discovered the other room with the hole?"

"Possibly," said Julin as he joined him in the corner to view the Egyptian newspaper. Marcus continued scanning the room with his torch while Penedora stood with Jilly who was now rhythmically stroking Gyp in her arms. He didn't purr and Jilly sensed something was wrong. "Gyp doesn't like it in here," Jilly told the others.

"I agree with Gyp," said Penedora, "I'm not sure about this room either. Can we go back and find another way to go?" She shivered. "I've gone really cold."

Marcus shone his torch to where Penedora was standing. "So you can feel it too Penny?"

"What?"

"The cold air."

She nodded.

Zac piped up, "But we're deep inside a pyramid, there shouldn't be any cold air circulating and the air smells so musty."

"Unless...." Marcus interrupted his brother, "there's a small shaft or vent that goes to the outside."

He shone his torch around the ceiling. Zac flicked his light around the room also.

"This cold isn't outside air," said Jilly, holding Gyp tightly in her arms, his tail fur raised and alert, "it's more like a temperature change wafting around the chamber. Spooky like!"

"I've found it!" Zac called out to the others. He bent down and shone his torch towards a gap between the floor and the wall near to where he was standing. "I can feel a definite draft coming from here. See Jilly, you are getting yourself all scared for nothing!"

"I trust Gyp," she responded, "something's not right."

Zac placed his hand near to the edge of the dark gap and he could feel a slight cold circulation of air on his palm.

Everyone gathered round to look. Zac tapped the stone wall just above the gap and a small piece of rock crumbled at his touch. He pushed a little harder and another piece of stone fell off uncovering more of the edging to the gap and allowing more cold air to waft through into their chamber. Julin stepped in and used his foot to help Zac remove more of the wall and in doing so caused a large slab of wall to crumble away in one go. The dusty sand spiralled up into Zac's nose and mouth causing him to sneeze and cough.

"Sorry Zac."

When the yellow dust had settled, they could see between the wall and floor edging that there was access to another room or corridor beyond. Shining the torch through the gap revealed nothing. It was still too dark to make out what was behind, or under, the chamber they were in. The gap needed to be made wider still.

"WHO'S THERE?" a voice shouted violently and suddenly. "CAN YOU HELP ME?"

Zac shrieked and toppled backwards onto his bottom as the voice from the dark hole took him by surprise. The torch fell from his hand and switched off.

Julin jumped five feet into the air with adrenaline flow when he heard the voice. He placed his hand over his heart and he could feel it pounding. Marcus shone his torch straight at the hole they had made and both Penedora and Jilly screamed. Gyp dived over Jilly's shoulder; his claws imbedded into her right shoulder as he went.

Everyone stood still for a split second in the semi-darkness. Zac scrambled to his feet, grabbing the torch again as he got up. He whacked it a couple of times and it came on again. He too shone it straight at the gap.

"I know there is someone there. Please help me." The voice came loudly again. It now sounded confused yet pleading. "Who's there? I know you are up there. Please help me."

Jilly put her hand over her mouth. She gasped loudly. Gyp immediately hissed at the hole and then jumped up onto Penedora. She took Gyp in one arm and put the other around her daughter's shoulders. Jilly's mind recalled her dream. The dream had been just a dream, yet here she was standing by the gap in the wall and this was reality.

"Jilly is that you?" came the voice responding to her sharp intake of breath.

She gasped again.

Nobody knew what to do, yet nobody ran. Fear had transfixed them to whoever was calling from behind the gap.

"It *is* you Jilly, I know it is. Help me, Jilly. Please help me."

The fear in her dream flooded back to her, the moment that would wake her violently lashing out in bed, or sweating from fighting off the unknown demon. The moment the thing, whatever or whoever it was grabbing her and pulling her through the gap and into the darkness beyond.

"Surely not," thought Penedora trying hard to focus on the voice, "it can't be."

"If someone's there, please help me."

It came again demanding.

"Steven?" Penedora answered hesitantly. "Oh my God, Steven, is that you?" Penedora dropped Gyp and rushed to the hole. She knelt down beside the gap and strained to see through it. Tears swelled in her eyes.

"Penny!" the voice responded urgently. "Penny?"

Both torches now shone down the hole in some attempt to see Steven in the darkness.

"Oh my God Steven, you're alive."

"Reach down Penny and take my hand," the voice instructed her.

As she reached her hand into the darkness Jilly screamed at her mother in fear. "No, don't!"

Penedora rapidly removed her hand and looked round. Jilly ran to her mother's side.

"It's evil. Don't put your hand down there."

"What do you mean Jilly? It's your father." Penedora looked at her daughter confused.

"Jilly?" The voice came again, "please help me."

"You're not my father," she yelled back, "I've seen you in my dreams. You are evil and want to hurt us. Leave us alone."

"No Jilly, it's a lie. I am your father. Please don't leave me here. Please help me Jilly."

"No! No! No!" she screamed back at the voice from the beneath the wall.

Penedora stood up and faced her daughter. In the dim light of the torches she could see the fear on Jilly's face. She grabbed her daughter's shoulders. "Tell me, Jilly. Tell me what's going on."

Jilly explained to everyone about her nightmares and what happened when she put her hand into the darkness.

"Then it grabbed me," she continued, "it was evil and it tried to take me down into the darkness."

The voice responded to her story. "They're only dreams, Jilly. I'm real. It's me, Steven, your father. Give me your hand!"

Nobody knew what to do. All eyes were on Jilly.

"If I reach down I will die." She was scared and unsure what was real. Were they just dreams, or a warning? She didn't know.

"And if we don't help him, we may never see your father again," Penedora followed on. She hugged her daughter. Penedora felt caught between the devil and the deep blue sea, literally. Allow her daughter to put her arm into the hole, and she could lose her into the darkness. Ignore the voice and if it *was* Steven, it sounded like Steven, then she could lose him forever.

Penedora feared opening up the hole to allow whoever stood on the other side through to the chamber. If it was evil tricking them, they could all perish and Thyme would never be saved.

Moments seemed like hours as the situation came to grid lock. Open the hole wider, or run?

Was Jilly being lured into the darkness or was Steven really behind the wall in need of their help?

"Jilly listen to me," the voice softened. "I too have dreams. In mine we also reach this point where you have a choice to save me by reaching in. But my dreams end when you run away and I'm doomed here for eternity. Can't you see that Seth has invaded your dreams to make sure you walked away if this opportunity ever came?"

Marcus gasped. Julin stepped back further from the wall. If this was really Steven he should know about the Egyptian book but how could he possibly know about Seth. Then again, if the voice belonged to Seth he would know about their quest and everything up to this point in time.

"Seth? You know Seth?" Marcus bent down to the opening.

"Yes, his brother put me here."

Marcus was surprised, "Osiris? Why?"

"As punishment for taking the book."

"So you did steal it."

"No I didn't, it was given to me."

"Then why punish you?"

254

"Because I took it across the stones to Thyme where they couldn't touch it."

"Couldn't touch it!" Zac butted in. "Do you know the trouble you have caused us in Thyme?"

"What trouble? What's happened? Who is this?"

"As if you don't know."

"How could I? I've been here for years," the voice replied angrily.

"Clever!" thought Julin. "Of course Steven wouldn't be aware of what was going on outside of the pyramid. Seth would though. So pretending not to know what was going on could mean it *was* Seth behind the wall, but there again, if the voice really was Steven, he wouldn't know what was going on back in Thyme." Julin began to confuse himself with his detective-like mind. There were only two ways to find out who was behind the wall. Just open it up or let Jilly put her hand into the gap and see what happened next.

"Why would Seth interfere with Jilly's dreams?" Marcus continued his careful questioning of the voice.

"To stop her saving me and returning the book to Osiris. If he put the thought into her mind through her dreams to run at this point, then I could never be saved."

"Why don't we just go without saving you and return the book to its rightful owner?"

"Because I can help you."

"How could you help us return the book?" asked Marcus.

"Because I know the way to Amentet."

The group above froze. The look of fear gripped them all. How did the person with the voice know so much about their intentions? Was it Steven below them, or Seth?

Marcus hesitated. "How do you know the way to Amentet?"

The voice faltered a little. "Because… I've been there!"

Faces again turned to Jilly and Penedora.

Julin continued pondering on the situation logically. He whispered to the others, "Surely if the voice was evil we wouldn't be standing here holding a polite conversation. It would have killed us all by now. I say we take the chance that it really is Steven behind the wall."

Gyp stalked his way over to the opening and sniffed at the darkness below, his yellow eye scanning for evil from the unknown. He looked over to Jilly, squinted and went back to stand behind her. This was her call, not his.

Penedora knelt down and put her face nearer the opening to get closer to the voice but made sure she wasn't close enough to be grabbed.

"Steven," she whispered.

"Penny?"

"If you've been down there for ten years why have you not tried to escape?"

"Because there is no escape when you cannot see your way out," he replied softly.

"But you could still feel your way around in the dark Steven. Surely you could have found this opening and dug your way out," she snapped at him. She couldn't believe Steven would sit still in a cell for ten long years and do absolutely nothing.

"I can't go far, I'm chained to the wall and… and I'm blind. Isis took my eyes as punishment. I'm blind, Penny."

It was out. The voice behind the wall sounded trodden and lost. The pain in his tone tore at Jilly's heart and the voice had called her mother Penny!

"Sounds a bit far-fetched to me," said Zac as Jilly pushed past him. She dived to the ground beside her mother and thrust her arm into the depths of the darkness.

"Take my hand, Daddy. I love you."

Steven grabbed his daughter's arm from the other side of the wall. It felt warm and loving. He had longed for this connection for so many years. Jilly could hear the chinking noise from the chains as her father reached up to her. Then she felt the iron bars around his wrists.

"Help me dig him out," she screeched loudly to the others.

Marcus was first to help, kicking the wall causing larger clumps to crumble beneath them into the chamber below. Julin used some of the old workmen's tools to gouge out large lumps of sandstone higher up and Zac pushed his hands against the stones as they loosened.

It took about twenty minutes for them to dig a hole large enough for them to squeeze through to the chamber that held Steven. It was on a slightly lower level to theirs so they had to climb through and down to reach the floor.

Once down, their torches lit up the chains attached to the far wall through big hoops and they could see the steel bands around Steven's wrists at the other end.

"What made you trust it was me?" Steven asked Jilly tearfully as he reached over to her and wrapped his arms tightly around her.

"It wasn't you I trusted," she told him, "It was me. I had to trust '*only in my higher self* ' and that was filled with love. Evil cannot love the way a father or daughter does, it therefore *had* to be you."

He hugged her tighter.

"Oh, and Gyp didn't hiss at you!"

Penedora made her way over to Steven and he sensed her presence. He held out his hand in front of him and she took it. Pure emotion swept over both of them as they connected. Then they embraced.

Penedora and Jilly just stood holding Steven, both wishing to never let go of him again. Tears fell from all three.

The whole scene should have had violins playing a romantic, happy ending in the background. Unfortunately this was no happy ending. This was just another beginning. There was still a lot to do before the tragic events in Thyme could cease. Marcus knew they should hurry on with the task ahead, but he also knew this was a special moment and the three people crying needed that special moment to last a lifetime.

To Penedora, Steven had not changed in over ten years. In the torchlight though, she could see that he had lost much weight and that his hair was now long, uncombed and matted. His face was worn with trouble and time and much of it was now hidden behind a beard. The soul, though, was still very much Steven. She saw past the holes set deeply under his eyelids. She remembered the loving blue eyes that once adorned his handsome face as they had lovingly wooed her when the couple courted as youngsters. She had shared her Age of Becoming with Steven and it was his soul she was holding tightly to, not the chained bedraggled prisoner who was now holding her tightly in his withered arms.

Jilly looked up at her father. He was quite tall and she noticed the yellow colouring of his hair underneath the dust and dirt of time. She winced at the sight of his eyes as his head bent down to acknowledge her presence beneath his shoulders.

"Do they hurt?" she asked him curling up her lip.

"My eyes? Not anymore," was his reply. "The pain I feel from losing them is deep within my heart. Not being able to see makes you totally lose control of all ability you once took for granted. I've spent the last ten years being held prisoner, eating what's put in front of me, sitting in constant darkness and only listening to the sounds of the dead as they roam the pyramid chambers."

Steven ruffled Jilly's hair and felt her face with his hands to see her in his mind through his fingertips.

"Having you here takes away any pain I may have once felt."

As a small child she was pretty. As a young lady he could feel her beauty appearing. His hands felt the lines of her jaw, her cheek and around her eyes and nose.

"You look like your mother," he told her lovingly. Oh how he had missed so many years of her young life. His heart was heavier now than it had been for the last ten years.

"Do you still have those appealing big brown eyes?" he smiled.

"Yes she does," Zac butted in sharply.

"A suitor for my daughter, eh?"

"Yes, sir. I mean, no, erm..." Zac fidgeted.

"It's okay lad. I may have lost my eyes but my sixth sense has trebled. I can feel what's in your heart just by being near you."

"This is Zac," Jilly blushed. So did Zac.

Steven let go of the two women and held out his arm. The chains clinked as he stretched.

Zac took up the offer and shook Steven's hand. "I'm Marcus' younger brother," he stated. "I'm sure you remember him but I was quite young when you, umm, left, so you probably don't remember me."

"Marcus? Then I'm honoured, young Zac." Steven bowed his head. "You must be proud of your brother now he has taken Highest Order."

All eyes turned to Marcus confused. He stepped forward to Steven.

"I'm Marcus. I was the one who questioned you earlier."

Steven raised his head quickly in response to Marcus' voice and turned towards him. "My Lord, you shouldn't have come. You should be in Thyme with your people. It is not safe here for you."

"My Lord? What do you mean?"

Steven could sense the confusion radiating from everyone.

"You don't know?"

"Know what?" questioned Penny.

"Did you not feel it happen?" Steven moved his head around to acknowledge everyone in the room. "Many hours ago, did none of you feel Nefron's passing to the Realm of Spirit?"

Everyone gulped in shock. Nefron? Dead? She didn't make it!

"Are you sure, Steven?" Penedora asked him.

"Very. Her spirit passed through me when she died. I thought everyone felt the passing of the High Priestess, especially you, Marcus, as you now hold the highest of order."

Marcus felt shocked at the thought of Nefron succumbing to the likes of the Egyptian Gods. She was far too powerful for them. He also felt angry that he had been too busy researching Egyptian history to notice her departure.

"Maybe we didn't feel it because we weren't in Thyme and were surrounded by mummified Egyptian spirits at the museum," comforted Julin as he touched his friend's shoulder.

Marcus held his head in his hands. "Why did none of us feel her? How did she die? Surely they didn't…"

"Don't blame yourself for Nefron's death, Marcus," comforted Julin. "There was probably nothing you could have done if we'd stayed. Nothing any of us could do under these circumstances."

"But if we had returned sooner with knowledge, we could have done something to save her."

The others shook their heads and lowered their eyes to the floor in disbelief at the predicament they all faced. Had they lost their quest already?

Was there now no hope for Thyme Hollow? Everyone felt numb from the news Steven had just given them.

"We heard screams when we crossed the stones. Do you think that..?"

"Don't think about it Zac," said Penedora, "If Steven felt the passing then it *has* happened. Maybe only Steven felt it on this side of the stones as he now has such high intuition." She took her husband's hand in hers and squeezed it.

"If this is true," said Marcus, "then I am the wrong side of the stones."

He paused. Everything had now changed for him.

"You must all go on without me. I must return to my people as their High Priest."

"But it will be too dangerous to go back now," quipped Zac. "Especially if they killed Nefron." Zac feared the same fate awaiting his brother's return.

"And too dangerous for him to stay here," Julin butted in, "everyone knows that the Highest Order should not cross the stones once appointed by our ancestors. Marcus is right, he has to return. It is his place and his duty."

The decision for Marcus to return to Thyme to face whatever had gone on after their departure was met with trepidation. Everyone agreed though, it was the right decision. The High Priest's place was by the altar at the Council Hall in Thyme. That was if the Hall was still there, of course! Nobody knew what lay ahead and nobody knew what Marcus would be returning to. The people of Thyme needed a spiritual leader and Marcus was now that appointed person.

"Someone needs to return with you," stated Steven. "You can't journey back to the unknown alone."

But who would be the best choice? Venturing forward would require much bravery but going back was knowingly going into a disaster that had already claimed the life of their High Priestess, the person who held most power and magic. Yet, Seth had managed to overcome even their most powerful ambassador. Home held no hope at this stage. Going home seemed futile, but necessary, going forward, just as frightening.

"I'll go with you," offered Julin.

"No. It has to be me," said Penny.

"No way Penny," snapped Steven. "It's taken ten years to find you, I'm not letting you separate from me again."

She placed her other hand over his and squeezed it. "You don't understand. Both Jilly and I are protected by Romanihum."

Steven looked surprised. He hadn't heard the word for years.

"Where did you get that from? No, don't tell me, the larder. I didn't think such potions still existed," he smirked. "No, I'm actually not surprised, Penny. You always were a squirrel with the old knowledge."

He felt comforted knowing that his wife and child were protected from the ones who had taken his eyes.

"Then I suggest Jilly should go back with you also. Maybe it will be safer in Thyme if the book is here. I assume you have their book?"

"Yes we have, but Jilly can't return with me," said Penedora looking at her daughter. "Jilly must go on with Gyp. With her protection and Gyp's guidance it's our only hope of returning the book to Isis and Osiris, and with you here and her dreams it's obviously all meant to be."

"I'm assuming Gyp is the cat who didn't hiss at me and who keeps rubbing up against my legs," he said, lowering his head to hear the purr clearer.

"I'll explain it all when we get going Dad," Jilly told him as she tried mustering up enthusiasm from the group. She was not going to be afraid any longer. Her mother would be fine and now she had her father back, Jilly felt empowered. "Firstly, how do we get these chains off?"

"I wondered when you were going to ask that. I've got just the thing," replied Julin, as he held up the hammer and chisel he had 'borrowed' from the upper chamber.

Everyone laughed. The mood lightened and a plan was coming together, even if nobody in the room actually knew what the plan was!

"I'd heard plenty of men working and socialising the other side of this wall many years ago then they suddenly stopped," Steven explained, as Julin started to hammer away at the chains around his wrist.

"Why's that?"

"Because they thought I was a curse," Steven chuckled as he saw the funny side of his plight. "I called out to them to help me and they ran. I heard them screaming all along the corridor. They must have thought I was the un-dead talking to them behind the wall. That's why I didn't cry out to you straight away, in case you ran. I knew Jilly would come one day and I was so afraid of scaring her away. My dreams were coming to me more often and more vivid. I just knew this moment was drawing nearer."

After much battering, the chains finally gave way and clinked heavily as they hit the floor of the chamber. Steven rubbed his wrists. "That feels good. They weren't tight, just annoying for so, so long."

He pointed to the wall to his left where a statue rested against the far wall. "The way out's that way. The guards come from that direction daily to feed me."

"What, from behind the statue?" asked Marcus.

"Underneath, actually; it moves. Well, I assume it's the statue that moves. I remember there being

266

one here when they first brought me to this chamber. I hear something large move every time they come and I've always assumed it was the statue."

"When are the guards due?" asked Julin.

"Not for hours. I have no concept of day and night anymore and hours mingle into oblivion when you are constantly in the dark. I am only aware of time by my sleep pattern and feeding times. I'm not hungry, but I'm quite tired, so I know I'm due for my period of sleep soon. Therefore, I know no one will be back to check on me for a long time yet."

"Beneath the statue, is that the way to Amentet?"

"Yes."

In the dim light, Marcus gently caught hold of his brother's arm. "I think you should return to Thyme with us."

"What about Julin?

"Julin knows more about Egyptology than you. He'll be needed for the journey to Amentet. Remember knowledge is important to us, our ancestors told us that."

"But, Jilly?"

"If nothing remains in Thyme Hollow, then I wish my brother to be with me to rebuild it."

Zac looked over to Jilly and his heart sank. He felt he had to comply with his brother's wishes, especially as he was now their High Priest but he too felt like Steven did; he had recognised his love for Jilly at last and wanted in no way to be separated from her.

Jilly wished also to have him by her side through the perilous journey ahead but knew it would probably be better for him to return with his brother, than go forward into the unknown. His four crystals were no match to the Egyptian Gods. She had Romanihum, he didn't. This worried her greatly now they were nearing the Underworld.

"I'll be Ok Zac. You go back to Thyme and I'll meet you there when this is all over."

Zac handed his torch over to Julin and moved towards the upper chamber. He scrambled awkwardly back up.

Steven placed his arm on his daughter's shoulder to comfort her. He could feel their torment but knew Marcus and Penny were right. Some had to go forward and some to return.

Penedora reached into Jilly's haversack and checked that the Egyptian Book and her spell book were still safely inside. She tied the flap securely and patted it down as she stepped away.

"Do you not want to take *your* spell book back with you?"

"No, Jilly. It is no longer mine. You have crossed the stones with it. It is a gift from me to you. When you return to Thyme, read from its centre pages."

"Why, what's on them?"

"It is a blessing from me to you. One which my mother gave to me and the same blessing you will pass to your daughter."

"Old customs stuff, eh?"

Penedora smiled. "Yes, boring *old* traditions!"

Jilly felt proud. She had reached the Age of Becoming and her Age of Transition was so close. She couldn't wait to start casting spells, mixing potions and meditating to connect with the Realms of Spirit. She so wanted all this Egyptian business to be over with, so they could all get back to normal. Whatever normal now was. She couldn't believe Nefron was dead. They were all really running on adrenalin and still in state of shock over the whole episode.

Penedora then reached into the little front pocket of her own haversack and picked out Steven's crystal. She placed the crystal in his hand and curled his fingers around it.

"You'll need this Steven; keep it safe."

He recognised it immediately.

"You brought it with you? How did you know I would be here?"

"I didn't. I just hoped."

"Where did you find it?"

"Uncle Gustus gave it to me."

"Uncle Gustus." His mind visualised the last time he saw his friend.

"How is the old fellow?" he chuckled with fond memories.

Penedora ignored his question and quickly kissed him on the lips, turned and joined Marcus by the opening in the wall. Steven felt the anxiety his question had caused her. How many people had they lost in Thyme. He was afraid to ask but did.

"How many have we lost since I brought the book over the stones?"

"Too many," she responded. He felt her presence move further away as he listened to her departure. Marcus helped her back up to the higher chamber. She grabbed Zac's hand and he pulled her to her feet. Marcus joined them. He turned and called back down to them.

"Good luck everyone."

"You too!" they shouted back as they heard their loved ones venture back towards the corridors of the pyramid and homewards; towards the stones of Thyme and to whatever or whoever was waiting for them.

"Our turn now," said Steven as he shuffled over to the statue.

Julin shone his torch on the statue. Closer inspection revealed how intricate the carvings were on it. Julin's eyes widened as he glimpsed the gold that shone back at him. Before him stood a tall wooden figure of an Egyptian guard standing on a large, square block of wood with one leg in front of the other. He was holding a long pole in one hand and what appeared to be a baton in the other. His head-dress displayed a small snake in front and clothing, which covered him from the waist to the knees, was tied like a towel after a bath and shone with gold. He was also wearing gold sandals and gold bracelets on both his upper and lower arms. The eyes had been painted white but the lips had been left neatly carved, with no colour.

Steven felt around for the baton. He grabbed the golden knob at the end of it and pulled it firmly downwards. He told Jilly and Julin to stand back as the whole statue creaked. It slowly revolved clockwise to reveal a set of steps beneath the wooden stand.

"Can you see the steps?" he asked.

Julin peered downwards. He could see the flickering of flames from light beacons dancing on the steps below and he could just make out the outline of a passageway.

"Where do they lead?"

"To other passages, steps and secret chambers. Remember it was many years ago when I actually saw the corridors, so please bear with me at each step. You'll have to describe everything to me as we go to jog my memory."

Turning off his torch and tucking in his belt, Julin took Steven's arm and helped him down the steps to the bottom. He stood for a moment scanning the passage ahead. Apprehension flowed through his veins but he knew they had to continue forward to succeed. Behind them, Jilly peered down the stairs and into the well-lit corridor. She turned to her loving cat by her side.

"This is it," she said and with that, they followed her father and Julin down beneath the statue.

Gyp shivered slightly.

"To Amentet and our journey by boat." they heard Steven muttering under his breath as he took his first steps towards the passage of adventure and hopefully, forgiveness.

Chapter 11

Small air vents lined the walls at regular intervals along the corridor. Cool night air from the outside world could be felt circulating around their heads. Time had penetrated the stonework for centuries, making the place smell musty and old. Flickering beacon lights on each side gave adequate light and added some heat. The ground they walked on was certainly not smooth or similar to a neatly laid patio in any way. Over the years, thousands of feet had eroded the centre of the corridor making it slope inwards. Workers and slaves passing back and forth; soldiers and guards marching beneath the heavy stones of the pyramids had taken their toll on all the sandstone pathways and corridors.

The passage was wide enough for Julin to walk beside Steven holding his elbow and directing his movement. Every so often, Steven would stumble a little and Julin would increase his grip helping his comrade regain balance. He could feel the bones in Steven's arms, which worried him. The thirty-six-year old looked worn and frail, but his inner determination shone. This man was eager to walk toward his captors. The very ones who took his eyes, his freedom, and cut ties to his loved ones. If these had been the good guys, what was

Seth and the bad Gods capable of? He shuddered at the thought. Deep down Julin was scared. His quest started with a good friend and grew to a group of strong willed fighters, three of which had now deserted him. Julin felt alone and vulnerable. His battle team consisted of a blind man, a young girl and a cat.

Coming to an opening on their right, Julin stopped Steven going any further by jerking his arm backwards a little. Steven took the clue and halted.

"We've come to a right turn. I can see this passage we're in continues up ahead, and the one on the right seems to slope upwards so I can't quite see the end of it," he said, bending slightly to try and look ahead. "Can you remember which passage to take?"

Steven pursed his lips tightly together and frowned. Jilly and Julin stood quietly to allow him to recall a visual picture in his mind of where they had reached within the tomb.

"Right, we go right."

"Are you sure, Father?"

"Yes. I'm mentally working my way back from where we're heading as well, just to make sure we are aiming in the right direction. It's very easy to get lost in this pyramid and one false move could spell danger for us all."

"What do you mean by danger?" Jilly looked horrified.

"Traps! The whole pyramid has traps laid by the original workers to prevent thieves from stealing the gold and treasures that surround the buried pharaoh."

"Isn't that just stuff of movies?" asked Julin.

"No. Where do you think all those movies got their ideas?"

"How come explorers haven't fallen foul of these traps?" Jilly queried. "The pyramid has a regular influx of tourists and explorers, you'd have bodies everywhere."

Steven smirked and shook his head.

"Only the surface has been skimmed, Jilly. Do you genuinely think that the *real* treasures in this pyramid have been discovered? Hardly, what the Egyptian Antiquities have on display in their museums is only half of what lies beneath these great stones. Remember I've seen the splendour and I've seen the horror of what lies beyond. These tombs are gateways to far greater things than what those the thieves have stolen or what has been archaeologically dug up. These sites are immense to say the least. Look beyond your knowledge Jilly, to what is really out there, there are realms you couldn't image exist. Feel the energy of what is really going on in here and around us." He tapped his heart with this fingertips.

Gyp curled his tail around Steven's ankle making him jump in surprise.

"Your cat?"

"Yes."

"He seems to understand everything I say."

"And more," said Jilly proudly.

"Let's bear right then," continued Julin, pushing Steven's arm in the new direction.

"Do all the pyramids lead to Amentet?" Julin asked his blind colleague.

"I believe all tombs do. How else could a soul pass through the Tuat to reach the Hall of Truths?"

"You certainly know your stuff."

"I've been in here a long time and have heard and learnt many things that even we mortals can't begin to understand."

"If every tomb holds the way to the underworld, why hasn't any such opening ever been discovered by archaeologists?" Jilly's question was quite rightly put, but she had sincerely missed the point her father had made to her earlier.

"Remember you have to look beyond what you know, Jilly. Why are we the only ones who know about the Stones of Thyme at the crossover point?"

"Only we can see them," she answered confidently.

"Correct. We know they are there because we see them, we use them and we have knowledge beyond those in the New World. Until someone here looks beyond what they actually see, Thyme will always be hidden."

"And the way to Amentet and the real secrets of the ancient Egyptians will never be discovered."

"Precisely!"

"I can see a door up ahead," Julin butted in.

As they approached, he could make out some hieroglyphic writing above the framework of the opening.

"There are some symbols above the door. I don't recognise any of them."

"Describe them to me," Steven asked him.

"Can you read hieroglyphs?" Julin asked.

"A little."

This impressed them all, even Gyp.

"There's a symbol of a ball. Directly underneath that, a sort of upside-down bowl and next to them two are three flag shapes. Perhaps it's a warning of some sort."

Steven cast his mind back to the books he'd studied and to things he learned while incarcerated.

"Paut… Paut," Steven said softly, "I think that means Paut Neteru. It's not a warning. The symbols are there to remind you that you are in the company of the Gods."

"Do you think we are being watched," said Jilly looking around them, "by the Gods? Maybe they already know we are here."

"I don't think so," said Steven confidently, "if they knew we were here we'd have been stopped by now. We definitely have protection from something or someone."

"Romanihum? Nefron?" said Julin.

"Who or whatever it is, let's hope it stays with us all the way."

"All the way?"

"This is only the start of our journey Jilly. There's a long way to go yet my love. Shall we?"

Julin followed Steven's invitation to open the door and with some difficulty, managed to heave it opened to reveal yet another chamber. Stepping inside, the room immediately impressed Julin. It was well lit and they could see the stunning artwork on the ceiling high above their heads. The walls were boldly covered from top to bottom with ancient inscriptions and pictures depicting stories of war, festivities and life in ancient Egypt. There were two small antechambers per wall; each inset with a finely carved statue pertaining to one god or another. Behind and above each carving was a brightly-lit beacon with dancing flames, highlighting these black and golden god statues.

"Wow!" Julin whistled with eyes wide open. He dropped Steven's elbow and ventured over to the far side of the room. Rubbing his fingers gently over the writing in amazement, he drew breath in awe of their beauty. He could feel the faint grooves and raised effect of the paintwork.

"Thousands of years ago, someone stood at this precise spot, with paintbrush in hand," he said. "How awesome!"

The room was indeed magnificent and Jilly stood, admiring it with her mouth wide open. Even the ceiling's brightly coloured paintings, depicting historical scenes, were still as fresh as the day they had been artistically designed by an Egyptian from long, long ago.

Treasures of all kinds were placed sporadically around the room, but neatly placed in their randomness. Jewels fit for royalty, hung around necks of statues. Julin and Jilly stood and gazed around at the sheer delight of the decor.

"Whatever you do, don't touch anything," ordered Steven.

"Booby traps?" asked Julin, who by now was very tempted to just pick up a ruby necklace or sapphire pendant to examine more closely.

"Everywhere," said Steven sternly.

Suddenly, without warning, the door behind them swung itself shut with great force and a loud bang echoed around the chamber. Jilly jumped out of her skin as she had been last through it. Her heart pumped rapidly as the rush of adrenaline flooded her body. Everyone froze, listening for the echo to subside.

"Jilly did you touch anything?" Steven snapped sharply at her.

"No. Nothing."

"Julin?"

"Not me."

"Look at your feet. Are you standing on anything?"

Jilly slowly looked at her feet. She dared not move. "Nothing I can see that's obvious."

"Am I?"

She looked across at the area beneath her father's feet. "No you're clear, it must be Julin." Her head turned towards his direction.

Julin too looked down to see where he was standing. He couldn't see anything immediately obvious, so he gingerly, with his left foot, brushed away some sand beneath him.

"Crap! It's me!"

"What is it?"

"I'm standing on a small marble slab of some kind and it's engraved with one of those Egyptian hieroglyphic symbols."

"Great! We're trapped!"

"Trapped?" said Jilly, as she turned to examine the door behind her.

"Do you wish me to describe the symbol to you?" Julin asked nervously.

"Pretty irrelevant now," responded Steven sarcastically.

"Won't it help?"

"The door has already shut!"

"What happens now then?" asked Jilly hesitantly. "Are the walls going to come sliding towards us or the room fill up with sand suffocating us all?"

"No, nothing *that* serious. We've just prevented ourselves from returning the way we came. The door we entered in will now be sealed."

Jilly tried to place her fingers in the miniscule gap around the door and the wall but nothing budged. "There's no handle on the door. Can we not use something to prize it open if we need to?" she asked.

"No!" Steven shouted at her. Don't touch anything."

"What about another way out? I assume there'll be another exit from this chamber." Julin looked around. "Otherwise why would you have brought us this way? You did say turn right."

Steven heard him move. "Don't move, Julin." he shouted, "as soon as you step off the slab our exit will also seal itself, so I suggest you stay perfectly still for a little longer."

"I thought you said this wasn't serious!"

Steven motioned to Jilly to assist him.

"I can't get my bearings but I know that in one of the corners of this place is a picture of a large eye, the Udjat-eye."

Jilly looked around.

"I think I can see one at the far end of the wall we just came from. It's the same as the eyes drawn on the figures of the people on the walls, but without a face around it. It's quite large too."

"That's the one. Now carefully go over to it, Jilly, and poke it."

"Poke the eye?"

"Yes. Press the black pupil of the eye firmly."

Very slowly, Jilly made her way over to the drawing on the wall, carefully aware of where she placed each foot. In amongst rows of pictures and writing was a large, black, Egyptian-shaped eye with an eyebrow neatly, but thickly, painted above it. She poked at the pupil of the eye with her index finger and waited. A large area of wall in front of her began to slide upwards revealing yet another passage behind. Steven began to count in his mind from the moment he first heard the wall door move to when the 'sliding of the heavy stone' noise ceased. "One thousand, two thousand, three…"

Jilly peered through to the next passage and tilted her head upwards so she could see where the large stone slab had slid up to another level above her. It seemed to hang there with no physical support such as a pulley system. As there was nothing visible she assumed the stone had been moved by a mechanism within the walls.

"Wow," she said, "you'd never have known this door was here." It reminded her of the large stone they had all seen at the bottom of the pyramid entrance.

Gyp crouched low, keeping as close to the wall as he could, and followed her out.

"Help me over to where you are Jilly," her father called.

She re-entered the chamber and very carefully steered her father through the new entrance and into the next passage.

"What about me?" called Julin, "Can I move yet?"

Steven called back, "You have precisely eight seconds from removing your foot from the slab before this stone slips back down again and seals your exit."

Still keeping at least one foot firmly on the slab beneath him, Julin spun round to face the exit behind him. "Eight seconds is ample time to make it over there," he thought.

"Remember eight seconds isn't very long as the stone will be getting closer and closer to the ground," said Steven, shattering Julin's positive thoughts instantly.

"Ready?"

"Ready."

Gyp, Steven and Jilly stood clear of the entrance to make way for Julin's mad dash to his only available escape.

"One, two, three." Julin took a deep breath and raising his foot from the marble slab, legged it as fast as he could in the direction of the now rapidly closing stone. He dived for the gap and rolled through the remaining space as the stone door came crashing heavily down just inches behind him. "I thought you said I had eight seconds," he snapped at Steven.

"Sorry. It obviously came down a lot quicker than it went up."

They laughed, mainly from relief rather than humour. Julin got to his feet, brushed himself down and checked in his back pocket that he still had the little Book of Pylons he'd taken from the Cairo museum. This was not how he envisaged the day would go. He had experienced virtually every emotion he could from the time he left the Hollow with Marcus, to flinging himself on the floor of a hidden passageway in the Great Pyramid of Giza. Not only was he now scruffy and sweating from adrenaline, he was still hungry.

"Right," he said, taking hold of Steven's arm's once more. "Well, there's only one way to go now, and that's onwards. Shall we?"

Gyp scampered off and Jilly kept an eye on her cat in front and on her father and Julin behind. "More steps ahead," she called back to them, "watch yourselves."

The steps became increasingly angled and they soon found themselves on a long, spiral descent. It became easier for Julin to go in front of Steven rather than beside him as the stairway narrowed. Steven held Julin's collar tightly with one hand and pressed the wall for safety with the other. Round and round they went for what seemed like forever. The air became cooler and thicker the lower they went. When the steps bottomed out they found themselves back on a level pathway. It was darker than where they had come from, but much wider.

Further along, they were met with a dead end. They stood before a large bricked-up, heavily-painted, sandstone archway. It completely blocked their path. Facing each other on either side of the arch brickwork was a statue of a huge black dog, sitting on a coffin. Every inch of wall and ceiling around them was masked in hieroglyphic symbols and small colourful pictures.

"We've come to a wall," Julin informed Steven, "and in the middle is an archway that is blocked and either side is a statue of a black dog. I recognise these statues," he explained, "they are of Anubis."

"Anubis, the Jackal god. Guardian of the underworld," Steven repeated.

"Are we near then?" Jilly asked hesitantly, studying the big black dog statues.

"Jilly, what you are looking at is the entrance to the Tuat."

She and Julin smiled at each other. They had reached their destiny.

Julin was relieved. None of them had died or been captured. The thought of being chained up for ten years really bothered Julin. Especially as Steven was so malnourished!

Jilly scanned the archway. She couldn't see any Udjat-eyes painted anywhere. "So, how do we get through?"

"Try once more, Jilly, to look beyond," said Steven gently, pulling his arm away from Julin's grip.

He held out his hands at shoulder height in front of him and stepped forward to the archway, then just kept going. The wall itself did not move. Steven walked through it like a ghost walking through an unopened door. Jilly and Julin stood watching in amazement as they witnessed Steven disappear. They heard a loud crash come from the other side and a yell. Jilly was first to plunge herself through the walled archway after her father.

Julin hesitated. He tried to follow but hit his head on the stonework.

"Ouch!"

Gyp looked up at him rubbing his head as he went through the wall with no effort whatsoever.

"Look beyond." muttered Julin. "If I look beyond to other possibilities… I can do this."

This time Julin succeeded in following through the wall.

Emerging on the other side, Julin could see Steven sprawled out a few steps down a wide, marble stairway.

"Are you okay, Steven?" he called down.

Jilly was already by his side attending to him.

"I forgot how close the steps were to the entrance!" Steven laughed, nursing his bruised elbows and knees.

"Are you hurt?" asked Jilly.

"I don't think I've broken anything accept my pride," he said rubbing his elbows.

Julin stood at the top of the marble flight, breathlessly taking in the most unbelievable sight he had ever witnessed in his life. The scene before him was even more 'awesome' than the last chamber he was enthralled with.

They now stood in a vast cavern, sparkling with gems and trinkets. The walls radiated every colour imaginable, glistening with gold and coloured limestone on the layers of rock. A stream flowed through the centre of the cavern edged by a marvellous patio of white and pink marble. No expense had been spared by whoever had built this cave. This place was definitely an entrance to a palace or to a realm well beyond comprehension of any mere mortal. It was stunningly beautiful.

Jilly and her father rested on the bottom step where he continued to rub the pain from his bruised limbs. Marble was cold and hard, so Gyp chose Jilly's lap.

"If this is the Underworld, where is everybody?" she asked.

"We still have a long way to go," said Steven pensively.

Jilly signed. This felt like one of the longest days of her life. Apart from the recent wedding, it also felt like one of the strangest. Julin eventually joined them and sat, one step above. Fiddling around his back pocket, he pulled out the library book Gyp had chosen for them and began flicking through its pages.

"I suppose we'll need this now," he said, pausing every now and then to read some of the written contents. "I'm sure we won't need all of these."

Backwards and forwards he rifled through it.

"Here's a good one," he read, "Spell Eighty Three. A spell for being transformed into a phoenix."

Jilly laughed. "Why would anyone want to become a phoenix? They get burnt, don't they?"

"Spell Thirty Three," he continued, "a spell for driving off a snake. Now, that could come in useful."

"Do you think there are any snakes down the river? I'm not too keen on snakes."

Steven felt for Jilly's hand and squeezed it. "You'll need all the courage in the world for this journey, darling. There are far worse things through the Tuat than just snakes."

Gyp's left ear waggled and turned, then both ears stood to attention.

Julin snapped the book shut.

Gyp opened both eyes. His pupils widened.

"As long as we all keep our heads, chant the correct spells and pray a lot, I think we can all make it through. Remember we have our crystals and most importantly, their book. They want it, so they're bound to let us pass safely down the river, snakes or no snakes," said Julin confidently.

"Don't be so sure, Julin," said Steven, tilting his head. "I can hear something I don't recognise."

"Do you mean running water? There's a stream," said Julin.

Steven held his hand up and motioned him to be quiet.

"Ssh! I can definitely hear something. Someone's coming. This doesn't feel good to me."

Steven stood up abruptly and tried in vain to hear from which direction the noise was coming from. An increasing rumbling noise headed downstream from their left towards them. Before their eyes, Jilly and Julin could see the water begin to rise upwards to form a great funnel. They too stood up abruptly. Gyp leapt off Jilly's lap as she stood, landing on all fours. His meow was loud and his back arched. Black fur stood on end as his claws protruded in readiness.

A great wind spiralled around them and Jilly screamed as it whipped against her face and body. A huge water spout rose higher and higher until it was bent over at the roof of the cavern. A face slowly emerged from the circulating water in front of them. It bellowed loudly at them, causing the whole cavern chamber to tremble.

"THIS IS AS FAR AS YOU GO," yelled the voice, "GIVE ME THE BOOK."

"What Book?" Julin shouted back nervously, his arm covering his face in fear and protection from the swirling water.

"THE ANCIENT BOOK, THE GIVER OF LIFE."

"We don't have it," Julin lied.

"GIVE ME MY SPELL BOOK," the face roared back even louder.

"Seth," whispered Steven, "I recognise the anger."

Seth! Julin and Jilly were rooted to the spot with fright. They knew this name and they knew what he or it was capable of. They were not surprised he was here. They had expected him to attack all day. But the furiousness of his voice chilled them to their bones. Jilly continued screaming as the wind continued to whip her. Gyp screeched and hissed.

"The book is not yours Seth. It belongs to Isis," Steven shouted bravely towards the direction of the voice.

Seth turned his attention to Steven and he grinned, a sickly smile as he recognised the impertinent human before him.

"STEVEN?" Seth bellowed, "YOU STILL LIVE. HOW CHARMING." Sarcasm from the face in the spiralling water funnel leapt swiftly towards Steven and a concentrated blast of spray blew Steven's light matted hair backwards.

"I SEE MY BROTHER STILL HAS YOUR EYES. I COULD GET THEM FOR YOU IF YOU PASS THE BOOK TO *ME*."

"I'll get them myself," shouted Steven defiantly at the face that was no longer in front of him. Seth had circled like a snake and was now behind him. Steven could feel the evil engulfing his space, but he was unafraid. As long as they had the book, he knew Seth would not kill them.

"I wrongfully took the book; I must ask for forgiveness myself. Osiris will give me my sight back when I return the book to *him*."

Seth screeched angrily at him, "YOU THINK MY BROTHER WILL GIVE YOU YOUR SIGHT BACK? YOU'RE MORE FOOLISH THAN I WAS. TWICE I TRIED TO RID THE WORLD OF HIS SOUL AND TWICE I FAILED. HE SHOWED ME NO MERCY, MY OWN BROTHER, THEN BANISHED ME TO THIS LAND OF FURY FOREVER. THIS TIME I WILL NOT FAIL. WHEN I SUCCEED, EVERY MORTAL AND SOUL THAT HATH PASSED THIS WAY WILL ANSWER ONLY TO ME... NOW GIVE ME THE BOOK."

"Never!"

"THE BOOK IS MINE. YOU TRY MY PATIENCE, MORTAL."

"Patience? You have none. You've been damned here for, now let me see, just a few thousand years and you want freedom already."

Seth screamed. The shrill was so loud, they had no option but to cover their ears.

"There's only one way out of the underworld for you isn't there?" shouted Steven above the roar. "The Spell of Life, from the Egyptian book. Sorry Seth, no can do."

Seth turned his attention to Jilly. A huge misty hand reached out from the water and scooped her from the cavern floor. She screamed, and Julin rushed over to try and grab her leg as she was promptly whipped upwards into the air. The hand stopped just below the ceiling and Jilly hovered there petrified.

"Jilly! He's got Jilly," screamed Julin.

Seth's huge snarling face blew Julin over and he fell hard against the marble floor.

"Let her go!" shouted Steven.

"GIVE ME THE BOOK NOW OR SHE DIES."

Stalemate. Steven was unsure what to do. Two choices were now in his hands - his daughter's life, or giving this evil God the book containing his life giving spell. "How could I have got her into this awful mess?"

Julin's intuition swept through him like a tidal wave. He stepped bravely forward to the edge of the stream and looked up at the human face of Seth within the swirling droplets. It had suddenly dawned on him that Seth was somehow unable to physically take the book from them, or he would have just killed them and removed it from Jilly's haversack.

"Jilly has the book in her haversack." Steven heard him say.

"Julin!" shouted Steven, flapping his arms in front of him, trying to locate where his friend was. "Don't!"

"It's OK Steven, trust me," he called back.

Bravely, Julin continued his conversation with the force in the water, hoping his hunch was correct. "Why do you not just take it? Why have you not killed us? What power do we have over *you* eh?"

"AARRRRRRRHH!" Seth grew angrier and angrier. His watery nose almost touched Julin's inner soul as he blew the short strands of brown hair from around Julin's face.

Julin stood his ground. He had obviously hit a nerve, but was unsure as to why Seth did not just take the book. He was puzzled.

"Surely if you're so great and almighty, you could just come and take the book from us without having to ask."

In one sweeping movement, Seth's hand came crashing to the ground as Jilly was flung violently onto the cavern floor below.

"WHEN YOU ARE ALL DEAD, I WILL CLAIM WHAT IS RIGHTFULLY MINE," Seth bellowed for the last time as his hand and face recoiled back into the waterspout and disappeared. The wind died down instantly and the water recoiled back into the stream. Seth vanished almost as quickly as his spirit had risen before them.

Julin rushed over to Jilly's soaked body and Steven fumbled his way across to where she lay, silent.

"Jilly! Jilly can you hear me?" her father pleaded.

"Is she dead?" Steven asked Julin as he fumbled around for her pulse.

"She can't be, she's protected by Romanihum."

Steven found her pulse. It was weak, but it was there. Thank god she was alive.

"I think she's been winded," Julin told him, "the haversack must have broken her fall. It's probably a slight concussion, that's all."

"Oh Jilly, how could I have put you through all this? I'm so sorry," said Steven as he cupped her head. His hand felt sticky. Her wet clothes and hair were cold to touch, but his hand felt weirdly warm. He fumbled around the back of her head to locate where the warmth was coming from. He wiped the wetness with his hand and held it up to Julin.

"Blood?"

Julin could see the redness in Steven's hands. He also investigated.

"It's not as bad as it looks. There's a cut to her head. It doesn't look too deep." He felt down her body. "I think she'll be badly bruised from the high drop but I can't feel any broken bones. Keep her still until she wakes."

He got up and ventured over to the stream leaving Jilly lying in her father's arms on the cavern floor. He ripped at a sleeve on his shirt and it eventually tore from the shoulder seam. Pulling it from his arm, he screwed it up into his palms and then bent down and cleaned it in the cool water. On his return, he squeezed the sleeve tightly until the last of the drips fell to the marble floor and then he flicked it open again. Julin bent down and carefully wrapped his cool, wet sleeve around Jilly's head to apply pressure to her bleeding cut.

Steven caught hold of Julin's arm as he finished the task. "Thank you," he said.

Julin then removed the backpack from her and, popping his torch inside a pocket, carefully rested her head on to Steven's lap. He left Jilly to recover in the safety of her father's arms.

Gyp crept out from behind the side of the stairway where he had hidden and made his way over to Jilly. He felt furious with himself for not being able to assist but knew there was nothing he could have done to stop her from being hurled to the floor. He was only a cat. He was also just a window, a looking glass for the gods to view these mortals and the whereabouts of the book. His eyes showed everything but his heart felt so much more. Gyp knew his journey was ending, but *how* he was unsure.

Julin sat and took the stillness of the moment to think carefully about their journey ahead.

'Six pylons, and just six hours to go,' he thought. Their outcome would be in the lap of the gods, but he held great faith that Jilly, her father and himself, could collectively convince Osiris and Isis to allow them all to go back home to Thyme Hollow. He opened the little book from the museum again.

Gyp curled up beside his best friend and rested his little furry chin on her leg. He liked these people, especially Jilly whom he loved very much. Spending ten years by her side, he had grown so close to her as he watched. He felt like a betrayer, a liar. Jilly believed he was her cat, but he was a slave to another. Oh how he wished he could talk right now.

Brin knew. The dog who always barked at him up at The Ridge knew he was different. Barking was a loud noise, but it didn't give his quest away. Now Gyp wished he could comfort Jilly and tell her the truth. He did not belong in Thyme. He belonged to these awful Gods. Gyp's true mistress was none other than Sekhmet, the lioness Goddess. She was known throughout the ancient world as the 'Eye of Ra'.

"The Eye," he thought, "so apt!"

Sekhmet would view the journey of the soul through the Tuat on her father's boat, towards the Hall of Truths. She could destroy any enemies of Osiris with fire and arrows. Her duty in Amentet was to protect the good and annihilate the wicked. Gyp hoped for their sakes that he had proven, beyond reasonable doubt that the people of Thyme were indeed good. What he saw, she saw. And Jilly, *his Jilly*, was pure of heart and soul and most definitely good.

Gyp mulled over in his mind the call for help Penedora made to distant spirits. Her Romanihum spell was powerful enough to reach these ancient lands. Sekhmet was indeed powerful enough to be their anonymous protector. Would the combination of their crystals, his mistress, and the goodness of their souls be enough to sway Osiris into believing them? They were innocent victims in the terrible circumstances they now found themselves in with Steven, unwittingly taking The Book of the Dead into Thyme.

His next thought moved to Seth. Gyp's little body shuddered under his fur. Seth was right. Once they were dead, Seth could just take the Egyptian book from them and the power of life would be his again to rain terror into the heart of every realm. They couldn't let that happen, and he prayed Sekhmet and Osiris wouldn't let that happen either.

Gyp didn't purr. He just lay there waiting for Jilly to wake up again. Steven sensed his presence and reached out and stroked him. "Who *are* you?" he whispered.

Gyp looked up at the man, but couldn't answer.

Julin hoped Seth would not return while he was busy reading about the Shat En Sbau.

"Book of Pylons - coming forth by night," he muttered, "now let's see what you can tell us about our little boat journey through the gates to the sixth hour."

Jilly's eyes flickered as she regained consciousness. Her head pounded with pain and she winced as she attempted, unsuccessfully, to get up from her father's lap.

Gyp scrambled to his feet as Julin rushed over to her side. "Jilly, are you okay?"

She struggled to open her eyes fully. Looking up, she finally focussed on her father. "How long have I been out?"

"Long enough."

Steven and Julin helped her sit up. She rubbed the back of her head and dislodged the make-shift bandage with her hand. She removed it and looked at the blood stain. "This is why I have such a headache huh?"

"Can you stand?" Julin asked.

"I'll try."

Julin took her arms and helped her to her feet.

Steven's legs had gone numb from sitting on the cavern floor with his daughter's head in his lap. He could feel the pins and needles rush to his limbs as he tried rubbing them to bring back the circulation.

"You two don't appear to be in very good shape," laughed Julin.

"We'll manage," Jilly said, dabbing the congealed blood on her head. "I assume we won."

"Seth's gone for now. But I've no doubt we'll be meeting him again on our travels."

"What about the boat? Have you found out anything about it?"

"I have indeed," said Julin enthusiastically. "I've been reading up about the journey through to the sixth gate; it appears that this also means the sixth hour. I figured out that the boat will arrive at sunset in the west and each section will take an hour to pass through. That way you end up at the Hall of Truths at the sixth hour and, if all goes well with Osiris, the boat continues on its journey and ends at the twelfth hour, at sunrise, in the East. It's only a theory, but it fits with the context of this book and information I picked up at the museum."

"But we've missed sunset," huffed Jilly. "That means we'll have to spend all day here."

"Not necessarily," Steven joined in. "Remember everything is relative to a given situation. Imagine time difference or, better still, time and place difference."

Julin and Jilly looked confused.

Steven tried to explain further. "What I'm trying to say is, I can't imagine the gods allowing a dead soul to wait around here all day until sunset if it had died during the morning."

Jilly smiled. She visualised a queue of dead souls waiting patiently through the day for a boat journey to their destiny.

"Let's suppose when we stepped through to the Tuat, *our* time becomes irrelevant and we begin time at a time that is relevant to here. When it is ready, I think the boat will come to pick us up to begin our journey."

"Regardless of what time it is?" Jilly said.

"Precisely. When the boat starts its journey, the twelve hours of the night begins."

"So then, we'll just sit and wait," said Julin.

This is what they did, but it still felt like forever before the boat of Ra finally made its way from the West up the stream, to collect them.

Spell 144

Taken from
The Book of the Dead

O you gates,
You who keep the gates of Osiris

O you who guard them

And who report the affairs of the
Two Worlds
To Osiris every day

I know you....
And I know your names

Chapter 12

Steven had taken the opportunity to wash in the stream. Julin helped him over to the edge and then retired to the steps with Jilly. Steven knelt down and leaned in. His hands swirled in the coolness of the water and he shivered as he dunked his head under. He brought his head out of the water and flicked it backwards. Running his hands down the length of his hair to remove the excess water, he could feel all the matting and tangles but for the first time in ten years he began to feel alive again. He felt free. Well, free from his chains, free from his cell, but free of his captors? No! He knew they had a long way to go till he was set free from the Ancient Gods of Egypt.

Gyp had curled up on Jilly's lap and with each stroke of his fur, sleep came as he focussed on the rhythmic sound of the water.

Steven was first to hear the distant sound of oars sinking into the water. Whoosh, splash, whoosh, splash, as each stroke brought the boat nearer. They each stood silently but apprehensively, in anticipation as the boat finally came into view. It was a fairly basic wooden boat shaped like a banana and was steered along by two oarsmen. One rowed at the front of the boat and one at the back. Both men wore short, sleeveless robes, tied at their waists by golden rope. They wore no shoes but the jewellery around their necks and arms was thick, heavy-looking, and obviously made from pure gold. Each had wiry, jet black hair that stopped at their shoulders. Heavy black kohl eyeliner was painted around the eyes. Neither oarsman spoke or looked around at the three people and a cat standing on the cavern bank watching their arrival.

Steven fumbled for Jilly's hand and she responded by gripping his tightly.

"Are there two gods in the boat?" he asked her.

"There are two men rowing, one at the front and one at the back."

"The front one will be the God Sa and the one at the rear is Heka," interrupted Julin, holding up his Book of Pylons. "It says Heka is the god who chants magical words on the boat journey, to allow the souls through the gates at each hour. If Heka does the spells, will I still need this book then?" Julin asked Steven.

"Which book, Julin?"

"Sorry. I'm holding the Shat En Sbau, Book of Pylons. The book I was telling Jilly about that contains spells to drive off snakes and things."

"Definitely. I think it better safe than sorry under these circumstances. If the book is filled with relevant knowledge of our journey to the Great

Hall of Truth, then absolutely. We must bring it with us."

There was very little noise or commotion as the boat came to a graceful halt before them. Up close they could see the wood had been ornately carved with lotus flowers and thousands of little hieroglyphic symbols. It had a feeling of calm radiating from its deck. As if by magic, a gangplank slowly edged its way from the side of the boat and lowered itself to rest on the marble platform in front of them. Neither Heka nor Sa moved a muscle to welcome them on board, nor did they speak, their heads facing forward and motionless as they waited for their dead souls to board.

The three mortals and the black cat carefully teetered across the plank. Julin helped Steven aboard and sat him down a bench. He could not see the table in the centre of the boat laden with food and he caught one of his many bruises on the edge as he sat. He winced.

Food had been the first thing Julin spotted when the boat sailed up. Upon this table was a vast array of fruit, bread and goblets of drink. In the centre of the food display was a disk containing the body of a beetle. On the outside edge of the disk was carved the body of a serpent. Jilly turned her nose up at the beetle; she wasn't too keen on bugs at the best of times.

Once everyone was settled, the gangplank magically withdrew back into the boat. The oarsmen re-positioned their oars and began to row once more.

"Do you think the food's for us?" Julin whispered to Steven.

"Food?" Steven held out his hand to feel for the contents of the table and his face lit up when he realised what he was touching.

"Definitely, I'm actually quite hungry!"

Steven took hold of an apple, felt its texture and shape, and then heartily bit into it. It had been a long time since he had eaten fruit.

Julin was eager to follow suit and grabbed at the bread. Ripping a small piece off the loaf, he tasted it.

"Foood!" he mumbled, spitting out a little crust onto his lip, "I'm starving and this tastes delicious."

Jilly nibbled at a few items herself and passed some tiny pieces below the table to Gyp. Her stomach was too knotted to consume a feast. She wondered how men could eat at a time like this! In fact, how could men eat all the time!

The boat headed slowly out of the cavern beneath their first Pylon, towards the night and their second hour. The stream, still shallow, opened up a little wider, as it flowed its way beyond the cavern into another world filled with blinding moonlight, but with no moon.

The oarsman stopped rowing and laid down their oars beside them in the boat. The front oarsman began uncoiling a long rope, which was laid before him at the bow of the boat. He threw it into the stream ahead and waited.

"What's happening?" asked Steven, "Why have we stopped?"

"Sa is throwing a rope to someone," Julin whispered back.

From out of nowhere, four thin and lanky men from the left side of the bank waded into the water and approached the boat. Between them they separated into their designated places and took hold of the rope, positioning it over their shoulders. In single file, two each side, they then pulled up the slack of the rope and heaved. The boat creaked as it jolted forwards and the boat's journey continued once more.

"There are four men in the water ahead of us pulling the boat by rope," Julin whispered, "they look like slaves."

"Maybe the river is too shallow to row," whispered Jilly.

"Just keep me informed if anything untoward happens," asked Steven, "we must remain vigilant."

His warning reminded them all that the boat trip and the feast was not a pleasant day trip but one filled with uncertainty and danger. The travellers remained silent as they listened to the splashes of the slaves tugging their boat through the water.

The further they travelled, the wider the river became and what once was a cavern turned into a vast openness and that turned into countryside. Even though the night was dark, Jilly and Julin could see both banks and the vista that began appearing before them. Each step forward, the wider their view became until they found themselves in a large valley sided by mountains. Surprisingly the temperature of the night around them did not change. To their left, twelve men stood on the bank watching their journey. A man near the centre of this queue was holding a large flag, shaped in the form of a jackal's head. On the right hand side of the valley were twelve more people watching as their boat passed by. On this side of the river the banner-man held a flag bearing the shape of a goat. Nobody on either shore moved or spoke a word.

The only noises heard in the valley of the first hour were from the four men up front, as they sloshed through the water pulling the boat, and from the three passengers and a cat inside, tucking into the food before them. Their long perilous journey through the Tuat to the kingdom of Osiris and Isis was now well and truly underway.

"This God entereth from the Earth into the arrit of the horizon of the West and he must travel 120 atru in this arrit before he arriveth of the Gods of the Tuat."

Sloosh, jolt, creak, sloosh, jolt, creak. The four beings in the water pulled the rope steadily and consistently, without speaking or pausing for a second to look to their left or right. The night air was still and silent and the three brave souls from Thyme spoke very quietly amongst themselves so as not to upset the karma within or around the boat. The atmosphere was almost subdued but with an eerie edge.

"How far do we have to travel to the second pylon?" Jilly whispered to Julin.

"Well we know it's going to take an hour and at this speed I can see why."

He fumbled in his pocket for the little black book and removed the torch from Jilly's backpack. He shone it on a particular page he found and Jilly read the inscription.

"What's an arrit or atru?" she enquired.

"I've no idea. I believe it means the sections between each pylon, like the area which we are travelling through now."

"So this is the first arrit?"

"I'm guessing, but that's what I think it means. Don't quote me on it, Jilly."

"And atru?"

"That must be some sort of distance, for example *miles* in our terms but again, I don't know how far one hundred and twenty atrus would be. I wish I'd studied ancient Egyptian a little better when I was younger!" he said with a smirk.

Jilly giggled at him.

"I don't think one hundred and twenty atrus will be very far. I think it's the speed we're going that makes this journey seem so long. Don't you want to just chivvy them up a little? It's all so monotonous: left foot tug, right foot tug. We'll be here all night at this rate."

"I think that's the idea Jilly!"

Julin turned to Steven. "Do you have any recollection of this journey, Steven, from when you were first brought here?"

"No nothing. I do *know* of the horrors of this journey though. Knowledge of this sort of thing is well known throughout Egypt. I remember being in the cavern where we boarded the boat and then nothing from there on. I found myself waking up in front of Osiris, being dammed in some sort of strange language and the next thing I remember being brought back through the pyramid, chained to a wall and unable to see."

"No trial or chance to explain your side of the story."

"None."

"Do you think Osiris will allow you to speak this time?"

"Oh most certainly, Jilly has their book. We haven't handed it over to his evil brother, Seth, so I'm sure he'll be more compassionate this time around."

"I do hope so," uttered Jilly.

The journey was very tedious and all three tried very hard not to become too complacent about the dangers that could lie ahead. Their journey may not have been too horrendous thus far, but this was just the first hour of the night and if any of the spells in the Shat En Sbau were anything to go by, then they knew they could expect all kinds of horrible and strange things up ahead.

Far in the distance they could make out the structure of a huge stone arch.

"I think I can see the second gate," said Julin, standing up to get a better view.

Jilly joined him.

"I think you're right. Father, we're nearing the pylon to the next hour."

Steven stood too, steadying himself so as not to bang anymore bruises. He could feel a sense of anticipation as the boat drew nearer and nearer with every pull of the rope.

The pylon itself was plain with no hieroglyphics inscribed upon its huge structure. It stood before them across the water like a large, thick bridge with two wooden doors sealing the access into the next realm.

The boat men ceased pulling the boat. They stood motionless in the water. Silence rained down on them as the boat occupants waited for something to happen. Then it came!

"SISSSSSS!"

Jilly screamed, "Aarrrrh!"

A huge snake reared up from the water to almost twenty feet above them spraying water in all directions. It stood on its tail with its head peering down at them. Green, yellow, brown; Jilly didn't have time to examine its markings and colouration before if came bearing down on her. Its enormous, forked tongue came swiftly towards them and ended inches from Jilly's face causing her to almost fall backwards, but Julin grabbed her. His reactions were sharp. The tongue coiled itself back into the mouth of the snake. Then it came again, this time hissing and lunging at Steven. Julin then grabbed Steven and pulled him aside just in time as the tongue whipped passed Steven's right ear. Jilly screamed again.

The four boat pullers cowered as waves battered their bodies, swamping them.

"SAA-SET. ARNOOAY NE ARDEY," came a loud voice from the rear of the boat.

"SAA-SET. ARNOOAY NE ARDEY," it came again, much louder.

The snake immediately ceased the attack on the occupants of the boat; his attention being drawn to the god Heka in the rear, who was now chanting loudly in ancient Egyptian tongue.

Julin scrambled for the Shat En Sbau, quickly flicking through it to find out what spell Heka was casting over the snake to help drive it away. His search was too slow.

Heka finished his magical words and the snake slithered silently back into the water and was gone. The waves receded to calm and gentle rippling returned.

Everything happened so quickly that everyone was left feeling totally shocked by the events. One minute they were steadily heading to the next gate, they arrived, then there was a snake attacking the boat and next it had gone. Steven hadn't had time to make sense of anything. He had been intensely listening to what was happening around him, then Julin had grabbed him sideways. He had heard hissing and screaming and then shouting from the person at the back of the boat. Then total silence. All this within what seemed like a nanosecond.

"Is everyone alright?" Steven asked, concerned for the welfare of his fellow traveller and his daughter.

"I think so," said Julin, checking himself.

"I'm fine too, Father," cried Jilly shakily.

Gyp jumped up on the table and began licking his back and tail. Water had splashed him in all the commotion and one thing he was not too keen on was getting wet. Jilly helped Julin pick up the scattering of food that had fallen to the floor of the boat in the attack. They placed it back into the upturned bowls and serving plates. Neither had any intention of eating anything else; their appetites had suddenly waned.

After the commotion had died down and without any instructions, the four men in the water scrambled back to their positions and picked up the slack of the rope. With a concerted tug, they began to pull the boat once more. Before them, the two huge doors of the pylon slowly creaked open.

The boat of Ra passed silently under the massive stone structure. Faint cries could be heard in the distance from behind them. Jilly and Julin turned their heads to see where the voices were coming from. The doors of the pylon had already started closing as they passed through into the next division. Wailing from where they had come from grew louder and more pitiful. The doors slammed shut and the noises of wailing could be heard no more.

"Do you think it was those people on either side of the river we passed earlier?" asked Jilly.

"I hope not," Julin replied, "whoever it was sounded in great pain. I wonder what was causing them to cry out like that."

Steven by this time had repositioned himself on the bench and had listened to all the commotion with great interest. He hadn't realised how close he had come to being struck by a forked tongue from a very thick, thirty foot Cobra.

"The souls you saw as we passed by the mountains are doomed to remain there forever. They cry out in desperation that one day the 'King of the Underworld' will let them out through to the next division," he explained.

"Osiris?"

"Yes, Julin."

"Wow if this is how the good guy treats people, just imaging if Seth ruled the world."

Jilly felt a great sadness for them all. 'What a depressingly horrid place,' she thought.

The second hour of the night seemed no more pleasant than the last. This area was not as vast as the last and they were quite near to the bank. This time, to their right, standing by the edge of the river, were twenty four humans who stood silently watching the boat as it passed by. To their left, they saw twenty men standing in a row with their arms tied behind their backs. Their heads were bowed down and their shoulders hunched. None of these men raised their heads to watch the boat pass.

"They look like slaves?" said Jilly, as she viewed each and every figure that they passed.

"Criminals and blasphemers," said Steven, remembering the tales he had heard over the years.

The boat continued to jerk forwards.

"What about those people, Julin?" Jilly pointed.

There were four people lying on their backs by the river, motionless. She leaned over the side of boat to take a closer look. "What are they doing?" she asked, studying them.

Julin raised himself off the bench a little to get a better look at where Jilly was pointing. He noticed the four people on the bank to which she referred. Then he noticed their bodies were lifeless and their gazes stuck.

"Look away Jilly. They're dead."

Jilly gasped. He shielded her eyes as he placed her head into his arms.

Nestling her face into Julin's shoulder she cringed, "That's horrible."

The four dead men lay with their eyes wide open looking up at the night. Blood could be seen horrifically splattered across their bodies and faces as if they had been slaughtered in battle. Julin and Jilly didn't look any longer to see if they could see any more wounds on their bodies. The red stains and fixed eyes were enough to remind both of them of the bad predicament they were in.

"Are you okay Jilly?" Steven enquired.

"She'll be okay," said Julin, "some of the sights down here are just as you warned us, bloody and barbaric."

"Would you feel better, Jilly, if you sat in between us?" Steven asked.

"I'm okay, Father. The bodies just took me by surprise. I'm not used to seeing so much death."

Approximately fifty minutes later they caught sight of the next pylon ahead. This time they took no chances. All three huddled up together on the bench and Gyp jumped down and stayed crouched beneath the table.

"Be ready for another snake," warned Julin.

They waited in anticipation as the boat slowly drew nearer to the pylon with every tug from the four men in the water.

"I can see people standing on the pylon," said Jilly.

"Who are they?" questioned Steven.

Julin saw them too, "Mummies, I think."

"Dead ones?" asked Steven.

"Not too sure. They're shrouded in linen, just like in the monster movies of the New World, but I can't tell from here if their eyes are open or not."

Nine mummified figures stood on a ledge just above the doors to the huge fortress, blocking their pathway to the next division. The entrance, again, was not carved or painted. It was plain and made of stone. It had a large overhanging ledge to its top with steps on either side to reach this high standing point. The shrouded figures did not move. Their clothing was old and decaying but still firmly wrapped from head to foot allowing no visibility of the body. Very tiny gaps in the bandaging at the top allowed the onlooker to make out where the eyes, nose and mouths were positioned on the head sections. The gaps were very small and dark. Jilly and Julin could not make out any facial features and wondered what actually remained intact, behind the mummified cloth.

"Here it comes," called Julin as the boat began to rock from the swelling water. Once more, on nearing the third pylon, an enormous snake reared up from the river before them. It hissed at the boat, but this time the attack centred on the four men at the rope, its yellow, scaly body twisting, turning and lunging aggressively before them as the men scrambled to the shores either side of the river. The boat rocked violently in the water and the three travellers held on tightly.

Loudly from the rear of the boat, Heka shouted to the snake to be gone, "AQEBI. ARNOOAY NE ARDEY. ARNOOAY NE ARDEY."
The huge, fearsome snake obeyed the commands of the God Heka and retreated into the river. Four frightened boat pullers and the occupants of the boat had escaped the lashing tongue of the snake. Turbulent rocking of the boat

ceased as the waves slowly settled. Calm once more restored. Without any instructions, the four slaves got back into the water and waded over to the boat. They took up their positions and grabbed at the rope. This time they hesitated in the water before taking up the slack.

"Where are these snakes coming from?" said Julin, scanning the depth of the water. He was puzzled.

Heka raised his arms high in the air and called loudly towards the huge fortress before them. The enormous doors of the pylon were still firmly shut and the mummies stood motionless on the ledge above. It was to these gods that Heka now chanted.

Julin reached into this pocket and pulled out the Shat en Sbau where he had placed it securely after the last attack. He flicked through its pages and stopped at Spell 144. He quietly read the translated text to Jilly and Steven as Heka spoke loudly in ancient language to the nine mummies guarding the third gate, the entrance to the next division of the night.

"The spell is aimed at the keepers of the gates," he explained to the others while trying to keep up with the chanting coming from the rear of the boat.

Jilly and Steven understood the gist of what was going on. One's welfare on this type of journey amounted to saying the right thing and keeping the right gods and snakes happy to enable the boat to pass safely through. Steven wondered how many souls didn't actually make it to the sixth hour for their judgement day. He then thought of all those souls who never made it on further to the twelfth hour and to ultimate peace in the afterlife.

~~~~~~~

"O you who keep the gates… because of… Osiris, O you who guard them…" Julin skimmed over the next paragraph to catch up with Heka's chants.

"I pass by in peace, I sail in the boat of Ra and my protection is the protection of the boat of Ra. Mine is a name greater than yours, mightier than yours upon the road of righteousness… The destructive one shall not attack me and those who keep their gates shall not be ignorant of me… I have caused the sacred boat to make its fair voyages; a way is prepared for me that I may pass on it. My face is that of a Great One, with the Double Crown… That's the crown that Osiris was wearing in one of the books at the library," he explained. Julin missed a little more of the translated text and just gave them the ending. "O you who are awake prepare a path for your lord Osiris."

He shut the book and looked up at the enormous structure before them.

"What now?" asked Jilly.

"We wait."

Heka now stood silently at the back of the boat with the God Sa up front who, for most of the journey so far, had done nothing, plus the four men in the water. They all waited patiently.

Steven could feel the eerie tension as the boat sat like a tiny bug in front of its predators wondering if it would be squashed or set free.

A little flicker of light caught Jilly's eye and she looked up. One by one a bright yellow light shone from the small eye gaps between the cloths on the mummies' faces. It looked as if someone had lit a torch from within their bandages. When the last pair of eyes lit up, the door to the third pylon creaked spookily and began to slowly open.

"We're going through," whispered Julin to Steven who was unaffected by the ghostly sight on the ledge. The boat jerked forwards and sailed beneath. Jilly refused to look up at the ledge. The glowing eye holes scared her. She had been taught in Thyme that the mirror to a person's soul was through their eyes. These eyes had no souls, just a yellow light shining from the dark sockets between the gaps in the cloth. Jilly didn't want to look to confirm if these beings were soul-less. She shivered a little as they passed through into the next hour of the night.

Behind them, the voices of those left behind in the previous division began to wail and cry out in desperation. The third set of doors leading to their fourth hour closed tightly behind them, drowning out the pitiful screams.

The structure of the third section of their journey took them totally by surprise. They were no longer in a valley or open air, but in a corridor. Both Jilly and Julin were so confused they shrugged their shoulders and stood studying the structure they entered. How could they have just gone from a marble cavern, to a mountainous valley, to a wide river bed to… to this? Their boat now flowed through what seemed like an ornate room with high golden walls. Their movement sent echoes back and forth within its boundary. Hanging all along the corridor at regular intervals were various spearheads. Each had a different motif or carving at the top of the spear. They gave the corridor a kind of museum feel, bearing the finest collection of an ancient armoury. The river had become just water along a corridor like a shallow swimming pool with sides. The gold reflected into the water and on the ripples coming from the bow of the boat.

The corridor turned sharply to the right and the boat hit the edge of the wall nearest to Jilly as the four men struggled with it to navigate round the corner. Steven lurched forward and grabbed the table in front of him as the boat rocked unsteadily. Jilly quickly ducked her head out of the way of a spearhead jutting out from the wall as the boat swung round. She clung on to the wooden side and the boat rocked in the water like a boat in a log-flume ride at an amusement park. With this ride though, there would be no flash photo moment or dramatic screams of laughter at the final water chute.

Once straight again, they could see they had entered another long corridor but this one was much wider than the last. Balls of fire could be seen up ahead, shooting across the corridor from the mouths of carved serpent heads, near to the ceiling.

"Will we make it through?" gasped Jilly.

"What can you see?" asked Steven.

"Fire!" replied Julin, "crouch down and cover your heads as we pass."

As their vessel passed beneath, they could feel the heat from the jets of fire above. Luckily the flames were too high to cause any harm.

Julin felt as if they were now on a ghost train ride at a fairground, where the carriage takes you this way and that passing scary models, dangling wet cloth, and the occasional pretend cobweb to catch the occupant unawares. He imagined that they would all appear at the exit to a roar of cheering relatives laughing and asking if the trip had been great fun. How he wished he was now in a fairground in the New World and not in the Underworld of the ancient Egyptians. On this attraction, the snakes, mummies, fire breathing sculptures and scary things were actually real.

The corridor again twisted to the right into a larger, more spacious one. Julin couldn't understand how the height and width of the water changed with each direction they took, yet they didn't need a lock to navigate. He understood magic but this was unexplainable. He could see the difference up ahead and when he looked back the scene was completely different and yet the water flowed at the exact depth and measurement of each division it ran through.

To their right they passed twelve holy shrines moulded into the corridor walls, with a carving of a god standing in each. The little carved statues were made of volcanic obsidian and bronze. Their glass eyes moved from right to left as the boat sailed silently passed them. Above each shrine was a snake. Not carved ones. These were alive. Each snake guarded its godly occupants with the occasional hiss or two to warn off potential thieves. To their left they could see twelve more statues but instead of being guarded by snakes, a channel of fire glowed menacingly beneath their feet. The statues did not appear to have been melted at all by the heat of each little fire. Instead the statues stood, brightly lit by the flames. Julin was still suitably impressed with the gold that was in abundance on this magical journey. He wondered if the ancient Egyptians knew of the sheer volume of riches they possessed and the value it held in the New World.

As they approached the next pylon, they could see it was much smaller than the last and was gaily painted with patterns and shapes all over. It shone majestically like a great painting at the end of the corridor. The serpent guarding the entrance was already in view and this one did not strike at the boat as it got closer. Its green snake-shaped eyes starred down at them. This time the boat halted much further back from the pylon and Jilly and Julin could see two mummies standing either side of the gate on ledges. They were similar to the last pylon. In front of the snake, they saw ten Egyptian men dressed as gods spanning the width of the river. The water went up to their waists.

The figure to the far left of those in the river stooped slightly as he leaned on what seemed to be a sword or staff of some kind. He appeared to be sleeping. Julin couldn't quite make out what god he depicted. Jilly, Julin and Steven prepared themselves for another snake attack.

Then it came. The snake hissed and leapt forward striking one of the gods before him, killing him instantly with the lashing of his strong forked tongue. With one quick movement, the god to the left who appeared to be asleep leaped forward and, lifting his heavy sword, struck the snake, cutting off its head, as it went forward again for its second, swift attack. The sharpness of the sword cut easily through the coiling neck. Blood oozed through the river towards the boat as the serpent's body plunged into the water, mutilated.

When the dead snake had fully submerged beneath the bloodied water, the nine Egyptian gods picked up the body of their companion floating on the surface and dragged him to the side of the corridor. They motioned for the boat to continue. The four boatmen took hold of the rope firmly and began to pull the boat towards the pylon. The gates opened and this time the four mummies remained motionless, as the boat passed by into the next hour of the night.

Steven was becoming exhausted by the noisy activity circulating around his head and ears. Jilly and Julin on the other hand were totally bewildered by everything they had seen and experienced so far. They kept Steven informed of every experience but felt their explanations came nowhere near the beauty and the horror they witnessed from the boat.

The next division was far busier than the last with activity going on all around their boat. They again sailed down a long, expansive corridor, which changed direction multiple times. There were fire-breathing figurines, fixed high on the corridor walls in alcoves, bearing golden shrines to various ancient gods. The river flowed down its centre with enormous columns bearing the weight of the impressive ceiling. Instead of rows of people on either side of them motionless or holding various artefacts, the occupants of this hour were full of life.

To their right they could see about twelve men in different costumes and varying crazy features all going about their business, fetching and carrying articles from around the stream but with no obvious direction or purpose. Everyone seemed busy doing nothing in particular. They were caught in a world of work for the sake of keeping busy. To their left they could see and feel the heat of a large lake of fire that stretched the length of the corridor. Walking upon the lake of fire were twelve jackal-headed figures, again dressed in ancient Egyptian costume with bodies of men. None of the half-dog, half-men showed any distress at walking on the fire and no one appeared burnt by the flames. The flames licked at their ankles as they wandered back and forth in no particular direction.

As the boat passed by the columns, one by one, huge serpents lifted from the shallow depths of the stream, stood tall on their tail, hissed a little and then retreated back into the water. Ten times this happened and each snake was a little different in colour, size and aggressiveness. The snakes were unthreatening but seemed to rise up in acknowledgement of the Boat of Ra passing by them.

Jilly leaned over the boat, confused. She couldn't work out how such large snakes could hide in such shallow water. The depth of the stream appeared waist high where the four men up front waded through it with the rope. Yet, the size of snakes seemed to signify that the water should be at least thirty to forty feet deep, if not deeper.

"How is this happening?" she asked Julin.

"I have no idea. The whole size-depth thing has been puzzling me since the second gate."

Jilly remembered her father's words and let her mind rest. She was to trust things beyond her knowledge and not just believe in what only her five senses could explore. Her hands flicked the water as she leant over to examine it more closely. The water was cold, but she let it ripple through her dangling fingers as the boat dragged her little hand backwards.

Leaving all the mayhem behind, the boat turned towards another direction into yet another vast hallway. The walls far to the side of the stream were plain at the bottom and midway, yet highly decorated and elaborately carved just below their top edge. Once more their boat had taken them out into the night and with this section void of a roof they could smell the evening air. It was dark. Even though they could see the great constellation above, there was no moon and no moonlight. Their eyes took a while to adjust and Julin switched on his torch to help them see beyond their boat.

It was in this division that they came across the most beautiful statue they had ever seen. Julin recognised it immediately as he shone his torch up and down the great carving. It was a thirty foot model of Osiris himself, Khenti Amentet, Lord of the Underworld. He was standing on a huge white marble block of granite and was encased in an oval shaped glass surround. His face was green in colour and his eyes were thickly painted with kohl eyeliner which swept from the tear ducts near to his nose, above and below the eye and out towards the ears. His eyes were black and his eyebrows were also heavily painted the same way. He wore a tall crown, totally covering his hairline, bending behind his ears and swooping low at the back of the neck. It was shaped like a fat champagne bottle with the neck rising upwards and instead of a cork or cap at the top, the end was rounded like a broom handle. Either side of the wide bottle-shaped crown were two further ornate fixings that looked like wings. A golden disc was engraved at the very front and the sheer size of the crown emphasised the fact that this type of headgear was only worn by the highest of order: the King of the Underworld himself. On his chin was carved a long, thin, black beard that curled up at the tip. His green neck was adorned with row after row of gold chains and necklaces made with the finest of jewels, ebony, carnelian, gold and silver. He wore two very thick gold bands around each upper arm. The body section was carved and painted white, with only very basic markings of body and legs. These fused at the bottom of the statue, forming one large leg and one set of toes.

"Wow!" said Jilly, "he is impressive."

"Statue of Osiris," Julin informed Steven.

Osiris' arms were crossed at the front and his green hands carried two items. The flail in his right hand resembled a golden whip with a bronze handle. The three large whips were strung together with bell-shaped toggles of red, turquoise and gold colour. The copper crook in his left was covered in glass and gold leaf. To either side of his casing was painted the symbol of the Egyptian eye that Jilly had poked in the sealed tomb. Jilly and Julin could feel the energy radiating from this statue as the boat nudged past. They both felt as if the statue watched their every move.

Further up they came to yet another impressive monument. This time the carving was of the God Horus. He was not so large as his father's statue, only about fifteen feet and not carved in the same level of grandeur. He was wrapped in a white skirt with gold bracelets on his arms and a large necklace neatly constructed around his neck. This statue had both legs and feet and neat little toes etched perfectly as the base. His head was not a carving of a man but of a bird and when Julin began to describe the statue in detail to Steven, the blood drained from Steven's face.

"You recognise the description?"

"Horus. Oh yes. That's the god that brought me here. Half bird, half man you say?"

"Yes."

"That's him then, Son of Osiris, taker of eyes."

The latter comment brought back the reality of what Steven had endured.

"You'll get them back Steven, I'm sure of it."

Julin touched Steven's arm to comfort him.

Jilly screamed and shot back from the edge of the boat as something nipped at her fingers. Julin jumped up and flicked something away from him with the back of his hand. The small figure of a scorpion made a splash as it hit the water and sank into the stream. Then there was another one, hurrying towards Jilly's feet inside the boat. She screamed again as she spied it scurrying across the floor. Julin kicked this one hard with his foot and it bounced backwards and rolled away. The two gods at either end of the boat flinched not, as scorpions came from every direction in their attack. The two gods stood their ground facing in the direction they were heading as little black scorpions ran over their toes and around them, across the deck and along the edge of the boat.

A three-headed being with a body of a monkey jumped from the edge of the corridor swam across to them and grabbed at the boat. It was hairy and all three of its faces were threatening and menacing. Using its long ape-like arms, it pulled itself up the side of the boat and hoisting itself over the rim, scrambled inside. Julin picked up the fruit bowl from the table and threw it at the monster spraying fruit everywhere. The three-headed thing brushed the bowl aside with its right arm and this too went splashing into the water. Julin lashed out at it again with another item from the table, this time connecting with one of its heads and sending the creature crashing to the floor of the boat, dazed.

By this time, Steven was standing and wildly waving his arms around his body picking off little creatures as he felt them crawl all over him. He had no idea what was scratching at his feet or clinging on to his legs but he knew by Jilly's screams that fight he must. Julin was whacking every invader within arm's length of his torch and Jilly was stamping her feet madly like a mad Irish jig, to crunch the scorpions beneath her.

Gyp hissed at the creatures from beneath the table, his claws giving him adequate defence as the attack came from all directions. Something grabbed Jilly's hair and she swung round to find herself starring into the eyes of a small reptile-like monster with dragon-like wings. It was hovering and flapping madly above her. She tugged her hair from its mouth and tipped backwards with the force as the creature let go of her long, wavy locks. Losing her footing she came crashing down backwards towards Julin who was by now balancing gingerly near the side of the boat, fighting off all manner of weird creatures. One second he was there, fighting, the next Jilly had accidentally nudged him awkwardly. He tried to regain his balance but had tilted too far. Julin toppled over the side of the boat and into the water. Both his crystal and the Book of Pylons fell from his jacket pocket as his body went splash.

"Julin!" Jilly screamed after him as he submerged beneath the dark liquid. She struggled to her feet and, leaning over the boat, held out her arm for him to grab.

"Julin? Stop the boat!" Jilly screamed to the men up front, but they ignored her and the boat continued relentlessly edging its way towards the next pylon.

Julin surfaced wildly splashing his arms about the water and trying to take in air. The noise of the battle echoed around the corridor and the boat rocked from side to side vigorously as the confusion continued. Steven and Gyp battled on with warding off the scorpions and other stranger creatures.

She spotted him as he surfaced.

"Grab my hand Julin," she shouted.

Julin swam back alongside the boat and reached up to her.

"Ouch!" Jilly was pulled backwards by the winged creature as it grabbed her hair again. Their fingertips slid apart. The pain from her roots made her yelp again as the creature pulled her hair much harder this time.

Losing his connection with Jilly, Julin then tried to pull himself up the side of the moving boat but couldn't get a grip. It was rocking violently and he just couldn't connect each time it came crashing down towards him. It continued onward. Julin was beginning to lose strength as he slid back under the water. He knew his chances of survival in the turmoil would be slim, if he didn't compose himself and keep up with the boat.

Jilly swung round and with a face full of hair she swiped at the creature behind her with her right arm. It went toppling across the floor of the boat and lay there recovering from her very powerful right hook. Gyp, with claw extended, took a swipe at it too, drawing blood from its scaly skin.

Jilly went back to the side of the boat and peered over.

"Stand up!" she screamed, but Julin went under again. Her mind could not understand how he was drowning yet the rope bearers were only waist high.

He surfaced gulping air and water as splashed around.

Steven could hear her shrilling cries as he battled on with the onslaught of attack.

"Stand up!" She reached out to Julin once more then let out the most blood curdling scream her lips had ever encountered. An enormous crocodile emerged from the depths of the water. With one swift lunge, it grabbed Julin between a set of ferocious teeth. Julin gulped up blood, as the crocodile bit down on him and took him under.

"Nooooo! Julin!" she screamed, "Julin!"

The crocodile began its death roll. With each lashing turn, it sunk lower beneath the water, dragging Julin further away from the boat. It never released its grip on its meal within its sharp, toothy jaws.

"For pity's sake, stop the boat," Jilly screeched as she made her way to the front where she tried to grab the attention of the God, Sa.

"Make them stop pulling the boat," she ordered.

He ignored her. She shook him violently, screaming at the top of her voice.

"Stop the boat!"

Sa remained undeterred by her protests and the activity around him. Jilly scrambled back to her seat, crushing another scorpion en route beneath her feet. She climbed over the bench.

"Make them stop!" she shouted at the rear oarsman. But he ignored her pleas also.

Jilly leaned over the back of the boat trying in vain to look into the depths of the water for any sign of splashing or a struggle.

"Julin!" she screamed again as the boat slowly jerked further away from where he had first entered the water.

"Julin!"

There was no sign of him.

As quickly as they had come, the scorpions began to disperse in all directions, screeching as they went. The winged reptile, bleeding and dazed, picked itself up from the floor and flew up out of sight. Steven was still sporadically flapping his arms in all directions, until he realised there was nothing around him to strike. The other hideous creatures withdrew back into the water. Some submerged beneath its depths while others swam to the side.

As the fifth pylon grew nearer, Jilly, exhausted from fighting, stared back towards where Julin had gone overboard. In the distance she could see no ripples, no movement whatsoever. Tears began to fall effortlessly from her face. The attack had finished, but the scars were deep. As the boat reached the gate, she felt she had no fight left in her to ward off a snake attack.

Yet this time, no snake came out of the depths. No mummies lined the pylon. The gates opened without fuss or drama. Steven and Gyp both comforted Jilly in her sobbing.

They could hear an evil chuckle coming from somewhere behind them, as their boat passed silently beneath the fifth pylon and into the next hour.

"Seth," whispered Steven as he held his daughter tightly. As the great gate silently closed behind them, all hope of seeing Julin alive again, were gone.

Chapter 13

"Hello! Is anyone there?"

Marcus slowly opened the bedroom door and peered in. Nobody answered. The room was void of personality.

"This room's empty too," he told Penedora as she stood watching him on the landing.

Zac called to them both from the bottom of the stairs, "It's empty down here."

"That's the eighth cottage we've tried and no sign of anyone," said Marcus, as he and Penedora made their way back downstairs.

"We've tried every cottage near the stones. Maybe everyone found refuge up at the Council Hall," she replied, "surely someone must still be around."

"Let's hope so, Penny. Let's hope so."

They clicked the light switch off as they left the house they had just explored and Marcus turned on his torch. Zac shut the front door firmly behind them.

It was still night time, and even though the evil fog had disappeared, Thyme still felt very different. There were no cottage lights on anywhere. Not a candle glowed in a back bedroom. Thyme was eerily dark and very silent.

As they made their way towards the Council Hall, all three remained vigilant. They had no idea what had happened in Thyme while they were across the stones but they were prepared for anything and everything. Penedora and Zac remembered the screams they heard behind them as they crossed the stones to Egypt. Both felt edgy and afraid of being confronted again by the Egyptian chasing them with a spear. The only noises in the vicinity came from the cracking of twigs beneath their feet, yet they still listened intently for any sounds around them other than their own. All three were very tired from their journey and very scared of what they might find when the daylight came.

They made their way to the steps of the Council Hall and looked up at the building they had come to love and respect. It too lay silent in the darkness.

"I don't hold much hope," said Marcus softly as he shone the torch over the windows and walls, "it looks deserted too."

Penedora ventured up the steps first and turned the door handle. She opened it easily and she stepped into the outer hall. Zac and Marcus followed. Zac reached over to the light switch and clicked it but the light bulbs did not respond. He flicked the switch a couple more times, but nothing happened.

"Lights are out."

Marcus went over to the large windows of the outer hall and shone the torch around the window ledge. He spotted the little box of matches and handed them to Penedora. "Looks like we'll have to revert to the old ways, huh?"

She smiled and relaxed.

"It's how we lived way before the New World came to Thyme," she replied, "and the old ways will be around a long time after we've gone!"

Deep down she was praying this statement would be true.

Marcus reached up and removed the candles from their holders around the walls and Penedora lit them one by one. He replaced them again and soon the lobby became bright enough for them to see each other better. Zac had already tried the main hall lights by this time and again, they had not responded. Penedora and Marcus took a couple of candles through to the main hall area and began to light the ones around the inner sanctuary. The final candles lit were the ones upon their altar. Penedora placed the box of matches on the altar next to The Book of Ancestors and the little bowl of crystals on display.

"I suppose this is all yours now," said Zac.

Marcus shivered. He hadn't really thought about it. His mind had been heavily focussed on finding the whereabouts of the people of Thyme rather than his place within the community.

"I'm sorry, I forgot," said Penedora apologetically, "I shouldn't have lit the candles on the altar." She placed her hand over her mouth in embarrassment of her actions.

"That's okay Penny. Ceremonial duties can surely wait. I haven't even been sworn in by the ancestors yet so let's forget this High Priest business until we've solved the mystery of where everybody's gone."

Penedora removed her hand from her face and bowed her head. "I'm still sorry," she whispered as she sat down on a chair in the front row.

Marcus followed her. He placed his torch on the seat next to him and relaxed back into the chair.

"Well what now then? The place seems deserted. Do we continue to check every dwelling or stay here until the others return from Egypt?" asked Zac.

"No idea."

"Me neither," said Penedora.

Zac wandered around the hall looking for inspiration and Marcus just closed his eyes to think clearly about the situation at hand.

"We could ask," said Penedora thoughtfully.

"Ask what?" said Marcus opening his eyes and swinging round to face her.

"What happened to everyone and where are they?"

"Who are you thinking of asking this time?"

"The same spirits I connected to before."

Marcus scrunched up his face. "Sorry, but I'm not too keen on that idea. A lot must have happened since we crossed the stones and I don't think it's wise to try any magic until we know what happened here."

Zac stood before his brother. "Remember, Penedora is protected by Romanihum and the unknown spirits did lead us to Steven."

"I'm still not sure," said Marcus unconvincingly.

"What have we got to lose? We haven't come to any harm so far."

"Sorry Zac, no! If the Ancient Egyptians and fog have left Thyme, there is no way in this world I would risk letting them know we are even here. Opening any magical channel now is just too risky."

"Think about it, Marcus. Something very sinister has happened to everyone. It's now your responsibility to find them. We can't just sit here and wait for something to happen. We have to take chances under these extreme circumstances just like Penedora and Jilly did. They weren't afraid."

"Oh I'm not so sure about that," Penny interrupted.

"But you did something, Penny. You tried and it worked. We have to try again."

Zac felt himself beginning to sound like Jilly. Angry at first, then doubtful, and now he too felt they acted correctly, when her mother connected to another realm.

They both looked at Marcus eager for his approval.

341

"What's the worst that could happen?"

"We die too!"

"Apart from that, what's the next worst that could happen?"

They waited for Marcus to think their predicament through. Carefully and methodically he weighed up all angles of danger in his mind.

"Oh all right. We'll try. But if anything goes wrong, don't blame me."

"What more could possibly go wrong that hasn't already happened?" she said.

"Do we need anything for the spells or requests?" asked Zac.

Penedora thought for a moment. Then her face dropped.

"Firstly, my potions are all back at my cottage and secondly, I don't have my spell book any more. I gave it to Jilly in Cairo."

Zac huffed. He slapped his thigh. "Great, now what can we do?"

He slouched into one of the chairs next to Penedora.

"I can't just sit here and do nothing. Particularly as Jilly is out there somewhere facing danger."

Penedora reached her right arm over to Zac and took his hand.

"Have faith, Zac. Jilly is going to be just fine, I know it. We'll just have to go back to mine and get my potion and then to Marcus' for his Book of Thyme."

"Will your potion work with my brother's book?"

"I don't know. We can only but try."

Penedora raised an eyebrow.

"Marcus's book – that's it! The Book of Ancestors. It's on the altar. We could use that. Or rather, I should say, you could use that." She turned to Marcus. "It'll have to be you who tries a connection for our answers and guidance. You are the new High Priest."

Marcus looked over at the altar. It still hadn't really sunk in. The power he now held and the responsibility that came with it. He was only twenty-nine and still so young to be so worthy a candidate for the job of High Priest. Yet, deep down in his heart, he knew he had been ready and capable for some time. But that was before the fog, the Egyptians and the mystery they were encompassed in. He had been brought up accordingly in the old ways and in the power of connection to ancestors like no other occupant of Thyme, apart from Nefron herself. Marcus was special, everyone knew that. Being so young and nowhere near 'elder' age, Marcus wasn't so much afraid, as apprehensive of his abilities. High Priest, with all the trimmings associated with the position, had been thrust upon him when Nefron crossed over to the spiritual realm. Restoring peace and harmony in Thyme Hollow was a priority. Keeping Penedora and Zac safe was another. Tradition was off the table right now; resilience and bravery stepped in.

Marcus got out of the chair and made his way over to the altar. He reached out to the Book of Ancestors and felt it with his fingers. This sacred book *was* now rightfully his. He turned to friends.

"Right, what am I asking for and who am I asking the question to?"

Penedora jumped up.

"I think we should try our ancestors first to see if the connection is back. If we have no luck there, then we could ask openly for any guidance from spirits of light."

"And if we open ourselves to the Egyptian Gods?"

"Then we shall deal with them and anything else they throw at us," said Zac defiantly.

He gingerly looked up at the ceiling to see if he could sense any wind beginning to pick up around the building but outside everything remained still.

'Phew,' he thought silently to himself.

The altar candles had already been lit so Marcus continued the proceedings by placing his own crystal beside the Book of Ancestors. Hesitantly his fingers slid down the curvature of the leather and opened it, revealing the dense, antique paper within. Marcus closed his eyes and raised his arms in prayer. Zac and Jilly stepped back from the altar.

"I am Marcus. I am of the Old Order. I am pure of heart, strong of mind and my soul is attuned. I call upon the ancestors of our forefathers and mothers to join us now, to advise us, to guide us and to assist in our time of great need."

Penedora and Zac had retreated to their seats. Marcus turned slightly towards them and let them know he was ready to begin. He turned to the Book of Ancestors and continued his asking for guidance.

"Cwym yun am ochorios
With love and light I ask thee, to share thy words
so true.
Guidance on our way ahead, is what I ask of you."

Marcus lowered his arms and waited. No wind came howling or blowing gently around them. No movement came from the book. Marcus looked back at Penny and Zac and shrugged his shoulders.

"No link?"

"Be patient," whispered Penedora, "you can do this."

They waited.

Nothing.

"Shouldn't we just go back and get your old potion?" Zac tutted.

"No, try again." Penedora waved her hand at Marcus to retry.

He did.

"Cwym yun am ochorios

With love and light I ask thee, with you I wish to speak.
With truth and love and courage, my people now I seek."

Marcus stood silently anticipating the pages of the book to turn and for its words of wisdom to appear before him.

A small wind came, very faintly at first. It tried to move the pages of the book but with no success. No writing appeared.

"The wind is too weak. Maybe Zac's right, we should go back and get your old potion?"

"Wait," she whispered, "you have connected to someone, Marcus. Listen."

He did. From above their heads he could hear a faint voice trying to speak to them. It faded and was gone.

"Let's try together," Marcus suggested. "Come up to the altar and link arms with me. It will make the link stronger."

"But that's not allowed," said Penedora hesitantly, "only you can cast spells from the altar and the within the Council Hall."

"These aren't normal times, Penny. Come, let's open our Chakras together and unite."

Penedora and Zac stood up and joined hands in circle with Marcus. Closing their eyes and allowing their minds to unblock obstructive emotions, they focussed on connecting with the faint voice in their heads.

Marcus guided them to visualise their 'chakras' within their bodies. He instructed them to mentally open each of these energy centres as he spoke aloud their colours: Red, Orange, Yellow, Green, Blue, Indigo and Violet.

"Visualise your Root Chakra. Imagine the colour red flowing through your body and up towards the world of spirit and beyond," he paused, as he let them see and feel the colour red at their feet.

"Now visualise the colour orange coming from your sacral centre. As you open this Chakra, blend it with the red as it flows upwards to Spirit."

As he softly spoke and their minds relaxed into opening their energy centres, their fears and trepidation began to wane. The power of their combined auras grew stronger the nearer they got to the last Crown Chakra; the top and most spiritual energy centre.

It took about ten minutes for them to open their channels enough for the voice to flow through again. It was soft and incoherent at first, then it grew stronger. The Book of Ancestors began to shudder as its pages flicked. The wind at their feet was still subtle but moved enough to give enough energy for the unknown connection to speak. They all heard him simultaneously.

"*It's me, Joseph,*" the voice whispered.

Penedora gasped, "Joseph?" She felt a sense of sadness, guilt and then hope.

"*Yes, it's me. Carmel is here too.*"

"Are you safe?" asked Marcus.

"Yes we are. We cannot cross over to our Land of Ancestors. There is a blockage, but we are in a safe place. We have heard you and followed your energy across the stones to Egypt and home but unfortunately there is nothing we can do to help. All links to Spirit have been severed."

"Joseph," Marcus continued, "did you see what happened here? Can you see where everyone is?"

"We cannot see, but we can feel the vibrations and sense what is going on. You are all in great danger. If the Egyptian Book of the Dead falls to the wrong hands, Thyme will be gone forever and you will die. This must be prevented. You must stop him..."

"We know, Joseph. Julin is returning their book as we speak. What of our people in Thyme?"

Joseph's soft voice began to fade as his link gradually diminished. "We are losing connection....."

"Joseph can you still hear me?"

"Our light fades, Marcus. We have little time..."

"Joseph, our people?"

The voice grew weaker and weaker. They strained to hear the last remaining words as Joseph's frequency faded quickly from their

minds. *"The children… below you… others…
scattered… corners… New Wor-… stones…
help… return…"*

Joseph vanished; their link cut. Zac was first to
open his eyes. He let go of Penedora's and
Marcus' hands. They followed suit.

Marcus grabbed his crystal from the altar and
placed it back into his pocket.

"Let's hope the Egyptians can't harm Carmel
and Joseph wherever they are resting."

"At least they are together on their journey
home," said Penedora reassuringly.

"What do you think he meant, below us?"
enquired Zac. "Spiritually below? Actually below
us?"

"Yes," said Marcus, "I think he meant *actually*
below us." He turned and grabbing the torch from
the chair, headed back towards the front entrance.

"Come on," he beckoned, "the vaults. I think he
was referring to the vaults below the hall."

Vaults? Zac didn't know there were any vaults
beneath the building. He often wondered though
what was beyond the little door on the right as you
entered the Council building. He'd assumed it was
an area for the High Priestess to change or rest.
Sort of like private quarters. Vaults; now that
sounded very intriguing indeed.

Zac and Penedora collected a candle each and
followed Marcus to the foyer. To their left was a
little, arched wooden door. Marcus turned the

large brass ring hanging from the wood. It was stiff. He used two hands to pull the door open as it rubbed across the floor. Before them were three steps leading down into a small room in which only Nefron, or the Priestesses before her, had ever entered. The room was pleasant and covered in a beautiful deep pile, purple carpet. A table rested against one wall and was covered by various articles used for prayers such as candles, crystals, bowls and a couple of potion bottles. A little wooden bookcase stood against another wall beneath a small window. Books of various sizes were neatly stacked on their shelves. Their titles ranged from *beginner's guides to spells and potions*, to advanced levels of *pagan chants and magic*. On the last wall to their left was a red velvet curtain.

"So I am right," thought Zac, "it is a little room of sanctuary."

"Must be that way." pointed Marcus, "behind the curtain on that wall. Whatever is behind it must lead to the vaults."

"Have you never been down here?" Zac asked his brother.

"No, never needed to until now."

"But you knew about the vaults?"

"Doesn't everyone?"

"Obviously not!"

He looked at Penedora. "Did you?"

She smirked.

They made their way across the little room and Zac helped Marcus pull back the heavy, red velvet curtain to reveal a set of wooden steps. They spiralled downwards into the darkness and out of sight. Marcus shone the torch at the steps before his feet and one by one they ventured downwards. Unlike the steps at the Great Pyramids of Egypt, none of them felt afraid of where these ones were taking them.

At the bottom, they found themselves on a small, insignificant landing with another door in front. It had a small handmade, iron latch. Marcus tried it and it opened easily. They stepped through and entered the vaults beneath the communal hall.

"Wow! Who'd have thought…" gasped Zac wide-eyed, as he gazed around the place. "and the lights are on!"

Flames from the large thick candles danced randomly. Dripping with wax, their light reflected the heavy stone coffins lined up in an orderly fashion around the vault rooms.

"Who do you think they belong to?" he asked his brother.

"Ancestors," replied Marcus as his swept an index finger over the lid of one of the coffins. He checked the tip of his finger and was quite surprised to see no dust on it. He wondered who kept the place clean and who had lit the candles.

"Important ones at that," said Penedora, reading one of the coffin lids. "The people of Thyme used to bury their Priests and High Priestesses down here until they decided it was best to cremate them."

"Has there ever been a High Priest, then? I mean before Marcus," Zac asked.

"Oh yes, way back," Penedora looked at Marcus and smiled, "but none in our generation, or the generation before that. Marcus is the first for a very long time. It's actually quite rare for a man to be so attuned."

"Then I'm honoured," said Marcus. "Or maybe I should say blessed. I should thank our ancestors for choosing me, and hope I please them in my work. First though, we need to find the children."

Marcus sighed. He was so sure the children would be beneath the hall, beneath their feet but the place was empty apart from the already dead and buried bodies of their hierarchy.

Zac had made his way over to an area where the stone walls had been carved to make shelves. He could see various pots and odd shaped wooden boxes on the layers of stone. He randomly picked up a pot. It was heavier than he'd anticipated it to be. He unscrewed the lid and examined the contents. He sniffed the grey granules but there was no aroma. Replacing the lid he noticed a label on the pot. Once the lid was secure, he tilted it sideways and read the little label.

"Oh my!" he exclaimed, scrunching up his face. "They are ashes. I'm sniffing dead dudes." He winced, replacing the pot on the shelf. "Does this mean your ashes will be kept down here when you've gone over to spirit?"

Marcus laughed at his brother. "I assume so."

A noise caught their attention from the far end of the vaults and they quickly turned round in the direction it had emanated.

"What was that?" whispered Penedora, her heart once more beating rapidly.

"I heard it too," said Zac nervously.

Marcus called over in the direction of the noise, "Who's there?"

A shuffle was heard coming from behind one of the stone coffins.

"Come out. We know you're there," he called again, louder.

A hand slowly appeared followed by a little frightened face as it peered over the lid of a coffin. It was a child. Her little blonde locks were tangled and across her face, but Penedora recognised her little frame instantly.

"Sofie!" cried Penedora and rushed over to her.

Then another little child stood up.

"Brendon?" Marcus rushed over too. "It's the children."

"How many of you are here?" asked Penedora as she hugged the little girl tightly.

"All of us," sobbed little Sofie as she held on tightly to Penedora.

One of the oldest survivors, Figg, stepped forward pushing a little lad in front of him.

"Jacob was the last I grabbed before they killed our High Priestess."

"She saved us all," sniffed Brendon, he began to cry.

"Every child was spared because she gave her life to save us. One worthy soul for the freedom of many lesser ones, they said." Figg gulped back his tears. He had to show courage as he was nearing the Age of Becoming and adulthood. "Nefron told us all to hide here. She told us to go quickly and not look back."

"Then they... they... they killed her, it was horrible. Jacob saw it all too." Little Sofie sobbed as the noise of screaming flooded back to her.

Marcus shook his head. The responsibility of the rank he now held was bigger than he could have imagined, but he knew at this moment in time, he was ready to make that commitment. Would he have given his life for the children? Yes, absolutely. Zac caught his thoughts as he realised the enormity of his brother's task ahead. If their book was not returned, would they come back for Marcus and show him the same fate he gave Nefron? But then, if Seth got hold of the book, they would all be killed. He shuddered to think any further.

The stillness in the vault was broken with the echo of activity as the children ventured out of their little hiding spots behind the coffins. Some were smiling with relief, some crying, but all were apprehensive of showing themselves and deeply scared of what was happening in Thyme. Their emotions turned to safety as each in turn was comforted in the arms of the friendly adults they knew.

"Is it all over now?" Sofie asked Penedora, her little green eyes blinking wetness.

"No not yet, but it will be soon. I promise." Penedora knelt down to her level and gave the little girl another tight squeeze.

"I want my mummy."

"Don't worry, Sofie. We'll find her. She'll be home again soon. They all will."

Penedora looked over to Marcus; her eyes pleading with him to reassure them all that they would win. He starred back at her but his soul could give her no assurance.

Penedora closed her eyes and hugged little Sofie harder still.

Ra's voice bellowed down at the little boat from the skies above. Yelling at them in an ancient tongue, he urged along the four front pullmen:

"BE STRONG OF ARM, FIRM OF LIMB, SWIFT OF FOOT AND BOLD OF SOUL TO MAKE YOUR SUCCESSFUL WAY TO THE HIDDEN CIRCLES."

Ra passed sentences of condemnation and doom on the poor souls on the left shore and to those worshippers standing on the right of the river he praised them for having spoken truth upon the Earth.

Jilly and her father huddled together in the middle of the bench fearing further attack from either side of the boat. They listened to the loud echoes of Ra's deep booming voice and the wailing of those on the left shore as they passed by.

The Pylon that separated them from the sixth hour was made of pure gold. The ancient carvings were etched deeply into it and standing on the ornate ledge high above their heads were twelve more mummies, shrouded and silent. The voice of Ra ceased. Further down the wall of the Pylon, either side of the golden doors, were two more ledges. Standing on the left ledge was a huge golden statue of a serpent and on the right hand ledge stood an equally-sized statue of a mummy wearing the head of a jackal. The doors looked solid and were locked together by a series of bolts and cog mechanisms.

On reaching the golden Pylon, Sa ordered his four slaves to stop pulling and lower the rope. This they did. The boat came to a halt. Casually the four slaves waded out of the water to the bank where they rested. From the rear of the boat, the Egyptian god Heka made his way to the front, carefully stepping over the fragments of food which had been scattered around the floor of the boat during the battle of the last hour. He joined his fellow traveller at the front and, side by side, they began to chant to the Pylon in ancient language.

Slowly, as did the keepers of the third gate, the mummies lining this ledge above them, one by one, opened their eyes. The golden gates, though, remained firmly shut. When each mummy had been woken by the two Egyptians at the front of the boat, Sa then left his position and moved to the right hand side of the boat where he bowed his head, saying nothing. Heka then placed himself in the centre of the boat and awaited instructions.

'Heka must be in charge of the boat and Sa in charge of the rope pullers,' thought Jilly, as she avidly watched their every move.

A deep masculine voice called out to them. It came from somewhere behind the golden serpent. Jilly soon realised that the voice was actually coming from the golden statue. She held tightly to her father in readiness of a snake strike, but it didn't come.

"I AM MAAB," it boomed. *"I AM KEEPER OF THE GATE TO THE GREAT HALL OF TRUTH. WHO WISHES TO ENTER?"* The statue itself did not move at all, just a voice called from within it.

As if reading from scriptures and spells from Julin's Book of Pylons, Heka replied. "I am Heka. I sail this night in the great boat of Ra. Hail to you, gods of the caverns, which are in the West. Hail to you, door keepers of the Underworld who guard this gate against those who bring news to the presence of Osiris. May you be wise, may you have power and may you destroy the enemies of Ra and smite the power of Seth who wishes to destroy us. May you make brightness, may you dispel darkness and may you guide us through your doors. May our souls pass by your hidden things, may you protect us and may you allow us to enter into the spirit of the kingdom of the great God and Goddess of the Underworld."

"Are you worthy of audience?" questioned the golden serpent.

"Hail to you, all gods who are in this Hall of Justice. I am pure from evil, I have excluded myself from the quarrels of those who are now living and I am not among them. I have given bread to the hungry, water to the thirsty and a boat to those who are boat-less. I have given forth the *soul* thou requested and brought forth the *cat* with the vision of sight."

Gyp flicked his tail. It went unnoticed.

Jilly watched as the head of the mummy on the lower right hand ledge opened its eyes and turned towards them with a stiff creaking movement. Another voice now came from that direction. Steven listened carefully to the conversation between the keeper of the boat and the keepers of the Pylon. He began to wonder if the soul and the cat they were referring to were Gyp and Julin but he was unsure.

The voice from the mummy statute on the lower ledge, spoke. *"Hast thou driven the evil from the caverns of the night?"*

"No. Seth lives on."

"As agreed at journey's origin, hast thou given the correct soul to alloweth you to enter beyond?"

"The correct soul has sunk beneath," Heka answered, "taken by the evil one, to live an eternal life beyond."

The passengers gasped. Steven understood what the conversation meant and believed now Julin was gone forever. If Julin *had* been the soul taken by Seth, and not by those of the Tuat, then there would be no bartering for his own life with Osiris within the Hall of Truths. Mulling over every sentence he would use in the presence of Osiris, Steven had even decided during the last hour to negotiate the return of his sight for the return of

Julin. He felt sick in the stomach. He knew they would never see Julin again.

'How could Osiris demand that one of them lose their life to enable the others to enter his Kingdom,' he thought angrily. This action made him no better than his blood-thirsty brother, Seth. Steven became furious with the whole affair and was now even more eager to confront these ancient Egyptian beings.

"A heart filled with anger may not enter this hour," stated the voice from the jackal-headed mummy.

Its dark eyes from behind the golden shrouding seemed to look straight into Steven's heart.

Heka turned round and stared at Steven.

"I think they mean you father," whispered Jilly.

Steven rubbed his mouth with his hand. His lips had dried up yet a small bead of sweat trickled from his forehead.

"Are you ok?" Jilly asked him softly.

Steven combed his long blonde hair with his fingers, from his forehead backwards and took a deep breath.

"We're in a situation here Jilly that I have no control over. I feel hate, hurt and anger, yet to succeed I know I must remain calm. You know they are talking about Julin don't you?"

"I guessed," she said lowering her eyes. "It means we will never see him again doesn't it?"

"I'm afraid so," he whispered back.

"Why do you think they chose *him*?"

"I'm not sure they did. He could have lost his crystal when he fell into the water and that gave them their opportunity but I can't believe they chose one of us like a raffle ticket prize."

"If they didn't take him by chance," continued Jilly, "do you think they decided Julin's fate *before* we even crossed the stones?"

Steven was unsure as to where all the connections had actually begun. He had been imprisoned over ten years, without sight and was unsure as to what had actually gone on in Thyme while he was away. He knew the whole mystery centred on the initial stealing of the old Egyptian Book but he was unsure as to the sheer scale of the revenge or where everyone fitted in with the story as it was unfolding. He had by this time realised though, that Jilly's cat was playing a major part in the episode and his own link to the trouble had escalated when he took the book across the stones to Thyme.

Jilly could feel her father's mind racing around searching for answers.

"Clear your mind," she told him, "you must not hold any grudges if we are to enter into the next hour and get back your sight. You are a good man, Father. Don't let them make you into something you are not. Hold your crystal and think of Thyme Hollow and of when we return home to the beauty of the woods."

Steven responded to his daughter's calm voice by feeling in his pocket for his crystal. He curled his fingers tightly round it and began to breathe deeply, bringing in memories of his cottage, his beautiful wife and of the courage of his child beside him. He put his other hand over hers and smiled.

"I can do this," Steven told her, "these gods are just like our ancestors. They hold great power, yet they listen to wisdom and reason." He smiled, or at least tried to. "We give them their book, they give me my eyes; we all go home."

Jilly squeezed his hand. Steven remembered the days when *he* gave the advice. 'Oh how she has grown,' he thought sadly, thinking of all those years he had missed. The anger of being imprisoned flooded over him and he couldn't control that feeling at all.

Heka smirked at Steven. "You have no understanding of the power of our gods. They do not listen. You are either good or evil and this measurement will be weighed against your soul. You must beg forgiveness for your sins, human; not barter for it, but beg. You must recite the spell for removing anger from the heart of the God of Justice before you may even enter."

"I don't know the spell," replied Steven, to Heka's voice.

"Then I will say it for you in your language and you must repeat it as I speak. Only then can we continue, unless you wish to remain in this division with the other lost souls, for eternity."

Heka waved his arms in the directions of the banks of the river as this time his smirk was aimed at Jilly. Her mind scanned all the scenes she had passed since boarding the boat with her father and the thought of either of them being damned amongst those weeping miserable souls on the shore sickened her.

"He'll recite after you," she called to Heka. "We must continue, Father," she whispered to Steven. "We have come so far, we must play by their rules. For Julin's sake, rid yourself of your anger."

She squeezed her father's hand again to relax him.

"Very well." Steven took a deep breath and let it out slowly. He repeated the exercise and this time took longer to release his breath. His body relaxed, easing his emotions. He released enough hatred to enable Heka to continue.

The Egyptian turned and faced the pylon again and began to chant to them slowly enabling Steven to repeat his words, sentence after sentence.

"Hail to you, you who descend in power, chief of all secret matters.
Behold, my word is spoken, so says the god who was angry with me.

Wrong is washed away and it falls immediately.
O Lords of Justice, put an end to the evil harm,
which is in me.
O you, companions of the God of Justice,
May this god be gracious to me and may my evil
be removed for you.
O Lord of Offerings, as mighty ruler, behold I have
brought to you an offering
So that you may live on it and that I may live on it;
Be gracious to me and remove all anger which is
in your heart against me."

When they had finished, Heka turned to Steven. "You have brought an offering to the gods of the sixth hour, haven't you?"

"We have a book which belongs to the God Osiris and his wife Isis. Our reason for being here is to return it to them."

"Reasons are not for you to decide," Heka said spinning his head back round again, "destiny is what brings you on your travel, not decision."

Jilly disliked this Egyptian god - boatman, whoever - immensely. Not only did he show shear arrogance towards them, he did nothing to help them save Julin. In fact, how could he condemn a man he didn't even know. Jilly wondered if he treated all his passengers this way.

Gyp, who had remained silent beneath the table for most of the boat journey, peered up at Jilly. His yellow marked eye blinked a couple of times, as pictures filtered through to somewhere else. He admired her courage and felt great sadness that their parting drew near. He began to feel hope that they would succeed and she would be able to return to Thyme with her father. He knew that Thyme would never be the same again after these many years of book searching and the recent killing and scattering, but he knew that given the chance, its people could begin to rebuild their lives again in peace. Hopefully, with the new gained experience they had learned that some books do not always bring the knowledge you are expecting in return for reading from their ancient pages.

"Are you now ready to enter into the Kingdom of Judgement, to the Great Hall of Truth?" asked the voice from the serpent statue.

"We are," said Heka.

"Then behold, your destiny awaits."

The cogs began to turn and the bolts slid aside, as the golden doors of the sixth Pylon opened. Mechanical trickery echoed around them. Jilly looked from side to side to see where the four rope-pullers were, but they didn't move from the shore. The doors were much heavier than the last ones but they didn't even make a ripple in the water as they spread apart. Magically, the boat began to move. It jolted slightly to start, and then picked up momentum as it slid smoothly forwards.

The boat of Ra carrying its two passengers glided majestically between the golden doors and before them. Jilly couldn't even begin to describe what she could see, as they entered into the sixth hour of the night and Kingdom of Osiris.

Spell 14

Taken from the
Egyptian Book of the Dead

Hail to you.

You who descend in power, chief of all secret matters.

Behold, my word is spoken:

So says the god who was angry with me.

Wrong is washed away and it falls immediately.

O Lords of Justice, put an end to the evil harm,

Which is in me.

O you companions of the God of Justice,

May this god be gracious to me;
May my evil be removed for you.
O Lord of Offerings, as mighty ruler, behold,
I have brought to you an offering, so that you and I may live on it.
Be gracious to me and remove all anger which is in your heart against me.

Chapter 14

Royalty in the great hall of judgement eagerly awaited their mortal presence. Marble flooring lay either side of the stream; lustrously painted drawings covered all of the inner walls. This vast building was nothing less than a truly regal expanse of magnificent opulence and splendour.

The huge Pylon gates of their judgement hour banged loudly shut as their boat glided to a halt on the right bank. This time, the narrow wooden gangplank began to emerge from the starboard side to allow disembarkation. When the gangplank finished extending and positioned itself safely on dry land, Gyp immediately leapt from the boat. Jilly skilfully guided her father's footsteps carefully down the gangway towards the beautifully polished marble.

As they stepped off, two young Egyptian ladies rushed up to them carrying what appeared to be white sheets. They beckoned Jilly and her father to take off their shoes. Jilly kicked off her little ballet shoes and told her father to remove his. The Egyptian ladies then helped Jilly and Steven wrap the white sheets around themselves. Jilly kept at least one hand on the haversack as the women manoeuvred her awkwardly into the cloth. They hooked the textile around her baggy burgundy sweater and tucked the end into the waist of her jeans. She flung the haversack back around her shoulders. Steven could feel the quality and softness of the silk garment.

As the two ladies retreated, another two came rushing up to them waving essence around their bodies. Steven coughed as the smoke rose up his nose. He was unprepared for the strong whiff of something smelly that was shoved under his face and around his body. He was usually very good with smells but couldn't quite make out what this essence was. 'Vanilla?' he thought, then changed his mind, 'eucalyptus?' It wasn't unpleasant, just very strong.

"I think we're being prepared for audience," said Jilly.

She was correct. Only white could be worn when being presented to the Gods and definitely no dirty shoes were allowed across the immaculate marble surface. Most souls arriving at this part of their journey had usually been attired correctly at their mummification. It was rare indeed for a soul to enter the Kingdom of Khenti Amentet wearing jumpers, shirts or jeans! Steven's memory of the last time he held audience here returned. He felt a stabbing of regret as he recalled on that occasion he was fortunate enough to witness the splendour of this great hall. He visualised Osiris seated above him as he stood there chained. Then he remembered the searing pain as they gouged out his eyes.

The immense chamber housed around forty other beings, all of Egyptian origin. Jilly viewed them as they stood staring back at her. Some of these Egyptians were human, while others had human bodies with heads of different animals. Jilly recognised a few from the paintings she'd seen within the pyramid and she recalled the statues of Anubis guarding the entrance to the underworld. That felt so long ago now as so much had transpired since they had all embarked on this perilous journey. Anubis was here now, in real life and as fearsome-looking as his statues. The ancient Egyptians had artistically depicted their gods to perfection on their tomb walls and on papyrus.

Considering Jilly was gazing at half-man, half-animal beings, she felt strangely unafraid of them now and certainly not as surprised at their presence in the hall as she thought she would be. She had grown up ten-fold in the last six hours, especially as her father was now by her side. She was puzzled to understand why these people wished to represent different animals. She assumed they chose masks according to their favourite animal or had characteristics most like when they were alive on earth, but she didn't know this for sure. In fact she wasn't sure of anything anymore!

Then Jilly saw him and the hairs on the back of her neck raised. She could see him at the far end of the chamber. Osiris. There he was, sitting at the top of an impressive flight of stairs in all his regalia. He was the spitting image of the large statue they had seen on their journey, apart from the fact this man had two legs and feet and was obviously very much alive.

When the women retreated and a hush fell amongst the crowd, Jilly guided her father forwards and, apprehensively, both prisoners made their way to where Osiris sat, watching their hesitant approach.

Positioned above them, his steps were paved with gold and his throne was a huge, square golden chair, carved on the arms and legs with equal blue and gold squares. The arm rests were made of two golden lion heads and Jilly could see that the back of the chair was a gold carving of two Egyptian people dressed in royal finery. She assumed these represented Osiris and Isis themselves.

"How pompous," she thought, "and what is it with all this gold?"

Hanging from the wall just above and behind the throne was another huge Egyptian eye, which seemed to stare down at the assembly gathered below. Jilly whispered what she could see to her father and his mind recalled the scene as if he had been there only yesterday. But he knew it had actually been nearly ten years since his feet trod the same path on which he and Jilly now found themselves. He could feel the tension radiating around the great chamber, as they stood below the greatest of Gods.

"He is staring down at us," Jilly told her father. "There's another black eye hanging on a curtain above his head. I think it's the Udjat eye again."

"No," Steven corrected her, "what you're looking at is the Eye of Horus. It represents that which was torn out by Seth, and restored by Thoth."

"They have a thing about tearing out eyes don't they?" she whispered back sarcastically.

"The Eye of Horus is symbolic of everything good, beneficial and pleasant," Steven said softly.

"That sounds positive to me," she responded. "Maybe that means you will get your sight back tonight."

"Let's hope so." Steven squeezed her arm with his other hand.

On their left, Jilly noticed an ape hurrying across the floor of the chamber with a large stick, poking it at a pig, urging it along. The pig squealed a couple of times as the stick connected with its rear end. When the ape was satisfied with its place amongst the onlookers it grabbed the pig to stop it running off elsewhere. It held the pig under its arm as its gaze returned to Jilly and her father.

Once the shuffling and general fidgeting had died down, Osiris raised his right hand.

Following Osiris' command, the Egyptian god Anubis made his way towards them and took his place to Steven and Jilly's left.

Anubis had the body of a man clothed in a golden garment embroidered with red chain-like loops, held with two straps. These were slung over his shoulders and tied at the waist with a red and blue ornate waistband. Placed on his upper arms were two broad black and gold bracelets and around his neck he wore a thick circular black and gold jewelled necklace. His face was not human. He had the head of a jackal. The snout and ears were much longer and thinner than that of a wolf and the colour of his head was jet black with gold eyeliner around his eyes and eyebrows. His face though was not hairy like a dog's, but smooth like skin. Jilly wondered if this man was also wearing a mask, attached to the wig, which extended down passed his shoulders at the back and in the front, to his chest. She bent her head round to take a closer look, but she soon realised there was no join between the head and neck and the wig was actually a part of him. She could see no stitching or string to hold the mask or hair in place. His jackal head blended into his body and Jilly could see he was real. She really was in the

374

presence of an ancient Egyptian God and not a man in a mask, and an extremely large and powerful-looking god at that. Jilly felt very nervous, so she shuffled in front of her father and he covered her protectively with his arms. This made her feel safer. Gyp sat as near to her as he could. This also gave her comfort.

From their right came another being; this man had the head of a falcon. He carried a sceptre in one hand which had a little hook at the end. In his other he held a large golden ankh, the symbol of Life. Round his ankles were clasped two golden bands. These were repeated on his arms; two around his wrists and another two on his biceps. Jilly was amazed by the tallness of his hat. It was shaped like a vase with something that resembled a large proboscis protruding from a butterfly.

This Egyptian took his place beside Steven.

Steven could sense the man beside him. His intuition was telling him something. Steven took a deep breath and let his unconscious mind enter his thoughts. He then turned to the figure standing to his right.

"Horus," he bravely muttered, "so here we are again."

The figure, half-man, half bird, nodded its head at Steven in acknowledgement. His eyes scanned Jilly standing in front of her father. Even knowing the human before him had no sight, he uttered no words in response. Steven was aware of the strength and power of the Egyptian God Horus. He could still picture him in his mind swooping down on him, as he lay on the ground after their collision, by the stones in Thyme.

From behind them, a figure of a woman emerged from the crowd and she nudged Anubis slightly as she slipped passed them all up the steps. She was tall and elegant and her jet black hair moved slightly as she glided up the stairs in a regal manner. Her long white dress clung to her waist showing feminine form. Like Horus, she wore gold jewellery around her wrists, arms and ankles, but it was her necklace that impressed Jilly the most. It was encrusted with many jewels and spanned from each shoulder, right round her chest and neck. Thick kohl eyeliner, applied heavily around the eyes, emphasised her beautiful facial features. At the top of the stairs, she bent down and kissed Osiris on the cheek and then turned to stand beside his throne.

'This woman can be none other than Isis herself; owner and reader of the Egyptian Spell Book,' thought Jilly.

The last Egyptian to join them in front of Osiris and Isis was Thoth, the scribe of the Egyptian Gods, the judge and jury, the man who was to decide if Steven and Jilly would live or die. He was considered the wisest amongst them and the Egyptians referred to him by his ancient name:

Djehuty. His dress was orange and white stripped and like most of the others in the underworld, it hung from long shoulder straps and was tied by a cord at the waist. Jilly thought this man looked kind.

Thoth carried a scroll and a writing implement. He nodded his head towards his left and immediately four slaves staggered forward from the crowd carrying an enormous set of scales. The wooden structure stood at least six feet in height and was cumbersome. Gold covered the wood at its mid-section, and at each end of the cross-section were two large shallow bowls. They swung precariously from their ropes, as the slaves manoeuvred it into position. They placed the scales on the floor by the steps and then scuttled back to join the other onlookers.

Jilly could see a little red and orange bird sitting inside one of the bowls as it swung side to side. Thoth bent down and with a quick flick of his hand, knocked the little bird from the bowl. It flapped away towards the roof of the chamber, squawking as it went. Still bent, Thoth then removed a small white feather from his waist and placed it gently into the pan in which the bird once sat.

He wore a very tall, ornate crown, dressed with two large golden balls, one at the base and one at the very top. There were a couple of snakes to the front and rear of the crown base, each with another ball stuck to its head. It had a rope-patterned rim which spanned beyond his shoulders. The headgear looked heavy indeed but Thoth moved confidently in this accessory. Jilly noticed he was quite an attractive man and she could see his shoulder muscles flex as he bent to remove the little bird. She was actually impressed the large crown remained firmly on his head when he bent.

As Thoth straightened again, Jilly caught her breath. She knocked her father's arm away with her elbow when she instinctively raised her hand to her mouth to prevent a louder gasp escaping from her lips.

"Are you ok?" asked Steven worriedly.

"Just taken by surprise, that's all."

"What happened?" he asked.

"Nothing, it's okay. I'm fine, really I am."

When Thoth stood up and turned to face Jilly again, his head and facial features were no longer human. His head had morphed into a bird with a curved neck and long bent beak. Two poky eyes sat at the base of his beak and he blinked at her several times when he realised she was startled by his transformation. One moment he was a handsome man and the next, half-man, half-animal. When the shock subsided, Jilly remembered this was no ordinary situation to be in and anything in this underworld was possible. Whichever form these Egyptians took, Jilly noticed the souls behind their eyes were all the same: powerful and mesmerising, but extremely hard to read.

Anubis spoke loudly as Thoth moved up a couple of steps towards Osiris where he rested to wait for the judgement.

"O ye who brings words true or false to me remember that it is Djehuty who weigheth them."

Osiris then spoke. He requested audience with whoever was here for the defence of the two humans who stood before him. Jilly scanned the hall to see which strange creature would step forward to act as their lawyer. She saw no movement from the crowd.

Gyp, who had always been by her side, did move. He curled his black furry body around Jilly's legs and then made his way up a couple of steps in front of them.

"Get back here," Jilly whispered to him, hoping he wouldn't get into trouble with Thoth or Osiris on the steps before them.

He ignored her and came to rest on the same step as Thoth.

"Gyp! Come down at once," she said firmly to him. Again he ignored her.

"Leave him," said Steven, "he is one of them."

"Don't be silly," she snapped at her father. "Gyp, come!"

Gyp began to shiver. Not from fear, but movement. Slowly his body began to stretch upwards and outwards. The shaking increased as he grew taller and taller from an upright cat-like position to what appeared to be a black furry figure of a baby in human form. He continued changing, growing larger before Jilly's eyes, until he stood before her, two steps up, as a young Egyptian boy. His fur began to recede, revealing skin beneath but the black colour remained to reveal an Egyptian garment, which clothed his semi-naked body. Jilly stood rooted to the spot, shocked. She witnessed her beloved cat transform into one of *them*. The enemy; the destroyer of her home and killer of two people she loved very much, Carmel and Joseph… and Julin… Gyp had done nothing to help Julin as the great crocodile took him under.

"How could you?" she cried, "why would you…" Words escaped her as a small tear appeared and fell onto her cheek.

All that remained of her faithful friend were his yellow eyes. They were now more human-shaped but the small mark to his left eye could still be clearly seen. He gazed back at her. In spirit, Gyp was still Gyp but now in different form only. His yellow glare penetrated her and Jilly began to see clearly through his eyes and beyond, deep into his soul. Confusion and anger began to slowly ease. They became connected mentally and Jilly realised she had nothing to fear from him.

'You are one of them, but on our side,' her mind questioned. Gyp stared at her, showering her mentally with warmth and kindness. He had not betrayed them, but had come to help.

'Don't be afraid of me, Jilly,' his thoughts responded.

She heard him loud and clear within her head. Gyp could read her mind and she his. She knew they were connected like soul mates ever since day one but hadn't really questioned their connection.

'Had he been telepathic all these years?' she wondered.

'Yes.'

She heard him again. 'I am still your friend, *your* black cat, the one who will always love you and be there for you.'

Jilly paused from her current thoughts and wondered if she would wake up in Thyme and find that everything had been a horrible dream. No. This was real, surreal even: men turning into animals, animals turning into men, friends being eaten by crocodiles. Of course this was real. This sort of thing happened every day, didn't it? The unfamiliar in which all her senses were being tested.

Isis broke the inner silence between the two friends. "You have my book?" she asked of Jilly.

Her voice was soft, yet authoritative.

"Yes," Jilly replied.

Jilly stepped forward and swung her haversack round her shoulder and placed it on the ground in front of her. Kneeling down, she lifted the flap of the haversack and pulled the drawstring loose to open it. Reaching in, she carefully removed the book. Gyp approached her and took it. He made sure their fingers touched hers reassuringly. Jilly looked deeply into his yellow eyes, as she handed it to him. Chemistry still flowed between them.

Gyp turned and made his way to the top step. He carefully handed the book over to Isis; he said, "As for whoever knows this book, they shall go out into the day, they shall walk on earth among the living and they shall never suffer destruction. This book I hand to you as a gift from a friend."

Carefully, Gyp retreated and made his way down the steps backwards, bowing his head in respect at Osiris and Isis as he went. He sat down on the bottom step to wait for Osiris to speak.

The silence that followed seemed like forever to Jilly. She couldn't understand what the problem was. They had their book back, what was everyone waiting for?

"What about my father's eyes?" she snapped bravely. "You've got your book back."

Osiris stood up and waved angrily at Thoth, who then spoke for him.

"You have no right to barter before Khenti Amentet," said Thoth on Osiris' behalf, "Osiris chooses to give your father his eyes back when he decides and because he chooses to, not because you request it."

"But that's not fair!" Jilly shouted back. "There must be someone in here who has some decency and fairness about them?" she said, looking around the room and back at Gyp, pleading for him to speak up for them.

"Silence!" shouted Osiris as he stood up from his throne, "how dare you judge us!"

"I apologise for my daughter's outburst," Steven called, trying to calm the situation, "it's just that we have travelled a perilous journey to return your book. My friends have ultimately suffered because of something I did, but I must reiterate, my actions were not intentional. You have imprisoned me here for ten years, yet I did not steal the book. I brought it across the stones to Thyme as an object of interest, for knowledge. Not as stolen property."

"Hush!" cried Osiris back at him.

Steven and Jilly fell silent.

Osiris pondered the situation for a moment, then spoke again, "I will give you back your sight… however… I do this not as reward for bringing back the book, but to enable you to see that which your actions have created."

With that, Osiris waved his hand across his face and miraculously at the same time, Steven's eyes were replaced. He could see. Well, sort of. Everything was too bright for him at first so he winced and shielded his sight from the glow of the gleaming gold and marble. He felt a sharp stabbing pain in his sockets as his eyes tried to adjust to the brightness. They began to water profusely as they adjusted to being back where they belonged. Steven knelt down and held his face in his hands until the pain subsided. Jilly knelt beside him. She felt at a loss as to what she could do to help.

For the first time in ten years, Steven gradually began to see again. Joy enveloped him as his daughter came into view. She was no longer the little girl he remembered picking mushrooms in the woods with her mother, but a young girl who was nearing womanhood. He could see why Zac was so reluctant to leave her. Jilly had grown up beyond his reach and attention. Oh, how he had missed so much of her life. Steven stood, taking Jilly into his arms. He looked down at her and the broadest smile lit his face.

"I can see you," he told her.

"I see you too," Jilly cried as she hugged her father back.

He caressed and kissed her hair as he held her tightly. His tears of pain turned to tears of joy.

"Now I will show you cause and effect," bellowed Osiris, interrupting their precious moment. "You will watch with your cherished sight all the pain and suffering you have brought upon yourselves by delving into things which you do not have the capability of understanding."

Once more, Osiris waved his hand across his face. Jilly and her father stood motionless at the bottom of the stairway, huddled together, awaiting their fate. It was the young boy Gyp who this time responded to Osiris' command.

Gyp bowed low and at the same time opened his arms wide to pay homage to the gods before him. Jilly could tell that Gyp had no option but to obey Osiris' command. His eyes were glazed and his manner subdued. This was not the stubborn, selfish but loveable cat she had grown up with. This was a young boy, with the heart and mind of someone from Thyme, but with the inbred ancestry of the ancients they all stood before.

"I acknowledge the Eye of Horus and am blessed in the presence of its power," he said softly.

Uncurling his body, Gyp then focussed upon the large eye on the curtain behind Osiris. Suddenly, his yellow eyes began to glow stronger and more vivid. The colour intensified as if someone had turned up the dimmer switch to full. Yellow rays of light flashed from his eyes like a beam of light connecting to the Eye of Horus on the wall above the throne. Like a projector, events from the past began to play out. Everyone assembled, watching the screen, as the story unfolded.

Jilly and Steven didn't recognise the man they saw entering a tomb and steal the ancient Egyptian book. They watched as Gyp screened the whole event as it unfolded to a terrible conclusion. The man had run with his book. He had lost his clothes as the wind tore them from his body. Steven and Jilly winced as the man in the movie was killed and crumbled to dust outside the Egyptian city walls.

Steven clearly remembered the next clip which showed the events surrounding his own trip to Egypt. He watched as he saw himself standing in the market place.

"This is when that man thrust the book into my hands," Steven called out, "there's your proof. I told you I had nothing to do with stealing the book."

"Silence!" bellowed Osiris, "you have no permission to speak."

Just as Steven had said, the images showed a man running pass Steven and thrusting an object into his hands. They watched the next clip of film in horror as they saw what punishment the unknown man had been given by the angry Egyptian gods. Jilly flinched at the fear on the man's face as the flames licked around his head, burning his whole body slowly to ashes. She turned her face away from the film. By the ending of this scene, a wind had blown the man's ashes into the sand and dirt of the hot Egyptian ground.

"Thank God her father had his crystal," Jilly thought to herself.

The silent movie continued to project from Gyp onto the Eye of Horus for some time, showing how Steven had brought the book across the stones and the outcome of his actions.

Uncle Gustus was shown using the book and trying its magic. Then they saw his death, followed by the swift demise of Brin. The loyal dog had tried to protect his master without success, from the evil spirits that attacked them at the Lodge.

The film moved swiftly on to the wedding of Joseph and Carmel. Jilly looked away, not wishing to be reminded of what happened that fateful day when evil swooped in and killed them too. She had been there and saw for herself the enlarged pupils in the staring eyes of her two dead friends, as they lay on the ground amongst their wedding guests.

Steven watched in total disbelief as time and time again scenes of death were shown to him. *His* eyes were focussed on the screen. He could not glance away. Osiris had transfixed them to watch everything that was being shown. Steven couldn't hear the screams of the people of Thyme in the images but he could feel their pain and fear as each death brought home the realisation that his actions had caused all this suffering. After witnessing the final act of barbaric justice as Julin was eaten by the crocodile of the fourth hour of the night, the screen flickered and went blank.

Gyp fell to the step floor exhausted.

"Now your eyes have images that will repeat in your mind over and over again as punishment," said Osiris proudly.

Steven's transfixed glazed was released and he immediately took the opportunity to look up at the Egyptian who sat egotistically upon his throne.

"Oh I agree, I will remember these visions for ever, Osiris, but I will hold no personal blame for the death of these people. Yes, I brought the book to Thyme and took it from your land. Yes, my colleague tried to use it. But, NO! None of us in Thyme are to blame for the cruelty you have bestowed upon us. You are evil, as evil as your brother. You are no better than Seth in your anger."

Steven swung round and addressed the crowd who had come to watch the proceedings within the Hall of Truth.

"There is no justice amongst you. *Any* of you."

He continued, "Did it never occur to you to just ask for your book back?"

"I have not caused these deaths," snapped Osiris as he leapt out of his throne, livid at the way

Steven had addressed him. "The *book* killed your colleagues, not *I*."

Steven was confused. "I don't understand. How can you not accept responsibility for all these deaths?" he asked. "You are a God, are you not?"

Osiris turned to Isis as she laid a hand on her husband's shoulders. She understood his power and strength, but knew of his kindness and humanity.

"You must explain to these mortals," she told him.

Calming down, Osiris sat back on his throne and looked lovingly at his wife. He continued calmly and methodically.

"My brother's evil and the Book of the Dead were what followed your people to their doom. This book, the *giver* of life, can only be handed over as a gift, never taken. It is the energy from this book that turns unlawful owners to dust even before they can hand it over to Seth or his evil followers. You see, this book is not just a book, it is power, pure energy. This Book of the Dead, or *for the dead* as you called it, can give life, yes, but it can also take life. Its essence is all about crossing the realms. Thus, it feeds on souls and it only rests when it is here, at the Great Hall of Truth. It knows Seth must never be given it; this would unleash the most powerful evil across the lands, killing everyone who stands in his way. The power of the book doesn't discriminate or judge people, it only seeks to return here amongst those that understand its magic."

Osiris looked at his wife, who smiled back at him.

"Only the reflective energy of your crystals saved those who handled it in Thyme and because the book was stuck there, *its* magic poisoned your land, not I. I just give justice to the wronged and punish the wicked. The book must *only* be used for good spells. Your Uncle Gustus set out to use it for good, for the young lovers, but he then trod where he shouldn't and began to wander through its pages, touching on the unknown. He read from its pages. The book did not appreciate this dabbling. And you... you, Steven, had no intention of returning the sacred book, so I ordered you here and took your eyes until you were worthy of seeing the truth."

Steven opened his mouth to speak but closed them again. Deep in his heart, he knew this to be true. Even though he had not stolen the book, it was not his to keep. When he took it across the stones, he had no intention of returning it to Egypt but to study it to keep it as his. He could feel its power and had agreed with Uncle Gustus to one day discover its secrets.

"The book has been returned," Osiris continued, "and so I return your eyes. This *is* justice. My son, Horus took *you* to ensure the return of the book. This we knew would happen. This was planned. I am not responsible for all that has happened since, you humans are, and the magical energy of the book are."

"You knew I'd come looking for my father one day?" Jilly interrupted.

"Yes. You had to hand the book over again as a gift. You have. You have given Isis back the book as a gift for your father's sight."

"So why were you so angry with me when I asked for his eyes?" she asked.

"Would you speak to your High Priestess the way you addressed me?" he responded.

Jilly lowered her face and shook her head. "No, never." She felt like a petulant child. "But what about Julin? He was a good person."

"That's right," added her father. "Are you stating that Julin's death was pre-planned? That you allowed the book *or* Seth to kill him, or was *that* just an accident of fate, the *book's* fault?"

Osiris took a deep breath and, leaning an arm on the armrest and his chin on his fingers and palm of his left hand, he answered Steven with a huge sigh.

"Your powers and understanding are so limited. You people of Thyme fail to see so much. Julin was destined to die for the sins of his fathers."

"Julin did nothing wrong," said Jilly, "in fact, it was he who helped more than anyone to return your book to save the rest of our people dying at the hands of Seth. Well, at the hands of the book, so you explained."

"You do not understand," replied Osiris, "a father is accountable for the wrongs of his sons and vice versa. A King is accountable for the wrongs of his people. Nation accountable to nation, and so on."

Jilly shrugged her shoulders.

"Then who was Julin accountable to? Uncle Gustus? My father?"

"No, his great grandfather, Harvay Julin Lawson, the very man who stole the book from the Tomb of Horus. The same man who struck a deal with the dead souls of the Egyptian Underworld so they could return from the dead to the realm of the living. The same man who originally set out to unleash evil, led by Seth, into the light of day, to quash the empire of the Underworld and Upper-worlds."

"But why did Seth kill him if they had made a bargain?"

"Unfortunately, he doubled crossed Seth and decided to keep the book for his own people. Those that live in Thyme Hollow."

Steven gasped.

"Yes. He decided to keep the book for the dead souls of Thyme, ancestors as you call them. He planned to resurrect them. But, as you have witnessed here today, he never made it back to the stones. The book chose death for this man, Harvay Lawson. Seth was left unavenged for the betrayal. Hence, Julin paid the price for his ancestor's actions and therefore the choice was not a difficult one but a necessary one. 'An eye for an eye', as you say. Seth had that right to choose punishment and the law of the lands below agreed. Julin died for the sins of his fathers."

"But that's unfair for Julin to be forever punished for someone else's errors," Steven pleaded.

"This is the way it is," said Osiris, "but, for your information, I took pity on his soul. His heart weighed light against a feather and for his goodness shown through his life, I allowed him to find his way home. He is with your ancestors in *your* land of spirit. Only his great grandfather remains amongst us. Oh and those that subsequently handled the book. Those and Harvay Lawson now sleep amongst the dead in the valleys below, whimpering pitifully as the Boat of Ra passes by him each night. Only your spell and crystal saved you when handling the book."

Jilly recalled the voices of those she heard en route to the sixth gate, and she wondered at which hour of the night Harvay was stuck in or if she had gazed upon his soul as their boat had passed through his division. Jilly then felt confused. How could Julin have already been judged? Surely his boat journey would have begun at the first gate, behind their boat!"

A slight twitch from the corner of Osiris' lip caught Jilly's attention as a smirked formed. He winked down at her.

"Now we must continue," he said firmly.

Osiris waved his hand again at the young boy Gyp who stood quietly below him on the stairway.

"I call again, upon your defence."

"Defence for what?" asked Steven. "You have your book, you have your 'eye for an eye' as *we* call it. You made me watch everything that has happened as punishment, so why am I being tried further?"

Osiris frowned. "You have entered the Great Hall of Truth. Like those before you, you cannot just leave. You have to face judgement for your life. If you pass the test, you may return home."

"And if we don't?"

"You proceed to the realm of the dead." came his flippant reply.

Jilly placed her head in her hands. She understood the laws and the reasoning but felt the whole situation was just so unfair. They really hadn't done anything wrong, especially not in her eyes, and the punishment was so harsh, so very harsh indeed. These Egyptians had unfairly judged the good people of Thyme. Her friends were honest and spiritual and their spells were used for only the good for nature and others. How could these Egyptians judge them? What right had they to judge them?

"Every right!" replied Osiris.

Jilly winced. She hated these gods reading her every thought.

"If you can read our minds," she said bravely, "then you will already know we are good, honest people. Well," she hesitated, "apart from one man who strayed, a long time ago, Julin's great-grandfather."

"It is for your defence to prove your innocence, not I to judge your actions."

Osiris looked at Gyp to continue with the trial.

Gyp spoke loudly so everyone in the great Hall of Truth could hear.

"Hear these truthful words I speak. I have judged the hearts of these who stand before you accused and I stand as witness for them that their deeds are righteous and their sins are from naivety, not gain or to cause harm."

Once more, Gyp obeyed the wishes of his lord and he began to project more images onto the Eye of Horus. This time, the movie was played backwards. Jilly and Steven watched as the images scanned Thyme, as it stood today, deserted and motionless. Not a tree branch moved, not an animal scurried amongst the trees in the wood and no person could be seen going about their day to day chores.

"Where is everybody?" Steven asked.

"Scattered to the four corners of the world."

"Who scattered them?" asked Steven.

"Seth, in anger, just as my brother once scattered me."

"What do we have to do to get them back?" he enquired.

"Search! Like I did." said Isis.

"What about Penny, Marcus and Zac? Did they make it home from the pyramid?"

"That is irrelevant to your defence," said Osiris.

"But I'd like to know," said Steven, "please."

Osiris ignored his questioning. The images displayed on the eye above him continued.

Nefron's face was clearly visible on the screen. She was obviously in fear of something. Behind her, they could see the children of Thyme huddling together. They saw what appeared to be a sudden commotion, whereby the children were running and hiding. Nefron was obviously standing her ground against someone or something. The vision became slightly blurred as if a fierce battle was going on too quickly to focus.

Then the image cleared again. She could be seen chanting. Nefron held her arms out at each side to enable the robe to shield the movement of the children behind her, from whoever was threatening them. Nefron was clearly protecting the children and pleading for their lives.

"They're in the Council Hall," whispered Steven, "all the children……"

Then they saw it. It came swiftly. Nefron was knelt, and lowered her head before someone or something which the film did not show. Gyp skipped the next scene and returned when all that was left of Nefron was her robe lying on the wooden hall floor. It was if she had puffed into thin air, or turned to dust! Steven gulped.

"That must have been the moment I felt her pass over," he thought. "Nefron surrendered herself to the power of the ancient Egyptian book to save the children. A life for a life, as we say!"

The pictures jumped from scene to scene travelling backwards and forwards in time. From Steven and Penedora enjoying a meal together in their kitchen at home, to where children were playing in the shallow water of the stream, by the shingles and rocks. They couldn't hear the noise of the laughter but the faces told a story of merriment and fun. Everyone appeared to be laughing and frolicking about on a warm sunny day. Jilly was there with her friends. They were shown scenes of people building the library, where everyone appeared to be chipping in with the hard work, and when their first book of knowledge was placed amongst the library shelves. The images also showed times of spell-making and the joy it brought to others. Next they were shown a prayer meeting at the Council Hall, to which a younger Steven and Penedora had attended. He could see his hand reach across to his betrothed while they were chanting and her response of brushing his hand with her fingers. Steven remembered these times vividly.

Gyp showed Osiris as many scenes of sacrifice, honour, love and happiness as he could in the short time he was allowed in their defence, and Jilly now believed he was their best chance of escape. Gyp had witnessed the kindness in Thyme and the love that radiated amongst those he had grown to know. She became grateful that their defence team was her best friend, her beloved cat.

At the end of the screening, Thoth moved down the steps towards Steven and reached out his hand, his small beady eyes peering at him from the base of a long hooked beak.

"Your crystal," he requested.

Hesitantly, Steven took his crystal from his pocket and handed it over to the long beaked-man. Everyone silently watched as Thoth placed Steven's crystal into the empty plate on the scales. The pan dipped towards the ground immediately, clanking loudly as it hit the ground.

Jilly gasped! It was too heavy.

"O Goddess, Devourer of the Dead, await. For if the scales show this man to be untruthful and unjust, you may eat his heart," said Thoth loudly.

The crowd leaned forward to see the judgement better, as intermittent whispering started amongst them. The Hall became alive in anticipation of the outcome of Steven's *weighing of his actions*. A hush then came. Steven's heart was pounding and he was sure everyone could hear it beating as loudly as he could. Nothing happened.

'Oh my God,' thought Jilly as she stood watching for even the tiniest of movements but the pan with the crystal remained nearest to the floor.

Still nothing. Jilly wasn't quite sure if she could see a smirk on Osiris' face. No, she was wrong. Slowly, extremely slowly, a slight twitch came from the pan holding the crystal. A gulp was heard from an Egyptian within the gatherers. Then the scales began to adjust themselves as the weight evened out. With much relief, Jilly and Steven watched as the pans began to swing up and down until the side with the feather went crashing to the floor. The other pan flipped up into the air making the crystal bounce within the pan itself. A loud cheer went up in the crowd. Steven didn't hold much hope of this happening, but he was so very glad it did. His crystal weighed lighter than a feather. He smiled a huge triumphant grin and Jilly hugged her father. He was surely pure of heart and proven to be a good man. This meant life.

Osiris waved his hand at Thoth who responded by removing the crystal from the highest plate on the scales. As he did so, the scales adjusted themselves again and the plate containing the feather jolted back up to align with the other. The Egyptian gods clapped as they saw the scales were perfectly balanced even though one held a feather. Steven's crystal had shown how light his heart was. It was full of love, love for his wife, for his daughter and his home. It was not often they saw a good man pass through the Hall of Truth, most were doomed to the Underworld. Osiris raised his arms to the crowd and the clapping gently ceased.

"Justice has been weighed. Your soul shines in the moon and glows in the sun, may you go forth among those multitudes of yours who are outside and may those who are in the daylight release you. May the gates of the underworld open to you when you go out into the day in order to do what you wish on earth among the living."

Thoth handed the crystal back to a very relieved Steven. The little red and orange bird swooped down from the roof of the hall and landed back in the pan on top of the feather and the pan clonked back onto the floor under its weight. It chirped twice as it settled itself comfortably. Thoth turned and walked away from the accused and beckoned his four slaves to remove the scales of justice from the hall. Jilly watched the birdman morph back into the handsome, muscular man she first saw.

Anubis and Horus both bowed to Steven and Jilly as a mark of respect and they too retreated into the dark shadows of the Great Hall of Truth.

"You have proved your intentions were not sinful when taking the book across the stone and that knowledge is all you seek. You speak the truth when your mouth is open and love is strong within you and your people. You may go home," said Osiris authoritatively.

"What about Jilly?"

"Sins of your fathers," said Osiris, "have you heard nothing I have explained to you?" He sighed as his patience waned with these mortals before him. He couldn't understand how with so much knowledge they still knew so little!

"As you are without sin, so is she," he continued, "your innocence is passed on through the generations and back again if one fails or succeeds. You are set free, so she is set free. An eye for an eye, tooth for a tooth…. as you say!"

Steven laughed. He hugged his daughter. He held her hands tightly in his and looked deep within her soul. "We did it! We're going home, love. We're actually going home."

"But what is left to return to?" Jilly asked him sadly.

Isis spoke, "Your people are scattered, not dead."

"You mean scattered to the four corners of the New World?"

"I found my true love with knowledge, and magic from my book made him whole again. I'm sure you Thyme people will figure this out."

Isis took the arm of her husband as they began to descend the royal stairs to leave the great chamber.

"Will *we* be safe to return home, and what of our links to our ancestors?" asked Jilly.

"Seth cannot touch you while the Book of the Dead remains here with me, and links to your ancestors will be at the Book's judgement, not ours."

"Excuse me," Steven called up to Osiris, "but how do we get home?"

When Osiris and Isis reached the bottom step, Isis spoke gently to Steven in response to his valid question.

"The Boat of Ra, of course. It will take you through the next six hours of the night to come forth by day. Once in the upper world, you will have to use your own spell book to transport you back to the stones. We cannot help you return, your crystals reflect our magic."

She turned away from him and continued with Osiris to make their way across the great marble floor to leave the Hall of Truth.

Jilly noticed Gyp still standing on the steps. He was looking down at her. She called loudly after Osiris.

"What about Gyp? What happens to him now?"

Osiris stopped. He thought for a moment and turned back to Jilly.

"That depends on Egypt," he said, "he may choose his own fate. He has free will to remain here amongst his people or to go back with you in the form he was given."

"As a cat?"

"Yes, as a cat."

"Forever?"

Osiris raised one of his large black painted eyebrows, turned his back to her and continued on his way.

"These mortals know nothing!" he muttered under his breath in ancient Egyptian language.

Jilly looked up at Gyp, not noticing the final departure of Osiris and Isis as they made their way out of the Hall. The three stood in silence, waiting for the other to make a decision.

Steven sensed the pain in his daughter's heart at the thought of losing her best friend. He moved away and their hands dropped as he left her side. Steven decided to head for the boat and wait for his daughter there.

Jilly climbed up to the same step as Gyp where she stopped and took his hands.

"I'll understand if you wish to stay here. It's your home. You'll be among your friends and family. My heart belongs in Thyme and I know I have to return there. I couldn't possibly ask you to remain as a cat just to be with me; however much I love you. So I'm going to just say a quick goodbye Gyp and go. I'm going to miss you so much."

Tears began to fall down her face. Jilly leaned towards him and quickly gave the young boy a kiss on the cheek, turned and headed back to the boat. Feeling that a quick goodbye was the best for both of them under the circumstances, she purposely didn't look back. The once black cat with the funny mark on his eye and knowledge beyond his years, stared back at her as she walked away from him.

Tears dropped from his eyes also. He felt a great sense of betrayal towards both Jilly and his Egyptian master as his duty in both realms was now over. He had been the porthole, the vision for the Gods to view these people ever since their book had been taken across the stones. Unfortunately, things became complicated when Gyp had grown to love Jilly. He ended up loving her and his life in Thyme so much that he had often forgotten his mission and blended in with the people of Thyme as if he really, truly belonged there. Egypt watched as he saw his friend and her father take off their white garments, put their shoes back on, and board the Boat of Ra. He then watched in silence with a broken heart as the boat slowly edged its way forward out into the seventh hour of the night towards morning.

Osiris, Isis, Horus and Thoth had all left. The crowd had dispersed. Jilly was gone and Egypt stood alone in the Great Hall of Truth. A large lump had formed in his throat and he couldn't shake off the pain of her goodbye in his heart. He let a much loved part of his life just sail away.

The beginning

A warm ray of sun glistened down upon Jilly's face, penetrating her eyes and waking her. She flicked her eyelids a few times and then opened them. She was unaware how long she had been asleep and how far they had travelled through the remaining gates. As she stretched, the black cat that had been sleeping snuggled upon her lap, slipped off onto the floor of the boat.

"Gyp!" she screeched, "you came!"

Steven was woken suddenly by the delight and celebrations his daughter expressed at seeing her cat once more.

Jilly bent down and picked Gyp up. She hugged him so hard and he couldn't purr, or breathe for that matter! Looking into his yellow eyes, she smiled radiantly at him. "I love you, Gyp. Thank you for choosing me. Thank you." But something was different. He no longer had a little black mark in the yellowness of his eye. Jilly looked deeper at it.

"Does this mean they are no longer watching us?" she asked him.

He winked. She remembered he could read her mind and now she knew what he was and who he really was. Suddenly she felt they were even closer than before. Their friendship had crossed over to the next level and now she knew their link was going to be stronger than ever.

"I'll always remember how you looked as a boy Gyp, and how you saved us, and everything about you," she told him. "Now it's my turn to look after you."

Gyp knew he had made the right decision. His home was where his heart was, not in the land he dwelled in for the last few thousand years amongst the souls of the dead ancient Egyptians. He loved being alive in the sunshine and rain and he loved being alive in Jilly's life. Being in her arms at this moment, completed him.

"Well I'm surprised you chose to come back with us, Egypt," said Steven. He stroked Gyp's head a couple of times. "I'm glad you did. Jilly would have been so unhappy without you."

Steven nudged Gyp on his furry chin with his knuckles.

"Thanks for looking after my daughter when I was, well, you know, and thanks for defending me and everyone at Thyme Hollow."

Gyp looked upon Steven's soul. He liked this man. 'Eyes suit you,' he thought, as he nestled himself back into the warmth of Jilly's embrace.

"I wonder where we are," said Steven looking around.

They had ventured from the dark of the hours of the night and had come out into some sort of stream bounded by tall reeds. On each side of them were fields: some were harvested, others had cattle grazing on them. The grass was fresh and green, and the water from the stream glistened in the early morning sunlight.

Neither knew how much further they had to go, as they had fallen asleep after the uneventful seventh Pylon!

There was no one to ask. Heka and Sa were not on board and no one was pulling the boat as it slid effortlessly through the water. A bowl of fresh fruit and plate of bread lay in the middle of the table before them. None of the occupants touched the food. Nobody had an appetite!

"We must be near to the twelfth hour," said Steven. "It's daylight and the sun is rising, so we've made it to morning," he muttered with his heart now even lighter than any feather Thoth could judge it against.

Jilly was unsure they had ventured through any more gates on this leg of their journey. Everything in the boat felt different and the journey itself felt different. Even the fact they all fell asleep shortly after leaving the hall of Truths seemed strange to her.

Gyp knew they had changed direction. Souls departing to the light went west to greet the sunrise on their final journey, to join their loved ones in the afterlife. Souls condemned to an everlasting existence of turmoil and pain, were sent back to the darkness of the East. This is where Seth sat upon his own throne. This boat journey was completely different. This was a journey to freedom.

They all decided to just sit back and relax and feel the warmth of the sun on their faces until the boat came to its natural end.

"Nobody hungry?" asked Steven.

Jilly shook her head and Gyp didn't even raise his.

"Me neither," said Steven. He couldn't wait to be in the arms of Penedora once more.

Jilly couldn't wait to see Zac again. She had so much to tell him. Gyp knew that however much Jilly grew to love Zac, *he* would always be number one in her heart. Their friendship would never be broken and Zac would have to accept this special bond he had with Jilly. But the future didn't matter to him right now. He was happy nestled back in her lap feeling the warmth of her hand as it gently stroked his fur.

It wasn't long before the boat gently changed course towards the reeds and nestled itself by the banks of the stream. They could see a wooden walkway onto the grass and it was here that the boat pulled alongside. The grass was lush and smelled fresh with morning dew. The gangplank creaked and extended as before, lowering itself onto the wooden sidewalk.

Steven disembarked first and this time he stretched out his arm to help his daughter off the boat. Gyp just leapt with glee from the edge of the boat onto the riverbank. He hated being in the Underworld. He always had. Apart from the abundance of food and gold, it was dark, dismal and full of weeping, wailing and sorrowful souls. Even the final hours for those who had survived the weighing of their hearts were filled with trepidation and sadness at the loss of their loved ones who had not been allowed to continue through to the afterlife of light. This time, his journey to fruition was filled with love, laughter and hope. Gyp had no hesitation in following Jilly home. He had spent thousands of years in the darkness, and the last ten years spent in Thyme recording life for the gods had given him light and purpose. Now he was free to be just him. Whether as a boy or a cat, he felt alive.

They watched from the shore, as Ra's boat creaked into action and continued its way upstream towards the first hour of the night.

"I wonder who is waiting for it to arrive this time," said Jilly.

"Hopefully someone who has led a good life," Steven replied. "I'd hate to be the one who followed our judgement hour."

They laughed. It came quickly and loudly as a way of releasing all the tension and pent up emotions from their journey through the night.

"Which way to the stones?" asked Jilly, looking in every direction.

"I'm not sure."

Neither had a clue which way they should head.

"I think we should use your spell book like Osiris told us to," Steven suggested. He scanned the area to see if anyone was in sight. "I can't see anyone, so I suggest we do a spell here and see what happens."

Jilly nodded. She took the haversack from her back and laid it in front of her on the grass. She removed her mother's spell book and held it to her chest for a moment. Jilly took a deep breath in.

"This will be the very first spell I cast on my own," she told her father apprehensively.

Steven was ecstatic. He had missed so much of his daughter's young life yet suddenly, here he was, witnessing her Age of Transition. He alone would be at his daughter's side when she cast her first spell and become one with the pagans and ancestors of Thyme.

"I have every faith you can do this Jilly," he encouraged.

Laying Penedora's spell book on the grass she took off the purple cloth it was wrapped in and placed a crystal beside it.

"Here goes," she sighed.

She stood tall over the book and raised her arms to the bright sun above her. She screwed up her eyes and thought hard for a few minutes. She opened them again.

"I don't know what to say."

Steven encouraged her, "Clear your mind and let the words flow."

Jilly closed her eyes and tried focussing her mind on nothing. It was hard after everything she had witnessed that night.

'You can do this,' she thought. 'Come on, Jilly stop thinking...'

Her mind came to rest and every time something popped in, she cleared it immediately. It felt forever until a surge of emotion flow through her young body as the words in her mouth flowed off her tongue.

"Amenie broth kelwin soothin, cwym y anartum bay.
With love and light I ask thee, to take us to the stone,
That will let us all cross over, to the place we all call home."

They stopped as quickly as they had come and Jilly opened her eyes again.

As always, they waited for the book to respond. A tiny spiral of wind blew up around Jilly's feet and spun up towards her head and then to the fingertips on each hand. Her hair was blown above her head and Jilly felt the power within and around her. She could feel the link to those beyond in spirit and she just knew her spell would be answered.

The pages of the book began to flick in the morning breeze and when they stopped, writing began to appear on the empty pages before them.

*Close your eyes and count to ten
And we will take you home again.*

"Wow!" she thought, "is that it?"

Her disappointment was an understatement. Jilly picked up the spell book and crystal and replaced them in the haversack. She called Gyp to her side as she sat down on the grass beside the riverbank.

Steven followed suit. "What's wrong?" he asked.

"I'm not sure. I thought it would be more mysterious, or difficult to do," she told him.

"Maybe our ancestors know you have been through enough already and don't want to challenge you any more than you need to be," Steven reassured her.

Gyp flicked his tail at her hand and she responded with a gentle rub of his head.

"I'm also afraid."

"Of what?"

"Of what we are going to find back home, in Thyme Hollow." Jilly lowered her head.

Steven lifted her chin with his fingers. "We have come so far," he said softly, "you cannot give up now. We don't know what awaits us, none of us do."

He glanced at Gyp.

"What I do know is that your mother is still alive. I can feel her essence. The children will need all of us when we return."

"You're right, they need us, whatever we find, we can overcome it."

"You can do this."

"I *can* do this," Jilly said. "I'm ready now. It's time to go home."

They stood up, held each other's hands and Gyp stood between their feet. Closing their eyes, Jilly began to slowly count, "One, two, three…."

~~~~~~~~~~~~~~~~~~~~~~

"Have you opened your eyes yet Jilly?" Steven asked her.

"No. Have you?"

"No. Shall we do this together?"

"Yes, you say when."

"When!" said Steven and he and Jilly opened their eyes together.

They could see the grass beneath their feet and the stream.

"It didn't work," sighed Jilly disappointedly, "we haven't even moved!"

Steven scanned where they were and it was the same place they had disembarked the boat. He laughed.

"No *we* haven't," he told her, "but the stones have. Look!"

Jilly turned her head around and she could see them. Joy swept through her immediately.

"We're back!" cried Jilly as she grabbed Gyp into her arms and raced over to the first stone.

It looked welcoming and familiar to them.

Steven hesitated for split second. It had been so long since he had ventured between Thyme and the New World. Gyp leapt from her arms in excitement and headed across first. Jilly giggled and followed him onto the first stone and then another until she was back in Thyme, her home; their home. When Steven crossed he felt good. At last he felt safe again and like Gyp, free from chains of imprisonment.

"Where to first?" he asked, "the cottage?"

"I think we should head for the Council Hall," suggested Jilly, "that's where everyone keeps congregating since this awful Egyptian business started."

"Then we'll go there first," he agreed.

As they made their way through the woods to the Hall, Steven felt a slight lump in his stomach. 'Please let everything be ok,' he prayed.

"Shoosh! I can hear someone," Marcus beckoned the children to be silent. They had remained at the Hall through the night waiting for daybreak. Marcus was first to hear the strange noise from outside the hall and immediately gathered everyone together. Rooted to the spot they starred apprehensively as Marcus made his way to the entrance. The door opened.

Penedora was the first to respond.

"Steven!" she shouted at the top of her voice. "You made it."

"Jilly!" Zac was second to realise who had entered their domain and he followed Penedora at great speed to greet his new love.

"The Book?"

"Safely back where it belongs."

"You can see! Oh, Steven, you can see again!" Penedora kissed her husband passionately.

The couples stood in the Council Hall hugging, kissing and grinning from ear to ear. Jilly and Zac were caught in a personal world of their own, totally unaware that her parents had stopped their own embrace to witness theirs. The young couple's cheeks turned bright red when they noticed everyone watching them. Zac let go of the young lady in his arms and coughed a couple of times to clear his throat.

"Welcome home Jilly," he said to her politely.

Steven and Penedora laughed. Steven slapped Zac on the back and smiled at him. They all laughed.

"She missed *me* more," thought Gyp flicking his tail around Zac's leg. He pushed passed him and made his way over to the younger children. A few of them bent down and made a huge fuss of him. He loved this kind of fuss. He actually liked being a cat. Gyp liked being in control!

Marcus seemed perplexed. He scanned the room for his friend.

"Where's Julin?" he asked. "Did he go straight home?"

From the clutches of his wife Steven eyed Jilly. He then glanced over to Marcus and lowered his head and shook it side to side.

"He didn't make it. I'm sorry."

Marcus felt a sudden pain in his heart at the loss of his very close friend. He turned and sat down on the nearest seat. Putting his head in his hands Marcus leaned forwards and closed his eyes to bring the image of his friend into his mind.

Steven left Penny's embrace and went over to Marcus. He laid his hand on his shoulder in comfort. He couldn't think of anything to say and he certainly wasn't going to explain about Julin's family history. That, he decided, would best be forgotten.

"What happened? Was it quick?" Marcus asked.

"It doesn't matter how he died," Steven replied, "he would wish you to remember that he died saving us all."

"I think I'd like to put his name above the library in his memory," said Marcus softly, "that's the least we can do for him. I'm assuming Isis has her book back?"

"Yes."

"And Seth?"

"We don't know. He can't cross the stones without the magic of the Egyptian Book of the Dead, so we are all safe… for now."

"As long as Isis has her book in the Underworld?"

"Yes."

Marcus hesitated. "I just have a gut feeling that maybe we haven't seen the last of Seth and the evil he spreads."

Steven wanted to tell Marcus of the energy and power of the Egyptian book and that Seth was only one component of the deadly danger they experienced, but decided now was not the time. Marcus had a lot on his plate with his new responsibility. He would tell him later, when they were alone.

Everyone paused for a moment to ponder over the recent events in Thyme. They were all exhausted. No one had escaped the power of the Ancient Egyptians, not even the children. The thought of Seth ever returning to Thyme frightened them all, but for now they had to move on in the hope, he couldn't, or at least wouldn't.

"Is this everybody?" asked Jilly loudly to break the moment of silence.

Marcus looked up and responded. "Yes, and no! The children are all here but we are unsure where all the adults went."

"We know," said Steven solemnly. "Anyone who had their crystal when the fog came has been scattered around the New World and those that didn't..." he hesitated as he could see the children listening to his every word, "well, they've gone before, to the home of our ancestors," he said confidently making the whole affair appear less traumatic to the children than it actually was.

"Does that mean they're dead?" asked a little voice.

"Is everyone dead?" another asked.

Penedora went over and put her arms around the little lad. "Some, but not everyone. Most of us carry our crystals everyday anyway and with all the events over the past few days most of us have made sure we carry them at all times. It's unlikely anyone's mummy or daddy have died." She looked at Marcus and back at the children. "I promised earlier we'd find everyone we can, and we will."

Still holding the little lad who by now had sunk his face into her chest, Penedora looked towards the sky in the hope that someone somewhere had heard her. She continued her hug as he snuggled in closer.

"Then Joseph was right," Marcus said, "our friends are somewhere across the stones."

"Joseph?" said Jilly excitedly. "You've spoken to him? Is he *alive*?"

"No. I'm sorry Jilly."

Her smile halted.

"We connected to his spirit and he told us that our people have scattered, but the link was severed before we could gain any more information."

"It was Seth that scattered our people," explained Steven, "he did it in anger and as punishment. He took revenge because he couldn't get the book."

"They could be anywhere over there," said Marcus.

"I'm afraid it's now up to us to go find them," said Penedora. "It will be a hard task locating everyone, and it could take forever, especially as no one had time to prepare spells for crossing back."

"Or had their spell books with them," continued Marcus.

"They may not even know we are coming," said Zac. "Just imagine if you suddenly found yourself in the New World alone with no one else from

Thyme and only a crystal to link back to home. No money, no home, no friends. That must be quite frightening."

"Especially to those who have never actually been across the stone before," interrupted Marcus.

Steven shook his head. He should never have brought the book across the stones. If only he could turn back time, but he couldn't. There was magic, and then there was magic. As Osiris had informed him, they knew very little.

"We need a plan," said Marcus standing back up boldly. He made his way to the altar and ran his fingers over the Book of Ancestors. "One of us each day will go across the stones to search for our friends, while the others stay here and rebuild our lives and care for the children." He turned to face his only remaining people of Thyme Hollow.

Marcus continued. "We can't just cross the stones and announce to the New World that there are spiritual people among them that know magic. It will start up the witch hunts of old again. We start with the first person we find, and grow our network from there, setting up circle groups. We'll put word out to everyone in the New World who is interested in crystals, potions, and meditation and anything to do with spiritual matters to join these circle groups and share ideas. That will, in turn, encourage our people out from hiding, or give them something to latch on to that is familiar to them. When each person joins our circle groups we can make another and grow them throughout the New World, intensifying until we trace everybody we have lost and at the same time bringing them home one by one. This is the best and fastest way I can think of to get them all back to Thyme safety."

"But won't New World people get suspicious?" said Zac.

"Not if we don't include magic and actual spells. We could teach the New World people our knowledge of the old ways and traditions that they are comfortable with and this in turn should spark interest in anyone from Thyme Hollow. Like advertising to a mass market, but not letting on we are actually trying to recruit our own kind in the process."

Penedora liked the idea. "So theoretically we will be flushing them out in the New World secretly to bring them home, and recruiting New World people to think more like us at the same time."

"Like-minded people always gravitate to each other so, hopefully, some of those people will be ours. We just have to check the circles each day for new recruits."

"We have to be careful not to release any of our knowledge of spells or magic to the New World folk," said Penedora, worrying about the effect these groups could have on the existence of Thyme.

"Definitely not," agreed Marcus. "We'll keep the knowledge within these circles as basic as possible. Just enough to entice our people to head home in the right direction."

The plan sounded great. It was simple yet could be very effective. They agreed to use The Book of Ancestors each day til their link grew strong enough again to ask them for any guidance and a starting point to what appeared to be a long and arduous task.

A new enthusiasm began to grow within the small group of adult Thyme Hollow residents. They had no clue how many friends had survived the evil fog and Seth's wrath, but they all vowed not to give up searching for every last one of them.

This was the beginning of a whole new chapter in the history of Thyme, the New World and for the Ancient Egyptians.

Osiris and Isis continued ruling together, weighing the hearts of the dead souls, as they journeyed through the gates by boat, to their Judgement Hour.

Marcus was Thyme Hollow's new High Priest. He knew he had a lot of studying to do to become as confident and knowledgeable as Nefron had been.

Penedora and Steven were on a new page of discovery themselves. They were like two newlyweds, together at last. Penedora took on the role of mother for the lost children of Thyme

Hollow and Steven volunteered to be first across the stones to look for those scattered to the far reaches of the planet.

For their daughter Jilly, her new episode had begun in a big way too. She had reached the Age of Transition and found a new love with Zac *and* had strengthened the old love she had with her black cat. He still closely scrutinised them all watching from his yellow, cat-shaped eyes, but this time he wasn't relaying their activity or thoughts to another realm. Gyp loved Thyme Hollow, he always had. This belonging warmed his heart. Gyp liked warm!

He stretched out his front legs and leapt up onto the window ledge to look out at the new day ahead. He flicked his black furry tail as he watched and waited for the story to unfold further from the chapter they were all currently in, to the one that lay ahead of them on the next page.

Deep in the Egyptian Underworld of sorrow and death, moans could be heard echoing along the corridors as Seth smiled to himself. He had already embarked on his next chapter.....

Printed in Great Britain
by Amazon

36990955R00243